MW01227191

Dammi Mille Baci

VIENNA CALLING
BOOK ONE

HYUNAH KIM

Published 2022 by Next Chapter

Edited by Fading Street Services

Wilhelminenberg

"*Willst du spazieren gehen?*" a soft male voice said, snapping me out of my snooze in the park. The warmth of the May afternoon and the blissful shade under the tree had wrapped around me like a soft blanket.

I opened my eyes to find where the offer for a walk came from: a young man with transparent, sparkling blue eyes looking over me with a faint, pixyish smile. His blond hair was tied up in a ponytail, and he wore a dark T-shirt and ripped jeans.

A strangely familiar face.

I was still half asleep, but slowly regaining consciousness when I asked, "Excuse me, are you talking to me?"

His dishevelled look and paint-stained hands led me to believe he was a worker from a construction site down the road. But his sharp nose, high cheekbones, well-carved face—like an ancient Roman marble sculpture—and his piercing, observant eyes said otherwise. If he was pretending to be an artist, he was doing a hell of a good job.

"*Oui, mademoiselle, je vous parle.*" (Yes, Miss, I'm talking to you) he answered in French this time. I enjoyed his subtle Austrian accent. And it all came back to me. That strange night a month ago... yes, of course, it was him.

April 1992 in Vienna: I worked as a make-up artist and stylist, and I shared a flat with some models in the 7th district, within walking distance of Mariahilfer Straße and Westbahnhof. My flatmates were invited to a party at a penthouse and extended the invitation to me. One of my flatmates knew a friend of the owner. I wasn't particularly keen on socialising with these models—I found their superficiality and self-absorption exhausting, although my profession required me to work with them. But that night, I was bored and eager to see this fabulous rooftop penthouse with a reported rooftop patio.

So, an hour later, I was in a spacious penthouse on the top two floors of a building near Stadtpark, overlooking Vienna. It teemed with models, photographers, hairstylists, make-up artists, booking agents, and people from advertising agencies, holding cocktails and canapés. They were all dressed in fancy designer clothes and formed clusters around the rooftop area, trying to impress each other and babbling over the loud music: praising, flirting, and kissing asses. And to make it worse, I was one of them.

Like it or not, I was invited to be part of this crowd because of my affiliation with the fashion industry. I had on a chic Sonia Rykiel black tunic and flowing black silk pants that matched perfectly. Now, who was mocking people who dressed to impress others?

Apart from the classy setting, the party was pretty basic. A few hours later, most people left, and those who stayed were mostly drunk, stoned, or high, lying around the upper floor of the penthouse.

I needed a bathroom, so I followed a long corridor that led across the flat and found a half-open door. I assumed it was a bathroom, so I went in. It was not a bathroom, but an airy room with floor-to-ceiling windows. It looked like a painter's atelier.

I stepped further into the room. The faint light from a lone

bulb allowed me to make out a few shapes—sculptures. My eyes gradually adjusted, and I recognised a few unfinished paintings. Further to the left stood a large table topped with brushes, tubes of paint, colours, and artwork materials. On the wall to the right was a vividly coloured painting that reminded me of Gauguin—the famous Tahitian black dancer with a flower in her hair. A sort of study for colours and shapes, maybe, after Gauguin? It was a well-executed reproduction at that.

I advanced, nearly kicking a small pile of canvases strewn carelessly across the floor, and I stopped abruptly to steady myself. Immediately, I heard an enraged force yell, "*Falsche Tür! Raus da!*" (Wrong door! Get out!)

The voice commanding me to get out startled me. I jumped and turned to face its source. A tall young man with shoulder-length golden hair stared at me from across the room, a scowl marring his face. But the moment I turned, his furrowed brow flew halfway up his forehead, his eyes grew wide, and his tightened lips relaxed.

I scampered through my mind for excuses, but to my horror, I realised I was under the influence of the pot I had smoked during the party—it was my first experience, and I only did it out of curiosity. I couldn't control my tongue. I started saying, "*Excusez-moi, je... suis vraiment... désolée...*" (Forgive me, I... am really... sorry...)

Oops. I was speaking French. I switched to English and stuttered again. Burying my face in my palms wouldn't save me from this embarrassment, let alone that I had broken into someone's private space. Worse, I was high and couldn't even coordinate a proper apology. *Quel horreur!* As I rushed to the door, he finally said, "*Doucement, mademoiselle,* (Easy, Miss), no harm done."

He understood me and responded in French. It calmed me down. "Are you with them?" he added, tilting his head towards the party. His lips curled up slightly as if mocking, and I caught a hint of underlying bitterness. The tone of his voice was unable to hide his contempt.

I said hesitantly, "Yes, but I'm leaving. Do you mind if I use the bathroom?" I was about to explode from all the drinks I had had.

"Sure, follow me." He led me across another corridor, into a room, opened the door and switched on the light.

"Use mine. The guest bathroom is congested with drunkards."

I stepped into the bathroom and stared at my reflection in the mirror. I was flushed from the excitement, my face all red and warm. I looked down at my watch—it was already 2:30 in the morning. I was light-headed and tired. The effect of getting high was now spreading across my body.

I rushed to the toilet seat and pissed like a racehorse, the sound of it like a thundering waterfall. The flush sounded even louder, like a water cannon.

Wait a minute, is this bloody hash heightening my senses?

I washed my hands and splashed some cold water on my face. A man's cologne sat close to the shaving kit in a cabinet next to the mirror. I opened the cologne and put it under my nose—fresh sandalwood mixed with a whiff of herbs—rosemary, a hint of basil, lemongrass, a touch of coriander, tilleul, and lime... a pleasant and manly scent reminiscent of the man outside the room. He must have been wearing it, although it was weak. He must have sprayed it several hours ago.

Wow, my nose is usually not that sharp.

Wait a minute. I'm standing in a stranger's bathroom. I need to go home immediately before I get myself into any more trouble.

I exited the bathroom into a bedroom. The room had a big window with a view of the stunning Vienna city lights. I could only wish for such a view from my bedroom window.

There was a simple bed next to a small bedside table with a standing lamp and a few books casually open on top. The bed was still made. Had the noise from the party kept him from sleeping? No wonder he was furious. I didn't see him at the party, so he certainly wasn't there, hiding out here somewhere in his corner.

But why did he allow these people to have a party in his house? Was he just renting a room in the penthouse? If that was the case, he had no say if the landlord invited this crowd.

I reminded myself I had no business in here and hurried out, only to find him standing a few metres from me, by the kitchen door. His eyes followed my every movement, his lips relaxed, and the trace of fury disappeared from his face. The curiosity in his eyes had a calming effect on me.

"I'm sorry to have intruded on you," I said. "Can you please call me a taxi?"

Instead of answering me, he handed me a glass of water. I was dreadfully thirsty. How did he know that? I took it with gratitude and emptied the whole tumbler. The fresh water blissfully coursed down my throat.

"Would you like some more?" he asked as I handed the glass back to him. His long, slender artist's hands had been stained with some colours.

"Oh, I could use some more cold water," I said, my eyes still locked on his delicate hands.

He led me to the kitchen and offered me a seat. Just moments ago, he nearly threw me out of his atelier, and now he was offering me a drink. It was a weird night. As soon as I laid eyes on the chair, exhaustion caught up with me. I found myself seated across from him.

"Look, I'm sorry to have scolded you earlier, but last time there was a party like this, one of my paintings disappeared." His apologetic voice was soothing, like whispers of autumn leaves.

"Oh, my God, I'm sorry to hear that. Were you able to recover it or find the bastard who stole it?"

There was a brief silence, and for the first time, he smiled. It was a joyful, beautiful smile. To my dismay, I had used the word "bastard" in front of a total stranger. I still couldn't control my tongue.

"No, I haven't found the bastard who did it." He sustained his sweet smile and put an insistent tone on the word.

I couldn't hold my giggles as he stared at me. Then I asked, "Are you a painter? Is this penthouse yours?" As soon as the words left my mouth, I regretted them. It was no business of mine. I tried to recover by adding, "I'm sorry to be so curious—"

He cut me off. "This apartment belongs to my grandmother. And I'm not a painter but an apprentice, currently assistant to a professor at an art school."

"My grandmother is a painter living in California." As I said that, his eyes grew wide.

"Is that so?"

"Yes. I practically grew up in her atelier, watching her paint. 'Art is a nourishment for the soul as food is to our body', she used to say."

His eyes twinkled and locked on me, with a radiant smile. "You have nothing to do with the unsavoury people at the party. What are you doing here in Vienna?"

I recounted my story—my year at a fashion school in Paris, my decision to move to Vienna after Munich, and what happened before that, and at some point in our conversation, I found myself back on the rooftop, but with him alone this time. Everybody else had left, except for a few who were wasted in the living room.

He said his grandmother rented the lower level of the penthouse to a fashion photographer. It was a prime location. Big enough for studio shoots and was close to the model agencies. The photographer occasionally asked to host parties on the rooftop. Though he reluctantly agreed from time to time, he never appreciated having people in his home because of the noise, drugs, and alcohol that came with the parties. They usually left him a mess or he missed a few valuables. That's why he was furious when he found me lurking in his atelier.

I lost track of time as I drowned deeper in conversation. Listening to his soothing voice—his English with a faint Austrian accent—was a pleasure to my ears. The building was practically across from Stadtpark; its view contributed to the experience. The

sweet scent of late spring/early summer with its flowers and plants in full bloom vibrated across the park. The night air was fresh and crisp, but soon the chill became unforgiving, and goosebumps formed all over my skin. He removed the dark woollen pullover he had on and tossed it to me. I appreciated his chivalry. "Thank you."

I didn't even have the courtesy to say no. I was cold. He was left with only a T-shirt on, but he didn't seem fazed by the cold. The starry night was beautiful. When was the last time I had seen a sky like this? Quite a few stars, including Seven Bears and Cassiopeia, twinkled, quietly watching us. I checked my watch again. It was almost 4:30 in the morning. I asked him for a taxi again.

"I will bring you home," he whispered. I followed him to the ground floor, into a big garage with an assortment of cars, including some collectables.

"My friend runs the garage. He's a mechanic," he explained as he opened the door of a small red Fiat. The car had certainly seen better days but was clean and well-maintained. He opened the garage door, only to find a BMW parked in front of the entrance. "*Scheiße!*" he exclaimed. "It must be one of the arseholes at the party. I will be right back."

He quickly disappeared upstairs. A few minutes later, he came back with a key in his hand.

"The guy is so fucked up he can barely stand."

I insisted I could go home by taxi, but he wouldn't hear of it. He got into the BMW and moved it aside, but there was another car parked in front. This time he went to the back of the garage and returned, dragging a motorcycle. I watched in disbelief, and my jaw dropped in panic. "No, I would never go on that thing," I said in a panic. "Never, never..."

"Come on, I will be careful and slow." He beckoned me and passed me a helmet and a leather jacket. He already had his helmet on and an old but stylish leather jacket. The next thing I remember was being at the back of his Ducati. At that time, I

knew nothing about motorcycles, but I found out later it was a fancy, high-end Italian brand.

Frightened as hell, afraid to fall and break my bones, and shivering madly, I asked myself how I ended up on this hellish ride in the wee hours of the morning with someone I had just met. I held him tight as if my life depended on it. The cold wind whipped through my body.

I cursed all the saints I could remember: St. Jude Thaddeus for hopeless causes to start with, St. Monica for abuse victims, St. Teresa de Avila for headaches, St. Thomas the Doubter for those who struggle with doubt, St. Dymphna for those suffering nervous and mental afflictions, St. Agatha of Sicily for protection from fire, St. Roch for those too sick to care for themselves, St. Cecilia for musicians (I'm a pianist), and at last, St. Catherine of Bologna for the BLOODY ARTISTS!

I cursed them all for putting me in this situation. I cursed them some more until I became too tired of it, and the resistance in my body wore out. I could only cling to this mysterious, mischievous, mystical individual who I knew practically nothing about. At this time of the day, the road was practically deserted. We were the only ones out and about. The leather jacket I had on was warm despite the harsh wind bashing me, and I started to relax and focused on the view ahead of us. Something was wrong. I didn't know Vienna well, but this was not the road to my place. Plus, we had been riding for quite some time. We should have already arrived by this time. Instead, we were heading towards the outskirts of the city.

Ohhh nooooo... my God—I hadn't given him my address! He never intended to take me home after all! The horror set in. *Where in the seven hells is he taking me? This is it. I'm done for. I am heading to my grave: to be murdered and buried in this foreign land.*

From classic Agatha Christie to Ruth Rendell, Ken Follett, and several other crime thriller authors, I had read them all with

great passion, and I knew a thing or two about homicides. All the indicators told me I was about to become a victim.

I was practically alone in Vienna with no close family or friends, and no next of kin. I had been carefully chosen as a victim. If I went missing, who would report it to the police? And who would identify my body if I were found dead? Those bloody models at the party? They sure as hell wouldn't give a flying fuck about my well-being.

Alright, lad, if you are going to do me in, strike hard and be quick about it. I don't want to suffer. Was he going to dishonour me first? In that case, I was not going down without a fight. I would defend myself tooth-and-nail until my last breath. I remembered one of my friends telling me what to do in such a situation: hit the motherfucker between his legs, kick him as hard as you can, with all your might, then run like hell and don't look over your shoulder.

Should I jump off and run when he slows down, turning a corner of the road? But there was one thing missing, according to Agatha Christie, for a crime to be committed: the motive. What motive could he have? What would he gain by murdering me? It just made no sense. If for some horrible, God-knows-what reason, he was a serial killer, he could not possibly have chosen me as a victim since he didn't even know of my existence until tonight. I was the one who had intruded on his personal space, not the other way around.

In my desperate analysis of the situation according to logic, order, and method, it just didn't add up. I wanted to verify something. I slowly reached up, trying not to make him suspicious, and moved my hand carefully around his leather jacket to see if there were any murder weapons in his pockets: a small handgun, sharp marine knife perhaps, or cut-throat garrotte, Ruth Rendell-style. Or even a ballpoint pen. I remember an action star in a movie killing a thug in a bar with only one ballpoint. Anything can be a weapon.

But I couldn't feel anything. No objects in his pockets.

Nothing whatsoever. He was clean. Or had I seen too many movies? While going through all these horrific details in my mind, we reached an off-road away from the main street, drove again for a while, and finally arrived at an open field on a hill overlooking a great wide space.

In the faint light of dawn, I could see green grasslands with Vienna vaguely in the distance. We were on top of a hill somewhere on the outskirts of Vienna, and the day was breaking. The sky turned pale pink, orange, and then mauve, and I understood something I had never contemplated until now. He didn't take me here to kill me. That was not his intention. He wanted me to watch the sunrise with him.

The thought of it became real as the landscape unfolded. The faint light before the sunrise slowly approached the meadow. The breaking of dawn produced a slow but persistent wake-up call of the morning.

Oh... this was the sweetest thing any man had ever done for me. He parked the motorcycle by a tree and helped me to my feet.

"*Alles gut?*" He turned around and smiled.

I looked at him in awe, stunned in silence, then struggled and managed, "Where are we?"

"Wilhelminenberg"

"What?"

I couldn't catch the long word. He put his lips close to my ear and pronounced each syllable clearly and slowly. "Wil-hel-mi-nen-berg."

His measured voice, the sweet scent of his cologne, and the natural smell of his hair and skin kept me immobile and dazzled. It was irresistibly sensual and pleasing, making my hair rise from my skin. The sun shyly peeked on the horizon, showing only its upper part between the multi-coloured sky but persistently penetrating the fog of daybreak across the field. The mystic atmosphere of dawn layered over pastel clouds around the horizon as the sun rose. It was fantastic, a pure moment of magic.

I looked up to find his face over me. For the first time, I saw his eyes clearly. Incredible, sparkling blue under this light of sunrise. It was too beautiful to be true—his sharp nose, high cheekbones, the perfect shape of his face, his lovely lips that I would kiss a thousand times, his fair hair slightly curled, falling to his shoulders... My jaw dropped in admiration.

Now, if this is not a sight for sore eyes, what possibly could be? At that very moment, time had stopped. I wished it would stop here forever, right here, right now. *Let it be the last sight I lay my eyes upon on this earth before I di*e. It took all my strength to not touch his lovely face.

Throughout the night, I noticed that he was attractive, but never recognised his beauty until this moment. He was strikingly handsome, heart-achingly beautiful, fabulously attractive, head-turning, drop-dead gorgeous. Or was I hallucinating?

Whatever it was, all these compliments arose in me, someone used to working with male models from around the world in Paris, Munich, Milano, and now in Vienna. He was God-sent, a rare creation of the universe. It occurred to me he was a piece of art himself, a masterpiece of the Creator of the universe. Was I dreaming? I unconsciously pinched myself in the leg. It hurt, to my delight.

"Come on. Let's go further up," he said, pointing to the hill above us with his head and offering me his hand.

I would go anywhere with you. I would climb every mountain on this planet if I could be with you.

I took his hand. It was icy cold from the drive, but his firm grip spread a strange magnetic sensation throughout my body. I was simply mesmerised by him. I was hypnotized into a state of semi-consciousness where I had no control over my body.

How would this delicate artist's hand move on a naked woman's body?

It was a thrilling thought, let alone if that body was mine. 'That will never happen,' I scolded myself. *Wake up, Hyunah! Why would a living Roman statue like him do that with me?* I should look like Monica Bellucci at least, and maybe he would think about it. *Wake up and be real,* I reminded myself again, sighing.

We finally reached the highest point of the hill, and the sun had crept up and out of the clouds. He turned and looked me straight in the eyes.

"What's your name, Mademoiselle?"

Oh dear, we haven't even asked each other's names yet! "Hyunah," I shyly croaked.

"What?"

Of course, every European had problems pronouncing my Korean name. This time, I put my lips close to his ears and whispered slowly but clearly: "Hyun-ah."

He repeated after me twice, flashing his boyish smile. He looked like a kid discovering his new toy. "I'm Axel."

I smiled back, looking into his mesmerising blue eyes. "Alright, Axel, nice to meet you."

He responded with a polite gesture. "*Enchanté*." To my amusement, he bowed like a medieval knight in shining armour.

"At your service, my lady."

I burst out, giggling. All we needed was a white Arabian horse tied to a tree nearby—instead of his Ducati.

He was admiring the sunrise, and I was admiring him. I took a picture of it in my memory and kept it in my heart forever. I forgot all the discomfort and exhaustion from that night and the dreadful thoughts I had in my mind on the ride here. I thanked the saints I had been cursing on the road.

Later in the morning, he dropped me off outside my building in Kaiser Straße, by the Zimmerman gym, above which was my apartment. He eased me off his motorcycle, and I handed him back the helmet and the leather jacket.

"Thank you so much for everything you've done for me. I enjoyed the sunrise as well."

"Pleasure is all mine, Mademoiselle."

He climbed on his motorcycle while I admired his long, slender legs in faded jeans. With his long fair hair and stylish black leather jacket on a Ducati, he mirrored an image of a rock star who'd be swarmed by madly yelling fans.

He put his helmet on and started the engine. Before he left, my eyes fell on the pullover I was wearing.

"Axel!" I shouted through the roaring engine. He looked back. "I have your pullover."

It was still cold, and he understood I was comfortable in it. He turned the motorcycle and came closer. "Keep it for now. Come by anytime to bring it back. You know where to find me. If I'm not in my atelier, just leave it with my friend in the garage downstairs. His name is Herbert. He usually knows where I am."

He gave me a swift, sweet, boyish wink through the helmet, leaving me enthralled by the ending moment of magic, desperately praying time would stop there.

And with that, he disappeared into thin air.

A Beagle in the Stadtpark

"Excuse me, are you talking to me?"

The memory of that night came back to me in mere seconds, almost coinciding with his response to my question.

"*Oui, Mademoiselle, je vous parle.*" (Yes, Miss, I'm talking to you)

I sprung up as if I had overslept my morning alarm and was about to miss my train.

"Axel," I croaked, suddenly losing my voice.

"My lady, at your service."

He smiled cheerfully, gesturing like a medieval knight. The memories of that beautiful sunrise in Wilhelminenberg flowed in.

I woke up fairly late the day after. Whether it was the most extraordinary night or the first time I had smoked pot, I was still light-headed and dizzy. It all seemed like a dream until my sight landed on the blue marine pullover next to my pillow. I took it on impulse and put it to my nose. The dazzling scents of sandalwood, rosemary, lime and bergamot hit me like a flare and reminded me of the mysterious young artist.

I drew the pullover tightly to my chest as if I was holding him. His pleasant masculine smell replenished my nostrils, the memory of the mystic rising sun delightfully pouring over his face, beaming on his sparkling, transparent blue eyes, sharp nose, high cheekbones, and amazingly carved face. His icy cold hand, well-balanced shoulders under his leather jacket, his long slender legs... all too good to be true.

Something beyond his stunning appearance had impressed me—his kindness to a total stranger, who broke into his private workspace. He could have called me a taxi and gone to bed. Instead, he offered me a glass of cold water, stayed with me, and talked to me when he would probably rather sleep at that hour. And he didn't hesitate to offer his pullover when I was shivering with cold.

He even took me to watch the sunrise. That was the sweetest thing any man had ever done for me. Was there any chance, any slightest possibility, that he liked me? Any prospect of a casual date? Or simple friendship? Taking a lady to view a lovely sunrise is a special gesture, is it not? Or was it just a spur-of-the-moment last-minute impulse?

He was an artist. I believe that artists tend to act upon sudden urges or unpredictable agitation, depending on their state of mind or emotions, not logic. So, if he suddenly wanted to watch a sunrise, he would have done so with or without me. I happened to be at the right time and right place, *et voilà*. Whatever his motivation, I was happy about his beautiful gift. I will never forget that. He was kind to me throughout the night, expecting nothing in return. A perfect gentleman. And what did I do? I searched for a murder weapon in his jacket. I have responded in kind, haven't I? I sighed in shame, grinning widely at the same time for the irony.

For the next few days, fashion shows and seances of photo shoots for advertising greedily controlled my days—and nights—and I drifted from contact with Axel until I found some extra time one afternoon after a casting. I went back to the penthouse to return his pullover.

The garage on the ground floor was open. I let myself in and looked around. "*Grüß Gott, bitte,*" (Hello, May I help you?) came a greeting from a welcoming man in a grey mechanic's uniform. Average height, and probably a few years older than Axel.

I struggled with my discordant German, scrambling to construct a greeting back and to enquire about Axel's whereabouts.

"*Grüß Gott. Kan ich sprechen mit Axel, bitte? Ist er da?*" (Good day. Can I speak to Axel, please? Is he here?)

He stared at me with his bright green eyes. Like the vivid green eyes of a curious cat.

"You must be Herbert."

"Ja. I'm Herbert. Axel is not here. He went to Prague this morning."

I doubted whether he already knew about me from Axel. He showed no sign of it.

"Oh, do you know when he will be back?"

"Maybe a week or two. He is there for an art exhibition. Is there anything I can help you with?" he offered.

I produced a neatly folded pullover from my handbag.

The moment I took it out, the unforgettable scent, faint but pleasant, hit my nostrils. I had the urge to keep it with me. Each day, I would smell it whenever I came across it and even sleep with it next to my pillow.

The thought of letting it go was unbearable. And I was sad Axel wasn't there. My heart was yearning to see him again. I should have come earlier. I had even carefully chosen my outfit—a nice cotton summer dress with floral prints. It looked natural, romantic, and elegant. The dress dropped at knee level, showing off my legs. My mom used to tell me I had pretty legs that needed to be shown. When I looked at my reflection in the mirror that morning, I agreed that it was not so hard to look at them.

But I had dressed up for nothing. I sighed again. "This pullover belongs to Axel. Can you give it to him, please?"

"Of course. I will give it to him,"

"Thank you."

I turned around, looking outside at the park across the street.

"It's a nice neighbourhood here. I would walk around the park every day if I were you."

He smiled. "I usually have no time for that, but yes, it's nice."

"Well, I should get going."

He accompanied me to the exit, where I said goodbye. As I turned to go, he said hesitantly, "May I ask who you are? Your name?"

"Oh, my name is Hyunah."

"Ok, nice to meet you, Hien-hah." He couldn't pronounce my name correctly, but I didn't bother to correct him.

"Nice to meet you, too, Herbert."

For some reason, I wanted to have a walk in the park. It was a nice sunny afternoon, and I thought it a pity to go home already. It was an unusually warm day for the end of April. The park was scattered with people sitting and lying on the grass, enjoying the late afternoon sunshine kissing their shoulders and hair. An overall happy and relaxed atmosphere. But I was NOT. I was disappointed. Axel was not there, and the only thing that reminded me of him was gone.

Spring birds chirped merrily above my head—seemingly communicating with one another—one bird singing, another one answering loudly, and a third barging in between to add an opinion. Probably a family reunion.

A sweet, gentle breeze caressed my forehead as if to console me. I strolled around the park for a while, stopped by the statue of Johann Strauss II, and found an empty bench nearby. I collapsed on it. My designer shoes hurt my feet. I removed them and put my feet up, thinking it wouldn't be a bad idea to sit on the grass like everyone else.

But that was out of the question. I didn't want to spoil my pretty dress, freshly pressed this morning.

Next time, I will wear jeans and a T-shirt with comfortable sneakers to sit on the grass like everybody else, I decided. How wonderful would that be? I also appreciated the calm and relaxing mood of the green lawn, trees, plants, flowers, dogs with their owners, and people outside the fashion industry. People who wouldn't judge you for your appearance, fame, wealth, or who you're sleeping with.

I had been working my butt off in this fickle industry for two long years already, and I'd begun to develop some doubt about it. When struggling with doubt, you are supposed to pray to St. Thomas, The Doubter. Would St. Thomas help me get through this? Most certainly not. I took a tramway. It brought me to the middle of Mariahilfer Straße. I trudged home from there, with the warm sunshine on my shoulders.

~

"Axel," I croaked, my voice harsh as I gasped for air.

"My lady, at your service."

I looked at him in disbelief. I never thought I would see him again. It had been almost a month since that night. It took me another moment to gather my wits. I had been asleep after all.

"Well, this is the second time you showed up unexpectedly, my lord. That is no way to treat a lady. You should announce yourself, you know."

His sparkling blue eyes lit up and a splendid smile beamed on his face. He enjoyed my witty response.

"My apologies, my lady. But I just came back from a war. I thought you would be pleased to see me alive." He bowed like a medieval knight and placed one knee on the grass. I giggled.

"And pray, what war was that? Art exhibition war in Prague?"

"Aye, my lady. After that, there was another battle near Krems, where I was summoned by Princess of Kraków, her royal highness; my grandmother."

I warmed up to the medieval play.

"I take it her royal highness is well and in good spirits?"

"Aye, my grandmother has been ill, but she's now recovering. On the way back, my second-in-command was ambushed and captured by enemies. And my horse was injured. I barely made it out alive, my lady."

"Then my lord is forgiven.

With my gesture of ease, he sat down on the lawn across from me. We gazed at each other in silence for a while. I couldn't believe he was right here with me, in the flesh. Of course, I wanted to see him again, but I had lost hope. After all, a drop-dead-gorgeous man like Axel is always swarmed by women. He must either have a girlfriend or be seduced by lots of hopefuls. Or he is probably a charmer, womaniser, libertine, heartbreaker, jilter, Don Giovanni, who changes his lass every two months. In any case, he was way out of my league.

I forced myself to accept the fact and gave up the idea of seeing him again. It was a one-time flirtation, a random act of kindness, *et voilà. C'est tout*. It was time to get back to reality. So, I made my peace with it, and a month passed. And now, he was back out of nowhere, and I was truly happy to see him again.

"It's good to see you, Hyunah."

He must have read my mind, and to my surprise, he pronounced my name perfectly. He didn't forget my name, let alone how to pronounce it correctly.

"Pleasure to see you again, Axel. I never thought I would see you again."

"And I never thought I would see you sleeping under a tree."

His eyes twinkled, with a naughty smile.

I was in T-shirt and jeans, with messy hair and no make-up. I must look horrible! With no make-up on, you could see the freckles I always tried to hide.

"I like it out here. It's calm and relaxing, away from the people I work with."

I tried to recover from the embarrassment of being caught out like this. This was the second time he had surprised me in a vulnerable state, the first time when I was wandering shamefully high in his private space, and the second time sleeping under a tree in the park. When would be the next time?

"And you look more natural and comfortable. I almost didn't recognise you."

The first time he saw me—I was in my fancy Sonia Rykiel, with my hair and make-up done. I must have certainly looked the part of the partying crowd. And today, I didn't recognise him at first, because he had his hair in a ponytail, not like the other night when his hair flowed freely on his shoulders. Also, I spent time with him mostly in the dim light of the night rooftop and the faint rays of dawn with foggy sunlight shyly unleashed through the pastel-coloured clouds.

And now it was broad daylight. It was amazing how the same person could look different with a change of hairstyle and different lighting. Even the colour of his eyes was a different shade of blue and vividly transparent, like a husky's. A pure delight, so beautiful that it hurt my eyes.

Wait a minute, what did he say? I look 'natural and comfortable? It sounded 'unattractive and untidy' to me. Certainly not a compliment to a lady.

"And you look shabby and scruffy," I snapped. His eyes observed me keenly. He must have learned I didn't like his choice of words in describing me. He grinned broadly.

"My fair lady, forgive my foul tongue and attire. I just survived the beastly war to be at your service again. I'm here again at your disposal. Please, just say the word, my lady. Your wish is my command."

He emphasised the word 'fair', pronouncing it clearly and slowly. He made me smile again. He was a charmer alright. Did he mean that? I was thrilled. Even if it was a lie to appease me, I still liked the sound of it.

Some photographers in Paris asked me to model for their portfolios, praising me as an 'oriental beauty' or 'exotic elegance', but I always told myself not to be flattered. They were using my Asian face to add some colour and diversity to their work. I always knew my limits.

To my amusement, several of the photos turned out to be

quite pretty. The photographers put some of them in their portfolios. But those pictures were the results of good lighting, backgrounds, hair, and make-up, clothing that suited the whole mise-en-scène, and the creativity of the photographers. They did wonders. Many times, I saw models so ordinary to my eyes look stunning in photos. There are many tricks behind fabulous shoots in fashion magazines and catalogues.

But I still wanted to believe Axel meant it when he insisted on 'fair.'

"My lord, I'm sorry you have suffered such a dire predicament. You are forgiven, and you have my blessing. It pleases me greatly you came back to me alive and well."

He bowed again. "Her ladyship is so kind."

We both grinned... wait a minute. Did he ask me something in German earlier?

"What did you say in German just a moment ago?

"*Willst du spazieren gehen?*" (Would you like to go for a walk?) he repeated.

"*Ja, gern!*" I said, accepting his invitation.

He stood up and offered to help me up. As I took his hand, his masculine puff of scent vibrated the air, dazzling, mesmerising, awakening my senses. I inhaled him for a brief second as he pulled me up, his smell, faint and subtle, irresistibly sensual, spread across my body. I drowned in his fragrance, drifting into semi-consciousness, losing control of my body... dreamy and dizzy. I pinched myself to gather my wits. It took all my strength.

While we strolled, I brought up something I was curious about.

"How did you find me here?"

"Because I could smell you from a mile away."

"What?"

I could see, out of the corner of my eye, his smile.

"I have a sharp nose like a beagle. I could pick your scent from my balcony."

Right. He lived right across the street from Stadtpark, where he could have a good view of the park. Was it possible he somehow spotted me from his balcony?

"What is a beagle? Some kind of hunting dog?"

"Yes, they have one of the most powerful snouts. And I'm like them."

With that, he gave me his sweet, boyish wink.

"So, you are a hunting dog, and I'm a stag?" I said with a gesture of dismay. I stopped by a tree and leaned against it. "I don't believe you."

He faced me with a glint in his eyes.

"Prove it," I said. "What is my perfume?"

He drew close and lifted my hair delicately. He put his nose to my neck and inhaled. After a reflective silence, he did it again. This time the tip of his nose grazed my skin, and an explosion of his herbal scent penetrated my nose, this time with a hint of Granny Smith apple... It was so sensual and pleasing... my hair rose from my skin, and goosebumps formed. He held my hair against his nose and closed his eyes.

"OK. *Le premier arôme* (The first aroma): Ylang Ylang, Rose, Jasmin. The French also call it '*note de cœur*' And... um... Aldehydes... Neroli... Citron *comme notes de tête* (top note). Let's see..."

He pulled himself close from behind and plunged his nose between my ear and neck and inhaled slowly and profoundly again.

"A hint of iris," he closed his eyes again. "There's vanilla; it's faint but definitely vanilla."

He sniffed my neck again, his beautiful face frowning with concentration.

"There's one more."

This time, he pulled my hair to his nose with his eyes still closed.

"Vétiver, yes, it's vétiver. Those are the last three *notes de fond*. The backbones of a perfume. I can't tell you the exact name of the brand, but these are what I can smell."

He opened his eyes. I couldn't believe it. My jaw dropped in amazement. Those were the exact nine components of the Chanel 5 I wore. It was an old-fashioned perfume, completely out of trend, but I loved it. I have been wearing it ever since. I liked its sweet, elegant mixture of Ylang Ylang, Jasmin, and Rose, and I also used to spray it in my hair.

"And your shampoo has mint in it." He came close again and sniffed from the back of my neck. "Your shower gel has orange blossom."

I looked back at him in total astonishment. All was true. I used mint shampoo, and my shower gel had a fleurs d'orange fragrance—my favourite—that I bought in Paris.

"Wow! big, wow. I'm, astoundingly impressed," I said. "You could tell each of the nine components of my Chanel 5. Have you worked for a perfume manufacturer before?"

"No, not really. But I did some training in Grasse in France. My aunt—the daughter of my grandmother—lives in Grasse. She married a French perfumer. We used to spend the summer there whenever we could. Every morning, we played a game of guessing scents with my aunt and uncle. I was pretty good at it. They even offered me to train to be a 'Nez', which is a French term for a scent master, to fabricate perfumes."

"Aha, that's why you speak French?"

"*Oui, un peu. J'ai fait aussi l'école de Beaux-arts à Paris pour une semester.*" (Yes, a little. I also went to Beaux-arts school in Paris for one semester)

"*A bon? C'est vrai?*" (Really? Is that true?)

"*Oui, mademoiselle. Quand j'avais dix-sept ans.*" (Yes, Miss. When I was seventeen.)

"*Oui, d'accord. Tu as du faire des sacrée stage à Grasse. Mais ça ne peut pas expliquer comment tu pourrais me sentir de ton balcon. C'est au de la capacité humane.* (Yes, alright. You must have had a hell of an internship in Grasse. But that can't explain how you could smell me from your balcony. It is beyond human capacity.) I still don't get how you could smell me from your balcony."

He grinned with a mischievous glint in his eyes. "The wind is blowing south-east in my direction."

He pointed to his rooftop. I followed his finger and could see his terrace on top of a building further away, partly hidden by a tree. He may have an extra-sharp nose, but it was still a far-fetched theory. Unless... oh, a book I had read not so long ago.

"You remind me of Jean-Baptist Grenouille!"

"Patrick Süskind?" He raised his eyebrows. "But I don't go around murdering women to collect samples of their scent."

"Did you read the book? I was fascinated by the story,"

"Of course. Patrick Süskind is a German writer. Did you read the book in German?"

"No," I replied. "The French-translated version. My German is not good enough to understand a whole book, but the French translation was well done. I read it in three days. Extraordinary plot. Süskind has a hell of an imagination. I give him '*chapeaux*'." I mimed throwing out a hat in admiration.

"Alright, Axel...let's say I believe you. But you should swear to all Gods and saints in front of me. Especially St. Catherine of Bologna for the Artists," I started. "She is the Saint who protects artists within her wings and blesses them with her wisdom. Swear to me by the name of St. Catherine, what you're saying is true, and I will believe you. If you swear falsely, not only you will lose her protection, but all your artwork will be cursed forever."

He stared at me calmly as I threatened him with nonsense.

"OK, Hyunah. I will tell you the truth of how I found you today, but you have to do something for me."

"I'm listening."

"Spend the rest of the day with me."

"What? You show up out of the blue and expect me to clear my schedule for the day?" I was thrilled but pretended otherwise.

"I'm supposing you don't have anything important to do, seeing you're idly enjoying the park."

"Alright, but I need to go home and make a few arrangements."

I lied. Vienna fashion week was over a week ago, and I had little to do. What I wanted to do was to go home and change into a new dress.

"Sure. I will take you home."

"And on one condition."

"Tell me."

"I would like to see your atelier. This time with your invitation, not as an intruder."

A fresh smile formed on his beautiful face. His eyes brightened as if refreshed by the memory. The memory of the night how he had first met me.

"Alright. Maybe tomorrow. It's a bit messy. I just came back, and things are lying around everywhere."

"No problem. I didn't expect you to show me right away. Take your time."

When we walked back to his place, Herbert greeted us with a broad, genuine smile.

He and Axel exchanged a few words in Viennese dialect, and Axel looked back at me.

"Hyunah, this is—"

"Herbert," I cut in. "We've met already when I brought back your pullover."

"Oh."

"Nice to see you, Herbert."

"Nice to see you, too."

Herbert watched us curiously. At first, he gave the impression he had never seen Axel bring a girl home. Or was it, 'Oh, a new girl this time'? I assumed I was not the first to waltz into this garage in his company. My heart skipped a beat. *Of course, women don't leave a handsome man like him alone. Didn't I know that already? Well, what the hell. Why don't I just enjoy the moment without over-thinking for once?*

"Do you mind if I take you home on the motorcycle?" Axel called.

"No, I don't mind."

It was still warm outside when we left on his Ducati. The wind blew more gently this time. I held him from behind, touching his slim waist through the light denim jacket he had on. To my amazement, the comfort I sensed was as if I'd done this several times. It was odd, considering how scared I had been the last time. The smooth cruise through Vienna provided stunning afternoon visuals. He drove carefully, stopping at every red light. How gallant. He was a gentleman alright.

He was the first person in Vienna who treated me with kindness, without expectations. Before him, everyone I had come across wanted something from me. What I could do for them or offer them. Maybe he just wanted to form a friendship with a lonely foreigner or a casual date with no strings attached. Nothing wrong with that. I could use a friend here. A friendship outside the business circle was a welcoming idea. Shortly, we arrived at my place. He stopped his Ducati outside the Zimmerman gym and removed his helmet.

"How much time do you need?"

"Uh... maybe thirty to forty-five minutes?"

It was 5:30 pm, and I wanted to have a shower first, freshen up, and then change into a new dress—make myself pretty.

"I will be back in an hour. Please wait for me out here," he said. I was oblivious to some models going up to my apartment as we talked, and they were watching us— well, more precisely, Axel. A hotshot booker called Pedro keenly observed Axel. Rumours said he had the biggest clients in Vienna and was friends with some of the top designers all across Europe.

Axel gave me a sweet smile with a swift wink before starting the engine. Late afternoon sunlight poured over his face, illuminating his sparkling blue eyes. His slightly pale face had a couple of blond strands escaping from the ponytail. His light blue summer denim jacket was in harmony with his bony shoulders... he was a vision. And I had no idea everybody behind me was staring at him.

"See you in an hour, mademoiselle."

He put on the helmet, and his Ducati roared. I stood for a moment, watching him disappear down the street. When I turned to hurry upstairs, the spectators jumped at me all at the same time.

"Oh, my, who is that sweetheart? Which model agency is he from?"

Pedro talked loudest and got my attention first. He took out his business card and handed it to me. "Can you have him call me please, darling? I have a client looking for a treasure like him for a TV commercial. And I'm more than sure that he IS our guy."

He leaned in and whispered, "It's for Hugo Boss."

"Wow, who is he?" Joanna, a model from New York, barged in. "He's smoking hot. Which agency is he at? Is he new in town?"

The group also included Paul and Anne, a couple from Melbourne, and Mark, a gay photographer from London, all stunned into silence and under the impression that Axel was a model. As I pushed past them, I blurted, "He is not a model, Pedro."

"What? Really? If a guy like that is not a model, it's pure waste. He could make tons of money. We will make him a model. Can you at least talk to him and give him my card?" Pedro shouted behind me. I was already halfway up the stairs, on my way to the door of the flat.

"I will try, but I'm almost sure he's not interested."

I dashed to the shower, frantically scrubbing myself with shower gel and shampoo. I stood for a moment under the running water, anticipating a date with the most gorgeous man I had ever met. My heart pounded, and I was dizzy with excitement. As I dried my hair, right before applying make-up, my roommate, Dorothe, a Danish model, came over.

"Oh, wow, look at you, Kim." Most people who couldn't pronounce my name seemed to agree on calling me, Kim. "Are you going out on a date? I heard you just arrived with a guy 'so wildly smoking hot', riding a Ducati. Is that true? I'm so jealous! You have to tell me all the details. Where did you find him?"

"Dorothe, I will tell you about it later. Now please excuse me. I need to get ready."

"OK, just let me know if you want me to help you choose a dress."

I got myself ready in a frenzy, applied my make-up, and tied my hair up in an up-style fashion to show off my neckline. After all, I was a make-up artist and stylist. I knew what I was doing.

After struggling with hairpins for ten minutes, I yelled out for help, and the girls flooded into the room. They debated about which way was the best until Anne, from Melbourne, came forward and took charge. She knew how to handle the pins, and her work was excellent. My hair looked nice. Just like I wanted it —pretty and natural.

I wore the same dress I had worn when I returned Axel's pullover. I appreciated the opportunity to wear it for him again. It was already 6:25 pm, and I had five minutes left. I chose water-drop-shaped pearl earrings. They complimented my romantic, natural, elegant floral print dress. For the finishing touch, I fiercely powdered my nose and sprayed myself with Chanel 5. I checked myself in the mirror, put my Ferragamo sandals on, and opened the door.

"Wow, you look beautiful, Kim. Very nice dress," Mark observed. He was openly gay and didn't hesitate to express his admiration of Axel. Everybody agreed with my look.

"Don't forget to give him my card, darling," Pedro added. He usually called me 'darling' when he had some favour to ask me. That's how it worked in the fashion business—anyone you could benefit from was addressed as 'Darling' or 'Sweetheart' or similar bullshit. Sometimes simply because they didn't know each other's names. What a load of crap.

Once I got downstairs, I realised how uncomfortable my designer shoes were. They would not do, since we were potentially going on walks. I went back up in a hurry and changed into more comfortable shoes before hurrying downstairs. My heart thundered wildly with each step of the way down. It was almost 6:30 pm. I anxiously watched the street, waiting for Axel.

Meanwhile, all heads from my flat were by the window, watching. They all wanted to get a glance at Axel. I scanned myself again. Oh, no.

"*Oh, shit, merde, merde!*"

If he arrived on his Ducati, how would I climb on with my knee-high dress? It was too late to go up and change. What should I do? Ask him to wait here while I changed again? Or invite him in? The models and Pedro would be all over him. He wouldn't like that, especially since he stressed he didn't fancy mingling with the fashion crowd.

While I debated, a small, red Fiat pulled over right in front of me. The driver, a strikingly attractive, tall, and slender young man in a dusty pink shirt and blue-grey cotton trousers, jumped out. I didn't recognise him at first behind his sunglasses until he swiftly removed them.

Axel! My eyes grew wide. He looked good enough to eat. He stared at me like a kid itching to open his gift.

"You look ravishing, my lady."

"And you look dashingly handsome, my lord."

He held the passenger side door open for me. I got into the car. A burst of cheers, whistles, and shouting erupted upstairs as we drove away.

Steffle & Hawelka

"If I'm not at home, then I'm in the Hawelka. And if I'm not in the Hawelka, then I'm on my way to the Hawelka."

I was reading what Alfred Schmeller (1920 - 1990), the art critic), once said about the Hawelka, an authentic old café where Axel took me after a long walk that evening.

We were barely two steps inside the café when the owner, who looked about a hundred and twenty years old but still alive and kicking, vigorously shook Axel's hand and greeted us with a very warm, wholly genuine smile. It was Leopold Hawelka, the man who had opened the café in 1939 with his wife, Josefine.

The inner decor depicted authenticity. The undeniably worn upholstered seats in the corner, the partially battered wooden chairs cluttered around marble tables, and the threads of frazzled velvet curtains... they were the witnesses to the lapse of time and its history. The entire interior desperately needed refreshing, but they had left everything untouched on purpose.

Time seemed frozen inside the café. It was reminiscent of Vienna in the old days. Hardly anything had changed since its founding in 1939. I felt a kind of nostalgia for its stubborn resistance to modernisation. It was only natural that the Hawelka, with its long tradition of hospitality, had gained its reputation as the post-war haunt of young artists, writers, and intellectuals. Andy Warhol, Arthur Miller, and many others visited.

Posters advertising local art exhibitions covered one side of the café. Axel pointed to the original artwork dotting other walls, explaining that some were accepted in payment for debts gathered up by broke artists, a sign of generosity by the owner of the establishment, to support poor young artists. No wonder this place was Axel's favourite hangout.

Mr Hawelka knew Axel well. He talked to him in Viennese dialect, and all the other tuxedoed waiters greeted him cheerfully. We settled into a corner table and ordered food and locally brewed beer. I was exhausted and famished after three hours of walking around Vienna. And I thanked heaven I had changed into comfortable shoes at the last minute.

First, Axel had taken me to a sidewalk café in Schweden Platz for an apéritif and some light snacks. Sitting outside, watching Vienna slowly transform into a blissful early summer evening, we talked while sipping local white wine from Krems—it was crisp and fresh to the palate initially, and pleasantly floral once swallowed. It was a nice surprise that Austrians made such a good wine.

And we ambled to Domkirche St. Stephan, snaking our way through Alt-Wien. Axel was familiar with every single alley and pathway in the old town. I found myself discovering a new face of Vienna while following him around. It was a wonder.

"Are you ready to do some steps?" asked Axel with a smile. It hinted a challenge as we approached the South Tower he called "Steffl." I learned later it was what the Viennese affectionately called the Stephansdom South Tower. There was no escalator to the 'Türmerstube' at the top, where you could enjoy a splendid view of the entire city. Instead, we had to climb three hundred and forty-three steps. It took readiness, fitness, and determination to complete the climb.

"Oh, dear." I breathed hard, but I was desperate to see the

amazing views. He stared at me warmly and said, "But you will be rewarded with a great view, I promise."

"Alright then, three hundred and forty-three steps it is!"

Axel had no problem climbing up the endless steps, but I had to stop three times to catch my breath before reaching the top. And there we were. The view was magnificent. The 360-degree entirety of Vienna spread out at our feet. The skyline was breathtaking. All the other tourists were busy taking pictures, and we were the only ones without a camera—too busy enjoying the view and each other's company. I was truly happy for the first time in a very long time.

I stared at Axel. With the mellow evening light, his fantastic, beautiful eyes sparkled, reflecting the sunlight. His eyes changed colour depending on the light around him. Admiring the beauty of the view, I said, "It's beautiful up here. Thank you for bringing me up here."

"My pleasure, Hyunah. You look lovely. I'm lucky to have you with me this evening."

It is ME who is damn lucky to have you. La vie en rose.

I pinched my leg to see if I was dreaming. I couldn't believe my luck. A drop-dead-gorgeous, living Roman statue was telling me HE was lucky to have me.

"I arrived in Vienna in December last year. Since then, I was always running around looking for a job but never had the time to enjoy Vienna like this. You must know Vienna well. Were you born here?"

"No. I'm not a genuine Viennese. I was born near Krems, where the white wine we just had was made. Some owners of the wineries there are friends of my grandparents. I grew up on a farm with horses and animals. My grandfather is a horse breeder."

"So, you grew up with your grandparents?"

"Yes."

As he didn't mention his parents, I knew he preferred not to talk about them. For once, I was not under the influence of anything, so I didn't make any undesirable comments like the first time we had met.

"Do you like horses? Did you grow up riding them?"

"I love horses, yes. When I was a baby, before I could even walk, they put me on horseback, starting with a small pony. I did some show jumping and horse-racing competitions when I was a boy."

Out of the corner of my eye, I observed his arms. Even under the dusty pink shirt, my professional eyes spotted his biceps and triceps, muscles naturally developed from doing sports such as horse-riding. He had a nice athletic body. I could tell.

I had been working with male models for two years, so my eyes were trained to recognise a nice body through clothing to ensure a good photo shoot for commercial purposes. But most of the male models achieved their muscles by working out and taking protein powder, and some fashion designers hated that. They wanted a naturally athletic body, just like Axel's. No wonder Pedro jumped at the prospect. An image of nagging Pedro came to my mind. I didn't want to ask Axel about such things now, but I had to do it at some point.

"I need to ask you something, and I think I know the answer already, but I need to get this over with."

"What is it?"

"You know, when you accompanied me home this afternoon, a booker from the model agency saw you and insisted I ask you if you would be interested in modelling. As a part-time job, I guess. I know how you feel about those people and the fashion crowd, but he was adamant about it. You know you are a very attractive man, right? He wanted to cast you for a TV commercial. He said you would make tons of money; I mean if you are interested in making some extra income."

Axel turned towards me. His smile was gone. His lips tightened.

"Do you think I would have chosen to be an artist if I wanted to make tons of money? These people think they can buy anybody if they propose money. Good heavens, no. Tell him I'm not interested."

"Alright, fair enough. I thought so, too. It was stupid of me to ask, sorry about that. Now tell me more about horses. How did you grow up with them?"

Axel produced a photo from his wallet. It was a picture of a beautiful white horse with a pretty blond boy sitting on top.

"Oh, my God, was that you? What a beautiful horse! How old were you?"

"Hmm... I must have been thirteen or fourteen. Her name is Frühling. She's my best friend. She's still alive now."

"Your best friend is a horse? That's interesting. In the world where we live nowadays, we find more connections and affection with animals, not humans. I kind of agree with you. They love you for who you are, not for what you can do for them. They never betray you, deceive you, abandon you, take advantage of you, or leave you as we wicked humans do."

He shifted towards me and faced me.

"Oh, young lady, you seem to have some anger within you. Not that I blame you. That's the reason my best friend is a horse. But a beautiful one."

We both giggled. While we admired the view, the sky grew darker... vivid pink, orange, and violet clouds gathered around the sun. Did he plan to see the sunset with me all along? Or did it just happen? Whatever the motive, I felt grateful someone was trying to show me beautiful things.

"You have a thing for the sunrise and sunset, right? This is amazing. I always find something wondrous about them. Each one of them I have seen so far is never the same. It's like Mother Nature is presenting us a different gift each time we watch it."

"It's my favourite moment of the day. Each time I discover different tones of colours around the sky. It reminds me of the beauty of nature."

"Speaking of which," I began, "can I ask you a personal question?"

He turned around and looked straight into my eyes.

"Go ahead," he said curiously.

"Well, I don't know you well. It's only the second time I've seen you. But I was wondering..."

Now he locked his eyes with mine. His eyes sparkled.

"Yes?"

"Why did you choose to be an artist? It's quite a difficult path, you know. And those who became famous, I mean, a good majority of them, suffered from hunger, personal tragedies, mental illness, depression, endless afflictions, and such... they never saw the light of day before they finished their miserable lives. Many of them only became famous after death. Van Gogh cut off his ear and shot himself in the wheat field. Nicolas de Staël, one of my favourite painters, jumped to his death from his balcony. Jackson Pollock drank himself senseless and drove into a tree... you see, none of them had a normal or happy life. But then, if you are normal, how can you be an artist?"

"I didn't choose to be an artist to be happy and normal. I had no other choice. I had a difficult childhood—a rough period I don't wish to remember. I was a shy child and incapable of communicating. The only time I was at peace with myself was when I played with horses and drew whatever the hell I wanted. It was not a choice but a means of survival to keep myself together and stay away from the agony I had. Probably the only way to express myself in some way. A teacher at my school noticed me as a kid with some kind of talent for drawing. Then my grandma sent me to an art school.

At seventeen, I went to École des Beaux-Arts in Paris for one semester. I learned a lot. The French people had quite a different approach toward the Arts. A breath of fresh air for me. For a shy boy who'd grown up on a farm, the different culture, I mean, the language, the way of thinking, the rich history, the food, the beautiful architecture, and the special atmosphere of Paris... everything seemed inspiring. They opened my inner eye, my gawky, blocked character, and my attitude towards the world of art.

"Parisians are unorthodox, liberal, expressive, and overly critical in every way. They say whatever they think, about any subject without the slightest hesitation. They called it '*liberté d'expression.*' (Freedom of expression.) Moreover, learning French was mandatory since all the classes were given in French. It kept me busy. It helped me put my rough childhood aside. I could forget about it for a while. It was fascinating. I'm sure you share some of these things with me. You have spent a few years there yourself. After that, I was admitted to the Academy of Fine Arts in Vienna. *Et voilà*. Here I am. Stages of the path to misery, as you called it."

"Oh, Axel, please don't say that."

By the time we climbed down another endless flight of steps, it was getting late. We were both starving and tired. Moreover, my feet hurt.

"We need to go somewhere very close, or I will pass out in the street," I threatened.

"Oh, we can't have that, can we? I know a good place."

And within three minutes, we arrived at the Hawelka. After a vigorous welcome from Leopold Hawelka himself, we finally collapsed into our seats at a corner table. I was relieved when the food arrived. I ordered Gemusestrudel, and Axel ordered sauerkraut. But instead of the usual potatoes and sausages, there were only potatoes with steamed vegetables on his plate.

"Oh, they forgot the sausages," I remarked.

"No, they made a special plate for me. I don't eat meat."

"Really? An Austrian who doesn't eat meat? Aren't you full of surprises?"

"I grew up on a farm with horses and animals. They are my friends. I can't imagine eating them. Seeing an animal that was once alive and running, being butchered, cut, chopped and cooked, makes me sick to my stomach."

Oh. It was lucky I'd ordered vegetable strudel. I ordered it because it was one of the few dishes that came with no potatoes or pork. After some months of living in Vienna, I was sick of

Kartoffel (potatoes) and Wiener Schnitzel (the famous Viennese pork cutlet). I just couldn't have them anymore.

"Aren't we humans wicked creatures?" I said. "We have been destroying nature, including all species of animals. Killing them for consumption is the less devilish part. Men have been hunting them for sport, slaughtering them for entertainment, like *corrida*. Explorers and poachers have been diligently extinguishing rare species of birds, mammals, whales, sea turtles, and reptiles... the list is endless. And this will never stop as long as humans are rampaging on this planet."

Axel's eyes twinkled on me with keen interest.

"You have sharp opinions and powers of observation. We destroy and create at the same time."

"My conscience is clear. I see very few things we do that give us joy. There's the ability to create. To create something out of nothing, with our imagination, endless searching, and a quest to understand who we are and why we are here. Maybe that's why art exists. It truly, sincerely, genuinely nourishes our souls. We are no different from animals if we can't create beautiful music, paintings, sculptures, architecture, or any form of art, for that matter. I am not an artist, but I am fascinated by artists' capacity to transform our emotions through a piece of art and move our hearts to make us happy or sad, depending on what they want to express."

Axel stopped eating. His blue eyes fixed on me with a dazzling flare, as if to pierce through my soul.

"Oh, don't look at me like that. I stopped eating meat a few years ago. I only eat vegetables, carbohydrates, and seafood. I ceased to eat your friends. Please."

We both burst into laughter.

He told me a childhood story. His grandfather found a stallion that had won some racing competitions. He was brought over to mate with mares at the ranch. And Axel, as a young child, innocently asked his grandpa why the stallion mounted at the back of a mare and made hideous whinnying noises.

"It's to look higher, my dear, to have a better vision," his grandpa used to tell him.

And innocent and naïve as he was, Axel believed it. He imitated a stallion humping on a mare, reproducing the same noises, mimicking an excited horse. I laughed until my belly ached and I almost choked on my food.

For dessert, Axel ordered Buchteln, a house speciality made with an original recipe from Josefine Hawelka—freshly oven-baked fluffy pastry filled with plum mousse, served only at night. It smelled delicious. And it was a delight. *I would come back here just for this.*

The mention of Arthur Miller on the wall came to my attention. I said as if I was thinking aloud, "It's sad most people only know Arthur Miller as a man who managed to get Marilyn Monroe. But he also wrote *Death of a Salesman*. It's funny how you are judged by whom you go to bed with, not for who you are or what you have accomplished."

"You are very keen on literature for a fashion stylist."

"Because I studied English literature at university. I have a bachelor's degree. I even wrote a thesis on *Symbolism in John Keats*, my favourite poet, in my last year to complete my degree. My keen interest in literature started with my father. He is a celebrated author in Korea."

"Then, if you allow me to ask, why did you end up working in fashion?"

"Ha-ha! Good question. When you graduate from a university in Korea, either you find a job or a husband who would give you the security of a home. Most parents want to marry you off, so you are sold like a mare. If you are from a good, wealthy family, you are listed on every matchmaker's agenda. Of course, there are always exceptions. A few people marry for love regardless of their parents' opinion. Once you're married, your husband expects you to attend to domestic duties: cook, do his laundry, clean the house and be obedient in bed to produce offspring. You are fenced in. Soon, you have kids, and your life becomes a boring routine. In the morning, you find yourself glad to see the back of your husband, relieved to drop the kids at school, and at night in bed, sex becomes a tedious routine, or you just want to skip it altogether, for heaven's sake.

"One day, you come across a handsome man in the elevator and fantasise about eloping with him. But it only stays in your mind because your social duty and role as a housewife will never allow such a thing. You're trapped in the system. And one day, you wake up in the morning and have this terrible urge to end it all. You look at yourself in the mirror and realise you are nobody. People don't call you by your name anymore. They refer to you as somebody's wife or some child's mother. You are absorbed into society, and your identity disappears. All you want to do is to jump from your twelfth-story balcony. Because life has no meaning. It gives you no more sense, joy, or purpose. Nothing matters anymore. You're a prisoner in this system of the society that guaranteed your security in the beginning, but you don't want it anymore. And that woman in the mirror would have been me in ten years. I knew it as clear as daylight. And I couldn't have that, could I? I mean, I'm not saying I wanted to be famous and leave my name in the history books, but I was sure as hell that I didn't want to end up like that.

"So, I had to find a way. If I wanted to find a job, the only option was to be an English teacher at a high school or to study for a few more years to become a university professor. It didn't appeal to me. Then I remembered how much I enjoyed my trip to Europe during the summer holiday of my last year at the university. Since childhood, I dreamed of going to Europe to travel around and see a different parts of the world. I had pen pals all over Europe, and I had been saving money to buy a plane ticket. I met a like-minded girl at high school, and we decided to travel to Europe together.

"So, we set off and travelled around many countries, using a Eurail pass for two months. Voyaging by train was wonderful. And I liked Paris a lot. I liked its artistic environment, beautiful architecture, and the lovely French language. And when I was trying to find a way out, Paris was practically screaming at me to come back. And I wished to find a job I could learn in Paris. So that I could earn my living to gain my independence and financial freedom. That way, I didn't need a husband to provide for me and, in exchange, be fenced in as a housewife.

"So, I talked to my dad. I asked if he and mom could advance me the dowry they would offer me upon my marriage, as is the tradition in my country. I would use that money to go to France and learn to work in fashion. And I would not ask for any more money if I got married one day. It was a bold move for someone like me who had a classical education and a conventional background. Being a writer and open-minded visionary, my dad agreed. I was incredibly lucky. *Et voilà*, here I am today."

Axel listened intensively without interrupting. When I was done, he nodded and smiled.

"Alright, my lady, now I understand. I could not figure out why a woman of your culture and education would choose to work in the fashion industry. Not that I don't appreciate *la mode*. Some high fashion I observed in Paris, '*Haute couture*,' they called it, is not only fantastic but also inspiring. I see the beauty and attraction to it. I only hope you have found what you have been looking for."

Later, long after midnight, Axel took me home. We had such a good time together, we didn't notice the time pass. He pulled the car over in front of the Zimmerman gym and opened the door for me. We faced each other in the street.

"I had a great time, Axel. Thank you for showing me around. I'm discovering Vienna with you."

"It was a pleasure for me too, Hyunah. And about discovering Vienna, I can help you with that. Would you like me to show you around a bit more? As a friend, I mean. You look like you could use a friend outside of your business circle. And I enjoy spending time with you. Would you consider that, Hyunah? Will you have me as a friend?"

He looked me straight in the eyes, his mesmerising blue eyes sparkling. It was a plea no woman in this world could refuse. And I had no intention of doing that. No girl in her right mind would deny such a sweet request. I was thrilled, and my heart started pounding.

"I would like that very much. I'm so grateful. I don't know how to thank you."

"Don't thank me yet. We have only just begun. So, you will have me as a friend?"

I will have you any way you wish. As long as I can see you. I will be a friend, companion, mate, lover, or even a slave. I shall scrub the floor of your atelier if that's the only way I can be with you. I will be anything to you as long as you will have me.

"I would be honoured, my lord."

"Then I will be your humble servant, my lady."

He stared at me. A pixie-like smile formed on his beautiful face.

"So, would you like to know how I found you this afternoon at the park?"

Oh, my God, of course. I was having such a sweet moment with him, that I completely forgot about our deal.

"Yes. Tell me."

"It was Herbert. He saw you going towards the park. He told me I might find you there if I was lucky."

So, it was Herbert who saw me. I had no idea. Since returning Axel's pullover, I went back to the Stadtpark whenever I was free. In jeans and a T-shirt. I used to sit and lie down on the grass. It had become a merry routine. And probably, unconsciously, I had a secret wish. I must admit I was hoping to run into Axel again, should he walk around the park when taking a break, as the park was only across the street from his place. But I never expected he would go to find me on purpose. Life is full of surprises sometimes, especially when you least expect them.

"Aha, so it was him. A human nose couldn't possibly smell me from that distance. A beagle, perhaps, but not you. You almost had me, though. Now when do I get to the end of my bargain? You said I would be invited to your atelier."

"Tomorrow, if you can. It's Saturday. I guess you don't work?"

"No, I'm free all day."

"Okay. Come by my place for coffee tomorrow morning. Ten or eleven, whenever it suits you. I need to tidy up my place and my atelier. It's messy."

"Alright then. Kill me tomorrow; let me live tonight," I whispered, dreamlike as if I were acting in a theatre. He watched me closely for a moment before he said, "Are you quoting Shakespeare? One of his tragedies?"

"Yes, my lord. I played Desdemona in *Othello* when I was at the university. This is the ending part where Desdemona realises that she is about to be done in by her jealous husband, Othello, who is full of murderous rage. She pleads for her life but accepts that Othello has the right to kill her if he wants to. She doesn't ask for her life to be spared, but only that her death be delayed until tomorrow. How tragic, and how sweetly poetic."

Axel pulled his eyebrows together in a frown and immediately dropped to his knees, spreading out his arms as if holding something in his hands.

"My lady. Let this sword pierce through my heart, should I contemplate such treachery towards you. I shall not live a day longer with that atrocity within me."

I burst into laughter.

"Arise, my lord, I have no such doubt."

He stood up and drew my hand towards his lips like a knight, with one graceful movement. He could be one hell of an actor, melting every woman's heart.

'What's in a name? That which we call a rose by any other word would smell as sweet.'

A quote I memorised from *Romeo and Juliette* streamed through my consciousness. Wait a minute. He said, 'if I would have him as a friend.' If I quoted *Romeo and Juliette*, he would be horrified and run away from me as fast as he could. I refrained.

"Coffee tomorrow morning, then. Her ladyship extends her gratitude, my lord."

"Good night, my lady."

He kissed my hand. His lips on my hand landed like a sweet breeze, a fresh zephyr caressing my forehead when I lie under a tree. *What would it be like, how would I feel, if ever he kissed my lips? That would not happen. He said he wanted to be friends. Not a couple. He was drawing a line between us so that I would not have a wrong idea about him.*

And that was fine with me. I would be anything he wished me to be. As long as I could see him. I still couldn't believe a drop-dead-gorgeous man like him would even consider doing anything with me, let alone be a friend and a personal tour guide.

The night was crisp and cool. I inhaled deeply, filling my lungs with the sweet air as I watched his car disappear into the night.

Klimt-Der Küss-Belvedere Museum

There was a trendy French bakery in Mariahilfer Straße that I had ached to visit since I heard about it. I stepped into the boulangerie. Axel had invited me for coffee this morning, and I wanted to surprise him with some authentic French croissants and pains aux chocolat.

And there was also my upbringing—*never go to someone's house empty-handed when invited. Even if it's for tea or coffee*, my mom used to chant. The buttery and yeasty smell of viennoiseries hit my nose as soon as I stepped in. The croissants, pains aux chocolat, chaussons aux pommes, pains aux raisin, baguettes freshly out of the oven... all looked authentic, just like in Paris. I bought every one of them, thinking there would also be Herbert and maybe other mechanics in the workshop.

When I arrived at the garage, I found Herbert and two other young mechanics working on a classic car, probably an Aston Martin like the ones in the old James Bond movies.

Herbert cheerfully greeted me. "*Grüßgott. Wie geht's?* (Hello, how are you?) Axel's waiting for you upstairs."

"Good morning, Herbert. Wow, what is this car? It looks awesome."

"It's an old Aston Martin. The photographer upstairs is going to shoot photos with it today."

"Oh, really?"

My professional curiosity got me wondering. Who is lucky enough to ride in a collector's item Aston Martin and get paid for it?

I took the elevator and got off on the sixth floor. A guy, probably the photographer's assistant, opened the door. I found people running around, preparing for a photo session. Models sitting by the mirror for make-up, a photographer checking his cameras and equipment, all sorts of wedding dresses on coat hangers and men's costumes that looked to be for a groom.

Two Austrian women, one older who appeared to be in charge, and the other younger, checked on all the items lying in front of them without a second's rest. It must be a shoot for some sort of wedding dress catalogue.

"Oh, Kim, is that you? You did make-up for me at the fashion show the other day."

I turned to the voice who addressed me. A tall, blonde Swedish girl faced me. She said to the photographer, "She's a make-up artist and stylist from Paris, Mike. She speaks fluent French and does fabulous make-up."

"Oh? Are you here to give us a hand?"

"Oh, no, no. I'm here to see Axel."

The photographer, Mike, approached me. "You mean the painter upstairs? You have to go to the seventh floor. He has a different entrance. The door that leads upstairs to his place is locked from his side. How do you know him? He has a gorgeous face and a perfect body. I asked him several times if he would pose for a photo. He declined each time."

The Swedish girl added, "Yeah, I heard he is smoking hot. But I've never seen him. He's a ghost!"

I saw her make-up—in my professional view, a disaster. It was overpowering and made her look like a dancer in the cabaret, not a bride. And I found out who did this job. Vicky, the hairstylist I met at the fashion show, was applying make-up to the other model. Oh, no. It happened so many times; the client didn't want to pay for a make-up artist and a hairstylist, so they hired someone to do both. Vicky must have said that she could do both to get the job. The consequence was miserable. But I was not hired for the work. It was not my place to say anything. So, I just suffered the misery. The Swedish girl whispered in my ear. Out of the corner of my eye, I noticed Vicky watching us.

"Don't you think my make-up is too strong? I look like a whore in a bar."

I couldn't agree more, but I just nodded quickly. My eyes dropped to a male model in a groom's suit. The tie was a wrong match with the shirt and the jacket. Oh, my God. So much for renting an expensive Aston Martin and going so wrong with the models. The lack of taste was quite apparent, and it was shocking, coming from people working in fashion. I sighed. The photographer seemed to catch on quickly.

"Listen, Kim, do you want to hang with us a bit? Give us some advice? We can give you a ride on James Bond's Aston Martin," Mike sweet-talked me.

Oh, you want to use me for free? I saw what he was getting at. "I'm sorry, it's tempting, but I can't do that. I'm expected upstairs."

"*Excusez-moi, j'ai entendu que vous venez de Paris. Je m'appelle Anne-Sophie, je viens de Paris moi aussi.*" (Excuse me, I heard you come from Paris. My name is Anne-Sophie, I'm from Paris as well.) I turned to a familiar French voice, and in front of me was the other girl. Her make-up was not fully done yet, but it was the same vulgarity. Quite a pitiful sight.

A bride's make-up should stay natural, romantic, and elegant. With brown tones, using a light touch of colour. Her eye shadow was bright violet, pink, and blue. She looked like a dancer at the Lido. All she needed was a feather in her hair.

She whispered in French, "*Je voulais juste vous demander votre avis. La coiffeuse Autrichienne m'a maquillée, et je trouve ça horri-*

ble. On dirait je suis danseuse de Crazy Horse, n'est-ce pas?" (I just wanted your opinion. The Austrian hairdresser did my make-up, and I think it's horrible. I look like a dancer at Crazy Horse, right?)

"Oui, je vois ça. Mais malheureusement, je ne peux rien faire. On m'a pas pris pour ce travail. Je suis vraiment désolée, mais ce n'est pas à moi de faire ou toucher quoi que ce soit." (Yes, I see it. But unfortunately, I can't do anything. I'm not hired for this job. I'm sorry, but it is not my place to do anything whatsoever.)

I whispered, hoping only the French model would understand me. Poor Anne-Sophie looked like she wanted to cry. I faced Mike. I drew him aside and whispered, "I'm not a photographer, but if I were you, I would go for a wide-angle, avoiding close up to the face. Don't show the make-up. It's inappropriate for a bride. Concentrate your image more on clothes. It's a catalogue for wedding dresses, right?"

"Yes. Are you sure you don't want to stay?" It sounded more like a plea.

"No, I can't. But why don't you make some extra shots in black and white so the make-up won't be so visible? You will only see the contrast of shades in the face. And it would look more romantic with the Aston Martin."

"That's a great idea. Thank you."

"And next time, hire me."

With a smile, I slid my business card into his shirt pocket.

The door leading upstairs to the penthouse flew open. Axel was standing there with a blue polo loosely hugging the contours of his upper body and faded jeans outlining his legs. He looked stunning, with the sunlight behind him softly kissing his athletic body, like a spotlight drawing all eyes towards him. All the chatter instantly died.

He said politely, *"Grüß Gott,"* (Good day) and he called me, *"Hyunah, c'est par ici."* (Hyunah, it's over here.)

He inclined his head towards his atelier. I ran up the stairs like a faithful dog, dashing to his master, but not before saying, "Good luck, everyone. Have fun with the Aston Martin."

"Ooh la la, qu'est-ce qu'il est beau! Il est canon... Quel beau gosse." (Ooh la la, how beautiful he is. He is hot... what a handsome boy) Anne-Sophie exclaimed behind me. *I know that, my dear.*

Once we were on the other side of the door upstairs, Axel locked the door. He appeared to be desperate to keep his privacy from this crowd. This way, it was like two independent flats with separate entrances. The rooftop terrace was only accessible from his floor.

He smiled, and I dived into the blue of his eyes. I wanted to throw myself in his arms and kiss him. Instead, I contented with a French-style *bise*, a friendly way of greeting common in France and parts of Europe. When I touched his cheek with mine, I picked up his divine scent.

"I'm sorry, Hyunah. I should have told you to come to the seventh floor to prevent you from confronting the people downstairs."

"It's alright. I saw Herbert preparing a fabulous Aston Martin for them."

"I know. He has a good car collection. He can give you a ride sometime."

"Oh, that's fantastic!"

I pushed the bag of croissants to his nose. "I brought you something."

"Smells like a French bakery." He raised his eyebrows. "Come on. I just made fresh coffee."

I followed him to the kitchen.

"I bought enough for everyone. I mean, for Herbert and his mechanics in the garage."

Axel asked, "Shall we invite them for coffee with us?"

"Sure."

"Alright. You didn't have to bring anything, but thank you."

He went to the living room to call Herbert. I loved hearing

him speak German in the Viennese dialect, although Hoch Deutsch was easier for me to understand.

"The car is ready. They can come up for a quick coffee."

A few minutes later, the guys arrived. Herbert entered first, followed by Ulf, tall with light brown hair, and Karl-Heinz, medium height, stockily built, with dark hair. All young, in vibrant shape. They would have no problem enjoying the French delicacies. They settled around the sofa in the living room.

Axel and I went to the kitchen. There was freshly filtered coffee ready to serve, but Axel took out an Italian Moka pot and asked, "Do you prefer filtered coffee or moka?"

"Moka. It makes the best coffee."

"I see you have lived in Paris. I also prefer Moka."

Moka was richer and stronger, just the way I liked. Plus, it went well with buttery croissants.

"Mais oui, mon cher, je suis devenu Parisienne." (Of course, my dear, I have become a Parisienne)

When the Moka was ready, he poured two small cups. With a sweet boyish wink, he went, "Let's taste one."

He took out one croissant and tore it in two. He handed me one half and the small coffee cup. We devoured it in a few bites and washed it down with a sip of Moka. It was divine. Axel closed his eyes.

"You brought Paris to me this morning."

I giggled.

"I miss Paris, too."

Could he and I travel to Paris together? Wouldn't that be sweet? Visiting all the museums until our feet hurt, seeing all the paintings there are to see, sitting on the sidewalk café drinking aperitifs...

I found a breadbasket in the cupboard and emptied all the contents into it. Axel took coffee and cups, and we marched into the living room. The delightful smell from the basket and the rich aroma of coffee filled the room. The guys' eyes grew wide. They talked cheerfully in Viennese dialect while Axel cut the fresh baguette and brought out butter and marmalade.

"I'm sorry, we're talking in Austrian, but Wolf and Karl-Heinz don't speak English."

"Oh, I don't mind. I will get used to Austrian dialect."

They chitchatted, joked, giggled, and enjoyed the French viennoiseries. This was the first time I experienced a convivial moment with friendly people in Vienna—normal people, away from the phoney fashion crowd. I liked it even though I didn't follow more than half of the conversations.

After half an hour, they all stood up. I looked at the table. They had wolfed down everything. Not even a bite of baguette was left.

"Impressionnant, n'est-ce pas?" (Impressive, isn't it?)

Axel whispered as if to read my mind.

"These are hungry wolves."

He beamed. We both laughed out loud.

Afterwards, we found ourselves in the atelier as promised. The place was bigger than I remembered—maybe daylight gave that impression. It was spacious, with a high ceiling. The top part of the atelier jutted out to the rooftop to gain height and extra light. The ceiling was of green and blue, tinted and translucent, glass panels.

The atelier was smartly placed in the corner of the building. The two sides of the wall faced outside, making one wall entirely of glass panels. The other wall next to it had a large French window with a balcony outside, allowing extra natural light in. Whoever designed this place was a genius.

On the right, I spotted the reproduction of Gauguin, the one I recognised—with the black Tahitian dancer. Sculptures stood in the middle as well as abstract paintings on canvases—others covered in cotton sheets. In a corner on the left, all kinds of drawing materials, colour tubes, brushes, and a variety of tools lay on the tables and were strewn carelessly on the floor.

A particular picture drew my attention. It was an abstract, with a certain pattern. Overall dark, with a dim light on the top left, like at the end of a tunnel. The light was faint, pale pink. It appeared to symbolise the painter's search for a way out from where he was, surrounded by darkness. It gave me a strange feeling of being locked up somewhere I didn't want to be, an expression of one's anguish. *Why would anyone paint such a thing? Why does an artist do what he does?*

I pointed to the picture. "You did this one, right?"

"Yes."

"Do you mind if I ask..."

"Yes?"

"It seems to me you were in some kind of trouble... or suffering from something... or locked up in a place you don't want to be in... when you drew this painting?"

Axel hesitated a moment. "Yes, you could say that."

"I'm just trying to understand. I don't know enough about paintings to say anything whatsoever. But I learned if you knew the state of the mind of the painter, you have more chance to see what he tried to express in his painting."

"You are right. And you know about paintings. Your grandmother is a painter. You grew up in her atelier. I see that effect on you. All you said is true. I was in a miserable state."

"Do you mind sharing with me what it was that put you into that state?"

His smile was gone. For the first time, the dark side of him showed. He frowned, the colour of his skin grew pale. His agony was genuine. Even though he tried to hide it, I didn't miss it—he was incapable of hiding his emotions. Maybe that's why he is an artist?

"It's... private."

"Alright, say no more. I understand. I don't expect you to share anything private with me."

"Oh, no. It's not that. I don't want to say things that might cloud our day. I just want to enjoy it, not go through my tragedy. Perhaps one day, but not now. Do you understand?"

"I do, Axel. No worries."

"But that painting was selected for a group exhibition I just attended in Prague. My professor had chosen it."

"Your professor had an eye for it for some reason. Something so expressive that makes people wonder."

Axel led me to the balcony. It was a nice, sunny day, and we had a good view of Stadtpark.

"Is this the balcony you talked about? Where you could smell me from?"

"Yes. If you look carefully, you can see the tree under which you were sleeping. If I had a telescope, I could have seen you from here, although you would have been partially hidden by the tree. Supposing I knew exactly where you were, of course. But I didn't."

"Until Herbert told you."

"Oh, he wasn't sure. He said you might be there."

He turned to face me. "Shall we go out? It would be a pity to stay indoors. I will take you somewhere you might like."

"Sure, can I use your bathroom before we go?"

"Sure."

He led me to his en suite room, which was as I remembered. I noticed a painting on the opposite wall I didn't see the last time—a sketch of a beautiful white horse. I recognised her.

"That's Frühling?"

"Yes. I was fifteen when I drew it."

A surprising talent for a young boy. Every little detail of a horse, the muscles, the hair, the expression of the face and eyes, the light illuminating the elegant body; it was all there. Even the shadow was right.

"It's a beautiful work, really," I said in admiration. "Was it done in the late afternoon?" I whispered, pointing to the shadows.

"No, it's an early morning shadow. I was an early bird. I woke up with the animals."

I proceeded to the bathroom and explored. There was a bathtub in the left corner, a shower booth on the opposite side, the washbasin in the middle, and the toilet to the right. It was a nice, spacious bathroom with a large window on the right wall.

A feminine curiosity rose in me, and I opened the cupboard. *Does he have a girlfriend? If yes, does she sleep here sometimes?* If a girl spends nights in a man's apartment, she usually leaves a trace —moisturising cream, a hairpin, a contact lens case, a toothbrush, or even tampons if she's careless. But there was nothing that hinted at a female's presence. I found an extra shaving kit, a razor, shaving cream, cologne, after-shaving lotion, a toothbrush, toothpaste, some aspirin, and a bottle of ninety per cent alcohol as a disinfectant, some bandages, and a bottle of medication with a label written in German. The bottle got my attention. It seemed to be prescribed by a doctor.

Why would a young, apparently healthy man like him need a prescribed medication?

I proceeded to use the bathroom and checked my make-up and my dress in the mirror. I had on a transparent tunic that flowed to my knees. Its soft silk material caressed my skin. A fluffy beige linen dress matched my linen trousers underneath. I admitted it looked elegant. I had trousers on so I could climb on the motorcycle, just in case. My hair was down with a simple hairpin on top. I washed my hands and got out, still wondering about the bottle of prescription medicine.

Axel had a jean jacket flung over his shoulder, ready to go out. "Shall we take the motorcycle? It will be nice in this weather."

"Sure."

We hit the road on his Ducati. The day was lovely. Sunny and perfectly warm, with a pleasant light breeze sweeping by. I cherished the opportunity to hold him from behind his back. I leaned my head on his back, feeling his body. A few times when we stopped for the red lights, he touched my hand, asking me through his helmet, *"Alles gut?"*

"Ya, alles gut," I would say.

After a short ride, we arrived on a quiet street in the third district of Vienna, on the south-eastern edge of its centre. We entered the ground set on a gradient, with decorative tiered fountains and majestic wrought-iron gates. A palace in Baroque style was spread upon us.

"Where are we?"

"We are at Belvedere Palace. It was built as a summer residence for Prince Eugene of Savoy. It has the Belvedere Museum."

I admired the stunning garden—its series of sculptures, fountains, cascades, and the magnificent Baroque palace.

"It is considered one of Vienna's architectural jewels," Axel explained.

"It's beautiful," I said in awe.

We stepped into the 'Upper Belvedere' that had a permanent collection, primarily dedicated to Austrian art from the Middle Ages to the present.

"You see an array of sculptures and paintings by Austrian artists. Ferdinand Georg Waldmüller, Heinrich Füger, Gustav Klimt, Egon Schiele, and Oskar Kokoschka," Axel explained as we advanced into the gallery. Indeed, it was an impressive collection of Austrian artworks.

We entered a dazzling, spacious room with a large painting that almost took up the whole wall. It was a shiny feast of golden leaves, a recurring motif of a woman and a man snuggled in an intimate embrace—*Der Küss*, by Austrian Symbolist painter Gustav Klimt. *The Kiss*.

The couple in the painting was wrapped in ornate robes, decorated in a contemporary Art Nouveau style. The man, wearing a crown of vines, was kissing the woman, who had a crown of flowers around her head. She was dressed in floral patterns. The man's face was hidden from view as he bent downwards to kiss the woman's cheek while his hands caressed her face. Her eyes were closed, and she had one arm around the man's neck while the other rested on his hand. Her face was turned upwards to absorb the man's kiss. The look on her face was so divine, peaceful, and dreamy, breathing in eternal happiness...

Time froze at the very moment of her romantic intimacy, a

pure moment of love, romance, and sensuality. It was so erotic I felt myself floating, drifting in fantasy and an endless sequence of magic, just by watching her lovely face.

"It's so beautiful... I don't think I have ever seen anything so beautiful..." I thought out loud, but Axel heard me.

"You look amazed." He was keenly observing me. My eyes moved from one beauty to another.

"C'est trop beau. Absolument magnifique..." (It's too beautiful. Absolutely magnificent...)

"Art historians also suggested Klimt is telling the tale of Orpheus and Eurydice."

"Greek mythology? Orpheus, the son of Apollo and the muse Calliope, who fell in love with Eurydice?"

"Yes. When beautiful Eurydice died from a snake bite, Orpheus made his journey to Hades to save his wife."

"And Orpheus was supposed to have Eurydice walk out to the light from the caves of the underworld, but without ever looking back at her."

"Exactly. Klimt seems to show the exact moment when Orpheus turns around to see Eurydice and loses her forever. As in this painting, the woman is slightly translucent, as if she is fading away."

"That's too sad. I don't want to believe the art historians. Too cruel to describe such a beautiful moment."

"It's beautiful, yes. Another suggestion is, that it is Klimt himself and his companion Emilie Flöge who modelled for the work. She was a fashion designer, by the way, a bit like you."

My vision produced Axel and me as lovers in an ultimate embrace on the flowery bed. His face turns downward to kiss me on my cheek, his fair golden hair falling onto his shoulder. I kiss him back with my eyes closed, one hand around his neck, the other gently posed on his other hand. His hand is fondling my face from behind.

"Dammi Mille Baci," I whispered to myself softly, dreamlike, without realising Axel was standing close enough to hear me.

"Give me a thousand kisses?" he asked, startling me.

"Oh, I thought of that from seeing the painting."

He smiled, his piercing, observant eyes on me as if to prod through my soul.

"Vita brevis est, Ars longa." This time I quoted Hippocrates.

"Life is short, art is long," Axel translated.

"Klimt is long gone, but his art is appreciated by millions of people every day. He lives through his artwork even today, and he always will. Isn't that amazing?"

"Aye, my lady."

We stayed a little longer in front of *The Kiss* before moving on to the other exhibits. I found some fantastic landscapes by Klimt. After spending quite some time in the museum and walking around the palace garden, tiredness and hunger started to creep in. Axel turned to face me. "Are you ready for lunch, my lady?"

"I am, my lord. I'm famished."

"Alright."

We headed back to the centre of Vienna and stopped near Hawelka. But Axel led me into a place called Trześniewski, a name impossible to pronounce. Through the showcase glass, I saw a wide range of colourful, enticing open sandwiches. My eyes grew wide with hunger.

"Take your pick. We will come back for more if it's not enough."

I was spoiled for choice, so I took one of each delicacy that I wanted to taste first. We ordered locally brewed beer and settled at a table. I took one bite, and it was delicious.

"How do you pronounce the name of this place?"

"Trześniewski"

"What?" I pricked my ears.

"Trześniewski."

"Come again?"

He pronounced it slowly, but I still couldn't get it.

"It's Polish. Franciszek Trześniewski was a Polish gourmet and cook."

"But how do you pronounce it so perfectly?"

"Because my grandmother is Polish. I learned Polish from her. I grew up speaking Polish and German. As a child, I spent more time with my grandma, and she always spoke Polish with me."

"How interesting. Your grandma is from Kraków, right?"

"Yes. She still has relatives there."

"I heard it's a historical city, very pretty."

"True. I like it there. Rich in culture and history."

"I would love to go someday. Also, Prague. Some people say it's the most beautiful city in Europe."

"Prague is one of my favourite cities in Europe. I go there frequently for art exhibitions. Would you like to see it?"

"Oh, yes. I would love to."

"I will take you there someday."

"Oh, how awfully kind of you. I always dreamed of Prague, especially after I read the novel *Unbelievable Lightness of Being*, by Milan Kundera."

"The famous Prague spring period in 1968? Under the invasion of Czechoslovakia by the Soviet Union and three other Warsaw Pact countries and its aftermath. I read the book."

"And Sabina, the mistress of Tomáš, is a painter."

"Yes. Alright. We will go to Prague."

We finished our meal. I was full before I could try anything else. Axel asked me, "Shall I bring you home, or do you trust me for the rest of the day?"

"I trust you till the end."

He gave me a gesture to hop on, and I obliged.

We set off, making a slow circle of the central area of Vienna, and headed out of town. We drove towards the outskirts of Vienna. Soon after, we crossed the Donau river. We arrived in a green area, a park with a view of the river.

"Where are we?"

"We're in Alte Donau."

The area teemed with people lying on the grass, sunbathing, some of them already swimming in the river, taking a boat ride, others strolling around, and also on their bicycles—a scene that you don't get to see in a city. I was in a different place. We wandered around for a short while. Axel found a spot under a tree overlooking the Donau. We settled in on the grass.

"This feels like a holiday in the countryside. Quite different from the centre of Vienna."

"I grew up in the countryside. I need my share of greenery sometimes, even in a pretty city like Vienna. I miss my horses and green fields."

"How many horses are there on the ranch?"

"Hmm. Between twenty and thirty. Young and healthy stallions who can race are sold, but a mare like Frühling stays to reproduce. Once, when I was a young boy, I got attached to a colt named Veloce. I won the race with him. When I found out my grandfather had sold him, I was so angry I didn't talk to him for a month."

"Oh, no. Your grandfather should have asked you at least before he sold him."

"I wished he had. But I would have never agreed to it, so he made the decision.

"Bad business, this horse racing."

"There is so much money in play in the equitation business. So many people are crazy about betting money and on the other side the others making a profit out of it."

"That's why I stopped racing. The whole thing just became disgusting. Using horses for money... I don't agree. But I don't agree with a lot of things we humans do."

"Right."

This was the right moment to pop the question.

"Can I ask you something?"

"Sure."

"Do you have a girlfriend?"

"Me? A girlfriend?"

He raised his eyebrows.

"Good gracious, no. I'm not in the situation to be in a relationship. And I don't want to. The last thing I need is a woman who wants to marry me and have children. I'm a poor candidate for that. I'm not even sure of my future. It will be irresponsible to drag anybody into this insecurity. My struggle and misery end with me."

I was dumbfounded. Of all the responses I expected, this was not the one I had in mind.

"Don't you think you are too young to be so pessimistic about yourself? I'm not talking about marriage or having a family. What I'm saying is you should have a way of being comfortable. Being in harmony with yourself. Do you understand what I mean?"

"I do. The only time I feel comfortable and in harmony with myself is when I'm with my horses. And probably sometimes when I paint. The horses understand me as no humans do. They give me something close to happiness. They make me forget my struggles. If I don't make it as a painter, I might consider being a horse-healer of some sort."

"Well, that's nice. You're maybe one of the rare horse whisperers who murmur in their ears to calm them when they are agitated or ease their troubles in a way no others do. That is a gift."

"I guess I have certain abilities to communicate with horses. But how could I not? I have been spending more time with horses than with people in my life."

"I've never been on horseback, except when I was a child. I could ride a pony in an amusement park for my birthday. But I've never been on a full-grown horse. I heard it's rather scary the first time."

"Would you like to learn?"

"Oh, I would love to, but I'm afraid of falling off."

"You won't if you are with me."

"Ha-ha! I have no idea how to handle it or straddle it. If it starts to go off or even begins galloping, I would panic."

He smiled. "I won't let that happen. You should have some more faith in yourself."

"How am I supposed to have faith when I don't know the animal I'm riding on? How do you communicate with your horse?"

"The relationship between you and your horse is equal, quite different from a dog and its master, as it is based on dominance and compliance. With your horse, it should be based on mutual trust and respect, and the horse must accept you as his rider, especially in racing competitions. You cannot force your horse to submit—it doesn't work that way. It's important to observe the horse closely. If it is bucking, scuffing, swerving, hopping, or whatever, you have to understand why. Only with understanding, patience, and empathy, can you work with your horse effectively. You need to see your horse with your mind and heart. Once you understand this, you can make it trust you. It takes quite some time, though, but once they trust you, the reward is so great."

"Wow, it's a true relationship. Like genuine soulmates—true love between two souls."

"If you say so, yes. And they would never betray you as humans do."

"I think I know why you don't want to get married. You already have a wife..."

He grinned.

I said, "... Frühling."

We burst into laughter. Then he went on.

"One horse out of a thousand dies after racing. They get fatal injuries that give the veterinarians no choice but to put them down. I've seen a few, and it's hard to watch—another reason for me to stop racing. But there are a few lucky ones with only minor injuries. These are either brought back to their owners to retire, or sent to the sanctuary to live the rest of their lives in care, managed by some generous families or animal protection associations. This is where I come in. I want to help heal these horses who have been traumatised, giving them comfort and assurance, using the knowledge and experience that I have gained since childhood. Trust me, with time and a bit of patience, they can heal. I've already helped a few."

"You are truly a benevolent soul," I said. He possessed a deeply generous heart for these amazing creatures. I almost wished to be a horse, to have his attention and care. His love for horses was unconditional.

Let me be reborn as a horse and have his love.

"What are you thinking?" he asked, staring at me.

"Oh, just that you have a heartfelt love for the horses."

He stood up, offering me a hand.

"Let's go back to my place."

I took his hand, and my heart pounded. He had that magic over me. A kind of euphoria, an exhilaration.

Climbing on his Ducati, I leaned my head against his back. There was stillness in the air as we passed by the Donau River as if life itself had been suspended. I noticed neither the noise of the passing cars nor the people walking by. The only sounds I heard were the roaring engine and the sporadic soft thud of his Ducati switching gears.

Endymion the Shepherd Prince and the Moon Goddess

There was a wild vibration in the air at the start and a mighty fall from a high cliff at the end. I ran frantically as if I were a stag, running for my life, from a bloodthirsty predator a few steps behind me. I could almost feel his diabolical grip aiming for my throat. And I found myself in front of an empty void at the end of a cliff. I couldn't see where it ended. I would rather die, falling from this vertiginous cliff, than be devoured by the demon alive.

I jumped... into the endless emptiness that became a black hole, swallowing me whole. The world turned around as I fell, swirling madly. I landed hard, headfirst, on a rock. My head was crushed in an explosion of red pulp in all directions, splashing the blood everywhere. I screamed and jolted awake.

Whether it was the horror of the predator tracking me, or the vertiginous cliff across my dreams that woke me in the middle of the night, I did not know. When I opened my eyes, my vision was altered. This was not my room in Kaiser Straße. I was on a bed with a desk nearby. The lovely view of the night projected through a large window on the opposite wall. On the desk was a small sculpture I couldn't recognise in the dark.

Now, where the hell am I?

I got out of bed. A sharp sting accompanied a constant

hammering on the left side of my skull. I stood on my bare feet. I still had on all the clothes from yesterday except for the long silk top. Quite apart from the severe headache, I was uncomfortable. I removed the clothes, except for my underwear. My clouded eyes found a T-shirt lying on the bed. I pulled it over my head and tiptoed out of the room to see where I was. *What sort of trouble have I got myself into?*

The long passageway that bent at both ends looked like a labyrinth, with my pounding migraine. I paused for a moment, then tried a few steps. I found a door ajar, and I peeked in. Under the faint light, a topless man with a toned back sat on a stool in front of a canvas. His blond hair flowed onto his shoulders. This was the atelier where I had first encountered Axel. Except for this time, it was me sneaking up on him. He was utterly focused on his canvas, oblivious to my presence.

I tiptoed backwards, and then I lost my balance and slipped. I held on to the doorknob to avoid falling, and the noise attracted his attention. He hastily threw on a T-shirt. My efforts to cling to the doorknob proved fruitless. I stumbled, hitting my head hard, with a sickening thud, on the wall to my right. Right before I bashed my skull on the wall, I felt a sharp pain in my left hand as I was losing my grip on the doorknob. I collapsed on the wooden floor, landing on my right shoulder, which hit the wooden floor with all my weight. I heard an alarming cracking noise.

Axel was already behind me.

"Are you alright?"

I grimaced with the intensity of the pain—along with my terrible headache.

Axel carefully held my head. "Does it hurt here? Tell me where it hurts."

His worried voice sounded distant as my vision blurred. It seemed like a dream where I could see myself from above. Axel bent over me with his hands around my head, trying to wake me.

"Please, stay with me."

His urgent voice brought me back to consciousness. Axel was

supporting my head with his left arm, cautiously feeling my forehead with his right hand. His eyes were wide open, looking down at me.

"Are you with me? Can you hear me?"

I came around and saw his gorgeous face.

"Who are you? You are so beautiful," I murmured without thinking. I was not myself yet. My consciousness started to creep back in, but I still didn't have control of my tongue.

Axel's forehead was furrowed with a frown, and despair showed in his eyes.

"Do you remember me? My name is Axel. I took you to see Klimt yesterday. The painting you liked so much... do you remember *The Kiss*? Now you are at my place. You are safe with me."

"Yes, I remember *The Kiss*... It was so beautiful... Klimt. Will you kiss me like that?"

Axel's brow was furrowed, and his eyes still held a glint of despair.

"Kiss me, please..."

He didn't seem to know what to do. He hesitated for a moment. To my delight, he drew himself towards me. He pressed a kiss on my forehead—like a sweet breeze brushing past me when I lay under a tree. A breath of fresh air stroking my forehead... such a lovely zephyr sweeping my moist skin, relieving me of my pain.

Momentarily, I forgot my pain, and my distress was gone. Then I snapped violently back to consciousness with a jolt, feeling sick to the stomach. I blurted urgently, "Take me to the bathroom. Now."

Axel lifted me in his arms. Within a few steps, I was in the bathroom. As soon as I was in front of the toilet, I gestured for him to get out. I needed to throw up. He didn't want to leave me alone, but I pushed him away, and he reluctantly complied.

I closed the door. The moment I opened the toilet lid, I erupted. It was like a huge explosion from my stomach, rocketing through my throat and mouth, each time with a violent jolt. I couldn't remember how long I had my head bent over the toilet.

I paused for a moment when it was over. I didn't want to run back here for a redo. Then another surge put me back over the porcelain bowl for the second session of misery. Finally, the turmoil calmed. I waited longer to give my body time to react again in case there was anything more left.

I was exhausted. I flushed the toilet twice to ensure it was clean, with no revolting debris left behind. I also cleaned the seat and the inside of the toilet bowl, leaving no trace. The lessons from my mother died hard. She rightly taught me to clean up after my mess, even amid the misery of a migraine, especially in someone else's house. I stood up, resisting the urge to collapse to the floor. I splashed some water over my face. I washed my mouth, gargling with water and toothpaste to remove the awful, bitter taste. I stared at myself in the mirror. I looked like hell.

Why didn't I go back home? Why did I stay with Axel until this time of the night? I had no idea. My watch showed three in the morning. I tried to remember, but my head hurt so much that my eyeballs felt likely to pop out. I opened the door and found Axel in the room. He rushed in. My legs collapsed beneath me and the moment I lost my balance, he braced me. He gently laid me down on the bed, pushing a pillow under my head.

"Are you okay? Feeling better?"

I nodded. My throat went dry. No sound came out.

"Hang on. I will be right back."

Axel came back with an ice pack wrapped in a towel. He placed it carefully on the right side of my head, where I hit the wall. The ice provided instant relief to my bruised head.

"You had better sleep in my bed tonight, in case you need to run to the bathroom again. I will sleep in the guest bedroom."

"Will you stay with me for a bit, Axel? Don't go just yet," I croaked. My voice came out husky. He seemed glad to hear it.

"You know who I am now? You asked me who I was a while ago."

"My head... hurts like hell. I don't know what happened."

"It's alright. It will all come back in the morning."

"Please stay with me for a bit."

"I'm right here, Hyunah. I'm not going anywhere. Now get some rest."

He tucked me in. It was maybe my imagination, but his hand stroked my hair. After emptying my stomach, I felt better, and the ice pack certainly helped.

"Please, stay with me," I murmured while drifting towards sleep.

He held my hand. With his arm around my shoulder, he whispered, "I will be with you, don't worry. Now get some sleep."

His soothing voice sounded like a lullaby. I fell into a blissful slumber. Unconsciously, I snuggled up to him and held his hand.

My body needed rest. A blissful sleep, like in a poem I admired by John Keats. In the Greek myth of Endymion, the shepherd beloved of the moon goddess Selene. The poet renamed Selene 'Cynthia'.

Endymion, the Shepherd Prince of Mt. Latmos, was brainsick and in a trance-like state. His sister, Peona, brought him to her resting place. He fell asleep. When he woke up, he told Peona of his encounter with Cynthia and how much he loved her.

Endymion went to the underworld, searching for his love. He ventured through the sea floor, where he met a beautiful Indian maiden. Endymion fell in love with her. Both of them rode to Mount Olympus on winged black steeds. Cynthia awaited Endymion there, but he forsook the goddess. Endymion and the Indian maiden returned to earth, and the girl told Endymion that she could not be his love. He felt miserable until he met the Indian maiden again, and she revealed that she was, in fact, Cynthia. She finally told him how she had tried to forget him, to move on, but in the end realised, "There was not one. No, no, not one. But thee."

I loved the beginning of this beautiful poem:

A thing of beauty is a joy forever
Its loveliness increases; it will never
Pass into nothingness; but still will keep
A bower quiet for us, and a sleep
Full of sweet dreams, and health, and quiet breathing.

Endymion, the Shepherd Prince, was Axel—symbolised by a thing of Beauty. And I: Cynthia. The two loved each other as mortal and immortal. My dream became such a sweet delight in a chamber full of endless joy.

Therefore, on every morrow, are we wreathing
A flowery band to bind us to the earth,
Spite of despondence, of the inhuman dearth
Of noble natures, of the gloomy days,
Of all the unhealthy and o'er-darkened ways
Made for our searching: yes, in spite of all,
Some shape of beauty moves away the pall
From our dark spirits...

Some shape of beauty moves away the pall from our dark spirits... Here goes my favourite line. How I used to read it aloud repeatedly during my university days! And now in Vienna, after I met Axel, this made sense.

All lovely tales that we have heard or read:
An endless fountain of immortal drink,
Pouring unto us from the heaven's brink.

An endless fountain of immortal drink would be the fresh glass of water Axel offered me, instead of calling me a taxi, when we first met. Why did he do that? The curiosity of an artist? I will never know.

All lovely tales that we have heard or read... Would our stories be 'lovely tales'? Could it be a narrative that I would tell my friends with joy later in my life?

~

The next morning, I woke up feeling a hand stroking my forehead. I opened my eyes. Axel's beautiful blue eyes were looking down at me.

How lovely to wake up to see him... *I should be sick more often*. The pain in my head from the fall was a lot better.

"How is my lady this morning?"

"Where am I?"

"You are in my room. You fainted last night."

"What? How...?"

My memory started to kick in. Hebert had invited us for dinner at the local beer garden. Ulf and Karl-Heinz were also there. Herbert wanted to celebrate his large profits from renting the Aston Martin with us. Then I remembered the wedding catalogue photo shoot and two girls with horrible make-up. And the ill-matched outfit for the male model. I wondered how the grotesque affaire went.

"We went to dinner with Herbert, right?"

Axel's face brightened; his eyes beamed with joy.

"Yes. I see your memory is coming back. How are you feeling?"

"I feel better now. Still sore from the bang to my head, but much better. I'm sorry. I barely know you, and I had to be sick this way in your home. Sorry."

"Please don't be. What matters is you are alright now."

"I was really out of it, wasn't I? Hallucinating and talking nonsense? I don't know what happened to me."

"We all had dinner together. You had a beer with your meal. I guess what did you in was the schnapps. The guys were having it, and you wanted to taste it. I remember you saying it tasted very strong and bitter, but you had it anyway, toasting with them. We all had a good laugh, and it was quite a party. Then you told me you had a headache. We went home and left the guys there."

"And what happened when we came home? Did I lie down on your living room couch?"

"Yes. You already didn't look well by then. You lay down for a while then passed out."

"Oh, my God. My mother will kill me! I drank like a fish and crashed on somebody's couch, at a man's house."

"Then you should be glad your mother is too far away to kill you." He smiled.

"You didn't drink like a fish. It was just a pint of beer and a shot of schnapps. But you are not used to drinking strong alcohol like schnapps, I guess."

"No, of course not. I don't drink that strong stuff that gives you the worst hangover in the morning. I don't know why I went for schnapps last night."

"We were having a good time, and you were swept up in the mood, I think. What I didn't know was what that schnapps would have done to you."

"I should never have had that shot."

If I hadn't, I never would have woken up in the morning to see Axel's beautiful blue eyes.

"I'm so sorry for all the trouble I caused. You should have just dropped me at my place last night. Why did you bring me here?"

He kept his eyes steady on me for a few seconds of silence. His eyes lowered. He had surprisingly long eyelashes.

"I felt somehow responsible for you. You would not have been in the beer garden if it hadn't been for me."

"If I were dumb enough to drink something I couldn't handle, it was purely on me. You had absolutely nothing to do with it. You cannot be responsible for my stupidity."

"That didn't stop me from feeling bad for you. And if you were to be sick and in need of help, you'd better be with me, not those models in your apartment."

"Oh, it was so kind of you, but you should not have done it."

"Now, can you sit up, or do you prefer to rest a little longer?"

"What time is it?"

"Half-past nine. Are you thirsty?" My throat was so dry it could crack.

"Yes."

"Alright. Hang on."

A few minutes later, he brought me a warm cup of something that smelled good.

"Drink it slowly."

He helped me sit up, pushing the pillow against my back. His hair and skin emitted the fresh scent of shampoo and shower gel. His hair was still wet. He must have had a shower while I was asleep.

"It's herbal tea, a tisane for an upset stomach. My grandma used to make it for me."

"Thank you."

I inhaled camomile, liquorice, lime, thyme and rosemary. I took a small, cautious sip. The aromatic beverage was soothing, and it immediately quenched my thirst.

"This is good. Don't you have something to do today? Am I not disturbing you?"

Slowly, my conscience began to return. I might have over-stayed my welcome.

"Today is Sunday. I can be a bit lazy. And I have her ladyship in my care."

He gave me that sweet, boyish wink.

I said, "Look. I don't know what you think of me, but this has never happened to me before. I hope you believe me. I have never passed out at a man's house like this. This isn't me."

"I believe you. There's always a first time for everything. Please don't be hard on yourself. Now, let's focus on how we can make you feel better. I'm not judging you if that's what you're afraid of. Now, relax. It's a nice Sunday. If you feel better later, we could do something, okay?"

I finished the tisane sip by sip, and my eyes fell on a T-shirt that wasn't mine.

"Is this T-shirt yours?"

"Yes. I left it on the bed."

I had passed out on the couch with my dress and make-up on. I must look horrible. I had to look at how dreadful I was.

"I need to go to the bathroom."

"Hold on. *Doucemen*t." (Slowly)

Axel helped me to my feet, supporting my arms and shoulders. I stood up slowly. My head swirled a bit. I managed to walk one step at a time to the bathroom door.

"Can I have a shower?"

"Of course. Can you manage without falling on the floor?"

He seemed in doubt.

"I will try."

"No more head-banging, please."

That made me smile. He smiled back.

"I think it would be better if you took a bath instead. You can't fall if you're already sitting in the tub."

That made sense. The shower could be slippery and dangerous in my condition. My head was still sore.

"You're probably right."

"Alright then."

He went to the bathroom. The water pouring into the tub sounded blissful. He disappeared for a moment and came back with fresh towels—a big one for the body, a small one for the hair, and a French-style *gant de toilette* (washcloth).

"Wow, you have a *gant de toilette* like the French?"

"Yes. I brought some from Paris and Grasse. My aunt lives in Grasse."

"Right. She married a French perfume merchant, right?"

"Yes. You remember everything."

He led me to the bathroom.

"I will leave you to have a soak. Take your time. Call me if you need help."

He grinned. "Let me know if you want me to scrub your back."

"Oh, if you are trying to sneak a peek at my naked body, it won't happen. Even though I see naked male models all the time, it doesn't mean that you can see me naked."

"You see naked men all the time?" He raised his eyebrows.

"Oh yes. They keep their underwear on, of course. But when it is work, and I have to concentrate on dressing them, it becomes routine. I don't even flinch nowadays. Nothing exciting there."

"Really?"

"Yeah, really, really."

He seemed unconvinced. I stepped into the bathroom, closing the door firmly. I had to pee first, so I opened the toilet lid. I first checked for any remnants from last night—I looked around meticulously, from the seat, lid, to the toilet bowl. It was spotless.

My face looked like hell in the mirror. My hair was dishevelled and tangled. Mascara was smeared all around my eyes. I looked as if I had just survived a war. My lipstick messily circled my lips. I sighed. Axel had to suffer this. I needed some make-up remover, but there was none. Ironically, I regretted he didn't have an ex-girlfriend, who might have left some make-up remover behind. I just had to scrub my face with soap and shower gel.

I undressed for the bath and plunged my hand into the water. Warm and nice. I found men's shower gel on the edge of the tub. I sprayed it under the running water. To my delight, I recognised the scent of Axel this morning. I eased myself into the tub, where the blissfully warm water soothed my tired body. I rested my head on the edge of the bathtub and took a deep breath.

My head was sore, but the pain was bearable. Given the shock I'd had last night, it wasn't too bad. I took the *gant de toilette* with my right hand and poured some shower gel on it and tried to rub my face first. Immediately, I felt a sharp pain in my shoulder. I couldn't move my hand. I could touch things with my hand, but the moment I tried to move and use it, it hurt like hell. I must have hit my right shoulder hard. I turned my head and saw a blue-violet bruise on my shoulder. So, I tried with my left hand, but my wrist hurt, swollen and bruised with a ghastly blue and violet shade. I recalled the pain I'd felt when I was holding the cup of herbal tea. I must have sprained my wrist somehow. *Merde. This is great.* As if the head bang was not good enough, I was practically handicapped. *I need help. But how do I do that without Axel seeing me naked?*

I called out Axel's name and sunk deep into the water up to my neck so he could only see my face. In a matter of seconds, he appeared. He opened the door, only enough to poke his head in, and peeked to meet my eyes.

"Yes?"

"Uh... I need your help, but I want you to blindfold yourself, so you don't see me naked."

"What?"

"You heard me. I hurt both my shoulder and wrist. I can't wash by myself. I need you to help me."

"Hyunah, I have to see you to help you. You can't ask me to blindfold myself."

"Then forget it. *Laisse tomber. Je vais me débrouiller tout seule.*" (Drop it. I will manage on my own), I blurted in French, and Axel pulled his brows together in a frown.

"Alright. I will do it your way."

"I will guide you."

"Wait a minute."

He disappeared again. *Was I being unreasonable? Maybe.* But having passed out on his couch, I didn't want him to think I was slutty. If I asked him to wash me, he would probably think I was trying to seduce him. Any man would think that unless I was badly hurt.

He came in with a scarf big enough to cover his eyes.

"Come closer."

He obliged. His eyes on me had a dubious look.

"I want you to wash my face first, removing this awful make-up. You can do it without the scarf."

"Okay."

It was getting hot in the bathroom with all the steamy water. A film of sweat formed on his forehead. The mirror was already foggy.

"And you can remove your T-shirt if you want. It's hot in here."

He smiled, staring at me. "Is that an order?"

"No, of course not. It's hot here, and you are sweating. I told you, I see naked guys all the time."

"Alright."

With one swift movement, he removed his T-shirt and tossed it in the wash basin.

For the first time, from the front, my eyes fell on his well-developed athletic body. His shoulders, his arms with well-defined biceps and triceps, and his torso with no traces of fat. It was a delight to watch. He was beautiful, a masterpiece of the creator of the universe. *If I could touch him, I would start with that amazing shoulder.*

He drew himself closer and took the *gant de toilette*, soaking it in the water. He gently ran it across my face to remove the smeared mascara first.

"I know. I look dreadful, right? With this mascara all over..."

"It's alright. Close your eyes."

He carefully went around my eyes.

"Why do you put on all this make-up? You look pretty without it."

"Do you think so?"

"Yes. You have nothing to hide. I like your freckles. Why do you hide them with all these products?"

He finally seemed satisfied with his work and continued to wipe my cheeks and around my lips. And there was my entangled hair to work on.

"Now, can I shampoo your hair?"

"Can you do that?"

"Sure."

He put some shampoo in his hands and worked it through my hair. He gave me a gentle scalp massage, carefully avoiding the right side of my head where I hurt. He carefully ran his fingers over the injured part of my head.

"Does it hurt here?"

"Yes."

"It's swollen. I think you should see a doctor."

"I don't know. If it continues to hurt, then I will."

"I can take you to my doctor."

"So kind of you, but you don't have to. You have done enough already."

"If it's a serious concussion, you have to have it seen. A head injury should never be taken lightly."

"Okay."

He tried to untangle my hair, carefully pulling it apart one strand at a time. It took him some time, but he was patient. He removed the shampoo, spraying water on my hair. He applied the conditioner through my hair.

"We need to wash your body now. Tell me what to do."

"Okay. Put your blindfold on."

"Are you sure this is necessary?" He gazed at me. His blue eyes twinkled.

"Yes. I'm sure. No cheating now."

He obliged. I checked the scarf was tight around his eyes. With the blindfold, his sharp nose and refined lips looked more gorgeous. I found him irresistible and evocatively sensual.

With his blindfold on, I can do a few naughty things... like touching him. I want to kiss him.

What would I do to him if I could have my way with him?

I guided his hand towards my shoulder. "You can rub my shoulders now."

I sat up so that my shoulders were out of the water. He went on scrubbing my shoulders from behind my back. When he arrived at my right shoulder, where I had the bruise, it hurt, and I yelped involuntarily. He stopped.

"What is it? Now I am going to see you. Can I remove this stupid thing, please?"

"Alright. Just a second."

I hid my breasts with my arms.

"Okay."

He got rid of the scarf.

"Oh, no. You have a big bruise on your right shoulder."

"Yes. I also hurt my left wrist."

I held out my wrist to show him the blue-violet bruise. He observed it.

"I see now why you can't wash yourself. I will help you, but I refuse to use this blindfold."

"No."

"Hyunah, please be reasonable. You are injured. I can't help you with blind eyes. Do you trust me?"

He met my eyes. His brow furrowed, and his eyes glinted with frustration. I just watched him.

"Do you trust me or not?" he pressed.

"Yes."

"What did you say?"

"I trust you."

"Then let me help you my way."

"But..."

"But what?"

I lost my words. He frowned, and the edge of his lips tightened.

"Alright, Hyunah, if you cannot trust me, get up now. I will take you home."

"No, Axel, I'm sorry. I do trust you. Please don't be angry. I'm sorry. It's just that... I'm so embarrassed... I hate it when things are out of my control. Please don't be cross with me...."

Tears welled up in my eyes.

Axel can't stand me anymore. He lost his patience with me. He wants to get rid of me. He is ditching *me. He will dump me at my place, never to see me again. Maybe I deserve it.*

Tears streamed down my face. I couldn't stop. *Quelle misère...* (What a misery)

Axel stared at me calmly. His frowned forehead eased up, and his lovely lips relaxed.

His eyes showed sympathy. He drew his hand to wipe my tears.

"It's alright, come on now, *doucement...* I'm sorry I snapped at you. Please, no tears now. Come here."

He drew me close and gently hugged me, stroking my hair. He gave me a shoulder to cry on, and I let go of myself. I was strangely liberated. With my left arm, I held him close, touching his warm shoulder. His skin was smooth and firm. His hair and skin smelled divine. Was the smell coming from the shampoo and shower gel he was using on me? I detected something more pleasant—perhaps his scent. I got dizzy with sweet solace in his embrace.

"It's alright. There now. Shh... shh..."

He whispered words of appeasement in my ear. His soothing voice was like a breeze as if to calm a crying child or cool off an agitated horse. That's it. He must calm troubled horses this way, whispering blissful sounds into their ears. No wonder he can help deranged horses. He had a magical talent for soothing emotionally and physically distressed animals. I had no idea how long we had been there in a tight embrace. At some point, he pulled himself away and wiped my tears. His mesmerising eyes portrayed empathy.

"It's alright. You are with me now. Okay? Now, shall we clean you up?"

He took the *gant de toilette* and put some more gel on it. He faced me and started to rub my neck, across my collarbone. I had my arms around my breast so he couldn't descend towards them. He went behind my back, my left arm, down to my hand. He did the same with my right arm but was extra careful on the bruised area of my shoulder. A sweet smile of satisfaction formed on his face, like a child playing with a toy. And I had gathered myself and had stopped sobbing.

"Feeling better now?" He grinned.

I nodded.

"Now, do you want me to wash you any further?"

"*Non merci, ce n'est pas la peine.* (No, thank you, it's not necessary.) Can you just remove the conditioner from my hair and rinse me all over with water, please?"

"Of course."

He pulled the stopper in the tub, and water started to drain from the bathtub. The sound of the water emptying was strangely soothing. I curled my body with my arms around my knees. The water was draining down almost to my feet now. He ran the water through my hair and body until no traces of soap were left on me. When he was content, he wrapped me with a big towel. I took hold of it and put it around my body.

Ha asked. "Wait, can I see your feet?"

"Yes."

He took my left foot and gave a careful look.

"Did you walk around here with bare feet? It's a bit dirty. I'm sorry, I didn't have time to clean up my place since I got back. May I?"

"Go ahead."

"Can you sit on the edge of the tub, so I won't wet your towel?"

He helped me sit at the edge of the bathtub and washed my feet, starting with the left foot. He guided my hand to his shoulder for balance.

I touched his amazing muscular shoulder and watched it as it moved. He took the cloth and patiently cleaned my feet, one after the other.

"I see my lady has found a smile again," he said, observing the smile he had put on my face.

"No one has ever washed my feet, except my mom when I was little."

"I told you. There's always a first time for everything."

His eyes sparkled with joy.

"Alright, my lady, you are clean now. You can get dressed."

I wished I had a second set of clothes to wear. I only had the outfit from yesterday.

"Wait. I can't let you walk barefoot on the dirty floor again. Hold on. Allow me."

He lifted me in his arms again and brought me back to the bed.

"Do you have your socks anywhere?"

"Uh, they must be somewhere, although they're not clean. I have to wear the same clothes I wore yesterday."

"Well, all my clothes are too big for you. I can't lend you anything that would suit you. Sorry about that."

"No worries. I'll get dressed. I have to go home now, anyway. I have already caused you too much trouble."

"No, you haven't caused me any trouble."

"By the way, what were you doing so late in your atelier when I found you?"

"Um... Sometimes I work at odd hours. I also have trouble sleeping."

"Oh, you mean regularly? You have trouble sleeping?"

He lowered his eyes. His skin colour turned rather pallid to my eyes.

"Yes. I have insomnia. It started when I became an adult."

"Oh, I'm sorry to hear that. Did you try anything to solve the problem?"

"I did. Sometimes it got better, and I slept well for a few weeks. But it started again. I usually sleep much better in Krems at my grandma's, where I can ride horses in the fresh air. But here in Vienna, it is not easy. So, I started running. It helped me to some degree, but the problem didn't disappear completely."

"I could never understand the pleasure of running—people sweating their souls out and torturing themselves. Why do that to your body?"

He smiled. "That's one way of looking at it. Now, how are you feeling? Do you want to rest in bed or get dressed?"

"I can get dressed. I feel better now that I've had a bath."

"If you want, I can give you a fresh T-shirt for now. To be honest, I would rather keep you in my care for another few hours to make sure you are okay. I'm an Austrian, and I speak German. If anything goes wrong, I know what to do, unlike your flatmates. What do you think?"

"Why are you being so nice to me? I mean, we've only known each other for a few days. You don't owe me anything. Why?"

He locked his eyes on me and grinned. "Because I'm a knight, and I serve my lady."

He gave me that boyish wink again.

"I practice fencing. I know my way with swords."

"Oh? You do fencing?"

"Yes. I grew up with it. My grandpa put me up to it when I was fifteen. He wanted to make a man out of me. I was a shy child. I have my armour and practise with my trainer when I'm in Krems. I did it obsessively until I became good at it. I even won some medals in regional competitions."

I understood now why he had such an amazing body. I knew he was an athlete, but not at this level of competence.

"Wow, you're a real athlete! And a genuine knight. I see many male models but rarely a man like you. Models mostly build their bodies in the gym with protein powder, but your muscles are made with real sports. May I?"

"May I what?"

"May I touch you?"

I don't know why I said that, but it just came out.

There was a twinkle of amusement in his eyes as he smiled.

"Whatever for?"

His lovely lips curled up slightly. His soft tone fondled my ears as it resonated calmly. My throat went dry, my heart started pounding, and my hands itched for his god-like body, sculpted like a Renaissance statue in Florence.

"I want to feel... um... what it's like... to touch an athlete... like you."

I invented an excuse, but it sounded ridiculous even to my ears.

"Then how can I refuse her ladyship?"

He gestured for me to go ahead. Trying not to hurt my shoulder, I ran my fingers slowly over his left shoulder. His skin was warm and surprisingly smooth. I held my breath as I passed my fingertips over his neck and the right shoulder. The morning sunlight from the window illuminated him, revealing the shiny golden hair on his chest and arms, and I stopped breathing. I marvelled at his perfection.

I went on, gliding over the firm and glowing skin across his back, following his spinal cord. My hands travelled over the front and back to the shoulder. I slowly ran my hand down over his heart. He stayed still while I explored his torso, but I could tell he was conscious of my every move. My hand stopped at his heart, and our eyes met. He calmly fixed his gaze on me without a word. His smile was gone, and for a second, I sensed some kind of alarm. I couldn't read his face or what was going through his mind. Could it be something more intimate? His eyes lowered to my naked shoulder and further down to my breasts, hidden by the towel. *Is this a masculine lust in his fixation on my body?* A second later, it was gone. I was confused. I put my ear to his heart and tried to listen to his heartbeat. Slow, close to stillness.

"Your heartbeat is slow. You use less oxygen than normal people. You must be excellent in sports of endurance, like marathons, long-distance swimming, and suchlike. The complete opposite to me."

"How so?"

"I'm not good at sports. I don't run well, I swim slowly, and I'm nervous by nature. Not an athlete like you."

"Do you want to improve that?"

"Oh, yes. But I don't know how. I never had a trainer."

"When you get better, we can work on that. Okay?"

"Okay."

I pulled my hand off his body.

"I will be back."

He stood up and stepped out of the room. I pulled the towel close.

What the hell have I done? He must think I'm a slut. What is going on with me? Do I have real brain damage?

Axel had returned. He was standing by the door, staring at me quietly with a fresh T-shirt in his hand. He came towards me and laid it next to me.

"Are you alright?"

"Yes. I'm fine."

I met his spellbinding blue eyes.

"Shall I put it on?"

"Yes, it's for you. Can I get you anything else?"

He also brought the old T-shirt I had worn. I took it and found my panties rolled inside. I thanked his discretion and sighed. He went out again, and this time, brought my socks.

"Thank you, Axel. I am embarrassed to make you go around bringing me these things. I'm so sorry."

"Don't be. I will be outside. You can get dressed. Okay?"

He disappeared again. I put my underwear on and carefully pushed my head into the new T-shirt. It was oversized, but the cotton comfortably wrapped around my body. I put my socks on. I got up slowly and attempted a few steps toward the outside of the room. Axel appeared, supporting me from behind.

"I've got you. Can you walk?"

"Yes, I think so."

"Let's go to the living room."

We advanced to the couch where I had crashed the previous night. I found my silk top carelessly strewn on the back of the sofa. I collected it and sat on the couch.

"I was a wreck last night, wasn't I?"

"It's alright. Now relax, make yourself comfortable."

He sat beside me, looking down at my legs. My eyes spotted another huge bruise on my right knee. It already had become blue and dark violet, similar to my shoulder.

"You hurt your knee too."

Axel gently ran his fingers over my knee, as he moved my legs on top of his lap. His hands, examining the bruise, gave me an incredible sensation of glee.

"Does it hurt?"

"I don't know where it hurts anymore."

I giggled. The whole situation became comic, and he laughed with me.

"Alright, my lady. The damage is done. Now, how is your stomach? Are you hungry?"

"Oh, no. I can drink a little, but I am not hungry at all. I'm afraid to throw up again."

"Do you want another cup of tisane?"

"That would be lovely. Thank you. But you don't have to bring it to me right away. Can you sit with me for a moment?"

I wanted him to keep his hands on my legs a little longer. He seemed to understand, and he smiled. He continued caressing my legs delicately, with the tips of his fingers touching my skin and rolling slowly, like a gentle breeze. His blissful stroking glided across my knees, thighs, and shins, up and down, onwards and backwards, alluringly and spellbindingly. It was a delight I had never known before. I desperately wished he would not stop. I was nearly about to shudder with pleasure.

Then the telephone sprang to life. We jumped as if a loud alarm clock had pulled us out of our sweet dreams.

"*Scheiße!*" Axel blurted. "Sorry, I have to take this."

He got up. Who could disturb him on Sunday morning? Someone close. He answered the phone. I understood none of the things he said. It was not German or Viennese dialect. It sounded similar to Russian. Ohhh... It was Polish. The person on the other end was most certainly his grandma.

Listening to him speak Polish showed me another side of him. He was a different person. Even though I didn't understand the language, I knew he was speaking it fluently, as if it was his mother tongue. And maybe it was. He probably started learning Polish before he learned German as a baby.

How many languages does he speak, I wondered? English, French, Polish, German... and what? Maybe some other Eastern-European languages? Amazing. He stayed on the phone, calmly listening to his grandma. A moment later, he started speaking rapidly, repeating the same phrase: *"Nie, to nie jest konieczne."* (No, it's not necessary.)

Then he hanged up. *"Scheiße!"*

"What is going on?" My eyes grew wide.

"We have to move to the terrace quickly. My grandma is sending me a cleaning lady. I said it's not necessary, but she's already on her way. A Polish woman who used to work for us in Krems."

"Oh, my God. When?"

"She will be here any time now. Can you change into your clothes?"

"Of course. Bring them to me, please? Now!"

He stepped out and came back almost instantly, holding my clothes. I started to hurriedly remove the T-shirt. A sharp pain stung my right shoulder. I screamed, and Axel helped. He carefully removed the shirt. I took the bra, and he fastened it. He pulled down the dress from my head slowly, zipped it, and went on putting on my pants. There was the silk top now—he passed it from my head again as I instructed. Now I was fully dressed, it was uncomfortable.

He ran to his room. He came back in a new polo shirt in pale violet and blue jeans. He looked stunning as usual, but he frowned. The moment he was about to guide me to the rooftop, the doorbell rang. We jumped again.

When the door was opened, there stood a stocky middle-aged woman wearing a colourful blouse with a dark skirt. Her brown hair was neatly tied in a knot. She was Eastern-European, physically strong, with a look of hard-boiled stubbornness on her face.

She greeted him with a wide smile, and Axel call her "Agnieszka."

She leapt to her feet to give Axel fervent kisses on his cheek as if she were his close relative. They knew each other well.

They talked in Polish, and soon she spotted me. Her eyes grew wide, her lips curled in curiosity. Axel introduced me to her in Polish, and turned to me, saying she was Agnieszka.

I smiled, and she smiled back. She turned to Axel and asked a load of questions. She was the type who enjoyed gossiping. Anything she learned today would be duly repeated to anyone around her, including Axel's dear grandma.

She continued to talk excitedly. Axel's politeness was shrouded in a frown on his face.

He drew me aside. "Let's go to the rooftop. Okay?"

"Okay."

He led me to the terrace. Once we were up there, he put his hands around his head and sighed.

It was a lovely, sunny day, and the rooftop was basking in the glorious morning sun. He took a big parasol and settled it between the two sunbeds on each side.

"You can lie down here. Do you want to be in the sun or shade?"

"In the shade."

He moved one sunbed so it would be placed in the shadow, and for himself, he didn't seem to care. His furrowed forehead projected his sulky mood.

"You don't look happy."

"Oh, I'm sorry. This wasn't supposed to happen. Normally, I clean the flat myself. I don't need help, but my grandma thinks otherwise and sometimes surprises me this way. Quite disturbing when I have a guest. I would have suggested that we went out, but you are unwell. So, we are stuck here with Aga. She used to be my nanny for a few years when I was a child. And she likes to talk."

I could see that from the way they exchanged conversations; I understood the familial ties between them. She looked at him with that affectionate expression that a nanny would have. So, Axel grew up surrounded by his Polish grandma and nanny. They certainly had spoken to him in Polish.

Was he closer to Polish than Austrian? He was perfectly natural when speaking Polish, as he was in German. Aga would ask Axel everything about me as a curious nanny would, and she would repeat everything to his grandma as soon as she could.

"I feel alright now. We can go out."

"Are you sure?"

"Yes. My stomach is settled now. I think we can go out. I can walk."

Axel pricked his ears. "In that case, I know exactly what to do."

"And what is that?"

"You will be sitting down and watching most of the time. You don't even have to walk so much."

"Yes?"

"Spanische Hofreitschule"

"What?"

"The Spanish Horse-Riding School in Vienna."

With that, his radiant smile returned. The lovely morning sun illuminated his golden hair and mesmerising blue eyes. I was once again fascinated by this God-sent beauty, a living Renaissance statue, and my Shepherd Prince.

Endymion, the Shepherd Prince, who fell in love with the moon goddess, Cynthia. And I desperately hoped I was that moon goddess to him.

"So, tell me: why is it called the Spanish Riding School when it is in Vienna, not in Spain?" I asked Axel when we finally settled in to watch the performance. We were smartly placed at the centre of the gallery, so we wouldn't miss the majestic stallions' moves and tricks. It was pre-noon Sunday, and the place teemed with spectators.

Living tradition—the values of the past blending with the passion of the present. That was the motto for Vienna's famous Spanish Riding School. The public could enjoy stunning displays of classical dressage by the Lipizzaner stallions. They also called this world-famous performance the Ballet of the White Stallions.

Axel grinned and passionately explained, "The 'Spanish' part of its name came from the horses that originated from the Iberian Peninsula during the Sixteenth Century."

"So, the species is originally from Spain?"

"Yes, today's Lipizzaner stallions are descendants of this Spanish breed—a cross between Spanish, Arabian, and Berber horses."

"So, they are a hybrid of three different species?"

"Right. And they were considered especially noble-spirited and well suited for the art of classical horsemanship."

"So, they are trained here, according to tradition?"

"Yes. The Spanish Riding School is an institution demonstrating the Renaissance tradition of Haute École that has existed for over four hundred and fifty years."

"Wow, four hundred and fifty years?"

"Aye, my lady."

He turned around and fixed his eyes on me. He looked like a child. Considering how grumpy he was just moments ago, it was a great change. Fortunately, I wasn't too sick to go out. My headache had diminished, and I felt a lot better.

"It's wonderful they have kept the good tradition after all, isn't it?"

"Yes. These horses are also known as dancing horses."

"Dancing horses? How do they dance?"

"Well, you are about to see it now. These Lipizzaner stallions are a dream to watch. They are Europe's oldest cultural horse breed. Their classic physique and grace made them perfectly suitable for the style of high school dressage."

"How amazing! So, how are they trained? Is there a specific method?"

"When they are around four years old, the horses leave the breeding stud at Piber and head to the Heldenberg Training Centre."

"Where is Piber?"

"There are three locations home to the Spanish Riding School. Their breeding stud is in the West Styrian village of Piber."

"And where are the other two locations?"

"Heldenberg in Lower Austria is the second site. It is here that the young, up-and-coming stars spend their first few years training. The Lipizzaner stallions also spend their well-earned holidays here, enjoying the fresh country air."

"Horses on holidays?" I giggled. "I'm glad they are well-treated."

"Oh, they are. They deserve it, I assure you."

"For how long?"

"Oh, I believe they get a six- to eight-week break during the year and sometime over the summer."

"And what is the third site?"

"The Winter Riding School in Vienna's Hofburg Palace. It's magnificent. Right where you are, my lady."

"So, we are now in the Winter Riding School?"

"Aye."

"I imagine this is a historical building?"

"Right. This Baroque building was built by Joseph Emanuel Fischer von Erlach during the 1729 to 1735 period. Primarily intended for horse-riding, courtly and equestrian festivities were held in the Baroque riding hall."

"How do you know all that? You talk like a trained tour guide. You could work as one."

He smiled and gave me his boyish wink. He went on.

"You asked about the method of their training. The methods used by the riding school are based on François Robichon de La Guérinière."

"Oh, he was French?"

"Yes. The movements were developed for battle. They strengthened the war horse's body and mind and make him a great athlete. All movements were based on those naturally done by the horse when at liberty in the wild."

"Oh, so it was developed to prepare for battle originally?"

"Yes. Classical dressage techniques are formed by cavalry movements and training for the battlefield. It is the art of riding in harmony with the horse." Axel paused.

"Alright. It's starting soon. I'll quickly explain what you are about to see. It begins with the 'Young Stallions'. They demonstrate 'All the Steps and Movements of the High School', where four fully trained stallions perform each of the movements seen in the Olympic Grand Prix Dressage test, including *flying change, passage, pirouette, and piaffe*. The horses are ridden in the double bridle to demonstrate their high level of training. Then '*Pas De*

Deux' is shown, with two horses demonstrating high school movements in a mirror image. Here we go. I will explain the rest later."

With classical Viennese music playing, four beautiful stallions gracefully trotted out, carrying their riders with deliberately delicate steps. Each horse took turns and showed passage, pirouette, piaffe, and the flying change, as Axel explained earlier. Next was the '*Pas De Deux'*, two horses moving around at the same time as if they were facing each other in a mirror. 'Work in Hand' followed, to show how the horses were trained for the school jumps. This demonstration included work on the diagonal, on the wall, and between the pillars.

The most spectacular act was *capriole*, meaning the leap of a goat. The horse leapt from a raised position of the forelegs straight up into the air, kicked out with the hind legs, and landed on all four legs at the same time. I was completely spellbound. It took ten years for these stallions to be fully trained to perform like this. I tried to imagine the work, effort and patience it took for these extraordinary creatures to perfect these manoeuvres, and the training required by the specialists.

After the performance, Axel explained to me at length how they were trained to step by step, following the methods. He told me it required an enormously powerful stallion to perform correctly. Only a few extremely talented stallions mastered the art of the 'Schools Above the Ground', which are the *levade, courbette, and capriole*.

I asked Axel, "What is *courbette?*"

"*Courbette* is when the horse raises its forelegs and hops forward on its hind legs. Only extremely strong and talented horses can perform five or more leaps forward before landing with the forelegs. But it's very rare they jump over four times. I was lucky enough to witness one. It was impressive, trust me. I saw it while I watched the dressage, during the training, not on a real performance. One of the riders is a friend of mine, and he allowed me to come and watch. I should say I was truly lucky to see the miracle that day. The extraordinary Lipizzaner stallion jumped five times before he landed on the ground. I still remember it like yesterday. They called him 'Winter wind'. It was his nickname, not his real name. I believe his foundation sire was Pluto."

"Wow, when was that?"

"Some years ago. I was at the beginning of my art school studies."

"Can we still watch his show now? Is he here today?"

"No. He's in Heldenberg now, on holiday. Probably humping a mare as we speak!" He grinned from ear to ear, and I laughed. I understood why he was so passionate about horses. These were indeed magnificent creatures.

The performance finished with the 'School Quadrille', comprising eight riders working in formation at the walk, trot, and canter, with flying changes, pirouettes, the half pass, and the passage. Classical music accompanied the performance and ended with the grand finale. A roar of cheering and applause followed.

"It was marvellous," I told Axel, as we got up and headed for the exit.

"I'm glad you liked it. Now, let's see if we can meet my friend back at the stable."

We waited until the crowd cleared out. I followed Axel through the stairs and a series of long corridors after passing a door that indicated *Verboten*. (Forbidden.)

We arrived at the stable where the stallions who had just performed were being led back to their stalls. The pungent stench of horse dung and urine hit my nose. The stable was bustling with people, moving Lipizzaners from one place to another. I was excited to see these majestic creatures so near me. They looked even more beautiful up close. *Can I touch them?*

Axel asked one of the horse carers something, and we followed in the direction he pointed. We reached one of the stalls. There was a stallion standing in a corner with a man bending over him. Axel called out, "Florian!"

The man turned and saw Axel. With a broad smile, he came

over to greet us. He looked some years older than Axel, medium height, slender, with blue eyes. He was wearing a traditional uniform: brown tailcoats, a bicorne-style hat, white buckskin breeches, white suede gloves, and black top riding boots. Axel told me later that the empire-style uniform had remained relatively unchanged for two hundred years.

He was one of the performers. I couldn't believe my luck. All the performers were good-looking with slim builds, which made sense. You should not only be fit to ride a Lipizzaner stallion, but also be lightweight. They shook hands, and Axel turned to introduce him to me. Florian, his friend, smiled at me. "Hello"

"Hello, it's such a pleasure and great honour. I loved the performance. It was magnificent."

"Thank you."

Axel went on, speaking to Florian in Austrian dialect, grinning and gesturing. The chat seemed to be about the horses. Axel was ecstatic. His eyes were ablaze with excitement. He turned around and met my eyes.

"Florian and I knew each other in Krems. We were both crazy about horses. When I went to Paris to the École des Beaux-Arts, he joined the training programme to be a rider at the Spanish Horse-Riding School. Sometimes I wish I had done the same."

He could have. He was fit and slender, a formidable athlete with a great passion for horses. Well, then we would not have met. I would not have wandered into his atelier. I thanked all the saints'f Axel decided to be an artist.

"I'm sure you would have been a wonderful rider, Axel. I do not doubt it."

He smiled. Then I wanted to ask something. "Uh, do you think I can touch the stallion?" I pointed to the amazing horse in the corner. "Can I pat him?"

Axel asked. Florian gestured me to come closer to the beautiful white stallion, watching us curiously. Axel whispered in my ear. "Let the horse smell you first. Go to him. Just be natural. Come on."

I approached the Lipizzaner carefully and let the horse smell me without raising my hand. He put his muzzle curiously over my shoulder and sniffed my neck. Axel drew closer and whispered in the stallion's ear. The horse pricked his ear and listened. He seemed to like it.

When the horse was calm and satisfied, Axel gestured for me to go ahead and pat him. I raised my right hand slowly and touched the stallion's neck, his head, and around his ear. He stayed still while I stroked him gently. His smooth hair strummed on my fingers, and I felt his strong muscles. The animal was formidable and healthy. I was excited to have this rare opportunity.

Axel gave the stallion gentle strokes all over his body as if to offer him a blissful massage while still whispering. The stallion drew close to Axel and nuzzled on Axel's shoulder, hair, and face, moving his ear up to Axel's lips as if he wanted to listen more. The horse loved what Axel was doing to him.

Florian smiled. "The Lipizzaner likes you both. Although he's used to humans, he rarely gets a pat from strangers. We won't let them. But Axel isn't a stranger to horses," he turned to Axel. "You always had a way with horses."

Florian looked straight at Axel and said something in Austrian dialect. Axel grinned broadly in response. He replied and I didn't understand what he said. How I wished I could understand what they were talking about, but something about their conversation and tone told me it might not just be about the stallion. There was something more intense and deliberate about it. *What could it be?*

"Alright, Hyunah, let this stallion have his rest now. We should be on our way."

Florian shook Axel's hand and mine. He had a firm grip like Axel's.

I said, "Thank you so much, Florian. I'm so grateful. It was nice to meet you."

"It's my pleasure. Nice to meet you too. Thank you. Enjoy your Sunday."

With that, we left the stable. The horse followed Axel's footsteps with its big curious eyes and neighed and snorted, seemingly saying, "Hey man, don't go just yet. Come back here and do what you've been doing to me."

Now I understood how Axel could help injured or distressed horses. He had a way of handling horses. *Is this what he was meant to do instead of painting?* Being an artist is far more difficult than helping horses.

It was around lunchtime when we headed out. People were out on the terraces of the cafes and in restaurants, enjoying a meal and a Sunday drink. Axel asked.

"So, how is my lady? How do you feel? Are you hungry or still at war with your stomach?"

"I feel better. I'm a bit thirsty. Maybe I can manage a light meal. I am not sure how my stomach will react."

"Please don't force yourself, give it a rest. I'm not so hungry, so it's really up to you. Tell me what you wish to do. Shall we go to a café nearby and sit outside?"

"That's a good idea."

"Alright then. Come with me."

I will come with you anywhere. I will go anywhere you lead me. Just let me be with you. The more I pass time with you, the more I want to be with you.

Soon, we were standing on the pavement, and Axel had his hand on my shoulder as he watched me closely.

"We have arrived. Here we are, my lady."

Before us was a place called Café Bräunerhof. It had some tables outside on the sidewalk, and only one or two tables were still available. We had only walked for a few minutes, so we were still close to the Spanish Riding School. The café was at Stallburggasse, in the inner Stadt of the first district.

Axel spoke to a waiter. The waiter answered, and this time I understood. If we waited for a few minutes, he would clear a table outside for us. As we stood waiting for our table, someone called Axel by his name. I turned in the direction of the voice. A tall, blonde girl, about the same age as Axel, faced us with a bright smile. She was slim, with a short summer dress showing off her long, pretty legs. Her big blue eyes complemented her face—like a porcelain doll with pink cheeks and long blonde hair flowing on her shoulder. The V-neck dress exposed the upper part of her glamorous breasts. She was stunning—the kind of woman every man would run after. She was in the company of another girl with brown hair, almost as tall as her but more ordinary.

Axel greeted her cheerfully and exchanged words in what I recognised as Polish. He introduced me to her, giving her my name.

"Hyunah, this is Alicja, a classmate in my school."

"Hello. Nice to meet you, Alicja."

"Nice to meet you, Hyon-hah."

So, she was a student at his art school. Not only was she beautiful, but also cultured. I was intimidated. I worked with models. I didn't get intimidated by beautiful men or women. But she was not a model, and she was even more attractive than most of the women I confronted. She could easily have been a model herself if she fancied it. And she had studied art like Axel.

Why was Axel spending his Sunday with me, not with this beautiful woman? Furthermore, she was Polish. They must have a lot in common.

Are all the Polish women beautiful like her?

My head started to hurt again. They continued talking merrily in Polish. I wished I could understand what they were saying. They were probably discussing school, artwork, certain professors, and such. The Polish language sounded appealing to me. It was similar to Russian but more elegant.

At one point, Axel said something with his beautiful smile. Alicja burst into laughter, throwing her head back, her long blonde hair flying in the air. What did he say that was so funny? I watched them in dismay while they were giggling together. Strikingly handsome Axel, stunningly gorgeous Alicja, all smiles... they looked like a perfect couple. I was an outsider. Blood rushed through my veins. I was shunned by these two amazingly beautiful creatures.

I started cursing all the saints. Why couldn't they talk in English so I would be included in the conversation? Maybe they were glad to speak their language for once. I understood that. But it didn't please me all the same. If I ran into a Korean friend here, I would certainly speak to them in Korean even if I knew Axel couldn't understand a word. I tried to convince myself. I should be more open-minded.

I needed to go to the bathroom. I didn't want to disturb Axel, so I walked into the café and asked a waiter to direct me to the restroom. He pointed towards it, saying, *"Geradeaus."* (Straight ahead.) I found the door to the restroom. As I grabbed the doorknob, a light touch on my shoulder made me turn around to face Axel. His smile was gone. His brow was furrowed.

"Are you alright?" he asked.

I was not alright, not after what I had seen. The image of stunning Alicja, with her long blonde hair flying in the air as she tossed her head, appeared in my mind like a movie trailer. How could I be alright? They were flirting. But I pretended otherwise.

"I'm fine. I just need to use the bathroom. I will join you shortly."

"Hyunah, I'm sorry that I talked in Polish with..."

I cut him off sharply by saying, "Oh, no problem. I understand perfectly. If I had run into a Korean friend here, I would have done the same."

Except that I didn't know any Koreans in Vienna. I pushed the door and entered the restroom, leaving Axel behind, standing there with a troubled face. Once inside, I looked at myself in the mirror. My bare face with no make-up was flushed red. I was not pretty. Anyone could see that I was upset. I told myself to be reasonable. I shouldn't be upset.

After all, Axel is not my boyfriend. And this is not a date. He made that clear. He wishes to have no girlfriend, and that includes me. We are just friends. He is kind enough to spend time with me, showing me around Vienna, when he certainly has better things to do... dating this Alicja, for example. Or is it possible they already dated? Axel could have told me that he didn't want a girlfriend and told Alicja otherwise. Then, why is he with me on Sunday instead of this pretty lassie? None of this makes sense.

After using the bathroom, I washed my hand vigorously until they hurt. My left hand was still swollen and sore. I poured some cold water on my face to cool down. Then I placed my hands around my head and closed my eyes. *Was Axel still flirting with Alicja outside?*

Theoretically, he had the right to do whatever he wished. He was a free man with no obligation towards me whatsoever. I was being unreasonable, like a spoiled child, and I hated myself for being such an ass. I decided to put this nonsense behind me. I should try to enjoy the rest of the day. There was no reason to ruin a nice Sunday. I should be thankful to Axel, shouldn't I?

Be smart, not stupid, I told myself again. When I came out, Axel was sitting alone at a table outside, watching the street. His beautiful forehead was furrowed. He had that dark shadow on his face that I saw in his atelier when I asked about his painting. As he looked up and saw me, he stood up and pulled the chair for me to sit.

Where did he learn to be so gallant? Was it his upbringing? Did his grandma tell him to do that for a lady? I sat down across from him. He stared at me closely.

"Are you alright?" he asked.

"Yes. I'm good. This is a nice place. Do you come here often?"

"Occasionally, in the summer."

Out of the corner of my eye, I spotted Alicja and the brunette sitting at a corner table some distance away. Alicja had her legs crossed, her short dress lifted as she sat, revealing her beautiful long legs as if to say, "look at me. I'm gorgeous." And she was. Everyone looked at her in admiration when passing by. Some men turned their heads to steal a second glance, even if they were accompanied by their wives or girlfriends.

I sighed. She was smoking a cigarette and smiling at a waiter, asking for something. The waiter talked to her much longer than necessary, smiling back and eager to do anything she wanted. Now she was flirting with the waiter. Oh, sweet Jesus, I hated her. I hated her even more because she was a smoker. I couldn't stand people who smoked in public. They didn't care if they were bothering other people; they were just so selfish.

Axel was still staring at me as if to read my mind.

"Hyunah. I'm sorry. I was rude to talk in Polish..."

I cut him short again. "It's alright, Axel. Don't worry about it, please. I understand. You seemed to enjoy talking to your friend."

"She is not my friend; she is a classmate."

"Look at her. Isn't she beautiful? Everyone can't stop watching her. Are all the Polish women so attractive?"

"You look more beautiful to me, Hyunah," Axel said softly. His eyes were watching my every move.

What did he just say? If he was trying to make me feel better, I appreciated the effort, but we both knew it was a lie. But it made me smile all the same.

"Oh, come on. We both know that's a lie. You don't have to tell me what I want to hear. Please. Let's be real."

But Axel had a perfectly honest face.

"No, I'm not lying to please you. The concept of beauty is individual. Beauty comes not only from the appearance but also from within. The inner beauty counts as much as your physique. Alicja may please the eyes of some people, but that's not what I would describe as 'beautiful'. A beautiful person is someone that you appreciate, also on account of her kindness, elegance, and how connected you are with that person. Someone you want to spend time with; someone who gives you joy, someone who makes you smile, someone you want to have endless conversations with, someone you wish to share many things in life. A beautiful person shines from within, as well as from the outer appearance."

"You're a charmer, aren't you? With all that sweet-talking."

"No, I just told you what I think. I may be a lot of things, but I'm not a liar. Ask Herbert. I always tell the truth. Look who I'm spending my weekend with. I'm with you, not the Polish girl behind me that everybody else is fussing about. Isn't that proof to you?"

Words failed me. He was being honest. He chose to be with me this weekend, and that was that. Was it possible he enjoyed my company just as much as I enjoyed his? Did he think I was kind, elegant, and shining from within? It sounded unreal to me. While I pondered the questions, a waiter came along.

Axel said, "Do you know what you would like to drink? We will order drinks first. Later, we will see if we want to eat."

Axel ordered a locally brewed draft beer for himself. I thought I could manage that.

"I will have the same."

"What? Seriously? No, Hyunah, I don't think it's a good idea."

Instead, he ordered a bottle of mineral water for me. I realised he was right. I had just had a nightmarish experience caused by alcohol. Any alcoholic beverage was a very bad idea indeed.

"You're right. I should stay away from the beer garden for a while. Especially schnapps."

"That would be wise. What are you doing tomorrow? I don't think you can work in your condition. You cannot even wash yourself."

That was a good question. I certainly couldn't work. I needed both of my hands in good shape to do make-up or styling. For the moment, I had little to do. Vienna fashion weeks were over, and there were no fashion shows scheduled for the near future. I should refuse all the castings for the moment.

"I honestly have no idea. I need to get some rest until I feel better and heal, I guess."

"Let me take care of you for a few days. You can stay in the guest bedroom."

"Oh, that's so kind of you, but I can't accept that."

"Why not?"

"I have already caused you enough trouble. I will manage by myself. I will be fine."

"You didn't cause me trouble. I'm partly responsible for it, too."

"No, you are not. Please, we already discussed that in the morning."

"Then let me take you to a doctor tomorrow. I will make an appointment."

"I don't need a doctor. I will be alright."

"You had a bad concussion and fainted. You had hallucinations. You should get it checked. I don't think you should stay by yourself tonight."

"For the moment, I feel alright. If anything goes wrong, I will let you know."

He didn't look convinced. His beautiful forehead was creased in a frown again.

"You are as stubborn as a mule."

I smiled.

"I guess I got it from my mother. She is so stubborn, it's easier to move a mountain than change her mind."

"So, does it mean you won't change your mind no matter what?"

"Maybe. Unless I have a major crisis. But I'm more flexible than my mom. I'm not stupid enough to persist with my idea if I realise I'm wrong."

"Alright then. I hope you realise I'm right."

The drinks arrived. Axel's beer looked tempting. He poured the mineral water into my glass. And I noticed something mouth-watering on the platter the waiter was carrying. It looked like some kind of dessert. Axel's observant eyes didn't miss it.

"It's apfelstrudel," he said as I was about to ask what it was.

My eyes grew wide. I could surely manage that.

"It looks delicious. Can I have that?"

"It's a Viennese-style apple pie. Would you like to try one? If you can't finish it, I will."

He grinned.

"Yes. I will have some."

Axel ordered it and something for himself.

"A cooked apple can't be too bad for your stomach." He raised his glass to toast.

"Here's to my lady, stubborn as a mule."

Here's to my Shepherd Prince.

I wanted to say that. But I restrained myself.

"Here's to our glorious Lipizzaners."

"Café Bräunerhof is well-known for being the preferred café of the famous Austrian writer, Thomas Bernhard. Every Saturday, there is live music here with a small orchestra playing waltzes and classical music."

"Really? We should come back for that. I like live classical music."

"If you like live classical music, we should go to Budapest. They have live music everywhere. Even in the streets, restaurants... the whole city is full of live performances. You have the impression everyone is a musician there."

"Wow, that sounds great."

"Would you like to go?"

"Yes, of course. How wonderful it would be."

"Well then, another city to visit for her ladyship."

The waiter arrived at our table. He placed the plate of apfelstrudel in front of me. The smell of cinnamon woke my palate with a promise of delight. Axel had a plate of colourful salad. That looked good, too.

I said cheerfully, *"Guten Appetit."*

"Go slow, Hyunah. Eat only what you can."

"Oh, you want to steal my apfelstrudel?"

I took a cautious first bite. It was delicious. With my clumsy, injured hands, I struggled with the knife and fork, trying to cut it into small pieces.

"Hold on. Give me your plate."

Axel took my plate and skillfully cut my apfelstrudel into small pieces. He put a small bite on a spoon with a bit of cream on top. He brought the spoon to my mouth with a gesture to open my mouth. I obliged and accepted the treat. Now he was spoon-feeding me.

Out of the corner of my eye, I spotted Alicja and her friend peeking a glance at us. Their eyes grew wide, watching Axel spoon-feed me apfelstrudel. I took the mouthful and closed my eyes blissfully.

"Oh, this is so delicious...."

"Wait, you have some cream on your lips."

Axel wiped the cream from my lips with his fingers and licked it. His lovely lips kissed me indirectly. The expression on Alicja's face turned into unbelievable dismay. Alicja and her friend stared at each other as if to say, "Did you just see that?"

An exhilarating sensation swept over me.

Ha-ha! This is what you get if you mess with my Shepherd Prince, I wanted to tell her.

I accepted another spoonful with a broad smile on my face, allowing him to have the next bite. Axel grinned while staring at me, enjoying the Viennese speciality from his hand, one bite after another.

The afternoon sunshine illuminated his fair hair, which seemed to become brighter the longer he stayed exposed to the sun. His spellbinding blue eyes were on me. He looked more beautiful than ever, with his pixyish grin from ear to ear.

My Shepherd Prince was happy. And so was I.

Kulebiak z Kapusta oraz Karpatka

I knew of a Korean restaurant in Kaiser Straße, only a few minutes' walk down the road towards Mariahilfer Straße. It was not an ordinary Korean restaurant. It was a North Korean restaurant run by North Koreans.

I always wondered what it would be like to dine there as a South Korean. Austria was one of the few countries in Europe where North Korea had an embassy, and it was only about a hundred metres away from my flat.

Most South Koreans, since their childhood, were given a grim picture of North Korea. The common belief was that North Korea was a cruel nation. Despite being the same people of the same race, the political propaganda forbade us from approaching any North Koreans, even overseas. I was exposed to the same teachings, so I was scared but awfully curious about these North Koreans. If I go in there as a customer, I wondered, what can they do to me other than serve me a meal? They surely wouldn't harm me? But so far, I hadn't dared to walk inside and taste the North Korean food.

Axel drove me back to my place that Sunday afternoon, after a long, relaxing lunch at the Café Bräunerhof. We both enjoyed our time together. When we arrived, and it was time for me to go up to my place, we were both reluctant to say goodbye. Axel fixed his eyes on me and asked one more time, "Are you sure you don't want to come with me?"

I wanted to join him, but my words came out otherwise. "Yes. I'm sure. I will manage by myself. But thank you. You are so kind."

He sighed in disappointment. "Well then, my lady. As you wish."

He got out of the car and opened the passenger door for me. I gave him a farewell cheek kiss, and as I was about to turn, he stopped me.

"Wait, you don't even have my number. How will you contact me?"

He took out a piece of paper from his wallet and scribbled something with a crayon.

His number first, then another one, after which he wrote the word, *Herbert*.

"Here's my number. Sometimes when I'm in the atelier, I don't hear the phone ring. In that case, call Herbert. He will pass the message."

I produced a business card from my handbag and wrote the private number of my flat with his crayon. My business card only had my agency's number on it. He took it and slipped it into his wallet.

"Call me anytime, even at night. I will come for you if you need me. Okay?"

"Okay. Thank you for everything. I loved the Lipizzaners."

"See you soon, Hyunah."

Regret started to creep in as I watched him turn around and get into his car.

Why didn't I just go with him?

His red Fiat disappeared. I stood there for a moment longer, watching the street. I sighed.

I climbed up the stairs, to find that the apartment was empty. It was a nice Sunday afternoon, and everybody was out enjoying

Vienna. I stepped into my room. I undressed carefully, trying not to hurt my right shoulder and the left wrist. The dress was uncomfortable, and I wanted to wash myself. I got into the shower and cautiously let the water run over my body. I took a bottle of my favourite orange blossom shower gel, only to find someone had used it without my permission. Half the contents were gone! It was about two-thirds full when I left the previous morning.

Shit. These damn models. They didn't have the courtesy to ask me if they could use my gel. Whoever did it didn't even bother to close the bottle. I felt furious. A sharp pain stung my right shoulder as I poured the gel into my hand. Any movement at all was hurting me. I couldn't properly wash myself without hurting either my shoulder or my wrist. I gave up rubbing myself and simply let the water run through my body. I turned around so the running water would sweep away the foam.

I finished my slow and careful shower, then stashed my shower gel and mint shampoo aside to bring to my room. No one could steal them again. Good heavens. I couldn't even have my products in the shower booth without fear of somebody stealing them! Wouldn't it be nice to find a place of my own? But I didn't know how to find another place in Vienna, and it could be more expensive than here.

I stepped into my room with the two bottles in a small container and the towel wrapped around me. As I sat on the small table before a mirror, the blue-violet bruise on my shoulder caught my attention. As I was drying my hair, I heard someone walk in. It was Joanna.

"Hey, Kim. How's it going? We didn't see you last night. Did you spend the night with that smoking hottie? Oh, my God, what happened to you?"

She fixated on my shoulder. Her eyes grew wide with excitement.

"Oh, my, my. You naughty girl! Did he go rough on you? Did he blow your brains out? Oh, my God!"

"I fell and crashed my head against the wall. I didn't sleep with him, Joanna."

"What? But you spent the night with him, right? If you didn't do a guy like him, what did you do?"

"We went to see Gustav Klimt."

"Who? Who is Klimt? Some Austrian movie star?"

I sighed. I knew some models were culturally handicapped, but they never ceased to amaze me.

"Joanna, not everything about seeing a guy is about fucking. You should make yourself wiser and learn about the culture a little, you know. Gustav Klimt is a famous Austrian symbolist painter."

As soon as the words left my mouth, I regretted them. I should not have said that. Not this way. Joanna's smile was gone. Her cheeks flushed red, and her eyes glinted with fury. I started, in an apologetic tone, "Oh, I'm sorry, what I meant was..."

But Joanna snapped sharply, "Oh, Kim. Don't patronise me. You think you are an artist from Paris? But you are no better than us. Stop with that artist crap attitude!"

I didn't respond. There was no reason to continue this conversation. She stormed out of the room and slammed the door. It was scarcely half an hour since I said goodbye to Axel, and someone was already yelling at me.

I clumsily wrapped my head in a towel and closed my eyes. Now I wanted to get the hell out of here.

Is it too late to call Axel and tell him I have changed my mind? What would he think if I did?

He must have arrived home by now.

I dried my hair with my aching hands, feeling miserable. I found a fresh T-shirt, comfortable shorts, and new underwear in a drawer. I got dressed. Every single movement hurt. Exhaustion started to catch up with me, and I lay on my bed.

My mind streamed through everything that happened over the past few days. It all seemed like a dream. My life had changed dramatically ever since Axel came to find me at the Stadtpark. It was only last Friday, but a lot had happened during these days. I had met him only a few days ago but it seemed as though I had known him for a long time. How was it possible? I had certainly never met him before, except for the first time one month ago. Did such a thing as 'past life' exist? That you had a life before you were born in this lifetime? My father believed in that. He believed in reincarnation, the rebirth of souls in new bodies. The people who were related to you in your past life would always appear and meet you again in this lifetime. Although it could be another form of relationship, there would always be a tie between the two people.

It was a convincing belief. Perhaps some people invented it to believe life doesn't end when you die. They wished to believe life continued even after your death, and you would be reborn in the next life as a different person. But in the next life, you would still find the people you were intimately involved with in the past life.

Was it possible Axel and I were close in our past life, if such a thing existed—husband and wife, or lovers, or any type of intimate relationship between two individuals? Or are we all afraid to die and do not want to admit life simply ends when you die?

However fantastic this theory was, I wanted to believe it. Axel was my Shepherd Prince, and I was his moon goddess Cynthia, and we were reborn in this life to resume our ties again.

Love between mortal and immortal. Endymion and the moon goddess, Shepherd Prince and the Greek goddess of the Moon and the wild animals, Artemis...

I must have dozed off. An annoying male voice with an American accent woke me up. He was in the living room.

"Yeah, man... yeah, I fucking did it, man, yeah, I stole it... yeah, I fucking won the bet. How did I? How did that happen?"

A loud laugh followed. I found the way he spoke vulgar, with f-words in every sentence. He continued.

"I was talking to this booker, you know? A crazy motherfucker, yeah... yeah, man... we were partying on the rooftop, some fucking artist's penthouse, yeah, he said, yeah... if I manage to steal one of the paintings... yeah, steal... no shit. We were all fucking high, man... The motherfucker said he would pay me for the flight back to LA... Yeah, no shit... yeah, so I did it, yeah... I sneaked into one of the rooms... yeah... yeah, man... I snatched the painting. Yeah, no joke, man... You will see... yeah, I said... yeah man, I will show you... muahahahahaha!" Another hideous laugh.

I sprang up. The back of my neck tingled. Was this the bastard who stole Axel's painting? I tiptoed to the door and opened the door just enough to listen to the conversation. He seemed to be on the phone. I pricked my ears and kept listening.

"What's in the painting... what? Yeah... it's some fucking hot pussy, man, yeah, almost naked... yeah... Muahahaha..."

The voice belonged to none other than Anthony, a guy from LA. He had that smug face you wanted to slap, always bragging about what he did, how much money he made, how he did this and that. I abhorred his unsavoury behaviour. He went on rambling.

"Yeah, man... are you coming to pick me up at the airport? Yeah... next Sunday... Yeah... I'm leaving... I got my ticket for free, man... yeah, no shit. Muhahaha... Muahahaha... I'm leaving fucking Vienna...."

I had to act quickly. This motherfucker (as per his favourite expression) stole Axel's painting to win a bet with a booker who proposed to buy him a flight ticket to LA if he could steal it, and he did. And he was leaving next Sunday. It could only be Axel's painting. How many rooftop penthouses in Vienna had an atelier in them? And frequently visited by the fashion crowd? This was it. The bloody bastard who got away with the painting.

Now I got you, you little shithead.

I had to find a way to retrieve it—quickly. Before next Sunday. Now, how would I pull this off? Confronting him was not a good idea. Threatening him? No. Talking to Axel was not a good idea, either. He was a kind gentleman, but he could lose his temper if provoked. I remembered how he reacted to my unreasonable behaviour this morning when I asked him to wear a blindfold: *If you cannot trust me, get up now. I will bring you home.*

He was decisive. He wouldn't let others treat him unfairly. I imagined what he would do to a guy who stole his painting. I didn't want to find out. Now what? Go to the police? That included Axel finding it out. So, no. There was only one thing to do—take it back quietly. As quietly as possible. For that, I needed to find out about the painting. Anthony described it as "some f---ing hot pussy, almost naked..."

So, was it a nude portrait of some woman? How big? That was important to find out. To get all this information, I had to go back to Axel's house again. I looked at my watch. It was almost seven in the evening. I had come back home around four-thirty, so I must have slept for a while.

I got up and put my jeans on. I tiptoed to the door. Anthony was still talking on the phone, thinking there was nobody around. He got off the phone and went towards the toilet. I got out of the room. There was no one around yet, so he thought he was not overheard. All the better. I wondered where Joanna was.

Anthony was sharing a room with Mike, the gay photographer from London. Their room was right next to mine. I peeked inside the room carefully. The door was half ajar, so I went in. Now, where did he hide the painting? The room had two single beds on each side. I noticed a wardrobe they shared. There were hangers with all the men's clothing on top. I looked inside each drawer briefly, between the socks and underwear. Nothing. I should get out before Anthony returned. There wasn't enough time for a thorough search now.

I left the room and saw no one in the living room, so I stepped into my room again. I took my wallet with some coins and went outside. The telephone in the living room only allowed incoming calls, the reason being that last year when anybody could make a phone call from the flat, some models called their home countries endlessly. And the *propriétaire* (landlord) had received an outrageous phone bill. But the models who were responsible had already fled Vienna.

Since then, only incoming calls were allowed. If you needed to make a phone call, you had to get out to the phone booth nearby. So, I went out to find a phone booth. I found an empty one nearby. I slid in the coins and punched Axel's number. It started ringing. I waited until it had rung several times, but no one answered.

Did I enter the right number? I tried again, checking the numbers one by one. This time, I let it ring at least ten times, but still, nobody picked it up. Is he in his atelier, I wondered? I saw Herbert's number, but since it was Sunday, the garage was closed. Axel didn't have an answering machine, either. But in any case, I needed to talk to him, not to the machine. Did he give me a false number? Why would he do that? Something was wrong. So, I returned home.

Some girls and boys were sitting around the living room table now. Pedro was there. He called me.

"Hello, Kim. How are you?"

"Hello, Pedro. I'm good, and you?"

"Fine. Have you talked to your sweetheart?"

"Yes. He's not interested."

"What? He's not interested?"

"No, Pedro. He's not up for it. Sorry."

"Well, that's a pity. He doesn't know what he's missing. Some guys would kill for this job, you know. It's a huge TV commercial. It will be shown on TV every day for several months."

"Sorry. No is no."

I went into my room before Pedro continued to nag me. Why didn't Axel pick up the phone? Something was amiss. I collapsed on the bed, feeling rather lost. While I pondered my next move, I heard a soft knock on the door. Was Pedro still going to nag me about Axel? Why couldn't he take no for an answer? I opened the door, ready to face Pedro, but found Mark.

"Someone is asking for you downstairs."

"What? Oh, thank you."

I hurried downstairs, wondering who it could be. I found nobody inside the building downstairs, so I pushed opened the door and stepped outside.

My eyes fell on Axel, standing there with his light denim jacket. The unexpected sight of him took my breath away. He was absolutely gorgeous. In the early evening light, his golden hair fell freely on his shoulder, his mesmerising eyes sparkled in cobalt blue. My heart leapt with surprise and joy. It started pounding wildly, and I could feel it pumping.

"I just came by to check up on you, I thought..."

Before he'd finished his sentence, I threw myself into his arms. I was so happy to see him. It was only a few hours since I had last seen him, but it seemed like forever. He flinched with surprise but held me back firmly in his arms.

"I just tried to call you. No one answered."

"Because I was on my way to you."

He stroked my hair with his delicate fingers, pushing me gently into his chest. He whispered, "Why did you call me?"

"Uh, because..."

"Yes?"

"Because, uh..."

"My lady?"

"Because I thought..."

His fingers travelled slowly to my neck, across my earlobe, and through my hair, caressing the back of my head. His low voice fondled my ears. "Did you change your mind?"

"Yes. I did. I... um... I want to come back with you."

"Good. I'm glad. Listen. Go to your room and pack some essentials for a few days. I will wait here."

And I obliged. I ran to my room in a frenzy, feeling my heartbeat pounding wildly with each step. I pushed the door to the flat and dashed to the room while everyone in the living room watched me curiously. I took a small travel bag and started throwing into it what I needed—T-shirts, panties, socks, comfortable cotton dresses, a pair of jeans, and a red silk dress I bought in Paris for going out (you never know), and a pair of shoes that matched the red dress. I wondered if I should take my make-up kit, but, having no time, I just took some powder and a few other products in a small pouch that already had moisturiser, body lotion, make-up remover, and a tiny sample of French perfume.

My eyes spotted my bottle of Chanel 5. I grabbed it and tossed it in the bag. I found a plastic bag and put my orange blossom shower gel and mint shampoo in it, fearing that someone would steal them. I hurled them all into the travel bag.

And I had business to attend to; I was determined to get that son of a bitch, Anthony. I would take the painting back before he fled Vienna. To do so, I had to prepare my ground first. I remembered his hateful, smug face and the unspeakable obscenity of the phone conversation. I must get him. He had no idea I was coming for him. Bloody selfish bastard. Stole a painting to win a bet and a free flight ticket. And proudly bragging about it. *I'm coming for you, bastard. And I'm going to get you.*

My blood boiled with rage. I put on a denim jacket and grabbed my handbag and the travel bag. My right shoulder hurt, so I put the travel bag across my left shoulder and took the handbag with my right hand.

When I got out, I found Anthony drinking with Pedro and Sam (a new guy from South Africa), loudly crunching crisps. The moment I saw him, I wanted to slap his face. Joanna was there, seated across from Anne and Dorothe. She glared at me. When I met her eyes, she ignored me and turned her face away. I felt bad for her. I should not have snapped at her like that.

"Are you going somewhere, darling?" Pedro asked me curiously.

"Oh, just for a couple of days. I hurt myself, and I can't work for a few days. I'm going to a doctor tomorrow."

"Oh, my God, I'm sorry to hear that. Take care of yourself. And say hi to your sweetheart. You know where to reach me if he changes his mind."

Yeah, right. I headed for the door, and Dorothe followed me out.

"What happened to you, Kim? You didn't come home last night. I thought you were having real fun with that smoking hottie."

"I slipped and fell in his flat and hurt my head. I will be alright."

"Oh, okay. But you still owe me all the details about this guy. How is he in bed? Fantastic, I imagine?"

Why is everybody thinking I slept with him already?

"No, Dorothe. We are just friends. Now, I really must go. See you later."

Before she opened her mouth again, I pushed the door and ran downstairs. When I stepped outside, to my surprise, I found Axel and Mark talking to each other. Mark had a small white dog named Poncho that he was out on a walk with. Everyone knew he broke up with his gay partner a few months ago. *Did he come down to walk his dog, or because he found an opportunity to speak to Axel?* Maybe both.

I didn't miss the fact that Mark's eyes were glowing in admiration of my Shepherd Prince. Mark was talking in his best charming tone while Axel was playing with the dog. His love for animals seemed to allow him to drop his guard against the fashion crowd.

Axel looked up and walked toward me to relieve me of the bags. Poncho followed him like a shadow.

"My car is parked down the road."

He inclined his head in the direction. Mark formed a subtle frown, seeing Axel go already. I quickly turned to him.

"Mark, do you want to walk with us to the car?"

"Oh, can I? I would love that, thank you."

Poncho jumped around Axel wildly, trying to get his attention. All animals loved Axel. He had a way with them. I had a word with Mark. Since we had little time, I went straight to the point.

"I need your help, Mark, and it's rather urgent."

"Oh, what can I do for you?"

"Did you guys introduce each other? My friend's name is Axel, and he is a student at the art school. Your roommate, Anthony, stole his painting during the party that was held at the rooftop penthouse."

"Oh, you mean Axel is the painter who lives in that penthouse? Nobody saw him. He never showed at the party."

"Right. And Anthony stole his painting to win a bet with a booker."

"Oh..."

Mark frowned, trying to remember something.

"I think I remember now. About two months ago, Anthony came back from a party with a painting. It was in the room for a while. Is that the one with a woman in it?"

"Yes! Did you see the painting?"

"Yes. It was a beautiful one—a picture of a very elegant lady on horseback."

"Oh, yes, that's it. Do you know where it is now?"

"It was in the room for a while, then it disappeared. I asked Anthony where he got it, and he said he bought it at an auction. That seemed odd to me. He is not the kind of bloke who would spend money on a painting. I never like that type. A pompous ass who brags all the time."

"Alright, Mike. Listen to me. Anthony is flying home next Sunday. We need to act now to get that painting back. And I need your help."

"Alright, what do you want me to do?"

"I need you to find out where the painting is. You're his roommate, right?"

"Yes, I can search the room when he is not there. Then what?"

"We are going to take it and bring it back to its rightful owner."

I pointed to Axel, who was merrily playing with the dog.

"Okay. Why don't we just whack the bastard and ask him where it is?"

"Well, it would get messy. I prefer to pull this off quietly. Are you with me or not?"

"I will help you any way I can. Axel is a painter? I thought he had something of an artist about him. That's nice. You're lucky to have him as a friend."

I saw a tinge of envy in his eyes. He liked Axel. A lot.

"Mark. When we retrieve the painting, we can all go out and celebrate it. How does that sound?"

"Oh. That would be lovely."

"So, listen to me. I will call you tomorrow morning, and you will tell me if you found the painting. I also need you to find out when Anthony is going to be out. So I can come and search the room myself."

"Okay. Call me at ten o'clock tomorrow. We will talk then, okay?"

"Okay. I appreciate your help."

"I did nothing yet. Let's talk tomorrow morning."

"Alright."

We arrived at the car. Fortunately, Axel had to park a little further away, giving me time to talk to Mark. To my amazement, we were standing right in front of the Pyongyang Restaurant, the North Korean restaurant I wanted to check out. I peeked inside. The restaurant was open, and I saw some people dining. I had a strange mixed sensation—creeped out, excited... I felt goose-bumps all over my skin. *On the other side of this glass, are there North Koreans serving dinner? Not killing or torturing people?*

Axel opened the trunk and hurled my bags inside. He offered a hand to Mark. Mark grinned widely as he shook Axel's hand. Poncho jumped around Axel as if he didn't want him to leave. Axel gave Poncho a gentle pat. The dog licked his hand excitedly.

"It was nice meeting you, Mark."

"Nice meeting you, too, Axel. Thanks for playing with my dog."

"A pleasure. Good evening."

"Good evening. See you around, mate."

Mark's eyes lingered on Axel a moment longer. We got into the car. And Poncho jumped onto Axel's lap before he could close the door of the driver's seat.

"No, Poncho, come here. Come here, I said!" Mark yelled after his dog.

Axel grabbed Poncho, who had no intention of leaving him. Poncho tried with all his might to stay in the car. While Axel tussled with Poncho, Mark advanced toward the dog to seize it, and his face brushed past Axel's strands of golden hair for half a second. Mark got the now-barking dog back. His face was flushed in a reddish pink.

"Sorry about that."

"No problem," Axel replied cheerfully. I smiled at the scene. It seemed the three of us, two humans and a dog, were all crazy about Axel.

"Are you alright, Hyunah?" Axel asked as he drove the car past the North Korean restaurant.

"Yes. I am fine. I feel better now."

He had a radiant smile on his face as he drove through Mariahilfer Straße.

The fresh, post-clean smell hit my nose as we entered his place. The apartment was wiped clean, with no traces of dirt anywhere. All the windows were wide open to allow fresh air in, and all the wooden floors were properly scrubbed. Every piece of furniture was meticulously dusted.

"Wow, your nanny did a great job."

"Yes. She did. She even cooked for us."

Us?

Axel led me to the kitchen. He opened the oven.

"She made a vegetable pie. She knows how to cook with no meat for me. My grandma taught her."

"Your grandma seems like a nice person."

"Oh, she is. I wouldn't be here today if it weren't for her. She's one of the most beautiful persons I know."

I remembered the concept of beauty he explained to me at the café earlier. His granny must be kind and elegant, shining from within. The mouth-watering smell of the pie suddenly woke up my stomach. Axel looked at me keenly.

"Are you hungry? You haven't had dinner yet, right?"

"Oh, I never have dinner before eight o'clock. And yes, I'm a little hungry."

"Alright then. Let's have dinner after I show you to your room."

He took my travel bag and handbag, leading me to the guest bedroom. The room was nicely cleaned. The window was wide open to air the room, and the bed was freshly made with new bed sheets that smelled of lavender. Axel brought me fresh towels, including a French-style *gant de toilette*, and laid them on the bed.

"Will you be alright here?"

"Oh, this is very nice. I wouldn't want you to see my room in my place. You would say the whole apartment is a big mess. Those models live like pigs in a pen. You have no idea."

"Really?"

"Yes. And they steal my things. Somebody used my gel douche in the shower without asking me. So I brought it here with me. They also steal my food in the fridge. I had five apples in the fridge before I left, but now there are only two left. Two months ago, I put on a note on my fridge, saying, *Please don't take anything out of this fridge without asking Kim*. And you know what happened? Some asshole drew a rat underneath, saying, *We are all rats here, Kim, and we like your food. Muhahahaha.* And they kept stealing my food. So I just gave up. I only buy minimum groceries for survival. They are real savages."

Axel's eyes grew wide in disbelief.

And one of them stole your painting. I will get it back to you.

"You can't have that, Hyunah. You cannot live in a place like that."

"What choice do I have? I don't know anyone here, except these people in the fashion industry. They all steal from each other, one way or another."

"Do you want to move out? To somewhere else? I can make some inquiries if you want."

"Oh, that's nice of you, but don't bother. I'm used to living like that now. Let's have dinner. I'm hungry. Oh, no. I'm sorry. I didn't bring anything for dinner. If I'd known we were going to have dinner here, I would have brought something. A bottle of wine, or a bunch of flowers... It's so rude of me... please excuse me... my mother would kill me."

Axel stared at me calmly. And with a smile, he said, "Hyunah, you are my guest. I'm pleased to have you as a company. It's just you and me in the house. You don't need to bring me anything. Please drop all that social courtesy when you are with me. I understand you had a certain upbringing in your family, but forget all those social manners with me, please. I don't need that with you."

And he showed me around the penthouse. He opened the door to a guest bathroom.

There was a toilet, sink, and shower but no bathtub.

"You're welcome to use my bathroom. I think you might as well use mine to wash yourself in the bathtub."

He flashed his boyish smile, and I didn't miss the playful glint in his eyes. I remembered the childish grin on his face as if he was playing with a toy, while he was rubbing me in the bathtub this morning.

"I will go set up dinner. Make yourself at home."

Axel disappeared into the kitchen. I went back to the guest bedroom and opened my travel bag. I needed to find out something about the painting. Mark said the painting was of an elegant lady on horseback, so it could not be a nude like I initially thought. Anthony told his buddy she was hot and almost naked. So, she was dressed, but maybe in a summer dress or something, where you could see her skin. What interested me was the size of the painting.

Was it small enough for me to carry it out in a bag? Was it big? If it was big, how big? Let's say I managed to find the painting; how would I bring it out of the room without drawing the attention of the curious eyes in the living room? If it was small, I could hide it inside Mark's portfolio, saying I was doing him a favour. That Mark asked me to bring it to him when he was outside somewhere. This could only be done if the picture was small. What if it was big? There was no way I could avoid being seen if I came out of the room with a big painting. And Anthony had to be out of his room long enough for the search. I could discuss it with Mark tomorrow. One thing at a time.

So, if the painting is big, there should be another way out. Can I bring it out through the window? Then I'd better have an accomplice down in the street waiting. I need someone I can trust. It could only be Herbert. He would gladly help me. I had to talk to Herbert, but the first thing was to find out the size of the tableau. Well, I must visit Axel's atelier to see if he had anything similar to the one that was stolen, which might be the same size. I got up and went to the kitchen.

Axel was slicing the tomatoes, lettuce, and cucumber on the cutting board to prepare a salad. He turned around to see me and smiled.

"Do you need anything?"

"Can I go to your atelier while you are in the kitchen?"

"Sure. It's open."

"Thank you."

I entered the atelier. As soon as I was inside, I started going through all his paintings, checking the different sizes. None of them was small, like portfolios. Before I left the atelier, I checked the bottom right corner to see how Axel signed his paintings. I looked at each tableau and found he signed *Axel* with one initial letter of his middle name and the family name in black ink.

I headed to the kitchen. The aroma of the vegetable pie being heated made my mouth water. Axel was laying the table in the kitchen. The table was small but big enough for two.

"Wow, smells good here. Can I do anything to help?"

"No need. Everything is ready. Tonight, we are having a simple salad and Polish vegetable pie. Does it suit her ladyship?"

"Oh, sounds great. What is Polish vegetable pie?"

"We call it *Kulebiak z Kapusta*. It's Polish cabbage and mushroom pie."

"What? I can never pronounce Polish words."

Axel pronounced each syllable slowly and clearly, and I repeated it after him twice. He served a bowl of salad, two plates and two glasses of mineral water on the table.

"*Guten Appetit*," Axel said cheerfully.

"*Guten Appetit*. Are you Polish or Austrian? You seemed to be closer to Polish. Your grandma is Polish, so was your nanny, and now you serve Polish specialities at home."

He smiled. "I am both. But as you said, I'm close to my grandma. I may tend to be more Polish at heart."

"My father is half Russian. His mother was Russian. Although we have no idea what happened to her since."

"What do you mean you have no idea what happened to her?"

"Oh, you know the situation between South Korea and North Korea?"

"Well, it was divided into two parts in 1945... by Russia and America? And there was a civil war... right?"

"Yes. Officially, we are still at war. We signed for an armistice, not a peace treaty when the war ended in 1953. My father lived in North Korea before the war, and he had to be a North Korean soldier during the war. He was captured by the South Korean army and became a war prisoner for two years on a small island in the southern part of South Korea. When the war was over, they gave him a choice: stay in South Korea or go back to North Korea. And someone told him to stay in South Korea, saying if he were to choose North Korea, he would die."

"That is quite a story. So, he chose to stay in South Korea."

"Yes. I wouldn't be here now if he didn't. I don't want to

imagine living in North Korea. The worst place on earth to live, with the most notorious dictatorship."

"Quite right. And a big tragedy, too. One nation separated into two like that."

"So, to answer your question, since my father stayed in South Korea, we couldn't hear anything from his family. There's no communication between North and South Korea, especially between civilians."

"So, you have no idea if they are alive or not?"

"No. Not at all."

"Oh, that's sad. So tragic. You said your grandmother was Russian?"

"Yes. I found out about it by chance. My father didn't tell me and somehow kept it to himself. I don't know why."

"Oh, I see now. I wondered why your hair is light brown, and it looks natural. You didn't colour your hair, did you?"

"No. This is my natural colour. I have never coloured my hair."

"And you don't have a typical Asian face. You have round eyes and high cheekbones, not like the Japanese geisha with moon-shaped eyes."

"Because I'm a hybrid. A bit like you. You are a good mixture of Eastern European. By the way, there's a place I want to go, but I'm scared at the same time."

"What is it?" He raised his eyebrows.

"This evening, you parked your car right in front of a North Korean restaurant. You might not remember."

"Oh, was that the restaurant you looked into curiously?"

"Yes. It's called the Pyongyang Restaurant, named after the North Korean capital. And I heard some rumours about it."

"What rumours?"

"Everyone working in there are secret agents appointed by the North Korean government to do some shady jobs."

"Shady jobs?"

"Some years ago, famous Korean pianist Kun-Woo Paik was

kidnapped inside that restaurant. They knocked him out with something, and he lost consciousness. He was with his wife, a famous Korean actress, at that time."

"And what happened?"

"They were about to be kidnapped to North Korea, but at the last minute, they managed to escape by a miracle. It's quite a dramatic story, like in a movie."

"And you want to go there?"

"Yes. I'm dying to see North Koreans. I've never seen any in my life."

"Do you want to go there tomorrow evening? Will you come with me?" Axel said cheerfully.

"Of course, I will."

"It can be dangerous, you know."

"I don't think so. If they want to harm you in any way, they have to get through me first."

"Then let's go tomorrow. Are you sure you are up for it?"

"Quite sure. I don't think they will do anything to harm you."

"We will find that out tomorrow."

He got up to check on the pie in the oven. It smelled delicious! As we sat to taste the pie, he asked. "What is Korean food like?"

"It's very different from European food. We eat a lot of vegetables, prepared in various ways with rice. And some dishes come with fish or meat. Tomorrow, we will find something for you without meat. Every meal comes with rice, soup, and various side dishes. Although how North Korean prepare their dishes, we will figure it out ourselves tomorrow."

"Sounds good."

We attacked the pie. I took the first bite that melted in my mouth with delicious cabbages and mushrooms, rich in herbs and aroma.

"Oh, this is good. Your grandma's recipe?"

"Yes. She removed sausages from the original recipe and put something else in to replace them. Do you recognise it?"

Axel watched my reaction attentively.

"Oh, what could it be? I have no idea. Why should I recognise it?"

"I think it's something you eat a lot in Asia."

As I struggled to cut my pie to get another bite, Axel took my plate and cut the pie for me.

"I have no idea."

"Here, take another bite."

He offered me a forkful of pie. I accepted it and tried to guess the mystery ingredient but still had no idea. I shook my head with my mouth full.

"It's tofu."

"What? There's tofu in the pie?"

He nodded, smiling. In fact, there was some texture melting like tofu.

"Yes, actually, yes. Now I see."

"It's part of my protein source. I also eat beans and seeds rich in protein. You don't have to eat meat to get protein, as most people think."

"If you like tofu, then you will survive Korean food. We eat a lot of it."

"Good."

I wanted to ask him something.

"Can you tell me what Florian told you before we said goodbye to him? I didn't understand it, but I'm curious. You smiled when he told you. What did he say?"

He tried to think a moment, his mesmerising blue eyes studying the ceiling. He seemed to remember.

"Oh, that."

"Yes, that. What was it?"

"Do you really want to know?" He had a playful glint in his eyes.

"Yes. Tell me."

"He said I have good taste in horses. He meant my beautiful

horse Frühling, in Krems. And he added I also have good taste in ladies. He meant you."

"Oh."

I tried to digest what I had heard. Did it mean Florian found me attractive? A lady a man with good taste would choose to go out with? It was obviously a compliment.

"Would my lady fancy a dessert?"

"Oh, do you have a dessert?"

"Yes. *Karpatka*."

"Sounds like a yummy Polish cake."

"Aye, my lady."

He showed me a plate of traditional Polish cream pie made of choux pastry with custard cream. It looked mouth-watering. Axel cleared the dishes and brought out two desserts. The delicious Karpatka was creamy and melted like a dream. Axel cut the pie into small pieces and offered me the first bite. I accepted the treat from his hand. He watched me eat with a smile on his face.

"You eat like a child," he said. "You have the custard cream all over your lips."

"And what about you? You also have cream all over your lips."

I lied. He didn't have cream on his face, but I took some cream with my fingers and rubbed it over his lips and face. He grabbed my hand to stop it.

"My lady is *déchaînée* (unleashed). This is not how a lady should behave."

"My lord is not himself. He is supposed to protect me, not to stop me from amusement."

With my clumsy hands, I managed to daub a few more smears of cream on Axel's face. Now, his beautiful face had cream on his lips and jaws. We played like children for a while, giggling, running after one another with cream over our faces and hands. I ran to the living room, and Axel chased after me. I took refuge on the sofa and sat there when he jumped me from behind. I had my back against him. He put his arms around me from behind and held me in place. I couldn't move at all; his strong arms firmly wrapped over me. He smeared some more cream on my nose and lips while I was wriggling to get away.

"My lord, I cannot move. It is so unfair of you."

"Why is my lady so rebellious tonight? What can I do to calm you?"

"Please stop. I can't breathe with cream on my nose."

"Will you stop rubbing cream on me if I let go of you?"

"I will. Please."

"You promise?"

"I promise."

"Alright. I'm going to count to three. At three, I'm letting you go, and you will behave like a lamb, okay?"

"Okay."

I stopped wiggling. He started to count.

"*Eins, zwei, drei.*"

He released me from his hold. I inhaled while removing cream from my nose. Axel turned me around to face him. He drew his hand to wipe the cream off my nose and lips. We were both panting from the playful run-around. Our eyes met. He looked funny with cream on his face, and I'm sure I did, too.

"There you go, my lady. Calm as a lamb."

He stared at me for a moment as I recovered my breath. His eyes moved around my face, my neck, and down through my T-shirt as if he wanted to undress me. I was sure he wanted to kiss me, but he didn't. He just stared at me calmly, without moving. Something was bothering him and kept him from kissing me. I saw the lust in his eyes, but he was controlling it firmly. He was obviously in conflict with himself. Whatever it was, it didn't please him. Finally, he whispered in a soft tone, "Let me help you wash your face."

He stood up, offering me a hand. I took his hand. *What was going on in his mind? Why didn't he kiss me?* Something stopped him. Why? He abstained with formidable self-control.

There was something medieval about him. He rode horses. He practised fencing. And how he was always so gallant with me.

Was it his grandma who raised him that way? I hoped I would meet her one day. I was sure she had played a great role in his upbringing. If someone could help me understand Axel, it was her. And Axel must have a deep affection for her.

I sighed as I followed him to the bathroom to get my face washed before going to bed.

When would I ever kiss my Shepherd Prince? Would he ever kiss me? Probably never.

I sighed again.

The Polish Book and Mon Petit Chou

Spring was in the air in the meadow. A myriad of flowers and plants were finally blooming after the long winter. A beautiful woman in a floral print dress, her lovely blonde hair freely flowing on her shoulder, was walking with her son. The child had just turned four years old. His beautiful, sparkling blue eyes and golden hair were just like his mother's. They walked along the riverside. The boy wanted to see the fish.

"There are no fish in the river, my dear. It's not deep enough."

"Can we go to the big river then?" the child insisted. His mother held him in her arms and kissed him on the cheek.

"We will go to the big river tomorrow, darling. There we can see the fish, alright?"

"Alright."

They continued their stroll along the river. Suddenly, the thunder clouds loosened. The small river filled up and turned into a big river, and before the child realised it, his mother had fallen into the river.

"Mama!" the baby boy screamed, but his mother was already gobbled up by the river, drifting away in the heavy torrent. The boy screamed and tried to go into the river to save his mother but couldn't move. His feet were stuck in the mud.

"Mama!"

As the child screamed, all became blurry with heavy rain and flooding.

~

I jolted awake, yelling like the boy whose mother was swept away. My throat was dry, and my voice didn't come out. I looked around. I was all wet, sweating as if I had just completed a marathon. As I tried to get up, my eyes fell on a thick book in my right hand. A ray of sunlight was beaming through the window. I was in Axel's bedroom. Why did I have a book in my hand? And why was I not in the guest bedroom? The book was in a language I didn't know—Polish. Why was I holding a Polish book in my sleep? I had no idea.

I got up from the bed and found slippers under the bed. I stepped into them and walked out of the room. The apartment was quiet. I called out for Axel. He wasn't there. I went to the kitchen. It was empty. The door in the living room opened with a clicking sound. I walked to the door.

Axel came in, dressed in his running gear—a T-shirt and shorts that showed off his long, slender legs. He was soaked with sweat. He held a paper bag. He smiled as we made eye contact.

"Good morning, Axel. Wow. How long did you run? You are dripping with sweat."

"Good morning, Hyunah. Oh, just five kilometres. But it was already warm outside."

He removed his running shoes and stepped in, putting the bag on the floor.

"What's in the bag?"

"Her ladyship's breakfast."

His forehead had a few strands of wet hair. "I need a shower first. Will you wait for me?"

"Of course."

He disappeared into his room. I took the bag from the floor

and brought it to the kitchen table. It was 7:30 in the morning. I opened the kitchen window and breathed in the fresh morning air. I used the guest bathroom and brushed my teeth. I looked at myself in the mirror. I looked better than yesterday, but my right shoulder and my left wrist were still sore.

I heard the shower running from his room. I imagined him all naked under the running water, the blissful water streaming through his athletic body, his gorgeous face, and wet hair. I wished my hands were not wounded so I could offer to scrub his back. I looked down at my sweaty T-shirt and went to the guest bedroom to change.

My mind drifted back to the thick Polish book. I remembered when Axel came into the guest room to say goodnight. I tried to sleep but couldn't, with all the things in my head. I tossed and turned for about an hour and started to count sheep in a meadow in my mind. I read somewhere it's what you should do when you can't sleep, but it didn't work for me. I got up and went to Axel's room. It was ajar, so I peeked inside. He was in his bed, reading a book. He looked up and saw me.

"Are you alright?"

"I'm sorry to bother you. I can't sleep."

"Do you want to come in?" He gestured me in. "I see you are reading. Am I not bothering you?"

"No. I was reading because I couldn't sleep. Come on."

I shyly went to his bed. He patted on the spot next to him, and I climbed on.

"What are you reading?"

"A book about the dressage of the Lipizzaner and the dressage in general of the other species of horses."

I glanced at the book. I didn't recognise the words. "Is it in Polish?"

"Yes."

"Okay. You're definitely Polish. You speak Polish, you have a Polish grandma and nanny, you eat *Kulebiak z Kapusta*, and now you're reading a Polish book."

"I also read in German, French, and English."

"Anything you can tell me about the book that's interesting?"

"Hmm... let's see. In the preface, it talks about something amazing. It tells the tale of an Irishman called Sullivan who lived two hundred years ago. His taming of furious horses had been witnessed by many. He would lead the animals away into a darkened barn, and no one knew what happened for sure when he closed the door. He claimed all he used were the words of an Indian charm bought for the price of a meal from a hungry traveller. No one ever knew if this was true, for his secret died with him."

"Wow, is that true?"

"As it says, the story about Sullivan is true, but no one knew how he calmed the horses. He took the secrets with him to his grave. All the witnesses knew was when Sullivan led the horses out again, all fury had vanished. Some said they looked hypnotised by fear."

"How fascinating."

"Here's another story. There was a man called John Solomon Rarey from Groveport, Ohio, who tamed his first horse at the age of twelve. Word of his gift spread, and in 1858, he was summoned to Windsor Castle in England to calm a horse that belonged to Queen Victoria. The Queen and her entourage watched in astonishment as Rarey put his hands on the animal and laid it down on the ground before them. Then he lay down beside it and rested his head on its hooves. The Queen chuckled with delight and gave Rarey a hundred dollars."

"That's impressive."

"Yes. He was a modest, quiet man, but now he was famous, and the press wanted more. The call went out to find the most ferocious horse in all of England. It was duly found—a stallion named Cruiser, who was once the fastest racehorse in the land. Cruiser was a 'fiend incarnate' and wore an eight-pound iron muzzle to stop him from killing too many stable boys. His owners only kept him alive because they wanted to breed him. To make him safe enough to do this, they planned to blind him. Rarey let himself into the stable where no one else dared venture and shut the door. He emerged three hours later, leading Cruiser without his muzzle and gentle as a lamb."

"Wow, is that a true story?"

"Yes. It's on record."

"What happened to Rarey?"

"The owners were so impressed, that they gave him the horse. Rarey brought him back to Ohio where Cruiser died on 6 July 1875, outliving his new master by a full nine years."

"Do you want to be like those men? Horse charmers? Or horse whisperers? It sounds just fantastic."

"Oh, I may have a certain ability to calm the horses, but I'm not a magician like these men in the book. These cases are very rare miracles."

My eyes fell on the book again. *How would it sound in Polish, with Axel's calming voice?*

"Can you read a few sentences from the book?"

"What do you mean? You want me to read and translate it into English?"

"No. Just read the book as it is written in Polish. I want to hear the Polish language. I find it pretty, and I would like to hear it with your voice."

"But you won't understand a thing."

"It doesn't matter. I just want to hear you read it."

He stared at me curiously. "Alright. If it pleases her ladyship."

He started reading the book in his soothing voice. I pricked my ears as I listened. He put the book in front of me on the bed and turned so he was behind me as he read it. He tucked two pillows under his head for comfort. He took hold of the book with his right hand. I held his left hand with my right hand, and Axel took my hand in return, giving it a gentle squeeze. He continued to read in his calming voice, his lips close to my right ear. After reading one page, he asked, "Do you want me to go on?"

"Yes, please."

He kept on reading in his mellow voice. The unfamiliar Polish became more familiar as he narrated in his measured tone and clear articulation of each word. The sound of it was like murmuring birds, a dreamlike whispering of a gentle breeze when I lay under a tree. I saw my Shepherd Prince singing softly to a herd of sheep in a green, endless meadow under the warm spring sun. A sweet smell of wildflowers brushed my nose as I laid my head on his lap under the shadow of an old tree.

He was strumming my forehead with his fingers, easing my pain, and relieving me of my worries. His delicate fingers stroked my hair as he whispered sweet words of comfort and the stories of Endymion. The Shepherd Prince who fell in love with the immortal moon goddess, Cynthia. He told me how much he loved her and missed her. And in my dream, I was that moon goddess.

Axel walked into the kitchen, and I woke up from my daydream. He had a towel over his shoulder, with his hair still wet. He was in a white bathrobe. He smelled of fresh shower gel and men's shampoo.

"I hope I didn't make you wait too long. Shall we have breakfast?"

"Yes."

"I think it's better for you to have tea rather than coffee for your stomach. I will have tea this morning too."

"That's fine. I like tea with my breakfast. Any kind of English tea will do. Ceylon, Assam, or Earl Grey..."

"I have English Breakfast Tea. A mixture of Assam and Ceylon."

"Perfect."

He boiled the water in a kettle and took out a teapot. He opened the fridge and brought the butter and marmalade to the table. An enchanting smell of freshly baked bread hit my nose when he opened the paper bag. There was semmel, also called Kaiser roll or Wiener Kaisersemmel—a crusty round Austrian bread roll. I also found some Schwarzbrot, a wholegrain brown bread that Germans and Austrians enjoyed. They all looked good.

I asked him, "Tell me, why did I wake up in your bedroom with a Polish book in my hand?"

"Oh." He grinned. His eyes had that playful glint.

"Last night, you asked me to read the Polish book to you, even though you didn't understand a word. You fell asleep while I read it to you."

"Oh, dear. I'm so sorry."

"Don't be. Did my voice sound like a lullaby to you?"

"It sounded soothing, yes. But I liked the sound of the Polish language in your voice. I didn't ask you to read the book to fall asleep. Please believe me. But why did I have the book in my hand?"

"My lady, I believe you. I have no doubt."

"And the book?"

"You fell asleep while holding my hand, and even while sleeping, you wouldn't let it go. So, I pulled my hand out and slid the book there instead for you to grab on to."

"Oh, dear saints. I'm sorry."

"Please don't be. For once, I slept well, too. And you slept like a baby."

Dear Saints. So, we spent the night in the same bed last night? Would the models in my apartment believe nothing happened between us after sharing the same bed? Most certainly not.

Axel stared at me in amusement. As the kettle burst into noise, he got up. To my surprise, he used loose tea leaves instead of tea bags. While I watched him prepare the tea, he explained, "My grandma loves tea. She always uses loose tea leaves instead of tea bags, so I learned to have tea this way."

"The more I hear about her, the more I admire her. I like to have proper tea with good quality tea leaves myself."

"You will get to meet her someday... if you come with me to Krems."

"Oh, I would love to."

"Then her ladyship will grace us with her presence in Krems," he replied cheerfully. He cut the Kaiser roll in half. "What would you like on your bread? Butter, marmalade?"

"Both."

He grinned boyishly.

"Good choice."

Axel prepared the semmel by spreading the butter first, and the apricot marmalade on top. He poured tea into two cups and placed one in front of me. He set the prepared bread on my plate.

"It's very good. I like the apricot jam," I commented, genuinely enjoying it.

"Made by my grandma."

"I love her already."

"Everybody loves her. She is one of the most beautiful people I know. I wouldn't be who I am without her."

"She must be a special person."

"She is. She makes everyone around her happy."

"Oh, really?"

"Yes. And she makes the best *pierogi*."

"What is *pierogi*?"

"Polish dumplings."

"Like ravioli?"

"Similar, but they are made differently. My grandma makes baked pierogi for Christmas. They are usually stuffed with potatoes, cheese, cabbage, mushrooms, buckwheat, or millet, then baked in the oven."

"Oh, sounds yummy. I would love to taste it."

"You will."

Then he gave me his boyish wink. I loved it when he did that.

"Hyunah, I'm going to call my doctor this morning to see if he can see you. I know him well, and he might be able to squeeze you between two appointments."

"I'm alright. I don't need to go to a doctor."

"Listen to me. You might be alright now, but a concussion can have a lasting effect. It will be a simple check-up. Please come with me. He will just examine you."

"Alright. If you insist."

"Good. He is around the corner. A few minutes walk from here."

Oh, I need to ask him about the painting. If I am going to involve Herbert, I have to be sure the stolen painting belongs to Axel. I am almost sure, but I should be 100% sure.

"By the way, you told me one of your paintings was missing the first time we met, right?"

"Yes. Why?"

"Oh, I was just curious. Why would someone steal it unless it had something nice on it? Was it a nude of a woman?"

"No, it was not nude. It was a lady on horseback. Why do you ask?"

Bingo! Now I had got what I needed.

I've got you, Anthony, you bastard. I'm coming for you. And I will get you.

Axel was watching me curiously. I answered casually, "Just curiosity."

I changed the subject. "This doctor you are going to take me to, he is not going to jab me, isn't he? I hate needles."

"No. He won't treat you before you are diagnosed properly. Don't worry, please. The doctor will do nothing without your consent."

"Alright. I have bad memories from my childhood. They jabbed me while I was crying."

"Hyunah, no one is going to do anything without asking you first. I promise you."

"You promise? No needles?"

"No needles. You have my word."

"Alright then. By the way, do you know what time Herbert arrives downstairs?"

"Usually by eight. He should be there by now. Why?"

"I'd like to know how it went on Saturday. You know he rented the Aston Martin to the photographer, right?"

"Yes."

"It was for a wedding catalogue. And the hairstylist did horrible make-up on the models. I'm curious to know how the shoot went."

"Alright. I need to finish some work in my atelier. I will be there if you need me, okay?"

"Okay."

I ran to the guest bedroom and hurriedly put on my jeans. This was my chance to talk to Herbert without Axel around me. I went downstairs in the elevator.

Herbert was already there, opening the shop.

"*Guten Morgen, Herbert.*" (Good morning, Herbert)

"*Guten Morgen, Hyon-hah. Wie geht's?*" (Good morning, Hyon-hah. How are you?)

"Fine, and you?"

"*Sehr gut, danke.*" (Very good, thank you)

There was no time to lose. I got straight to the point. "Herbert, I need your help."

Herbert's green eyes grew wide.

"What can I do for you?" he asked curiously.

"One of the guys in my flat stole Axel's painting. I just discovered it yesterday. And I need your help to retrieve the painting."

"Oh, really? How do you know the painting belongs to Axel?"

"I talked to his roommate who saw the painting. And I asked Axel about the missing painting just now. The description matches perfectly. It's a woman on horseback."

"Oh, I saw that painting. It disappeared after a party two months ago—you know, the loud party with fashion people. Axel was very upset. I remember it clearly."

"You saw the painting? How big was it?"

Herbert traced the size of the painting in the air. It seemed big enough, so it had to pass through the window.

"Listen, I know the guy who stole it—an asshole called Anthony. He is leaving Vienna this coming Sunday, and we have to get the painting before he flies out. I'm going to find out where the painting is hidden. His roommate will help me locate it, and if it's in the room, it will have to be brought out through the window. I need you to stand by and get ready on the street, under the window, to take the painting. And I want to do this quietly. There are always people sitting in the living room right outside the bedrooms. If I came out with a big painting from Anthony's room, they would be curious. Do you think we can ask Ulf and Karl-Heinz to help us?"

"Two extra men can always be useful. I will ask them. When do you want to do this?"

"To decide that I need to talk to Mark, the roommate. And I will let you know."

"Did you tell Axel about this?"

"No. I think he shouldn't know. What do you think?"

"Better he doesn't know. He is usually gentle, but he has a temper. If he finds out who stole his painting, he would go straight to him and give *der Oarschloch* (asshole) what he deserves."

"Oh, really?"

"Yes. He is highly trained in combat sports through fencing. In three movements, the guy would be on the floor. I'm not joking. Don't tell him anything."

"But don't you need an épée to fence?"

"Fencing is a combat sport. You learn all the basic movements of offensive and defensive. And you learn how to attack. If you know all the skills, you don't need a weapon to hurt someone. Trust me. You don't want Axel to get angry at someone, especially if the guy stole his painting."

It made sense. So, I was right not to tell Axel. I wanted to do this as quietly as possible.

Anthony wouldn't even know what was coming for him.

"So, you are with me on this, Herbert? Can I count on you?"

"Yes. You can count on me. And I will talk to Ulf and Karl-Heinz. Just let me know when you need us."

"I will. Thank you."

I went back up to Axel's place only to find I had forgotten to leave the door open so that I would not have to disturb Axel. The door had locked automatically when I closed it. I had to ring the bell. A moment later, I heard his footsteps towards the door. I felt my heart beat in harmony with each of his footsteps.

The door opened. Axel was wearing an Indian pink polo and faded jeans, with his hair still wet. He looked good enough to eat. *How I wish I could kiss him. When would that happen?*

"I'm sorry. The door locked automatically when I closed the door."

"Come in." He stared at me curiously. He must have been wondering why I had to go down to talk to Herbert first thing in the morning.

I headed to the guest bedroom. It was time for me to wash myself. It was a quarter to nine. I decided to take a shower. I had to call Mark at ten, which would give me enough time to wash and get dressed. I took my favourite orange blossom shower gel and mint shampoo from my travel bag. I picked up the fresh towels Axel gave me and headed to the bathroom. The shower in Axel's bathroom was bigger and looked more comfortable. I set my shower gel and shampoo next to Axel's products. At least no one would steal my things here.

I let the water run until it reached a comfortable temperature. I slowly lifted my right shoulder to see if I could move it without pain. It still hurt. When I moved my right hand slowly, it seemed alright, but a sharp pain stung me as soon as I tried to squeeze the shower gel. My left hand was no longer swollen like yesterday, but I couldn't move it without pain. There was no way I could wash my hair and body in this condition. It was embarrassing, but I had to call for Axel's help again. I hesitated a moment, and as I was about to call out his name, there was a knock on the door.

"Are you alright? Do you need my help?" Axel said through the door. I cut the water to hear his voice.

"Yes, I need help."

"Okay. Hold on. I'm coming in."

A rustling of clothes tickled my ears. My heart started thumping.

He is removing his clothes. How much is he undressing himself? Oh, my dear saints. Am I about to see the naked body of a Renaissance statue? He saw me naked, but I only saw his naked torso. Blessed all the saints, I'm about to see my Shepherd Prince in the flesh.

My throat went dry, and my heart continued pounding—so loudly I could almost hear it.

The door opened slowly. Out of the corner of my eye, I spotted his underwear, black boxers with a thin white stripe on top. His amazing, athletic body was too good to be true. My eyes gazed at his long, slender, toned legs, and upwards. He opened the door to the shower booth.

"May I come in?"

"Yes. Come in."

I had my back towards him with my arms around my breasts, facing the wall.

He said calmly, "The floor is slippery. Let's sit down."

He gently put his arms around my shoulder, pushing me to the floor. I sat down on the floor with him behind me. He placed each of his long legs around each side of my legs, brushing my skin with his. The shower booth was big enough for us to sit down comfortably. He took the shower head and opened the water, letting it run until the temperature was warm. And he sprayed the water on my legs.

"Is the temperature okay?"

It was warm but not hot, just blissfully pleasant.

"Yes. Fine for me."

He let the water course all over my body, from my head to shoulders, on my chest, down to my stomach, and along my arms and legs.

"I see you brought your shampoo and gel."

"Yes. If I had left them in my flat, they would be gone in a few days."

"Do you want me to shampoo your hair?"

"Yes, please."

He took my shampoo, poured a small amount into his hand, and worked it through my hair. The fresh smell of mint perfumed the air in the shower stall, allowing us to inhale its vibrant scent. He gave me a blissful scalp massage with his delicate fingers. He whispered in my ear as he continued.

"Does it please her ladyship?"

"*Oui.*" (Yes.)

"*Oui?*" (Yes?)

"Oui, mon chou." (Yes, my sweet).

"*Quoi?*" (What?)

"*Mon petit chou, parce ce que tu aimes bien chuchoter à l'oreille.*" (My little sweet, because you like to whisper in my ear.)

"*Je suis ton petit chou, parce ce que j'aime bien chuchoter à l'oreille?*" (I'm your little sweet because I like to whisper in your ear?)

"*Oui, mon chou, tu aime bien chuchoter à l'oreille.*" (Yes, my sweet, you like to whisper in my ear.)

"*Tu as inventé ce jeu de mots?*" (Did you invent this pun?)

"*Oui, j'ai inventé ce jeu de mots.*" (Yes, I invented it.)

Axel wanted to know if I invented this wordplay in French, and I did. I called him "*Mon petit chou,*" *chou* means cabbage in French. But saying '*mon petit chou* ' would mean 'my dear', or 'my sweet'. But I also called him 'chou' because he was Polish, and he ate the cabbage. I said, 'You are my sweet,' because '*tu aimes bien chuchoter à l'oreille'*—you like to whisper in someone's ear.

"Did you pick up this wordplay by yourself, or did you have a French lover who taught you?"

"By myself. I invented it."

"But you did have a French lover, didn't you?"

"Do you really want to know?"

"I do. Tell me. What was his name? Jean-Jacques? Sebastian? Philippe, Laurent, François?"

Julian. The French bastard who left me for another woman only a year after I met him. I curse the day he was born. I was deeply hurt—the reason I left Paris.

A week after I broke up with Julian, I took a train to Munich. I had a friend there, a Danish girl called Olga, who was a model I had met in Paris. She told me I could stay with her for a few days and look for a job in Munich if I liked it there. So, I went to Munich and stayed there for a few months before I went to Vienna.

I said, "I dated a French guy named Julian for about a year. He left me for another woman."

"He broke your heart, didn't he?"

"Yes, but you know what he said when I asked him, 'how could you do this to me'?"

"What did he say?"

"*Oh, la la, Hyunah, ne le prend pas trop sérieux. C'est la vie.*" (Don't take it too seriously, it is life.)

"I'm sorry. He sounds French alright."

"But you know what happened to him a month later?"

"Tell me."

"*Il as été plaqué par Nathalie—*" (Nathalie ditched him)—"and she married a handsome doctor. She was only using Julian to make her future husband jealous. When she got what she wanted, she dumped him. After that, he called me in Munich, begging for forgiveness, but I cut him off, of course. He even sent me letters to Vienna. He got my address from a mutual friend in Paris, but I sent him back all his letters without even opening any of them."

"I say he got what he deserved."

"Yes."

I blurted solemnly, "*La vengeance est un plat qui se mange froid.*" (Revenge is a dish best served cold.)

Axel burst into laughter.

"So, her ladyship had her revenge."

"Damn right, I did."

As Axel washed off the shampoo from my hair, I asked him, "And you, did you have any lovers when you were in Paris?"

"Oh, I was only seventeen."

"It doesn't matter. A gorgeous guy like you, the French women wouldn't have left you alone. I'm quite sure. Now tell me."

"Do you really want to know?"

"Oh, yes. Come on."

"Unlike you, my story is unethical. Immoral."

"Oh, la la, I like unethical stories. You were a naughty boy, weren't you? Anyone who lives in Paris experiences a fling or a love affair. At least one or two. Now tell me, how many women did you have?"

"I only had one fling."

"Okay. Now we're talking. Tell me what happened."

Axel paused a moment, finished rinsing my hair, then applied a hair conditioner.

"When I was studying art à l'École de Beaux-Arts, I met a woman much older than me. She was thirty-three. She was walking her dog near my school, and she let me pat her dog. And we started talking. She had an apartment nearby. When I told her I was at art school, she said she had some original paintings by well-known artists in her place. She offered to show them to me. She said she had a Nicolas de Staël. That got my attention, and I followed her to her apartment. She was a married woman, and her husband was a rich businessman who was passionate about art. When I arrived at her apartment, indeed, there was a genuine Nicolas de Staël in her salon.

"Her husband was often travelling for business, and I guess she was bored and needed company. And we became close. Whenever her husband was away, she would invite me to her place, and I went to her. I liked her salon with all the paintings. They were a private collection you cannot see in a museum. Quite a privilege, in a way. I knew I was her toy boy, but I didn't care. I didn't mind pleasing her as long as nobody found out. After two months, I finished my semester, and it was time for me to go back to Austria, and my little affair ended there."

I paused a moment to process what I had just heard.

"So, you had a fling with a married woman?"

"Yes. I told you it was unethical."

"Was she pretty? What was her name?"

"She was beautiful. I was young and stupid. I couldn't resist a beautiful woman and her salon full of nice art. It was a long time ago."

"What was her name?"

"Oh, what does it matter, her name?"

"I told you the name of my ex. Now tell me. Sophie? Valerie? Caroline? Vanessa? Marie?"

"Her name was Geneviève."

"Have you heard from her since?"

"No. Of course not. We both knew what we were doing. The story ended when I left Paris. *Et voilà.*"

"You know Nicolas de Staël is one of my very favourite painters?"

"Yes. You told me. You also said he jumped to his death from his balcony in Antibes."

"What was in her salon?"

"Oh, it was one of his *paysages* (landscapes). I liked it a lot. The colours he used, the composition..."

I imagined drop-dead-gorgeous Axel with this beautiful French woman in the salon full of beautiful paintings. Certainly, an unethical affair, but it portrayed a pretty image in my mind. I was not shocked, but I felt sympathy for him in a strange, inexplicable way.

He was attracted to an older woman. Was there a chance he was suffering from Oedipus Complex? Oedipus, a character from

Greek mythology, unwittingly killed his father, Laius, then married his own mother, Jocasta.

"And how long ago was that?"

"If you are asking me how old I am. I'm twenty-two. It was five years ago."

So, he is two years younger than me.

He took my orange blossom shower gel and applied it to the *gant de toilette*. He started rubbing it gently on my back, neck, and arms. The sweet scent of orange blossom vibrated delicately in the shower stall. We both stopped talking and inhaled the blissful perfume for a moment. And he diligently passed the *gant de toilette* over my legs, stomach, around my breast and shoulder. His legs were almost touching my skin. The foam from the shower gel also spread to his legs, arms, and probably to his chest, although I couldn't see it. He was sitting behind me the whole time. His boxers were all wet.

"Shall I rinse you now?"

"Yes."

Using the shower head, he poured water on me everywhere. When I saw most of the foam was washed out, he half stood up and placed the shower head back in its holder. He sat back behind me again, taking the same position. Now we were both under the soothing water streaming over our bodies. He wrapped both of his arms around my shoulder and gently pulled me towards him. My back grazed his chest, his firm and smooth skin against my back.

He didn't move, keeping his body against mine under the running water. His face on my shoulder half turned towards my left ear as if he wanted to say something, but no sound came. I tried to turn my head to face him, but he held me a bit tighter so I couldn't move. He whispered, "My lady, will you allow me to stay still like this? If it pleases her ladyship? Just a little longer?"

His voice carried a pleading tone. I had no wish to refuse it. I held his left hand and squeezed it. He took it as a yes and drew me a bit closer to his chest. Now, he was holding me from behind, our naked bodies touching, his hair brushing my shoulders. He smelled divine. I inhaled deeply.

Whatever conflict he was suffering in his mind, I did as he wished. I hoped he would tell me what was going on in his mind, but this was not the right moment to ask him. I'd let him decide the right moment to open up at his own pace. I supposed all this had to do with his unhappy childhood.

We stayed in a close embrace for a little longer with the water flowing over our bodies, holding each other's hands. The sound of the water was like gentle rain pattering over the window in autumn. We were immobilised and hypnotised, with no control over our bodies. All we could hear was the sound of the constant rain. There was stillness in the air as if life itself had been suspended.

From the distance, the doorbell rang. We were startled back to our senses. Axel helped me to my feet, opened the shower door, and passed me the towel I had left over the sink. He put on his bathrobe. He exited the bathroom to check the door.

As Axel was talking in German with whoever was at the door, I wrapped myself in the towel and dried my body. The bathroom was foggy with the steam from the shower. I wiped the mirror with the end of my towel and stood staring at myself. A strange sensation swept over me, triggered by an inexplicable embrace under the strumming water. Time had stopped for that blissful moment. As if life had been suspended.

It seemed long, but at the same time, too short. It was useless to ask him or myself what it meant. What mattered was we were getting closer in an unusual way.

The Power of Inductive Reasoning

The pungent smell of bloodshed spread across the battlefield. A young North Korean soldier, just turned twenty, was lying next to his comrade's lifeless body. It was a brutal scene of devastation and the worst combat as far as he could remember.

Bullets flew everywhere, grenades exploding as far as his blurred vision could reach. Most of his comrades seemed dead. The rest of them were severely injured and putting them out of their misery appeared to be the only merciful thing to do. He looked around. To his horror, he was the only survivor in his squad.

Was this incredible luck or misfortune? If there was anything worse than death on the battlefield, it was to be captured by the enemy—the South Korean army. The soldier whispered to himself, *"Why think separately of this life and the next when one is born from the last?"*

He believed in reincarnation. If he died here today, he would be reborn in the next life in a different body. But he would still be around. Keeping this in mind brought him serenity as a man ready to die. He had no business being here in this brutal war. The only thing that dragged him here was that he was born in North Korea.

Being born to a White Russian mother and a North Korean father, he spoke fluent Russian. Right before the war, he was teaching Russian at a high school. The blood of his comrades was smeared over his handsome face. He muttered again, *"Why think separately of this life and the next when one is born from the last?"*

He jolted awake when a sharp piece of metal stung him behind his head. Someone was aiming at him with the end of a rifle.

"Get up, you red brat!"

It was undoubtedly a South Korean accent he was not used to. He slowly got up with his arms over his head. And that was it. He was now a captive.

"Are you ready to order, Miss?" A North Korean waiter, a small man with sly eyes behind his glasses, watched me with a wicked smile. The first North Korean man I ever saw in person in my lifetime. While looking at the menu, I was thinking of my father during his days as a soldier in the war.

"*You can never forget the pungent smell of bloodshed once you smell it,*" he said. And as I stared at this North Korean waiter standing in front of me, I found he looked no different from any other South Korean. The only differences were his heavy North Korean accent and his out-of-date attire.

Axel was also watching him curiously. He looked relaxed but was ready to act quickly if necessary. Before we entered, I gave him a briefing and provided him with the address of the South Korean embassy in Vienna and their twenty-four-hour emergency number in case anything happened to me. I also let him know my passport was in my handbag. Axel assured me repeatedly that nothing would happen, but I still prepared him.

But now, this waiter looked more like a comedian than a ruthless secret agent. He talked with a lot of humour. He narrated his first few years in Vienna and how things differed from his country.

And I enjoyed his North Korean expressions (quite different and never heard of) and heavy accent, a bit like my father's. My dad was eighteen when he went to the war, but he still had a North Korean accent.

I ordered *Bibimbap* for Axel, a popular Korean dish with rice, mixed vegetables and beef but asked them to remove the meat. I ordered tofu miso hot stew with seafood for myself. I also ordered *Kim-bop*: a seaweed roll with spinach, eggs, pickled radish, mushrooms, and some other vegetables inside, asking if they could remove the meat as well. The waiter hesitantly accepted our reason for opting out of meat. As far as I knew, meat was a treat for North Koreans.

I had had a busy day. I had talked to Mark in the morning. He tried to search the room while Anthony was out but couldn't find anything. He looked everywhere, from Anthony's bed, under the bed, all his closet, drawers, wardrobe, anywhere that had his belongings in the room, but nothing. So, I told him I would come in the afternoon if the bastard was out of the way, to search with him.

Axel took me to the doctor at 11:30. An Austrian, Dr Steiner received us. He was probably in his fifties, with grey hair and glasses and a pleasant smile. Axel accompanied me. They seemed to know each other well, as they exchanged casual conversations in Viennese dialect.

Dr Steiner spoke excellent English and began with questions about how the injury happened and its symptoms. I told him what had happened, and Axel added something in rapid German. The doctor nodded knowingly.

He explained, "A concussion is a mild traumatic brain injury. It can occur after an impact to your head—" (which was my case) —"that causes your head to shake quickly back and forth. It results in an altered mental state that may cause unconsciousness. Axel said you were unconscious for a while?"

"Yes. For a brief moment."

"And what happened?"

"I woke up and vomited."

"Do you still have pain in the head?"

"A little."

He inspected my eyes with a small lamp. Axel explained to me later that Dr Steiner was also a certified athletic trainer, and he fixed Axel each time he had an injury from his fencing training. Now I understood how they knew each other well. Axel must have injured himself frequently.

The doctor let me remove my T-shirt and examined my right shoulder. I had a mighty bruise. He carefully touched my shoulder in various spots. To my amazement, he asked me how I had met Axel. I explained the funny situation of how I wandered into the atelier, looking for a bathroom. I was relaxed, and I smiled at the memory.

With a swift movement, he pushed my shoulder, and it made a cracking sound. It hurt like hell, and I screamed, jumping at the shock. He smiled and explained, "You had dislocated a bone in your shoulder. I just put it back in its right place. Now, can you move your head from right to left and vice versa?"

I moved my head slowly as he indicated. Strangely, my neck turned more easily than usual. As a certified athletic trainer, he was also an osteopath. Many athletes dislocated their bones from violent falls or shocks, and he was used to fixing them.

Axel said, "Dr Steiner fixed me many times, Hyunah. Sometimes it was much worse than you."

The doctor asked me to lift my right arm slowly. I could lift it without pain, but I was still in shock.

"Tomorrow morning, you will feel much better. But avoid doing any sports for a few days, and rest."

The doctor was smart. He had asked me about how I met Axel to distract and relax me.

Was it so obvious in his eyes that I loved Axel? Was it written all over my face?

He examined my left wrist and checked various spots.

"No broken or misplaced bones here. Just a few more days of

rest will let you recover. I will give you some pain relievers and ointment to apply locally. I will also prescribe something to relieve your headache."

He checked my heartbeat, pulse, and weight.

"You have a low pulse. Lower than normal. Do you have cold sweats sometimes?"

While I pondered about it, Axel told him something in German.

"Axel said you were sweating cold on the night you fainted. Has it happened to you before?"

I couldn't remember. "No, I don't think so."

"Okay. Next time it happens again, you may need to check your body temperature. Cold sweat may lead to hypothermia."

Dr Steiner addressed Axel in German, and Axel answered back with a smile. The doctor seemed to be explaining to Axel what to do in case that happened again and prepared a thermometer nearby.

Why is he saying that to Axel? Does he think Axel is my boyfriend or something? We haven't even kissed, for heaven's sake.

"And no more schnapps for our pretty lady. That will be all for today. Do not hesitate to come back in case you need me. But I think you will be fine in a few days, young lady," Dr Steiner added cheerfully.

We went to a nearby pharmacy. We came out of the pharmacy with a bag loaded with medications, enough for a week, as prescribed. Axel had to go to the art school to see his professor, so we had a quick lunch— sandwiches and Polish sour cucumber soup, cooked on the Aga—at his place.

Axel drove me to my flat in Kaiser Straße.

"It would be better if we meet for dinner early this evening," I suggested to Axel.

"Alright. See you this evening."

"See you soon, Axel."

We bade our farewells in the usual French-style *bises*, but it was strangely awkward. In the name of Saint Valentine, I wished to know what was going on between us. My last Saint Valentine's Day came to my mind. I was in my apartment in Vienna, spending the evening alone, eating a cold meal. That day, I received a letter from Paris, from Julian. I didn't know how he managed to send his letter to my address on Valentine's Day, but he did.

Julian's father was from Rome, so he was half Italian despite being born in Paris. He spoke fluent Italian. He used to teach me Italian. He called me '*Amore mio*' and said a lot of words of love in Italian. When I got his letter that morning, I hesitated. After having spent all morning dithering about it, I finally opened the letter. I had lied to Axel about not opening the letters. My feminine curiosity got the better of me. I went to the kitchen, boiled the water, and used the steam to delicately detach the seal without damaging the paper over the seal.

I went to my bedroom to read it. He opened the letter by saying, "*Je regrette...*" how much he regretted his stupidity and the way he left me... if he could turn back the clock, he would, to fix what he had broken... but if I could find it in my heart to forgive him, he would come back to me on his knees... and he quoted an old Italian song called *In Ginocchio da te* (On My Knees to You), by Gianni Morandi. It was a song we used to listen to together after making love, lying naked on his bed.

At last, he said this letter would be sealed with a thousand kisses. He finished the letter by saying, *Ti do Mille Baci* (I give you a thousand kisses), *Amore Mio* (my love).

It was a sweet letter. I read it over and over again until I knew the Italian song by heart.

I carefully put the pages back in the envelope, folding his three-page letter just the way it was originally folded. I found paper glue and sealed it delicately. Afterwards, I pressed the letter with the iron in low heat and took the trouble to lay a cotton kitchen towel on top of the envelope as if to iron a silk blouse. All the traces of the letter having been opened had completely disappeared.

I found his previous letters, sent to me in Vienna, including a Christmas card last year, and lunar New Year's greetings at the end of January this year. I went out and bought a big envelope and slid them all inside. I trudged to the post office, passing by the lovely displays of chocolate and flower shops promoting Valentine's Day. Couples kissed in the streets. The whole town was in love except me.

At the post office, I wrote Julian's name and address in black ink (he always hated black ink). I mailed the big envelope with no return address. Even though he would know it came from me, I was sending him a message. This was all he would get from me after what he had done to me.

I left the post office with no regrets. I was liberated. All these months of hatred and anger seemed to be evaporating with each step as I shuffled my way back to my apartment. On the street, I made eye contact with a handsome man coming out of the flower shop with a beautiful bouquet of dozen roses. I smiled at him. He smiled back.

That evening, while I was in my bedroom, Anne, a tall blonde girl from Melbourne, came to ask me a favour. She was going out with her boyfriend Paul, a fitness trainer in the Zimmerman gym downstairs, to a fancy restaurant for Valentine's Day. She asked if I could help her with her make-up.

I said, "Of course, Anne. With pleasure."

I did a fabulous job and made every girl in the flat jealous. Anne looked stunning in her fancy evening dress. She proudly walked around the flat as if she was on a catwalk during a fashion show.

After most of the girls and boys went out, I sat alone in the living room for dinner. Three girls without dates that night invited me to go out for a drink, but I turned them down politely.

"*La vengeance est un plat qui se mange froid*," I repeated to myself. I found a leftover meal from the night before, a rice dish with stir-fried vegetables and eggs. I brought it out directly from the fridge and had my cold meal of vengeance with pickled radish, washing it all down with a glass of cold water. Alone.

The night I discovered Julian was cheating on me, I fumed with murderous rage—I wanted to put a knife through his heart and scoop his eyes out from his hatefully handsome face.

I cursed and insulted him in three languages—French, Italian, and English. I packed a suitcase of what I needed for the night and stormed out of his apartment. He followed me out, telling me I could spend the night at his place. He would sleep on the couch. But I just couldn't stand him anymore. I was shaking with rage. So, he offered to drive me wherever I wanted to go, but I would have none of it. I just wanted him out of my sight.

It was the end of September, and Paris was bustling with art exhibitions, expositions of all sorts, concerts, and all kinds of venues, and all the good hotels were fully booked. After having called over twenty hotels, I found a hotel near Place d'Italie.

It was a shitty two-star hotel on the street behind Avenue d'Italie. As soon as I checked into my room, I opened all the windows. It smelled of mould as if the room hadn't been cleaned for a month. I turned down the covers and the bed sheets. It looked like they had been there forever without being changed. It was a cheap, shitty hotel, and this was what I got. I cursed all the saints throughout the night.

I didn't bother to remove my clothes. I slept with my jeans and long sweatshirt on to avoid touching any surface of the bed. I found a towel from the bathroom and tucked it under my head over the pillow.

I could have called Lydia, a French friend of mine who lived in a small apartment she shared with her sister near Montparnasse. She would have gladly offered me a couch in her living room, as she had done a few times before. But she would be curious about what had happened, and I would have had to talk to her.

That night, I didn't want to talk to anyone. I wanted to be alone. I was terribly upset. Julian and I had moved in together in June at his suggestion. It was his new flat in a nice area in Paris. I hesitated for a few days about whether or not I should leave my place to move in with him. I was foolishly in love and left my apartment to live with him near Place Monge, in the 5th district, an area with all the charms of Paris. And look what had happened.

While I was lying in the shitty hotel room, staring at the shady ceiling, I made two oaths to myself: never trust a man, and never move in with a man without a backup plan.

From then on, I always kept a place of my own where I could take refuge in case the relationship went south. I did not want to be in a position where I would have to stay in a shitty hotel like this or ask someone for a favour.

As I pulled away from Axel's brief French *bises*, I inhaled his divine scent. The strands of hair that escaped from his ponytail brushed my face at the same time. His mesmerising blue eyes fixed on me curiously, as if to wonder what was going on in my mind.

I watched his car drive away for a moment then I walked up to my flat. Mark was sitting in the living room, waiting for me.

"Hello, Mark. How is it going? Where's Poncho?"

"I'm fine. Poncho is with my assistant today. Look, Kim, the painting is not in the room. I looked everywhere. I really can't think of anywhere he could have hidden it, the bloody bastard."

"Okay. Let me have a look at the room myself. Where's the bastard now?"

"He's out. We are clear for at least an hour."

We entered the room. I could see the place had been ransacked. All the drawers were open, every closet turned upside down, the wardrobe wide open, the table, the beds. Mark even took the trouble to remove the sheets from Anthony's bed. But there was no painting. I rummaged through the room. Nothing.

I asked Mark. "Did you look on top of the wardrobe?"

I pointed to the tall wardrobe standing in the corner of the room.

"No, I didn't."

"Give me a chair."

Mark grabbed a chair and placed it in front of the wardrobe. I carefully climbed up on the chair while he held it steady. I searched over the wardrobe. It was very dusty, but there was no painting. I passed my hand everywhere, but it was just a dirty wooden surface. I climbed down in disappointment, then sat on the chair for a moment to think.

"Do you have a flashlight?"

"What for?"

"I want to see behind the wardrobe."

There was a narrow gap big enough to hide a painting between the wardrobe and the wall.

"Let me see."

Mark went through his things and produced a small emergency flashlight.

"Can you switch it on?"

Mark turned on the flashlight.

"Can you shine the light behind the wardrobe so I can look?"

"Sure."

I peeked behind the wardrobe. It was dark, and I couldn't see well. Unfortunately, I didn't notice any objects. I asked Mark, "Do you want to look?"

Mark stared through the narrow gap. He inspected the space thoroughly.

"There's nothing here."

"Shit. Where did the son of a bitch hide it?" I thought aloud, collapsing on the chair.

I blurted. "Where is his suitcase?"

"What? His suitcase?"

"Yes. The bastard is leaving next Sunday. He must have a suitcase to pack his things in."

"Oh."

Mark considered a moment and said, "I remember his old suitcase that was in the room. He said it was old, and he wanted to buy a new one. He must have thrown it away since it's not in the room anymore."

"It means he's going to buy a new one?"

"Most certainly. If it's not here already, it probably means he hasn't bought it yet."

"It's possible he's out there somewhere buying one as we speak."

"Yes."

"Do you know anyone he is close to? A friend, a buddy he often hangs out with, or a girlfriend?"

"Hmm. I don't think he has a girlfriend, but I've seen him in a bar drinking with a few buddies."

"Okay. Do you know any of them? Are any of them a booker?"

"Oh, maybe. Let me think..."

"Which agency represents him, do you know? Is it Flare?"

"I think he's with Flare, yes. But the booker I saw him with didn't work for Flare."

"Do you know which one? Which agency does this other booker work for?"

"What are you getting at, Kim? Why do you want to know the booker?"

"Because it was a booker who dared him to steal the painting. He made a bet with Anthony. He said if Anthony could steal a painting from the penthouse where they were partying, he would buy him a flight to LA."

"Oh, that's it. So, Anthony stole the painting to win a bet and fly home for free?"

"Yes. Exactly."

"How do you know all that?"

I drew close to him and whispered, "Because I overheard the bastard's phone conversation yesterday afternoon. I happened to be in my room when he was calling his friend in LA. Thinking he was alone in the flat, he bragged about how he stole the painting and won the bet. He didn't know I was in my room and overheard the conversation."

"Oh, bloody hell. That's how it happened. Now I understand. So, you want to know who the booker was. His partner in crime?"

"Bingo. Now you know the whole story. So, do you know the booker he was having a drink with? What's his name?"

"Oh... I believe it was Matej. I think he's Czechoslovakian. He works for Next."

"Matej? He is a booker for Next Agency?"

"Yes. A nasty piece of work. He has a bad reputation. Always manipulating people."

"Alright, Mark. I have a feeling Matej might be our guy. If he put Anthony up to this, he may be our missing piece in the puzzle. Now, we all know things in this apartment are not safe; they steal things here. They stole my food from the fridge and my shower gel from the bathroom. Nothing in this apartment is safe. So, if Anthony valued the painting, he might have asked Matej to keep it for him. There's a good possibility the painting is with Matej now."

"You're right. Most probably Matej has the painting."

"Yes. It also makes sense Matej gets to enjoy the painting for a while before Anthony takes it back to LA."

"Are you sure Anthony is bringing the painting with him? Not giving it to Matej as a trophy?"

"Oh, I'm sure. He told his buddy in LA he's going to show the painting to him. One thing he enjoys is bragging. He will take the greatest pleasure in showing off the painting. He is definitely bringing it with him."

"Alright then. Now, what do we do?" Mark asked, rather lost.

"We're going to pay Matej a little visit."

"What?"

"Yes. We're going there now. To meet Matej."

"But what are we going to do there?"

"You're going to say you might have a client for his models.

Invent a job for one of your clients. To have an excuse to visit the agency. And we will ask some questions. You will say you brought me with you because I will be the stylist and make-up artist for the job. It's common for a photographer to visit an agency with his staff, to look for models, right?"

"Yes, it is common. They won't be suspicious in any way. They will be interested in booking their models. They will not be curious why you are there with me."

"Okay, then. Let's go."

Before we left, I made sure Mark put everything back in its place in the ransacked room. Any traces of anyone searching through his belongings would make Anthony suspicious. I couldn't help him with my clumsy hands, but I scanned over the room meticulously once he had finished, to ensure it looked like it had never been disturbed.

After, we headed to the Next Agency in the centre of Vienna by tramway. I asked Mark during the ride, "How do you keep all your cameras and equipment in the flat? You know they are not safe there, right? They are also very expensive."

"Don't I know it! Some bloody bastard stole one of my camera lenses when I first arrived. After that, I've been keeping all my equipment in a very heavy suitcase and I lock it with a key and bring the key with me at all times."

"Of course. Moreover, these people come and go. Not many people stay in the apartment for a long time. It's very difficult to find out who stole what. You should be careful."

"So should you."

"Oh, I know."

"May I ask you something, Kim?"

"Sure."

"How do you know Axel?"

"Oh, I happened to wander around in his atelier by mistake during the party at his penthouse. About a month ago. You were there, too, right?"

"Yes, I was there. But no one saw him that night except you."

"Oh, it's because he doesn't enjoy partying with the fashion crowd. He never showed himself at the party."

"And how did he find you in his atelier? Wasn't he surprised to see you there?"

"Oh, he was furious. He scolded me in German and asked me to get out. But I went in there by mistake. I was looking for a bathroom."

"Then what happened?"

"I was completely embarrassed about trespassing. I apologised, stuttering every word. I was mortified."

"And what did he say?"

"He said, *Doucement, mademoiselle*. No harm done."

"That's it?"

"Yes. Then I asked him if I could use a bathroom."

"What? You wandered into a stranger's private space and then asked to use his facility? You certainly had some nerve, Kim!"

"Oh, wait a minute. I did that after apologising for the intrusion. Wait. Now I remember. I asked if he could call me a taxi, after using the bathroom. I was badly in need of a bathroom, you know, after all the drinks during the party."

Mark chuckled, like the Englishman that he was. "So, did he show you to the bathroom?"

"Yes. He let me use his bathroom."

"Did he call you a taxi?"

"No."

"No?" Mark asked. "Why not? It must have been late then, right?"

"Yes, it was two-thirty in the morning."

"If he didn't call you a taxi, then what?"

"Hey, are you interrogating me or what? Don't you think you're too curious?"

"Oh, I'm sorry, Kim. I didn't mean to pry, but it's such an extraordinary story. Never heard anything like that. I'm sorry for being so nosy. My apologies."

"Apologies accepted. How do you find Axel? Isn't he beautiful?"

"Oh, my lord. He is the most gorgeous man I have ever seen in my life. He looks like a dream. Too beautiful to be true. When I first saw him with you on his motorcycle, I was sure he was a model you worked with. I thought it was kind of him to give you a ride."

"Well, he is not a model. Pedro is nagging me to try and convince him to be a model. He is adamant, you know."

"Well, I don't blame him. I would love to take some pictures of him. Do you think he would agree?"

"Oh, I doubt it; I heard he turned down every proposal. There's a photographer downstairs in his penthouse, you know. He's asked him several times already. He is just not up for it. He doesn't like people like us who work in the fashion business."

"Then how come he spends time with you? Aren't you one of us?"

"Oh, I sure am. I don't know. Maybe he finds something in me that's interesting. Wait, isn't this our stop?"

Mark looked out and stood up.

"Yes. We have to get out now."

We got out of the tramway. We were in the First District, where most of the model agencies were.

"So, what's the plan?"

"We'll play it as I said. We'll pretend to have a client who's looking for models. Just say you want to see some models; first of all, their portfolios. If Matej asks who the client is, just say it's for a casual wear catalogue and play along, okay?"

"Okay."

"Mark, the main purpose of this visit is to find out if Matej is behind this theft. It's important to find the painting. If Matej is responsible for this, the chances are the painting is somewhere in his apartment. But for now, let's focus on finding the booker who dared Anthony to steal the painting, alright?"

"Alright."

"What you need is order and method. Like Hercule Poirot, who is always telling that to his friend Hastings. Or you can also start by eliminating the impossible like Sherlock Holmes; '*When you have eliminated the impossible, whatever remains, however improbable, must be the truth.*' We have already eliminated one impossible fact. It was impossible to find the painting in the room. So, the truth is elsewhere. Trust me, we will get to the truth."

According to Sherlock Holmes, we all need to form a process of our own when observing situations using the power of inductive reasoning. Sherlock Holmes never used deductive reasoning to assist him in solving a crime. Instead, he used inductive reasoning. Deductive reasoning starts with a hypothesis that examines facts and then reaches a logical conclusion. For deductive reasoning to work, the hypothesis must be correct. Inductive reasoning starts with observations that produce generalisations and theories that lead to hypotheses. So, my inductive reasoning started with the observation of the thief's room.

While observing his room, I realised quickly the painting was not in the room. Then the question was, *why?* Why was the painting not hidden in the room? Because Anthony, as a thief himself, knew very well that his valuable painting was not safe in the apartment. So, what would his next move be? He would call for help from the only person in Vienna who knew about his crime. The booker who made the bet with him. So, as a hypothesis, without confirmation, I supposed it was Matej. The one and only partner in crime, the one who gave him the idea to steal the painting.

As we got off the tramway, we walked for a few minutes to the street where we found the model agency, Next. We went up to the second floor of the building. The door of the agency was open, and we stepped inside to find a few girls and boys standing around, chitchatting and complaining about their daily life in Vienna, how it was better in Hamburg, where they had more castings with bigger jobs and more money.

On the wall of the agency, I saw various composites and photos of girls and boys they represented. There were tables with bookers sitting behind them, mostly talking on the phone. Mark asked a woman at the desk for Matej, and she went to the back of the office to another room to call him. I heard a male voice coming from the direction in which the woman had gone. He was talking on the phone, so we waited another five minutes. We decided to gather some composites from the wall as if we were interested in hiring the models.

The models watched us curiously. Finally, a man emerged from the back. He was middle-aged, with brown hair, and had a beige shirt on. The look on his face somehow reminded me of a weasel. When he saw Mark, he tried to smile but still looked unpleasant. On first impression, I didn't like him already.

"Hello, Mark. What can I do for you?"

You can tell us where you hid the painting, you sly weasel.

"Hello, Matej. How's it going? I'm looking for a boy and a girl for a prospective client. Oh, this is Kim. She's a make-up artist from Paris who will work with me." Matej nodded to me with his weasel face, and I mirrored the gesture. "What type of job is it?"

"It's for a catalogue for casual wear."

"And what is the budget of your client?" He went straight to the point.

Mark played along. "Oh, if the client likes the model, we will talk about the price later. Just show me what you have, so we can have an idea."

The boys and girls had stopped talking and were all listening to our conversations.

"Sure."

Matej showed us some of his besties and let us choose freely from the wall. I went ahead and picked some composites as if I was interested. I chose one with a brown-haired boy with a pleasant smile. He was dressed in smart casual wear. I asked Matej if he could make a few colour copies from his book (a model's portfolio that shows all the good photos) directly, apart from the composites.

"Of course, he's one of our best working boys. He is rather expensive, though."

He disappeared through the corridor and opened the door to a room that had a copier. I quickly snatched another bundle of composites of a blonde girl and followed him as he entered the room and said, "Excuse me, can you do this one, too?"

I was right behind him when he entered the room, so I had a good view of the room. I peeked inside the copy machine room and spotted what I was looking for. On a corner next to the copy machine, there was a brand new, big, grey suitcase with the price tag still attached. I also managed to check the price tag, which had a *20% discount* written on it in red. It was a sale item that had just been purchased. Matej looked back at me and took the composites of a girl I handed him.

If I was lucky, that big new suitcase belonged to Anthony. He had just bought it and brought it to Matej. If that suitcase was Anthony's, it would be inside that piece of luggage that the painting would be transported. But of course, the case could also belong to anybody in the agency. Anyone could buy a new travel bag, especially these models who travelled around from city to city all the time. It was also common for models to leave their luggage at the agency before they took their train or plane, while they did their last-minute errands in the city.

I had also left my suitcase at my agency the day I arrived in Vienna, while I was visiting rooms to rent. And it was common for agencies to store those suitcases in a place like a copy machine room, like mine was, since there was enough space there, and it would not bother others. But it was unusual to have a brand-new suitcase with the price tag still on it. The models usually left their used bags. So, I supposed the grey suitcase could belong to Anthony. He needed to buy a new one. If Matej had the painting, at some point, he would put it in that suitcase. From now on, we needed to monitor that grey suitcase.

Mark stared at me curiously when I walked back to him. He must have wondered what in heaven's name I was doing when I chased Matej to the photocopier room. I just smiled. We gathered some more photos from the wall to play along with the scenario when Matej came back with colour copies. He slid them all into the big envelope and handed it to Mark.

"Thank you, Matej. We will let you know if my client wants a casting, okay? Have a good day."

"Sure. Just call me. Good luck with the job. Bye, Mark. Bye, Kim."

Bye-bye asshole. We are coming for you.

We walked down the stairs in silence. As soon as we were on the street and safely out of earshot, Mark asked, "What was all that about? Why did you follow Matej to the copy room?"

I grinned broadly. "Elementary, my dear Watson."

"What?

"Come on, Mark. We have things to do."

"What are you thinking so hard about, my lady?”

“Elementary, my dear Watson.”

Axel looked up from his *bibimbap*. My mind was still on the inductive reasoning of Sherlock Holmes.

“Elementary, my dear Watson? Are you playing Sherlock Holmes with me? I’m the slow-paced Watson?”

“Oh, no, I never considered you slow-paced. I mean, compared to brilliant Sherlock Holmes, everybody else is slow-thinking, you know?”

“But why are you thinking of Sherlock Holmes now?”

Axel was halfway through his *bibimbap*. To my amusement, he enjoyed the Korean speciality. He didn’t eat it to please me; he liked it. He tried every single side dish, including kimchi (fermented cabbage with garlic, ginger, and spicy pepper powder—a very symbolic Korean dish), telling me it was not so different from sauerkraut. Most foreigners either hated kimchi or loved it. And I was glad Axel was the latter. And of course, he loved my tofu stew and *kimbap*. Everything they served was surprisingly good and in generous quantities.

“Oh.” I quickly invented an excuse. “I was just thinking, if that Korean waiter is a ruthless spy, I have to be clever like Sherlock Holmes to outwit him."

"Hyunah, I don't think he means harm to us. I don't understand what he says, but I know he is harmless. He's just doing his job, and he seemed to enjoy talking to you."

Axel was right. The North Korean waiter was harmless indeed. There was also a small woman (they were all small, these North Koreans) who served us the dishes. She was a bit plump around her waist, with her black hair in a tight knot behind. She wore a hideously unmatched blouse and skirt. She talked slowly with a North Korean accent and kept glancing at Axel. Of course, she was not used to seeing a gorgeous man like Axel. She also stared at me curiously.

I was wearing a fancy designer dress from Paris—a long black dress with transparent lace over the neck and shoulders and a thigh-high slit. One could see my legs between the dress when I sat. Sensual, but not slutty. If Axel didn't want to kiss me, I wanted to provoke him at least. He eventually kept peeking at my dress under the table. Each time he lowered his glance towards my legs, I was secretly satisfied. I was teasing him.

I'm yours if you want me. Kiss me. Press your lovely lips to mine. And you can have me.

This evening, Axel had come to pick me up from my flat. He waited for me downstairs in the street as usual. He never even thought about venturing into my apartment. He didn't want to confront anybody. Even though he had no idea one of the guys in there had stolen his painting, he wasn't keen on socialising with them... except Mark, because he had a dog, and he was nice.

In my experience, gay people were always kind to me. My best friend in Paris was a gay hairdresser named Xavier. After I broke up with Julian, he stood by me and let me stay in his apartment until I left Paris. I had Lydia, of course, but Xavier was there for me without asking loads of questions like Lydia. He was a friend without the feminine curiosity.

Before I left for Munich, I had quite a lot of things with me I couldn't bring. I gathered all my stuff and carried it from Julian's apartment with Xavier's help. It was such a painful moment when I packed my things at Julian's apartment; Julian wasn't there, of course. Instead, Xavier was at my side, silently carrying my suitcases without a word. And I was grateful for his graceful gesture.

The day after I left Julian, he called Lydia, asking for me. Lydia told Julian she didn't know what had happened to me (as I had specifically instructed her to do) and asked him to explain what happened between him and me. Julian didn't say he cheated on me. Instead, he said we had a big fight, and I left.

Mark had that kind of kindness in him. The kindness and generosity I frequently observed among gay men. I knew he had a huge crush on Axel, but of course, Mark knew Axel was a straight man and not interested in him. But he helped me anyway, without expecting anything in return.

I spent some time making myself pretty for dinner with Axel. My hands were better. I felt less pain, with all the medications and ointments prescribed by Dr Steiner. When I was ready at around 7:30 in the evening, I went downstairs.

I came across Mark, who had come back from his assistant's place with his dog. We talked for a moment while I waited for Axel.

"So, Miss Sherlock Holmes. Tell me what to do now."

I had already told him about the discovery of the grey suitcase and my hypothesis about it. "Now we need confirmation that the new suitcase belongs to Anthony."

"How do we do that? By asking him, 'Hey, Anthony, I saw a brand-new suitcase at the Next Agency. Does it happen to be yours?'"

"Of course not. Listen to me. Anthony likes to brag about things, right?"

"Yes. So?"

"We are going to use it to our advantage."

"How?"

"Just tell him casually that you need to buy a new suitcase, and ask if he knows where you can buy one for a good price. Don't forget to ask him about a good price, because he bought his suitcase with a twenty per cent discount and I'm sure he'd like to brag about it. Ask him where you could find one."

"Then what?"

"If we're lucky, he'll brag about how he found his new suitcase, possibly a Samsonite, with a twenty per cent discount, at a store in the centre of Vienna."

"And then?"

"Thank him for the tip, and ask him, are all the colours in the sale?"

"Okay."

"Then he might say, 'Oh, not all the colours are on sale, just the blue one."

Or he could say blue and grey. Or all colours. But usually, the classic models like black or blue are not on sale. Usually, they put green or grey on sale. If he says he bought the grey one at twenty per cent off in the sale, bingo. That pretty much confirms the grey suitcase in the copy room belongs to him. Listen. Tomorrow I'm going to the centre of Vienna to find a Samsonite shop near the Next Agency. You can come with me if you want. We need to know if Anthony bought his new suitcase, and for a twenty per cent discount. And one more thing; can you go and find Anthony's composites in his room? I need his photos."

"What, now?"

"Yes. Give me Poncho. I will keep him while you're up there. I saw Anthony's pictures in the room this afternoon. He likes to brag about how handsome he looks in the pictures. He will gladly give you some. Come on, be quick."

"Wait a moment."

Mark handed me Poncho's lead and went upstairs.

I looked down at the dog. Poncho watched me as if to say, "Are you going to play with me or what?"

I talked to him in a friendly tone, "*Allez Poncho. Tu va être sage avec moi, d'accord?*" (Come on Poncho. You'll be good to me, okay?)

I patted him on the back, and he tried to jump up at me with his dirty paws on my designer dress. I stepped back. I didn't want the dog pawing at my expensive dress and staining it.

"*Non, Poncho. Arrête! Tu va abîmer ma robe. Non, arrête!*" (No, Poncho. Stop! You're going to ruin my dress. No stop!)

Immediately, a sharp whistle from behind surprised me. As soon as Poncho recognised the person behind me, he sprinted past me. I let go of the lead immediately. I turned around to find Axel, in a classy blue marine shirt and jeans, looking stunning. My heart started pounding.

When he saw me in my dainty dress, his eyes grew wide.

"You look ravishing, my lady," he said, as Poncho jumped around him excitedly, wagging his tail.

"And you look good enough to eat, my lord."

I ran to him and leapt to my feet to give him a *bise*. He put his arms around my shoulders and drew me close to his chest. His calming voice fondled my ear as he lowered his lips towards my earlobe.

"Would her ladyship prefer to eat me for dinner rather than the long-awaited North Korean meal?"

I smiled and whispered back into his ear, "Her ladyship will keep you as her dessert if it pleases his lordship."

Axel grinned from ear to ear. "At your service, my lady. I'm your humble servant."

As we were standing there in our sweet embrace, whispering into each other's ears, we didn't realise Mark was already behind us with the photos of Anthony folded discreetly in his hand. We pulled away from each other.

Axel greeted him with a smile. "Hello, Mark, how are you?"

"Hello, mate. I'm good, and you?"

Mark's face brightened with admiration. Poncho continued to jump around Axel, nagging him to play with him. He was wagging his tail excitedly.

"I think our little fellow here needs some attention," Axel said and started talking to Poncho cheerfully. He took Poncho by the lead and started running with him. The dog followed him like a shadow.

While Axel was away with Poncho, safely out of earshot, Mark handed me the composites. I slid them quickly into my handbag. The last thing I needed was Axel seeing this thief's photos.

"Can you ask Anthony about the suitcase, or shall I do it myself tomorrow when I get the chance?"

"No, Kim, I will do it. You never talk to him in the flat. It would be more natural if I asked him, as his roommate. Call me tomorrow morning. I will let you know if I can come with you tomorrow. I have a testing tomorrow, but it hasn't been confirmed yet."

"Okay. I will call you. And Mark?"

"Yes?"

He looked at me.

"I appreciate your help."

"Oh, don't mention it. I haven't done much yet."

"Are you kidding? You already helped me a lot."

"I hope Matej is our guy."

"We will know soon."

We strolled behind Axel and Poncho as they played around in the street. The road was inclined and sloped towards the Pyongyang Restaurant.

"You are all dressed up. Where is Axel taking you this evening?"

"We're going right into my enemy's territory. If we don't survive this, you have to promise me you will get that bloody bastard for us."

"What? What are you guys up to?"

"We're having dinner at the North Korean restaurant just down the street. If we don't come out alive, you will get that nasty brat for us, okay?"

"Nonsense! You guys will be alright. Nothing is going to happen to you. Axel won't let anything happen to you."

"Do you think so?"

"Oh, yes. He will protect you. He must like you a lot, from the way he's looking at you."

"Really? How do you know that?"

"Anyone can see you guys are drawn to each other. You look good together."

We reached the restaurant, and Poncho was in Axel's arms. He turned back towards Mark and me while the dog licked the side of his face. He handed Poncho back to Mark, despite the dog wriggling and trying to stay with Axel. Mark gathered up his dog and turned around as we entered the restaurant. I felt a bit sorry for Mark. He looked rather lonely. I made a mental note to pay him back for his help and kindness.

"Can you help me with the zipper, please?" I asked Axel. We had come home from a delicious dinner at the Pyongyang Restaurant. My dress had a zipper on the back. I had Dorothe's help when I got dressed in my flat, but now I only had Axel to help me.

"Sure."

I turned my back to him so he could see the zipper. Axel approached. I pulled my hair up so that it wouldn't get in the way while he unzipped my dress. He took hold of the zipper and pulled it down slowly. His gesture was so smooth as if he was used to doing it frequently.

Was he used to undressing women? If so, whom? Geneviève in Paris? That was five years ago. My feminine intuition told me otherwise. If he didn't have any girlfriends, he certainly had a lover. Or lovers.

As inductive reasoning taught me, I observed his fluent gesture of undressing a woman. That led to a pattern. The pattern would help me understand his behaviour and mindset.

"Is there anything else I can do for you, my lady?" Axel's calm voice brushed my ear from behind.

Oh, yes. There is. You started to undress me. Why don't you finish the job? You can do that by kissing me first. Kiss me. And I will kiss you back. Press your lovely lips on mine. Please. Kiss me.

Before I answered, he said, "Hold on. Wait."

He disappeared. I was in the guest bedroom. My mind started turning wildly.

What is he doing? Will he come back half-naked? Will he kiss me finally? What is he up to?

His footsteps made my heart race. I turned to face him. He had my ointment in his hand. *Oh.* I sighed. So that was it... to treat my wound. He helped me to remove my dress and let me sit on the bed. I was wearing a matching black lace bra and underwear from La Perla I bought in Paris. This brand was well known for its sensual and stylish undergarments. It cost a small fortune. I thought of the conversation I'd had with Dorothe.

As she helped me with my dress while I prepared to go out to meet Axel, she said, "Oh, my God, Kim. You look so sexy. You're doing him tonight, aren't you? I bet he won't wait five seconds to jump you."

"Well, that's the idea. But he won't bite. We haven't even kissed yet."

"What? Do you expect me to believe that?"

"Yes. It's true. He just wants us to be friends."

"Oh really? What's wrong with him? Is he gay?"

"No, I can assure you he is straight. I know a gay man when I see one."

"Then what's bothering him? Oh, no. Is he terrible in bed? He has problems... you know?"

"Oh, please stop, will you, Dorothe? Now, I have to go."

I ended the conversation there but gave her the benefit of the doubt. What if she was right? But the whole idea was hideous. The moment I got out of my dress and found myself seated there in my La Perla items, his gaze fell upon them immediately. He looked as if he had just received a gift and was about to open it. He was a man alright. I was secretly satisfied. I sat on the bed. He sat behind me.

"Do you want this off, too?"

He touched the opening of my bra from behind.

"Yes, please."

He removed it in two seconds. He knew how to undress a woman all right. He unclasped the bra swiftly as if he had done it many times. He definitely had lovers. That ruled out Dorothe's hideous idea—the idea that he could not perform in bed was complete nonsense. I wondered if he was a good lover.

Axel applied the ointment on my right shoulder, and my left wrist. He was calm and completely in control of himself. He stood up and turned slowly to the door. There was a split second of hesitation.

"When you're ready, come to the kitchen. You need to take your medications after dinner."

He went out.

What? This is it? Will we stay friends forever? Maybe I'm not good enough for him? Alright then. I will be what he wants me to be for him. As long as he will spend time with me, I will be whatever he wants me to be.

I put on a long T-shirt as a nightwear and went to the kitchen.

The Plague Column (die Wiener Pestsäule) is a Holy Trinity column located on the Graben, a street in the inner city of Vienna. It was erected after the Great Plague epidemic in 1679. This Baroque memorial was one of the most well-known and prominent sculptural pieces of art in Vienna.

The next morning, I was standing in front of the column at 11:30 am. The column was in the heart of the shopping district in Graben. I thought of all the victims who died during the plague in the dark ages. At that time, there was no proper medication, let alone vaccines against the disease. The only weapon was the immune system. Those who had strong immunity that could fight off the virus survived; the others who were less lucky perished one by one. Sort of natural selection!

The area was bustling with life—tourists, shoppers, and business professionals. I had my own business to take care of. I strode towards one of the shops that sold suitcases, travel bags, and other travel items. And this shop, barely one hundred metres from the Plague Column, was only five minutes walk from the Next Agency where Matej was. This was my fifth shop. The other four I had visited before gave me no results.

I stepped into the store and went straight to the big suitcase compartment. I found a large size Samsonite suitcase like the one I had seen in the photocopying room, but there weren't any grey ones. The navy blue and black ones were not on sale.

"May I help you?" A young woman approached me with a smile.

"Oh, yes." I smiled back. "A friend of mine is leaving Vienna, and I want to buy him a gift. I know he needs a big suitcase like this, but I wanted to know if he had bought it already. In that case, I'll need to buy him something else." I produced his photos from my handbag and showed them to her. "It's him. Have you seen him? Did he buy a suitcase here?"

She looked at the composites carefully.

"Is he a model? He's cute." She smiled.

Oh, tell me about it. A bloody selfish bastard. A thief.

"Yes, he is a model. Did he come here to buy a Samsonite suitcase like that one?" I pointed to the same model in blue.

"Can you wait a moment? I will check with my colleagues."

"No problem. Thank you."

She went away with the photos and came back a few minutes later with another shop assistant, a woman in her middle age, a typical Austrian. She said, "Yes. I think I remember him. He bought a grey suitcase. The last one that was on sale. It was last Saturday, I think."

Bingo! I wanted to jump with satisfaction. I almost wanted to give her a hug.

"Oh, so you saw him? He bought the grey one on sale?"

"Yes, it was twenty per cent off."

"What about the blue one? It's not on sale?"

"No, the classic navy blue suitcase is not on sale, sorry. Only the grey ones, but they are sold out."

"Okay. Thank you very much. I think I need to find something else for my friend. Thank you."

"Have a good day."

Yes! After visiting five shops in the morning, I found a match.

Here I come, you little piece of shit Anthony. I'm coming for you. And I will get you. You think you can get away with stealing the painting? Get ready for a little surprise, you filthy bastard. No one messes with my Shepherd Prince. I'm getting his painting back.

I went to find a phone booth and called Mark. He answered after two rings.

"Hello, Mark? It's Kim. How are you?"

"Kim, I was waiting for your call. Listen, I didn't have a chance to talk to Anthony. He came back late last night, and this morning..."

I cut him short: "There's no need, Mark. I found the shop where the bastard bought the suitcase. Just now. You don't have to ask him."

"Wow. Miss Sherlock Holmes. You are becoming a detective, aren't you? I'm impressed."

"Are you working today?"

"Yes, but not until this evening. I'm using the evening light."

"Then can you meet me at the Graben district? If you're not busy?"

"When? Now?"

"Yes. Now. If you can. I will take you to lunch if you hurry."

"Okay. Give me half an hour. Where do we meet?"

"In front of the Plague Column on Graben."

"You mean the tall white statue with gold decoration on top?"

"Yes. Come on, hurry. I'm getting hungry after visiting all these shops."

"Alright, alright. I'm coming. See you there, Kim."

"See you soon, Mark."

This morning, I had woken up alone in the guest bedroom. My watch said a bit after 7:30. As I got out of bed, I moved my right arm slowly. I felt much better than yesterday morning. All the medications and ointments Dr Steiner gave me yesterday were working. They did wonders. The door of the room was ajar, but there came a soft knock.

"Yes?"

"Are you up, my lady?"

"Yes, come in."

The door opened. Axel was standing by the door. He was in his running gear. His beautiful face was drenched with sweat, and his strands of hair escaped from a colourful hair band over his forehead. He looked like a model shooting a catalogue for sportswear.

A sight for sore eyes. He was so beautiful my eyes hurt.

Would he sweat like that after making love? Something tells me he is a formidable lover. He would give all of himself completely until his heart would burst, and he'd sweat like that. Would he give himself to me someday? Would he ever kiss me, his body rushing against mine passionately until my heart burst? When would that happen? Would it ever happen?

"Breakfast in fifteen minutes? Is that okay for you?"

Sweet Santa Maria, I will have you for breakfast, my prince.

"Sure, sounds good. Did you run?"

"Yes. Seven kilometres this morning."

He smiled. I wanted to jump on him and kiss him. He looked so lovely. He disappeared quickly into the shower. I sighed and got up to brush my teeth in the guest bathroom. I looked at myself in the mirror. Next time, I would wear something prettier, like a laced silk gown in Indian pink I bought from La Perla.

As I went to the kitchen, I could hear the sound of the shower from Axel's bathroom. I opened the window of the kitchen to let the fresh air in. I found the kettle and poured water into it for tea, then I opened the fridge and took out the butter and apricot jam I liked. And I found the cutlery in the cupboard and brought out knives and spoons for the bread and marmalade.

Being close to Stadtpark, I could hear the birds chirping from here. The fresh morning air refreshed my skin. Axel's cheerful whistling and footsteps made me start. He was in a white bathrobe like the previous morning, with a towel around his wet hair. He smelled divine. Was it the shower gel he used or his shampoo? Or his scent? Would that shower gel and shampoo smell just as good on another person? Most certainly not, I reckoned. He had a natural scent that smelled amazing.

He was holding a bag—probably with the fresh bread in it—and a small box. He put them on the kitchen table and opened the box. Oh... my eyes grew wide. There was a small strawberry tart just big enough for two. It looked delicious.

"*Oh, la la! Tarte aux fraises. J'adore ça!*" (Oh, la la! Strawberry tart. I love that!)

"Ça te plaît ?" (Do you like it?)

"*Mais oui, ou est ce que tu as trouvé ça? Ça as l'air trop bon.*" (Yes, where did you find that? It looks too good.)

"*Juste au bout de la rue.*" (Just at the end of the street.)

"*C'est trop gentil. Tu est adorable.*" (That's too nice. You are adorable.)

Axel put the kettle on and prepared tea. He cut the strawberry tart in two and placed a piece for us each on two small plates. And he asked me, "How is your shoulder this morning? Are you feeling better today?"

"Yes. I feel better. My shoulder doesn't hurt anymore. All the medications and ointment given by Dr Steiner are working."

"That's great. I thought her ladyship deserved a *friandise.*" (A treat.)

"Oh, I love strawberries. This is the first time I've had strawberries this year."

"Then you should make a wish. The first fruit of the year demands a wish."

"How did you know that? It's a French tradition."

"Uh... my aunt in Grasse told me. She knows all the French customs."

"She lived in France for many years, right? And her husband is French." Axel gave me his sweet, boyish wink. My heart melted.

"Make your wish, my lady."

"Alright then."

I closed my eyes and put my hands on the plate.

May the Shepherd Prince kiss me. On my lips.

Axel locked his eyes on me. "What was the wish?"

"Oh, I can't tell you. You should keep your wish to yourself until it becomes true."

"Is that so?"

"Yes. Absolutely."

"Well, then. I hope you will get your wish."

Yes. You can kiss me right now.

Instead, he got up to prepare tea. I sighed as we sat with our tart and cups of tea. Axel cut a small piece from my plate and moved the spoon towards my mouth. I accepted the treat from his hand. And he took one bite. It was delicious. The fresh strawberry with the custard cream and the *pâte sablée* (shortbread dough) melted in my mouth like a dream. Whoever made this tart should be blessed.

"*C'est trop bon. Vraiment délicieux.* (It's too good. Delicious.) You should tell me where this bakery is, exactly."

"Oh, this is dangerous. The owner of the shop would see you arriving from far away."

"It's difficult to find a French-style patisserie like this in Vienna. And they make it perfectly."

"The pâtissier of the bakery is French. The owner told me."

"*Parfait. J'y vais.*" (Perfect. I will go.)

"Listen, I talked to Herbert about you. About your living conditions in your flat."

"What? My living conditions? That I live among savages and thieves?"

"Yes. Exactly. Herbert has a small studio that's empty. He can rent it to you."

"Oh, really? Axel, I told you you didn't have to worry about it."

"Listen, Hyunah. Herbert has a small building he has built for his family. It's a second-storey building. The ground floor is occupied by his elder sister and her family, first floor by his younger sister. And the second floor used to be Herbert's place when he was living with his wife. Now he has built a house across from the building, on the other side of the garden, to live with his two kids."

"What about the wife?"

"He got divorced."

"Oh, dear."

"Anyway, he is willing to let you the studio on the second floor. I've seen the place. It has a bedroom, kitchen, and a bathroom. All for yourself. It's big enough for one person. You don't have to share a flat with those people anymore. What do you think?"

"Where is it?"

"Ten to fifteen minutes walk from here. In a quiet neighbourhood."

"It's kind of you, but..."

"Will you think about it?"

"Oh, of course. I sure will."

"Herbert doesn't need to rent the studio. But he's doing it as a favour for you because I asked."

"It's very kind of him. Thank you, Axel. It's so nice of you."

"Just let me know if you want to visit the studio. I will take you there."

"Alright. Let me think about it. Okay?"

"Okay. I think you will be much better there. No one ever will steal anything from you. And the area is nice."

It certainly was an interesting offer. Plus, it was within walking distance of Axel. I would have my place. I wouldn't have to be stressed about my things being stolen. I could buy anything I wanted and put them in the fridge, knowing everything would be there the next day. I thought about taking it before Herbert changed his mind.

"Is there a tramway to get to the centre?"

"Of course. There are several that run directly to the inner district. A few of them pass right by Stadtpark."

"When can I visit?"

"Whenever you want. The studio is empty. All we need to do is ask Herbert."

"Okay. Great. I will let you know."

"What are you doing today?"

"I'm going to the centre. I need to go to my agency this morning."

"I will drive you there on my way to school this morning. Can we leave around ten?"

"Sure. That's perfect. Can I use your phone?"

"Of course. In the living room."

The beautiful white towel laced with sky blue and pale pink was beaming at me through the window. I'd been watching it on display at a shop while roaming around, waiting for Mark. The price was exorbitant. Who would pay that much money for a towel?

'If there's a tall tree you cannot climb, don't even look at it.' —a proverb I used to hear.

Was that fancy towel a tree I couldn't climb? Was Axel a tree I couldn't climb?

I looked at my watch and started making my way towards the Plague Column.

Oedipus Complex

"Trześniewski"

"What?"

"Trześniewski"

"Come again?" Mark pricked his ears.

"Trześniewski," I pronounced it slowly, as I had learned from Axel, but Mark still couldn't get it.

"It's Polish. Franciszek Trześniewski was a Polish cook."

"But how do you pronounce it as if you know how to speak Polish?"

"Because I learned it from Axel. He is more Polish than Austrian."

"Oh, my word, Kim. You're a piece of work. You speak English with a French accent. And you pronounce Polish words as if you speak Polish fluently. And you look Korean. Where are you from, really?"

"Ha-ha! I'm a mysterious woman." I giggled.

Mark shook his head in dismay and gulped his beer. We sat around a small table at the Trześniewski for a gourmet lunch.

"The Austrians also call it 'unpronounceable delicacy'."

"Even the Austrians can't pronounce it? But how do you pronounce it so perfectly?"

"Because Axel read me a Polish book while I fell asleep."

"What? Did he translate it for you?"

"No, he just read it to me in Polish. It must have penetrated through to my mind somehow."

"Why would he read you a Polish book in bed?"

"Because I asked him to."

"Whatever for? Why ask him to read you a Polish book? You don't understand a word."

"I don't, but I liked the sound of the Polish language. It's so pretty."

"Alright, Kim. You guys are made for each other."

"Oh, Mark, you have no idea. He hasn't even kissed me yet."

Mark's green eyes grew wide. "Oh really? He hasn't kissed you yet? But you slept in the same bed, and nothing happened?"

"That's the thing; nothing happened."

"Is it possible that he likes boys?" Mark's eyes twinkled.

"No, Mark. Don't even think about it. He is straight. He had a lover before... a WOMAN."

"Then what's wrong with him? Something is fishy."

"I know. It's really weird, isn't it? I suspect he has an Oedipus Complex."

"English, please."

"Oedipus Complex. Ever heard of it? Oedipus is a character from Greek mythology. He unwittingly kills his father, Laius, then marries his own mother, Jocasta, unaware that she is his mother."

"Oh, I think I've heard of that."

"Yes. This theory was later proposed by Sigmund Freud, the Austrian neurologist, in his book, *The Interpretation of Dreams.*"

"You mean Axel has that complex?"

"Yes. He said he was always attracted to older women. He might take comfort in them, trying to find the image of his mother."

"What's with his mother?"

"You see, that's the thing. He never talks about his mother or his parents. He grew up with his grandparents."

"Maybe his parents passed away."

"Probably. Tell me, you saw the painting, right? How big is it?"

"Oh, big like this..." Mark gestured. It certainly would fit into Anthony's grey suitcase.

"Okay. It's almost confirmed that the grey suitcase I saw at Matej's agency belongs to Anthony. Thus, Matej is the partner in crime."

"Now, what do we do?"

"We keep an eye out for the suitcase."

"How?"

"I think we should wait until the suitcase appears in your room. Anthony will have to pack his luggage sooner or later. As long as the painting is with Matej, we can't do much about it. So, we sit tight until that happens."

"And when it appears in the room, how do we get the painting out of the suitcase?"

"That's where you come in. I want you to take him out for a drink or dinner as a way of saying goodbye. If you can organise it with some other guys in the apartment, it will be perfect. I need as few eyes as possible in the flat while I search for the suitcase. And there's one more thing: we need to find out how we can open the suitcase. Anthony would most likely lock it before he leaves the room. Does the suitcase have a key? A code? The similar suitcases I saw yesterday were locked with a code. I assume Anthony's suitcase has the same system, but you never know."

"How do we get his code?"

"We can only guess with no certainty. Starting with his birthday. Do you know his birthday?"

"No bloody idea. I told you I never liked the brat."

"Then we should search for his passport. I hope he doesn't go out with it all the time?"

"I honestly don't know."

"I need to go back to our flat to find his passport. We need to find a clue to open the damn suitcase. While you searched for the painting, did you happen to see his passport anywhere?

"Oh, let me think. I saw some of his papers in one of his drawers, but I didn't look—because I was looking for the painting, not his passport."

"Right. Okay. Let me worry about that."

We enjoyed every bite of the Polish delicacy, but my mind was with Axel throughout. His delicate hands over my body when he washed me this morning, had left his mark on my body and mind. And the conversations we had. Yes. The conversations.

After breakfast, I hurried downstairs to talk to Herbert. I first thanked him for his offer to rent me the studio. And I asked if Ulf and Karl-Heinz would join us. They were in.

"That's good news. We need all the help we can get."

"Oh, they will do anything to help retrieve the painting. Just let me know when we can assist you."

"I will. Oh, when will be a good time for you to show me the studio? I'm interested."

"How about tomorrow evening? I finish at six o'clock."

"Okay. Great. And how much would be the rent per month?"

"Oh, I'm not doing this for profit. I'm doing it as a favour because Axel is a good friend of mine."

He told me the price. It was ridiculously cheap—not even half the price I paid for my apartment. Was it a normal price or a friendly price (most likely)? What I paid for my apartment was likely to be a rip-off. The models didn't know the market price in Vienna. My mind was already made up. *I'm getting the hell out of the shit hole, away from the savages and thieves.*

"That's fine with me. Thank you."

"Axel told me about your injury. How are you this morning?"

"Oh, I feel better. Thank you for asking. See you later."

"See you later."

I got into the elevator. As the door was about to close, someone stepped inside. I looked up to find myself face to face with Mike, the photographer who rented the Aston Martin for the wedding catalogue. He recognised me and smiled. "Hello, Kim. How are you?"

"I'm good, and you?"

"Fine. I've been thinking of calling you. I have a job for you next week if you are interested. I need a make-up artist. A good one, this time."

"Oh, of course. What is it for?"

"It's for men's clothing."

"When next week?"

"I haven't got the confirmation from the client yet. But I will keep you posted."

"Sure. No problem."

I would be fully recovered from my wounds by the following week. I asked Mike, "How did the wedding catalogue job go?"

"Oh, do you have a minute? I can show you some of the shots that came out."

It was not yet half-past eight. I had time.

"Of course. I would like to see them."

I followed him. He had a table in his room with all the A4-sized photos lying scattered on it.

"You gave me the idea of shooting in black and white to avoid the horrible make-up by Vicky. They came out quite nicely. Look."

I moved toward the table and browsed through the photos. I chose one of them and pointed it out to Mike. The black and white shots of the couple, on top of the Aston Martin, looked beautiful and romantic. The background was a small country road with trees on one side.

The bride had her eyes closed, wearing a bright smile, while the groom bent towards her to kiss her on the cheek. It looked quite romantic, just as a wedding catalogue should be. The awful make-up wasn't so visible in black and white, especially from the distance of a wide-angle shot.

"I love this one."

"So do my clients. They will use it on the front page of the catalogue. Thanks to you, Kim. To be honest, I didn't intend to shoot in black and white. Now you see, it looks romantic."

"Oh, yes. It's a beautiful shot. Bravo."

"Thanks to you."

"Oh, Mike. I didn't do anything."

"But you gave me the idea. Next catalogue job is yours."

"Wonderful. I will be happy to do it."

"I will keep in touch with you for next week, okay?"

"Okay. Are you from Australia? Your accent is unique."

"How did you know? I'm from Melbourne."

"In fashion, you meet people from everywhere. I worked with a few Australian photographers and models in Paris. You are far away from home. How did you end up in Vienna?"

"Before coming here, I was in London for a year. It's a tough market. There are too many star photographers. Quite hard to find a job in London. A friend who was a make-up artist there convinced me to go to Vienna, so I followed her here."

"That's great."

"How come you speak English with a French accent? You are from Paris, right?"

"I lived there for a few years. It seems the French language somehow altered my English."

"That's interesting."

"Alright. I should get going. It was nice talking to you. See you later, Mike."

"Nice talking to you, Kim. See you later."

As soon as I got out, I ran to Axel's apartment. The door was slightly open for me this time. As I stepped in, the water was running in Axel's bathroom. I walked towards the sound and found Axel by the bathtub. He turned towards me. He stopped the water and smiled.

"Her ladyship's bath is ready."

He had the *gant de toilette* in his hand, ready to wash me.

"We have time for a quick bath this morning. Come on."

His fabulous athletic arms were on display. He complemented the sleeveless shirt with jogging shorts, revealing his long, slender legs. His hair was tied up in a ponytail. His mesmerising blue eyes beamed in the morning light. He looked like a character out of this world, unreal and unbelievable.

Can any creatures of this earth be so pleasing to the eyes of human beings?

His beautiful face, usually pale, was slightly pink from the steam. I stood for a moment in front of this striking vision, enthralled and hypnotised, unable to control my body.

"Are you alright, my lady?"

His low voice fondled my ear like a dream.

"I'm alright. My lord is so kind as to give me a bath."

"It is my duty to serve you, my lady. Please." He gestured towards the bathtub with one graceful movement of his right hand. *Oh... I had to undress myself first. How do I do that with this living Renaissance statue watching me?*

"My lord, pray, I beg of you to turn around while I get myself ready."

Axel gave me a pixyish smile. He stood up slowly with his eyes on me, took a few steps towards the door and went out.

"I will be outside."

I undressed and soaked my hand to feel the temperature of the water—blissfully warm and lovely. The bathtub was filled halfway, so when I plunged in, the upper part of my body was out of the water. I sat with my arms around my breasts before I called out for Axel.

Each step Axel took toward me made my heart pound. He knelt, placed his arms at the edge of the bathtub, and grinned.

"Can you move your right shoulder like this?"

He lifted his right arm and made a slow circle that made his shoulder turn around. I imitated his movement slowly. I could do it painlessly.

"Do you feel any pain?"

"No."

"Now try with your left arm and see if you feel the same."

I did as he said.

"Now move both of your arms slowly, at the same time."

I followed him as he demonstrated the movement with both of his arms. His biceps and triceps moved along. He seemed satisfied as he watched me move.

"I think Dr Steiner fixed you alright. You cannot move your arms like this with a dislocated bone."

He drew his right hand and showed his palm towards me.

"Now, try to push my palm with your right hand. *Doucement*. Go easy. Gently."

I pushed my hand towards his and our palms touched.

"Push it a little harder."

I did, pushing my hand a bit harder towards his. I felt no pain.

"Now, can you push my palm downwards?"

I pushed his hand towards the floor.

"Now, I will push your hand horizontally. Try to resist it."

He pushed my hand gently, then a bit harder. I could resist his hand with no pain.

"Good. Let's give it a rest now. I think you will be fine by tomorrow." He gave me that sweet, boyish wink that always melted my heart.

"How do you know all that? I mean, to check my shoulder?"

"I learned it from my fencing coach and Dr Steiner. I've dislocated my shoulders several times while training. Now show me your left wrist. Try to grab my hand. Gently."

I grabbed his wrist.

"Does it hurt when you move?"

"Not so much as before, but I feel a bit of discomfort."

"Alright."

He grabbed my left wrist and turned it slowly. "How about now? Do you feel uncomfortable?"

"Oh, just a little."

"Do you feel discomfort all the time or only when you move?"

"Only when I move."

"Alright. Now, can you open this bottle?"

Axel handed me the shower gel bottle. I held it with my left hand and opened it with my right hand.

"No. Try to open it with your left hand."

I tried. This time it hurt. My left hand was not fully recovered.

"Okay, stop. Your left-hand needs more time to heal. Don't force it. Avoid using it or lifting anything with it. Give it a rest for now."

Axel delicately let go of my left hand.

"Shall I shampoo your hair?"

"Yes."

He squeezed a bit of my mint shampoo onto his palms and applied it to my hair.

"By the way, I talked to Herbert about the studio. He can show it tomorrow evening."

"Good. I will take you there. We can walk so I can show you the road. There's a shortcut through the park."

"Oh, so we can enjoy the park at the same time."

"Yes, my lady."

Axel gave me a blissful scalp massage. *Oh... heaven.* I inhaled his divine scent. He ran the water through my hair to remove the shampoo and applied the conditioner.

I asked, "I'm not prying, but do you know why Herbert got divorced?"

"His wife cheated on him."

"Oh, no."

"Herbert practically raised his two kids by himself."

"What about his wife? She didn't take care of her kids?"

"Not really. I don't know the details."

"Oh."

Axel went on. "Nowadays, it seems marriage does more harm than good to many people."

"That I agree. It's social boundaries people have created to unite two families. Marriage is not just a union between two individuals; it's a union between two families. You don't always have the luxury to marry someone for love."

"Well, unfortunately, that is true. That's why I don't believe in marriage."

I asked Axel, "You don't believe in marriage?"

"No. I shall never get married."

"Never?"

"Never. Marriage is a contract. You cannot sign on a piece of paper to promise to love someone for good. It goes against human nature. You cannot promise love. We humans have a fickle mind. That's why a lot of marriages cannot work."

Axel's response was firm.

"You are right. Listen. Do you know three people a married woman would confide her secrets to?"

Axel's eyes twinkled. I detected an amusing glint of curiosity.

"No. Tell me."

"A married woman would confide in her secrets to her lover, her hairdresser, and...?"

"And who?"

Axel pricked his ears.

"Her private detective."

Axel laughed. He applied some shower gel to the gant de toilette and started rubbing on my shoulders and back, working his way down to the spinal cord.

"Where did you hear that?"

"Hercule Poirot."

"Oh, Agatha Christie's detective? The Belgian detective with a moustache and an egg-shaped head?"

"Oh, have you read Agatha Christie?"

"Who hasn't? My grandma read a lot of it."

"I've read almost all her books. The queen of crime stories. It's classic but always fun."

Axel's hands moved towards my neck and arms. When he reached my neck, he stopped a moment and stared at me. His beautiful blue eyes sparkled, and his forehead tensed slightly. His lovely lips curled up a little.

Does he desire me?

I took the chance and held his hand. I met his gaze. I couldn't see what was going on in his mind but his piercing eyes were observing my every move. I said shyly, "My lord, if his lordship fancies the pleasure of my company, I will be happy to please his grace."

Axel locked his eyes on me for a while without an answer. As the silence filled the void between us, I grew impatient and got embarrassed. I cursed the saints. I should have shut my bloody mouth.

Axel slowly removed the *gant de toilette* from his hand. His voice was ever so soft, almost whispering: "My lady, I'm your humble servant. I can't possibly think of it."

"Pray, forgive me, my lord. I just thought..."

He took my hand and drew it to his lips. His gaze fixated on me; he closed his eyes briefly while he kissed my hand. He changed his tone. His voice was more measured, and he articulated every word clearly. "Hyunah, I invited you to my place to take care of you. Because you were injured. You are still not well. I can't take pleasure by taking advantage of the situation."

"And I'm grateful for all you have done for me. I'm sorry for jumping to a false conclusion. I know you want me just as a friend. Nothing more..."

"Please, don't get me wrong. You are lovely. Any man would be lucky to have you. You are one of the very few people I enjoy spending time with, and I don't want to ruin it by doing things in haste. Do you understand?"

I breathed deeply. I didn't answer. His smile was gone, and he pulled his brows together in a deep frown. His lips tightened, his cheeks flushed slightly, and his eyes studied the floor.

"Look. I had a few women in my life. None of them ended up well. I mean... when they got close to me... The thing is... um..."

His beautiful face contorted. He was desperately rummaging for the right words.

"I don't do well with women... I cause them more pain than happiness... more harm than good...."

He looked me in the eyes. His blue eyes were achingly beautiful but troubled. His brow was furrowed, and his lips tightened more.

"I can't do that to you, Hyunah... I don't want to hurt you..."

"Axel, why do you think you will hurt me?"

"You don't know me... not in the least... I'm sorry... I probably have done things... behaved in a way that might have confused you... for that, I apologise. For your own sake, Hyunah, it would be better we stay as friends."

"Alright. You are in pain, just talking about it. Listen, I will be what you want me to be with you. If you wish for my friendship, you shall have it. Now, please don't give me that face. I like you better when you smile."

Axel looked up, and our eyes met. His eyes held unspeakable pain I had never seen before. He looked completely lost. He took my hand and drew it to his lips. Without closing his eyes this time, while his lovely gaze was still on me, he kissed my hand. His kiss gave me a sensation of sweet exhilaration. His face brightened up a little.

"I am grateful, my lady."

He resumed washing me. We stayed silent for a moment. He applied my orange blossom shower gel over my neck, arms, the upper part of my breast, stomach, and legs. After that, he took my left foot and patiently rubbed it with the washcloth, then he worked on my right foot. He did it with utmost care. At some point, when he rubbed my right foot, it tickled me, and I started giggling.

"Oh, did I tickle you?"

He looked up and smiled—a sweet smile. Whatever had given him pain seemed to go away. As I observed him, he slowly returned to himself and regained his self-confidence. I was relieved.

~

"Do you want a cup of coffee? I looked up. Mark was watching me curiously. We finished lunch, and my mind went back to my morning with Axel.

"Oh, sure."

"I would love a cup of tea," Mark said.

"Ha-ha, you are English alright."

"Yes. In England, coffee tastes horrible. Tea is always a better choice."

Later, Mark and I went to one of the shops I had visited earlier. I wanted to check the locking system. I found the same suitcase but in blue and asked if they had the grey one. It was sold out. I asked if the grey model had the same locking system with the code. The young man answered, "This model has the same locking system with all its models, no matter what the colours are."

Okay. So, the grey suitcase opens with a code, too.

"Oh, because a friend of mine has just bought the grey model, and he set the code the first day. Then he forgot the code. How can he open it again?"

"Your friend must come to the store with his suitcase, and we will open it for him," the shop assistant said firmly. Shit. I thanked him, and we left the shop. I looked at my watch. It was a bit after three.

"Mark, I need to go back to Axel's place to get my bag. Do you want to come with me?"

"How far is it?"

"It's by the Stadtpark."

"Oh, right, I remember. I can hang out with you a bit."

"Okay. Let's take a tram."

We walked to the tramway stop. On the way, I talked to Mark

about what had happened this morning with Axel. I wanted to have a second opinion. In my experience, gay people were always good listeners.

"You know what? This morning Axel told me he wanted to stay friends with me, nothing more."

"Oh, did he really say that?"

"He didn't say 'nothing more, but it's more or less the same. He doesn't want things to change between us."

"And what about you, Kim? Do you want him to be more than a friend to you?"

"To be honest, yes. But I think it's hopeless now. Maybe I should get out of his apartment now. I don't want to overstay my welcome."

"You guys have been together a lot lately, right?"

"Yes. We have been seeing each other every day since Friday—day and night. I think I'm not good enough for him."

"Oh, Kim, I wouldn't put it that way. But it won't be a bad idea to give the lad a bit of space."

"So, you think I should leave now?"

"Oh, I don't know. But giving him a break for a while wouldn't hurt, I think. But it's your call. You should do as you feel. Don't blame me if something goes wrong. Only you can decide. It's not for me to say, really."

"That's right. It's my call. I think I will get out of there now. He has done enough for me already. I don't want to be a burden."

"Don't exaggerate, Kim. You're not a burden to him. I think he likes you."

"Well, all the more reason to give him some space. It wouldn't hurt, as you say."

The tram halted at a stop at Stadtpark. We got off and walked along the park towards Axel's penthouse. Axel told me this morning he didn't know when he would be back from art school, but if I came back before him, Herbert would let me into the apartment since he had a spare key.

We reached the garage downstairs. Herbert and his two assistants, Ulf, and Karl-Heinz, were working. Mark's eyes widened as he noticed the collection of classic cars. Herbert came to greet us.

"*Grüß Gott.*"

"Hello, Herbert. This is Mark. Mark, this is Herbert."

I lowered my voice and told Herbert. "The thief that stole the painting is Mark's roommate. Mark will help us get the painting back."

"Oh, good. I see you're organising it well. Any progress?"

"Yes. For the moment, the painting is with the booker, who is an accomplice to the theft. But my guess is the painting will arrive inside a grey suitcase the thief bought recently. When it appears at the apartment, I will call you. This is the address."

I took a piece of paper from Herbert and wrote down my address.

"The apartment is on the second floor, and I need to find a way to bring down the painting through the window. We cannot move it outside the room through the living room; too many curious eyes in the apartment."

"Maybe we can use a rope around the painting and lower it down through the window," Herbert suggested.

"That's an idea. We can't throw it down. It might break."

"I will think of something. Leave that to me. How will you get the painting out of the suitcase? You cannot just walk into the boy's room and take it?"

"Let me worry about that. I got this. I am going to give the bastard the taste of his own medicine."

Herbert smiled. "We're going to do it together. Just let me know when we can do it."

"Oh, I will. Just sit tight and wait for my signal. Okay?"

"Okay."

"By the way, I'm here a bit early. Can you let me into Axel's apartment? I need to get my bag."

"Okay. Are you leaving?"

"Yes. I have to go."

Herbert took the key, and I followed him. I turned to Mark, who was still drooling over the vintage cars.

"Mark. I'm going upstairs to get my bag. Can you wait here? I won't be long."

"Okay."

As we went upstairs, Herbert asked me, "Why don't you wait until Axel comes back? Are you in a hurry?"

"Oh, I have things to do. I have to go figure out how to open the suitcase. We only have a few days left before Sunday. We can't have the bastard flee with the painting, can we?"

"No. We can't have that. But..."

Herbert hesitated. I saw something was bothering him.

"But what? What is it?"

"No, nothing. It's not for me to say..."

"Say what? What is not for you to say?"

"Nothing..."

Herbert was conflicted. He wore a frown. What was he not telling me? The elevator door opened. He unlocked the door, and we entered the apartment. Herbert stayed by the entrance.

"I will wait here."

"Okay. I just need a minute."

I went to the guest bedroom and gathered my belongings. I made the bed I had slept in and smoothed the covers as nicely as I could. I took a paper and a pen from the desk and left a note for Axel.

Went back to my apartment. Thank you so much for your help and all you have done for me. I will be back tomorrow around 18:00 to visit Herbert's studio. Gros bisous, Xox Hyunah'

For a split second, I wondered if Axel would be upset if I left like this, but I rubbished the idea. Mark said it wouldn't hurt to give him a break. And I might have overstayed my welcome. I got out of the room, holding my travel bag and the handbag, and Herbert kindly helped me carry my travel bag.

"I will be back tomorrow evening at around eighteen hundred hours to visit the studio. You finish at that time, right?"

"*Ja, genau.*" (Yes, exactly.)

"Alright then. See you tomorrow. Thank you, Herbert."

"See you tomorrow."

I waved at Ulf and Karl-Heinz, who stood by. They waved back. Mark oozed with excitement after having a good look at the impressive car collection.

"Did you like those cars, Mark?"

"Wow, they are amazing. I could use them for my photos."

"Someone already did. Do you know the Australian photographer upstairs who is sharing the penthouse with Axel?"

"Uh... I think I saw him at the party. I recognised his accent, a bloke from Melbourne, right?"

"Right. He had a wedding catalogue job last Saturday, and his client rented an old James Bond Aston Martin. I saw some of the shots this morning. They came out really nice."

"Oh, what a lucky tyke."

Mark helped me with my travel bag to the tramway station. Something Herbert said bothered me. He asked why I didn't wait for Axel. *Should I have?*

There was a couple in the distance on the tramway publicly displaying their affection. There was a time I would have found it vulgar and indiscreet. But not now. The man was good-looking, but the woman he was kissing was rather ordinary. She was plump and nothing special, but he seemed to be so much in love with her.

The man's dreamy eyes showed love with such intensity, I wondered what the woman did to him to make him so crazy about her. Was she amazing in bed? Or was she very kind? Did she have a great sense of humour? Or did she have a heart of gold? Or did she worship the ground he walked on? Whatever it was, the man was kissing her so tenderly, holding her in his arms and stroking her hair. It made me blush.

I wondered what I would do if Axel wanted to kiss me in public. I would let him have his way if that's what he wanted. He could kiss me in the middle of the goddamn street or in the café or on the train. I would gladly kiss him back like that couple were doing. Hell, I would let him take me, leaning against a tree in the middle of the forest if that's what he fancied.

But he didn't want me that way. I was crestfallen, disappointment carrying me away. I turned my head from them. I couldn't watch them anymore. It was torture.

"It's our stop."

Mark stood up. I sighed and followed him out of the tramway.

A Promise at Kahlenberg

There was a big fight going on at the apartment when we arrived.

Marcia, the thirty-three-year-old ex-model who ran the apartment, was having a row with her boyfriend, Klaus. Klaus was a young Austrian boy of barely twenty (I suspected he was even younger), who didn't have a regular job but lived off his older girlfriend, Marcia. He had a pretty face, medium height, pleasant body, light brown hair, and dreamy green eyes. He had the kind of look many gay guys would have a crush on and many girls would love to go out with.

The lucky girl was Marcia, who provided him with shelter, food, and more in exchange for the pleasure of his company. Everyone in the apartment knew Klaus was Marcia's toy boy, and Klaus was living off her money. It was a fair deal, but they frequently got into nasty fights. Everyone in the apartment had to suffer the noise. They would lock themselves in their room, yelling and throwing things for hours.

On my first day, I arrived at the apartment during one of these furious fights. I had to wait until the fight was over before Marcia could show me to my room. Their fights usually ended with either passionate make-up sex or Klaus storming out, only to come back a few hours later, dragging his feet, tail between his legs. And Marcia would always have him back. He was just too cute to cast off. It became a routine, and after some time, everybody stopped paying attention to their fights.

Marcia was Brazilian, as was Pedro, the booker, and they were close friends. When Pedro saw Klaus for the first time, he made Klaus a model. I suspected it was Klaus who was stealing my food. He was a nasty, spoiled brat, and Dorothe told me it was him who drew a rat on my fridge with the words, *We are all rats here, and we like your food, muhahaha*.

While everybody was distracted by the fight, I followed Mark to his room. Anthony was not in the apartment, and I was determined to search for the clues to open the suitcase. I went through Anthony's drawers: all sorts of papers, including the contract with Flare, his agency, and some other things that were of no importance to me. But no passport. He must carry it around with him. I opened another drawer to find his photos, composites, and his portfolio. Still no passport.

"There's no passport here. He carries it with him when he goes out. He must be doing shopping where they ask for your passport to get the tax refund," I said in disappointment.

"Yes. Most certainly. Now, what do we do?"

"There's not much we can do but wait till he comes back."

"Then what? Tell him, 'Hey, dude, where's your passport'?"

"We wait until he goes into the shower and search his pockets."

"What if he removes his clothes in the bathroom with the door locked?"

"I already checked that. Anthony goes to the shower in his bathrobe. He leaves his clothes in this room. He's not stupid enough to leave his passport in the bathroom where it can get wet."

"Alright. Then we can't do anything now."

"No."

Mark stood up to go.

"Wait. Where are you going?"

"To get Poncho from my assistant."

"Then leave me something that belongs to you before you leave—some camera equipment, or a lens, or something."

"Why?"

"Because if I'm searching Anthony's pockets while you are out, and the bastard comes in, I need an excuse to be here. If you leave me something that belongs to you, I will tell him you asked me to bring it to you as a favour because you're shooting outside somewhere, and you need it. It should be something that you need while shooting. Something to do with a camera, or some other equipment. Not too big or heavy, though."

"Aha. You thought of everything?"

"I am trying. I can't have that son of a bitch getting suspicious."

Oh, no. This isn't going to work.

"Oh, shit! I'm a bloody idiot. Does Anthony know you keep all your camera equipment under lock and key in your heavy suitcase?"

"Yes. He knows. Since my lens was stolen."

"Then he would think I'm stealing something from you. You have to leave me the key to the suitcase. That's the only way he would believe I am doing you a favour. You would only give the key to a person you trust. And he knows that."

"Oh, Kim. Then you have to promise me you will not lose it."

"I won't, I promise."

Mark produced a small key from his pocket and gave it to me.

"Do you have a second key?"

"Yes. But I don't want you to lose this."

"I won't lose it, okay?"

"You'd better not."

"See you later. Good luck with the testing."

"Oh, it's nothing exciting. See you later."

"Thank you for the key. I promise I won't lose it."

Mark left the room, and I entered my room. It looked messy compared to the nice guest bedroom at Axel's penthouse. I sat on my bed. I might have made a mistake leaving Axel's place the way I did. I should have at least told him in person. I got up. I needed to call Axel.

I stepped out of my room. Klaus and Marcia were still exchanging verbal blows. Objects flew around, crashing on the floor and the wall.

I got out of the apartment to go to a phone booth. I found one, but it was occupied, so I proceeded towards Mariahilfer Straße; the one by the French bakery was also occupied.

Shit. Shit. Merde. Merde. Merde. I walked towards the post office. At the post office, I finally found a free booth and went in.

I called Axel. It rang several times with no answer. I called again and let it ring at least ten times. No answer. Maybe he's not home yet. I looked at my watch. It was a bit after five o'clock. *Why don't I call Herbert? He could tell me whether Axel is there or not.* I rang Herbert's garage number. After three rings, someone answered. I recognised Herbert's voice.

"Hallo."

"Hello, Herbert. This is Hyunah."

"Yes. What can I do for you?"

"Have you seen Axel? He didn't answer his phone. I was wondering if you've seen him."

"Axel came home half an hour ago. He came home with flowers and a cake for you and was disappointed you had left."

"Oh, my God! Where is he now?"

"I don't know. He left the flowers on my desk and gave me the cake."

"He left? To go where?"

"I don't know. He took the Ducati and drove away."

"He didn't say where he was going?"

"No. He just climbed on his motorcycle and took off."

"Oh, no. I made a mistake, Herbert. I should not have left like that. Oh, shit. What am I going to do now? Where do you think I can find him?"

"He took the Ducati. He could be anywhere now."

"Oh, no. Can you tell him I am sorry when you see him?"

"I think you should say it to him yourself."

"But how? I don't know where he is now."

"I am sorry. I don't know where he went. Maybe he came to you?"

"No, he didn't come. If he left half an hour ago, he would have arrived at my place already."

"Well, I'm sorry. I don't know what to say."

"Okay, Herbert. Sorry to bother you."

"I am sorry. He seems to like you a lot. I've never seen him buy flowers for anyone."

Oh, dear Saints. Holy sweet mother Mary. I'm in big trouble. What a bloody idiot I am.

I bitterly regretted it, but now it was too late. I should not have left like that.

"Okay, Herbert. Sorry about all this. See you tomorrow."

"See you tomorrow. I hope you will find him."

"Herbert? Are you there?"

"Yes, I'm here."

"Do you mind if I come by now to put the flowers in the water?"

"I will be here until six o'clock."

"I will be there as soon as I can."

I rushed to the tramway station. While I waited, my heart pounded out of control. The tram to Stadtpark arrived, and I jumped on it. When I arrived at the garage, Herbert was standing by the entrance. He looked worried. He showed me the box of cake and the flowers. It was a bouquet of lovely blue irises. The iris flower took its name from the Greek word for a rainbow and the Greek goddess of the rainbow, Iris. Did Axel like rainbows? I took the box.

"Do you mind if I bring these upstairs? Can you open Axel's door?"

"I don't mind at all. Come on."

Herbert took the key, and we went upstairs via the elevator.

"Do you have any idea where Axel could be?"

"He could have gone anywhere on his Ducati."

"He wouldn't do anything to hurt himself, would he?"

Herbert turned towards me. He raised his eyebrows.

"Do you know him well?"

"Not really... I only met him a few days ago. Apart from the first time I ran into him, which was a month ago. All I know is that he is kind and a perfect gentleman. I also think he's very sensitive. I know he loves horses, and he is more Polish than Austrian. He grew up with his grandparents and is close to his grandmother. And he is an artist who appreciates beauty. That's all I know."

"That's a start."

"And you, how well do you know Axel?"

"Oh, well enough, I guess. I've known him for several years. He's a good friend of mine."

"Do you think he was upset?"

"He didn't say anything. But I could tell he was disappointed you were gone."

"I was an idiot. I wasn't thinking straight. Now I regret it. Do you think he will forgive me?"

"Do you like him?"

Herbert answered my question with a question.

"Oh, yes, I like him very much."

We arrived at the seventh floor, and Herbert unlocked the door. As we entered, something crunched under my feet as my shoes grazed tiny pieces of broken glass on the living room floor. The shattered pieces seemed to be parts of a tumbler.

"Watch out. Be careful with your feet," Herbert said. He went to the kitchen and brought a broom to gather the shards. I stood there, flabbergasted, not knowing what to do. Herbert finished up and went to the kitchen to discard the broken glass. I followed him with the blue irises and the box of cake in my arms. As Herbert carefully tossed the remains of the tumbler into the dustbin, I asked him, "Do you have any idea where Axel keeps a flower vase?"

"Um... Maybe somewhere here or in the living room cupboard..."

He checked every cupboard and closet in the kitchen but couldn't find one. I saw a carafe and asked him to pull it out. It was big enough to accommodate the bouquet. I ran some water in it from the sink and removed the transparent package surrounding the flowers. I put the flowers in it. They looked lovely. My heart skipped a beat. I felt a knot in my stomach. I opened the fridge to find a space for the cake box. I moved a few things up and down and made room for the box. I carefully slid the box into the fridge.

Herbert looked at his watch. It was almost six o'clock.

"*Es tut mir leid*. (I am sorry.) But I have to go. My kids are waiting for me at home."

"Oh, please, you have done enough already, Herbert. You should go now. Thank you so much. I'm sorry to bother you like this."

"I hope you will see Axel soon."

Herbert took a piece of paper from the kitchen table, scribbled something, and handed it to me.

"Here's my phone number. Call me if you need anything."

"Thank you. It's so kind of you."

I walked him to the door.

"So, you will wait for Axel here?"

"Yes. I hope he will come home soon. I don't know anywhere else he could go."

"Okay. See you tomorrow."

"See you tomorrow, Herbert."

Herbert left. I went back to the kitchen and opened the fridge. I took out the box and carefully opened it. There was a mouth-watering Forêt Noir, my favourite chocolate and cherry cakes. I closed the box and slid it back into the fridge. I went to the living room and called my apartment. After several rings, someone answered.

"Hello."

It was a male voice with an American accent. To my horror, I recognised Anthony's voice.

"Hello, this is Kim. You are Anthony, right?"

You bastard, thief, son of a bitch.

"Yeah. What do you want?"

How bloody impolite, you piece of shit. What do I want? I want you to give me back the painting.

"Did anyone call me or come to see me?"

"I don't know. I just got here."

"Can you get Dorothe for me, please?"

"Hey, I'm not your secretary. Why don't you get your butt over here if you are so curious?"

What? You bloody fucking bastard! Is that a way to talk to a lady? Fuck you, asshole. Go to hell.

My blood began to boil. "Listen, dude. It's urgent. I need to talk to Dorothe. Put her on to me right now!"

"Oh, Jesus Christ."

He called out for Dorothe. He didn't bother to say to "hang on", or "wait a minute".

After a moment, I heard Dorothe's voice. "Hello?"

"Hello, Dorothe?"

"Kim. What's up?"

"Oh, thank God. Listen, something happened, and I need to know if someone called me or came to see me."

"You mean your sweetheart? Ducati Man?"

"Yes. Did he come?"

"Uh, not that I know of. Do you want me to ask around?"

"Yes, please, can you do that?"

"Okay, hang on."

Dorothe asked the others in the living room. There seemed to be several around. I heard different voices discussing it.

"What? Who? Oh, the Ducati Man? Kim's sweetheart? Yeah,

you know the guy, the smoking hottie… with a blonde ponytail? Of course, I remember. What about him? No, he didn't come by today… You? You haven't seen him? No. I don't think so… Oh, you mean the blue-eyed guy on Ducati? No? Nobody saw him?"

Dorothe came back to the phone.

"Kim? Are you there?"

"Yes. I'm here."

"Nobody saw him today, sorry. What happened? What's going on?"

"Oh, I will tell you later, Dorothe. Thank you. See you later."

"See you later, Kim."

I hung up the phone and sighed. He didn't come to see me. So, he was not in the mood to meet me. *Was it a good idea to stay here and wait for him?*

Mark, the only person I could talk to, was out on a shoot. *What should I do now?*

I went to the atelier and stepped out to the balcony. I had a good view of the front of the building. The main entrance was down below, next to Herbert's garage. If Axel arrived on his Ducati, I could see him from here. *Maybe this is where I should wait for him, so I know he is on his way up before he arrives at the door. And I will beg him to forgive me. What if he doesn't want to see me anymore? What if he says, 'Go home. We're done.' Or, 'Leave me alone.'?*

My mind started turning wildly. I stood outside on the balcony, going through all the scenarios that could happen when he arrived. None of them was good. There was a chance this was the last time I would see him. I imagined myself back to my life before I met him… so dreadful and unbearable, I could hardly breathe. My eyes scanned the street down below, but no sign of Axel.

I felt dizzy, so I sat on the floor, leaning against the wall to my right. I was wearing jeans with a simple T-shirt, so it didn't matter where I sat. None of it mattered now.

Where in hell is Axel? Did he go far? Is he alone, or did he go to see someone? Why did he bring me flowers after having told me he wanted us to be just friends? What is really going on in his mind?

Goosebumps formed over my body. I was scared. I was scared as hell of losing Axel. *Is he the forgiving type? Does he have the heart to tolerate the mistakes of his friends? Does he have the kindness and generosity to forgive?* I had no idea. One can never know a person entirely. As a matter of fact, I really didn't know Axel. What did I know about him? I couldn't tell much to Herbert.

My eyes fell onto the park down below. I remembered the afternoon when he came to wake me up from my sleep. His mesmerising blue eyes, his pixyish smile, his untidy and dishevelled look... his hand stained with multiple pigments... his sharp nose, high cheekbones... perfectly carved face... piercing, observant eyes... Even before he told me, I knew there was something artistic about him. His unusual sense of observation... extremely developed nose... his delicate touch on the canvas... all signs of his exceptional gift and talent.

Time passed while the stream of consciousness ran in my mind. The sun was shining low now, casting a long shadow over the trees down in the park.

The roaring sound of a powerful engine pulled me back to reality. I leapt to my feet to see Axel on his Ducati down below, slowing down to a halt. He removed the helmet and shook his head. He moved the motorcycle inside the garage. With my heart in my mouth, I ran to the door.

The number of the elevator changed from "3rd floor" to "0" and back up slowly. 0...1...2...3...6. My heart thumped so loudly, that I could hardly breathe. I jumped at the '*ting*' sound as the elevator arrived on the seventh floor.

I breathed deeply, closed my eyes, and opened them again. The elevator door opened. Axel was wearing the blue polo and faded jeans from this morning. His pale face was flushed from riding, his brow furrowed, his forehead frowned, and his lips closed tightly. His beautiful eyes met mine.

His eyes grew wide as he stepped out of the elevator. The door of the penthouse had shut behind me and had locked automatically. Without saying a word, he unlocked the door. I tried to say, "Axel, I am sorry..."

I followed him inside. He looked at the floor. It had been swept clean of the broken glass. He slowly turned to face me. His voice was ever so soft, almost whispering.

"Why did you come back?"

"Because I made a mistake. I was stupid. I should not have left like that without telling you. I'm so sorry."

What he did afterwards was not what I expected. He went to his room and came back with his light denim jacket and another one of similar fabric and headed towards the door. He gestured for me to follow him without saying a word. I obliged.

He pressed the elevator button. As the elevator descended, I observed him. His face was calm. I couldn't read his mind.

"Axel, where are we going?"

When we arrived downstairs, he went straight to his Ducati without answering me. He put on his denim jacket and handed me the other jacket and helmet. We were going for a ride, and I had no idea where we were headed.

"Hop on."

His voice was decisive. He wasn't asking. He climbed onto his motorcycle, putting on his helmet. I wore the jacket and put on the helmet. I climbed behind him. Anything was better than being left alone. I couldn't let him get out of my sight.

The next thing I knew, we were on his Ducati with the wind thrashing through our bodies. Instinctively, I held him by the waist, his denim jacket touching my chest. I was afraid of the speed. The Ducati sprinted through the streets of Vienna. Axel was driving faster than usual. Something boiled inside him. *Where is he taking me? Is he driving me back to my flat to dump me there? Am I about to be jilted?*

As we passed the outskirts of Vienna, and away from the city, I was relieved. This was not the way back to my place. At least he was not dumping me. Whatever destination he had in his mind, I didn't care as long as he was with me. With Vienna behind us, we drove for another twenty minutes. The picturesque cobblestone Höhenstraße came into our view.

After a few minutes, we arrived at Wienerwald, forested highlands that formed the north-eastern foothills in Lower Austria. We were at least fifteen kilometres from the centre of Vienna. Why he had taken me all the way out here, I had no idea.

We drove up the hills, towering over a good view of the vineyard. Finally, we reached the summit. He got off his motorcycle and helped me to my feet. He was still behaving like a perfect gentleman. We reached a point offering a panoramic view of the entire city of Vienna and the vineyard down under the hills. When we stopped moving, I asked him, "Where are we?"

"Kahlenberg."

The sun was going down over the horizon. The sky turned bright pink, and vivid orange colours surrounded the setting sun, illuminating the wide field of the vineyard and the skyline of Vienna in the distance. It was beautiful.

Wilhelminenberg from a month ago came back to my mind. How scared I was on the way there and the surprise that followed afterwards. *Why did he bring me here? Is this lovely sunset part of what we are about to discover? A sort of parting gift? It was certainly poetic. A courtship started with a sunrise, to be ended with a sunset. Which is worse? To be killed or to be ditched?"*

I would rather die at his sword than be forsaken by him.

My knight. My lord. My Shepherd Prince.

Let your holy iron pierce through my heart. I would rather die than be jilted by you.

Let your beautiful face be the last thing I see on this earth. Come on. Do it. I'm not afraid of dying. But I'm afraid of being abandoned by you.

A low voice reached my ears.

"Look at me, Hyunah."

I turned to face him. The lovely light of the setting sun beamed on his face, ever so beautiful, with his fantastic blue eyes and shiny golden hair freely falling on his shoulders. He was hypnotic. I was hopelessly, incurably, madly in love with him.

All I could manage was: "Axel, I am so sorry..."

He cut me off before I said anything further. "Instead of apologising, I want some answers from you, Hyunah. If by any chance, all this is too much for you... I mean, staying at my place and having me around you all the time... waking up with me, spending time with me... if it has become somewhat difficult for you, and maybe that's why you left without saying a word to me in person... you only need to say so. Then I will take you home and leave you in peace..."

"No, Axel, no... that's not what happened!"

What he said was so absurd I wanted to scream, but my voice came out hoarsely.

"Then tell me why. Why did you leave without telling me? Look me in the eye when you answer. Why did you pack up and run from me?"

I met his eyes as he asked. He was calm; his voice was low as usual, but under his furrowed brow, his eyes glinted, revealing his frustration.

"Listen to me, Axel. You are the most beautiful, kind, and generous person I know in Vienna. I love spending time with you. I loved every minute I spent with you. And I like you. This afternoon when I left, I wasn't thinking... I wasn't thinking clearly... please, don't get me wrong... I thought it was you who needed some time off from me... that I have become somehow a burden to you... I thought I had overstayed my welcome... I thought..."

My throat went dry. I breathed deeply. Axel's piercing blue eyes locked on mine as if to see through my soul. He asked, "Is that true?"

"Yes. I couldn't be a burden to you."

I turned towards the sunset.

"*Regarde moi dans les yeux quand tu me parle. C'est vrai ce que tu dis?*" (Look me in the eye when you talk to me. Is it true what you said?)

"*Oui, c'est vrai. Je te jure.*" (Yes, it's true. I swear.)

He sighed. His furrowed brow relaxed, but his eyes moistened as if tears were about to well inside.

"What have I done to you, Hyunah? For you to feel that way?"

His beautiful forehead was furrowed again.

"Is it what I told you this morning in the bath? Is it? When I said we had better stay friends? I saw the disappointment in your eyes. Is this what it's about?"

I stared at him in dismay. He was pointing out something I hadn't considered until now. Sure, I was disappointed, but it was not really the reason I left. Part of the reason was the business with the painting.

I was too preoccupied with finding out how to open the bloody suitcase. But how could I tell him that without revealing the story of his stolen painting? I couldn't. But in my mind, unconsciously, I was crestfallen and probably trying to find a way out to spare the embarrassment. It was embarrassing to be rejected by a man. This morning, I offered myself to Axel, but he wouldn't have me. No matter what he gave me as an excuse, I didn't really understand why he would not have me. And I was deeply scarred by Julian.

"No, Axel, it's not that."

"You don't look so convinced yourself. Please tell me the truth," he pressed.

"No, it's not what you said. I swear. I thought I overstayed my welcome."

"No, you haven't. It was my idea. I invited you to come. I want to take care of you until you are recovered. And I will be true to my words. You can count on me."

"Are you sure I'm not bothering you? Wouldn't you rather be alone? I don't want to disturb you in any way."

Axel's gaze was still on me. The setting sun illuminated his drop-dead gorgeous face. The warm light showed his magnificent blue eyes, amazingly sculpted cheeks, chin, forehead, lips, and sharp nose, along with the shiny golden hair falling to his shoulders. The same face I admired so much in Wilhelminenberg... now he looked more beautiful because I was in love, though hopelessly. He didn't feel the same way about me. His face looked more relaxed now, and the frustration was fading. And his calming voice melted my heart thousand times over.

"You don't disturb me. Didn't I tell you, you were one of the few people I enjoy spending time with? I meant every word. Now, will you do one thing for me?"

His eyes had that same pleading look as when he had kissed my hand in the bath this morning.

Anything. I will do anything for you.

"Yes. Tell me."

"Promise me."

He put his right hand to his chest, towards his heart.

"Promise me you won't do it again. Promise me you won't leave without telling me first. And look me in the eye."

I met his eyes again. *I will happily look into your eyes, my Shepherd Prince. Let me do it for the rest of my life. Let me wake up in the morning to see your eyes, blue as an ocean. Blue as a lake on a sunny morning.*

"I promise."

"Say it again."

He drew his hand, showing me his palm. I touched his palm with mine.

"I promise, in the name of Saint Catherine of Bologna for the Artists. I shall never leave your presence, pack up or run off without announcing it to his lordship first. If I ever rebel against my lord again, let your holy iron pierce through my heart. My life is worthless with such treachery."

Axel gave me his word in return.

"I promise to be your humble servant, my lady. I swear my loyalty to you and you only. If I ever rebel against my lady, let this holy iron pierce through my heart. My life is worthless with such treachery."

Axel knelt, his left knee touching the ground. With one graceful movement, he raised his arms above his head, as if holding a sword towards me.

"My lady, give my sword your blessing."

"I would be honoured, my lord."

I stretched my arms as if to hold the invisible sword he offered me. With the gesture of holding the hilt with both of my hands, I swung it from his right shoulder to his left, touching his shoulders slightly with the holy iron.

He was on his knees, bowing his head in front of me like a medieval knight. The magnificent sunset beamed over him. It was like a scene from a movie. A knight in shining armour pledging his oath... a splendid sight beyond description... a sight I would never forget... a sight I would carry to my grave. I wondered if I deserved such an honour.

The warm, wistful sunset lightened his shiny golden hair, his well-balanced shoulders, his athletic arms, and his long slender legs. I pinched my leg to see if this was a dream. It hurt, to my delight. I inhaled deeply before I spoke.

"Arise, my lord, as my knight. The one and only. You grace me with your presence. You honour me with your oath. Arise, my knight."

Axel stood up gracefully, drawing my hand towards his lips. He kissed my hand. His lips touched my hand, with a quiet breath, like he did when he took me home from Hawelka.

His lips brushed my hand like a sweet breeze, a fresh zephyr fondling my forehead while sleeping under a tree. *What it would be like, how would I feel if ever he kissed my lips? Would it never happen? Never?* I sighed.

Is my simple wish, to be kissed by my Shepherd Prince, too much to ask? I made my wish this morning with the first fruit of the year. I prayed to all the saints my wish would be granted someday. And soon.

When Axel faced me, I saw him smile for the first time this evening. His brow and forehead relaxed, and his eyes twinkled with satisfaction. I was relieved. I breathed deeply. The sun went down under the horizon, and the air began to freshen. I asked Axel, "Is there a place where we can get a drink? I could use a drink. We both could, couldn't we?"

"Yes, we could. Just up there."

As Axel led me up to the panorama terrace at the highest point of the mountain, he shyly offered me his hand. I took his hand and pulled it towards me. I leapt to my feet and threw myself in his arms. He hugged me hard. My heart would likely burst out.

He whispered in my ear, "What did you just say about me?"

I whispered back, "That you are the most beautiful, kind, and generous person I know in Vienna?"

"Umm... after that."

"That I loved spending every minute with you?"

"Hmm... after..."

"That I like you?"

"Say that again. I can't hear you."

"I like you."

"*Wie bitte?*" (I beg your pardon?)

"*Ich mag dich.*" (I like you.)

"*Comment?*" (What?)

"*Je t'aime bien.*" (I like you.)

"*Ich mag dich auch.*" (I like you, too.)

Axel whispered in answer.

"*Wie bitte?*" (I'm sorry, what?) I asked him, still whispering in his ear,

"*Lubię cię,*" he murmured.

"Is it Polish? Say that again."

Axel repeated in his calming voice, slowly, articulating every syllable, "*Też cię lubię.*"

I said it after him twice, slowly and persistently, until we both grinned from ear to ear.

Axel pointed to the tall viewing tower, Stefaniewarte, built in 1887 and named after Crown Princess Stefanie of Belgium. Just below the summit, I found the Baroque St. Joseph's Church. Axel told me the black Madonna in the chapel made it a popular pilgrimage sight. From there, we arrived at the panorama terrace. It was a restaurant and a café offering not only beautiful views but also Viennese delights—and our well-deserved drinks.

Later that night, Axel drove me back to my apartment. He stopped the Ducati on the sidewalk below.

"Can you wait for a few minutes? I will grab my bag," I said.

"Why?"

He smiled. His eyes had a playful glint. I put my lips to his ear.

"Because there is a delicious *forêt noire* waiting for us at your place."

He grinned. "Alright."

I rushed back to my flat.

There was a commotion in the living room, with several people sitting around. Pedro, Mark, Sam, Paul, Anne, Dorothe, Joanna, and a few other models from outside were all yelling and whistling excitedly, drinking.

At the same time, Marcia was screaming her lungs out from her room—but a different kind of screaming this time. It was not a fight. To my amusement, Marcia and Klaus were fairly busy with each other, having passionate make-up sex. Everybody in the apartment could hear Marcia moaning and screaming with pleasure.

They cheered on, mimicking pleasure:

"Yeah, baby, give it to me!"

"Come on, baby, harder!"

"Ahhhhhhhhhh... yeah, yeah, oh, ohhhhhh, do that again..."

"Go, Klaus! Give it to her!"

"Oh, baby, I'm coming..."

I couldn't help myself but smile. I stepped into my room, found a small rucksack, and threw in what I needed for the night.

When I came out, I locked eyes with Mark and mouthed, 'See you tomorrow.'

He nodded. I waved him goodbye. Dorothe followed me out to the door.

"What's happening, Kim? You and your Ducati sweetheart okay?"

"Yes. There was a small misunderstanding, but now we are good. He's waiting downstairs. See you, Dorothe. And thank you."

"See you, Kim."

I ran downstairs. Axel was waiting patiently on the sidewalk. Marcia's screaming and the loud cheering could still be heard from the street below.

Axel asked, "What's going on up there?"

"Oh, they are having some fun."

Axel started his Ducati. The roaring sound of the powerful engine dominated the sound upstairs. We began our way back home, racing through the streets of Vienna by night.

Adventure of the Stolen Painting

Herbert's house was on the other side of Stadtpark, a pleasant ten-minute walk from Axel's penthouse through the beautiful foliage of early June.

Axel led me across the park on a lovely sunny afternoon. Herbert's studio, our destination, was in a quiet neighbourhood on a boulevard. Angela, Herbert's six-year-old daughter, opened the gate. Angela was a pretty girl, with light brown hair and green eyes like her father's. She leapt to her feet to greet Axel, and Herbert came out with his four-year-old son, Felix, in his tow, followed by a shiny black Dobermann named Pezzi, wagging her tail as she ran straight to Axel.

The studio was on the second floor of the building, to the left of the entrance. Across the small garden was Herbert's house, a single-storey house Herbert had built some years ago. The studio was nice. There was an open bedroom with a queen-size bed and a small living area with a fully furnished kitchen. A table with four chairs was placed in the kitchen for use as a dining table. There was also a bathroom and a wardrobe set on the wall.

It was a clean and spacious, fully furnished, one-bedroom apartment with a view over their garden. I quite liked it. Big windows were gulping in daylight. All this, for less than half the price of my shitty flat. Oh, and I had my fridge.

"Well, this is good enough for me. I will take it," I told Herbert, soon after I looked around the apartment.

"Alright then. It's empty, so you can move in whenever you want."

"I will let you know as soon as I know when I can move in. Thank you, Herbert."

Axel smiled in agreement. Afterwards, we went down to the garden and sat around the wooden table, where Herbert offered us refreshments.

Felix, a harmlessly mischievous boy, wanted to play with Axel. While Felix, Axel and Pezzi played in the garden, and out of earshot, Herbert asked me, "So, how did it go with Axel last night?"

"I waited for him until he came home, and he took me on a ride to Kahlenberg."

Herbert smiled. "It's a nice viewpoint for sunset over the vineyard. Axel took you there after what happened?"

"Yes."

"It's a romantic getaway for couples. He must really like you to take you there after what you did."

"Oh, no. He only wants me as a friend. Tell me, did he have any girlfriends you knew of?"

"Hmm... He is very discreet about his personal life. I've never seen him bring a woman home. You're the first, as far as I know."

"Really?"

"Yes. I know he has issues with women. He rarely talks about it. I guess he tries to stay away from women for his own reasons."

"What reasons?"

"I am not sure. You should ask him yourself. Give him some time. If you're patient, he will open up to you."

"I'm really confused. He said he wanted us to stay as friends, but he brought flowers for me. He is sending me mixed messages. Yesterday, he took me to see a lovely sunset and asked me to promise I would never leave without telling him first. What is really going on in his mind?"

"I think he doesn't know it himself. He is in conflict with himself. He is deliberately trying to suppress his feelings for you, but sometimes he cannot resist his impulse, so when he passes by a flower shop, he ends up buying flowers for you. He is an artist, after all. He doesn't act upon reasoning but tends to act upon sudden urges. How he reacts depends on his state of mind or emotions of the moment. I know it's confusing and unpredictable. But that's Axel."

"Alright. Do you think he will open up to me someday?"

"Oh, yes. I believe he will. You just have to be a bit patient with him. Allow him some time. He will come around when he is ready. He is a benign soul, blessed with kindness and generosity. You will get to know him soon enough. Trust me."

Felix ran towards Herbert. Axel came to sit with us, and the conversation ended. As I watched Felix cling to Herbert and listened to Axel and Herbert talk merrily in the Viennese dialect, I wondered if the day Axel would open up to me would ever come.

I snapped out of my sleep. My throat was dry, and my voice didn't come out. I had the same dream as I'd had a few days ago—a beautiful woman drowning while her child watched. I was drenched in sweat.

I slowly got up, still recovering from the nightmare, when the phone rang in the living room. It rang persistently and stopped. My watch said a little after 7:30, time for Axel to come back from running. I was in the guest bedroom. I got to my feet. *Why do I have this strange recurring dream?*

The phone started ringing again. *Who is calling Axel at this early hour of the morning?* It could only be one person: his grandma. Something urgent must have come up. Should I answer? Hell no. The phone was still ringing, and the door clicked open. Axel. His footsteps approached the phone. He answered and talked in Polish. It was his grandma. He stayed on the phone for a moment; his usual calm voice sounded agitated. I left the room and walked to the living room.

Axel was in running gear—shorts and sleeveless shirt, colourful hair band around his forehead, sweating profusely. He turned around and saw me. He flashed a lovely smile that melted my heart again. He said something twice, "*Będę tam jak najszybciej*," (I will be there as soon as I can) before he hung up.

"How is my lady this morning?"

"I am good. What is going on? It's your grandma, right?"

"Yes. I need to go to Krems today. Let me explain to you over breakfast. I will take a shower now, okay?"

"Okay."

Axel disappeared into the shower. I went to the kitchen. Fresh morning air brushed my face. The kitchen window was already open. The birds sang merrily. I prepared the kettle for tea and set the table for breakfast. My right arm and my wrist were recovering well.

Soon, Axel's rhythmical footsteps fondled my ears. He appeared in his white bathrobe and the towel around his wet hair. As soon as he put the kettle on to boil, he said, "My grandma found a troubled horse nearby. There was a fire in the barn in the village nearby last week, and one of the colts was quite badly burned. It wasn't a fatal wound, but the horse was traumatised. He wouldn't let anyone near him. They had to sedate the colt to treat his injury. For several days, he has been refusing to eat. He is agitated and aggressive. The owner called my grandma and asked if I could help. The vet suggested putting him down, but the owner insisted he wouldn't allow it until I had seen the horse."

"Oh, poor horse. Do you think you can help?"

"I hope so. I can't let the vet put him down when the colt doesn't have a fatal injury. There's always a way to help a horse."

"When will you leave?"

"As soon as we are ready. The owner brought the colt to our

stable this morning, and my grandma is keeping an eye on him now."

"Okay. As soon as we have breakfast, I will get ready."

"No problem. The horse is safe with my grandma for the moment."

"What about college?"

"I don't have much to do today. I will call my professor."

"I will go back to my place. I need to talk about moving out and start packing."

"I will drive you on the way. I'm sorry I have to leave like this. Will you be alright without me, Hyunah? How is your shoulder? And your wrist?"

His eyes widened, showing concern.

"Oh, please, don't worry about me. I'm healing well. You should go and help the poor horse before they put him down. Don't let them kill the colt if he has a chance to live."

"I won't. I will do all I can, trust me."

The kettle whistled, and Axel prepared the tea.

"So, you are well known as someone who helps troubled horses?"

"Well, word gets around in the small village. I've already helped some horses with various problems, but I've never dealt with a horse with burn wounds before."

He looked up to meet my eyes. "When do you think you can move out?"

"Hopefully, this Sunday."

"I will be back to help you. I will take you to Herbert's place."

"Go and help the horse first, then we will see."

As soon as we finished breakfast, I rushed to the shower. I could manage to take a shower on my own now without Axel's help. I got dressed. When I had finished packing my rucksack, I asked Axel, "Do you mind if I make a quick phone call to Mark?"

"No, not at all. Go ahead."

I called my apartment. Mark answered promptly.

"Hello, Mark. It's me. Any news?"

"Yes, Kim. The package—" (we had decided to call the grey suitcase that so that no one would understand) —"arrived this morning. It's sitting in the room. You should come over."

"I'm on my way. See you in a bit."

"See you, Kim."

I felt a surge of satisfaction spreading all over me. The very suitcase with the stolen painting was now in the room! When we were at the garage downstairs, while Axel opened the trunk and hauled in his luggage, I ran to Herbert. "Wait for my signal. We're doing it."

Herbert nodded.

"Okay. We will wait for you."

Axel and I stayed silent during the short ride to my flat. I was too preoccupied and worried about all the possible scenarios. I guessed Axel was also preoccupied with thoughts about the injured horse.

"Are you alright?" Axel asked. He pulled the car over in front of the Zimmerman gym. I heard this gym was where Arnold Schwarzenegger used to train before he became famous in Hollywood.

"Oh, I'm fine."

We bade our farewell with *bises*. Before Axel got into the car, he turned around and looked me in the eye. His mesmerising blue eyes seemed to be sunken slightly as his brow tensed.

"Take care of yourself, Hyunah."

"You too, Axel. Go and help the poor horse."

And he drove away.

When I entered the apartment, I found Mark and Poncho waiting for me in the living room. Most of the models were out.

"Hey, Mark, how are you doing?"

Instead of answering, Mark mouthed silently, pointing to his room.

"He is in the room packing his suitcase."

I whispered, "Let's go in."

"And what?"

"Just act like you have something to show me. Grab your portfolio and pretend to show me some photos. As if we are going to work together. I will lead the conversation, okay?"

"Okay."

Mark led me into the room. Poncho was behind me and entered the room with us. Anthony was busy packing his suitcase. All the drawers, closets and the wardrobe were open. The brand-new grey suitcase I saw at Matej's agency was wide open on the bed. If the painting was in there, the bastard must have put it at the bottom and hid it with his clothes spread on top.

"Hey, man," Mark said casually as we came in. Anthony looked at me as if to say, 'What are you doing here, Kim?' with his smug face. The moment I saw his pompous ass, I wanted to slap his face. My blood started to boil.

I asked Mark, trying to sound casual, "Show me, Mark. What kind of make-up do you have in mind? If you can show me a few examples in your portfolio, it will help."

Mark played along. "Okay, let's see."

Mark opened his portfolio, placing it on his bed. I sat on Mark's bed, pretending to look at the various photos on the portfolio. Mark sat on the other side, pointing at some of the shots.

"You see, something like this. I like this kind of strong make-up on the eyes, giving contrast to the pale face."

"Oh, it goes well with her dress, too. Like in the Sixties."

Out of the corner of my eye, I spotted Anthony sneaking a glance at us as he packed. He seemed to be thinking, 'Why can't you guys do it in the living room?' I couldn't care less. We continued our charade while Anthony moved about between his drawers, wardrobe, and suitcase. I pretended to look at the photos, but all my attention was on the grey suitcase lying on the bed a few metres away from me. I said to Mark, "Okay. I think I have an idea. Let's go and have some coffee."

"Sure."

We got out of the room. I led Mark to the kitchen. Poncho followed us in, and I shut the kitchen door. I whispered, "I think the painting must be at the bottom of the suitcase with a layer of clothes spread on top."

"That is most likely."

"There is no guarantee the painting is in there."

"What do you mean?"

"Matej is a sly weasel. I don't trust him. He could have changed his mind and kept the painting for himself and given Anthony something else."

"Do you think Anthony is stupid enough not to check the painting with his own eyes?"

"Well, you never know. Let's hope he verified the painting when Matej brought it to him. Otherwise, things would get complicated."

"That's much worse than getting it out of Anthony. We don't even know where Matej lives."

"That's the thing. I hope that is not the case."

Footsteps startled us, and Klaus came in. He was a young boy with a ravenous appetite. He must be hungry, spending all his energy with Marcia.

"Hi, Klaus. How are you?" I said.

He looked at me with his dreamy green eyes.

"I'm fine, and you?"

"I'm good. Is Marcia around? I need to talk to her."

"She is in the shower."

"Okay, thanks."

Klaus opened the big fridge where Marcia kept her food, and he took out a cup of strawberry yoghurt. *Aha, it's you who's been stealing my strawberry yoghurt all these months. Eat up, pretty boy. But your days of devouring my food are over. I'm getting the hell out of here.*

Poncho became agitated, running around the apartment. As Mark went out with Poncho, I stepped into my room. I went to the window and opened it. The noise of the street with cars passing by immediately bothered me. I leaned over and peeked at the window next door, the room Anthony was in. The street down below seemed too far down. We needed a rope to lower the painting down safely. It was at least a nine-metre drop from the second floor to the ground.

Marcia's voice came from the living room. I went out to speak with her.

"Hello, Marcia. How are you? Can I talk to you for a minute?" I asked as she had breakfast.

"Sure, Kim. What is it?"

"I'd like to move out. I found a nice place to stay."

"Oh, okay. When do you want to go?"

"As soon as possible."

"You paid the rent till this Sunday, right?"

"Yes."

"Then you can move out on Sunday."

"Thank you."

Klaus looked at me curiously.

"So, you are leaving us, Kim?"

Yes, sorry. You can't steal my food anymore, pretty boy.

"Are you coming to Anthony's going-away party on Saturday, Kim?" Marcia asked.

"Oh no, I have to pack my stuff, and I'm rather busy on Saturday. Is everyone going?"

"I guess most of us are going, except one or two maybe."

"Where are you guys going?"

"I think some pub in town. I will give you the address if you change your mind."

"Okay, give me the address. I will see if I can drop by later. What time are you going there?"

"I guess from around eight o'clock in the evening. I will let you know when I have the address."

"Okay, thank you."

I was glad to find out that Anthony and most of the people in the flat would be out of the way on Saturday. I took my wallet and went downstairs. As I walked down the street towards the phone booth, I saw Mark with Poncho. I ran to them.

"Hey, Mark. I just heard you guys are going out on Saturday night for Anthony's going-away party."

"Oh, yes, I forgot to tell you."

"You're going there, too, right?"

"Yes, as you suggested. Most of the people agreed to go."

"That's good news. Listen, I need you to do one thing for me. Can you sit next to Anthony and make sure he drinks? The more he drinks, the better. Make sure to pour him drinks non-stop. I want him to be drunk and careless."

"Alright, I can manage that."

"And the moment you guys are leaving the pub, please call me. I need to know when I should clear out of the room."

"Okay. I will call you when the party is over before Anthony arrives home. Hope you can open the bloody suitcase. See you later, Kim."

I strode towards the phone booth nearby and called Herbert.

"Hallo."

"Hello. Herbert. It's Hyunah. We're doing it on Saturday evening. From eight o'clock on. The people from my apartment will be out in a pub for a going-away party for Anthony. And we need a rope to lower down the painting. I think it would be nice if you could come here to have a look. What do you think?"

"I can come during my lunch break. Can I come after lunch at one-thirty?"

"Sure. It's great that you can come. You have my address, right?"

"Yes. I know Kaiser Straße."

"I will meet you in front of the Zimmerman gym at one-thirty, okay?"

"*Alles klar*. (Understood.) See you at one-thirty."

When I was back in my room, I took my own large Samsonite suitcase. I might as well start packing. I opened all the drawers, the closet, and the wardrobe.

~

"I mean, no offence, Kim. But it's hard to believe what you're saying."

Mark shook his head in disbelief. We were having a quick lunch at my favourite French deli in Mariahilfer Straße, where they had a few tables outside the bakery on the sidewalk. We arrived early to secure a table. Mark had a big baguette sandwich, and I chose Quiche Lorraine with salad. I told Mark about what happened at Kahlenberg, how Axel pledged an oath, his left knee touching the ground in an untimely and medieval fashion.

"But it's true, Mark. Why would I lie to you?"

"It's not like he asked you to marry him. Who kneels to a woman these days unless to ask for her hand in marriage?"

"Axel doesn't even believe in marriage. He would never ask me to marry him. He hasn't even kissed me."

"Then what was the oath for?"

"He promised to be my humble servant and swore his loyalty to me."

Mark chuckled like an Englishman.

"I'm sorry, but it sounds too fantastical. Are you sure he didn't travel through a time machine from the Middle Ages? It's as if he was swearing his loyalty to his royal highness or his queen."

"Are you saying he is crazy?"

"No. I'm saying it's just unbelievable."

"You think he's rather unreal, right?

"No, Kim. I didn't say that. Maybe he had very special and old-fashioned education. I don't know. You said he grew up with his grandparents?"

"Yes. He's very close to his grandma. And he is a perfect gentleman."

"Well, all I can say is he's a very special man in every way. And you're one hell of a lucky girl, you know that?"

"Yes, I know. I pinch myself every day."

Mark roared with laughter again.

"Promise me you will tell me what happens next. Maybe he will go to war for you in your next adventure."

"Oh, Mark, please. Stop that. I won't tell you anything if you keep laughing."

"Alright, alright, your royal highness. I swear I won't laugh again."

Mark was still grinning broadly when we left the deli. It was almost time to meet Herbert. We walked back to Kaiser Straße, where Herbert was already waiting in front of the Zimmerman gym.

"Hello Herbert, I hope I'm not late?"

"No. I got here in advance. So, which window is it?"

I showed him the window, pointing upwards with my fingers. Herbert took a careful look at Anthony's window, shading his eyes with his hand and squinting against the sun. He asked, "Is there someone in the room now?"

I turned around to see Mark.

"I'll go upstairs and let you know." Mark ran upstairs.

"Do you want to see the room from inside the apartment, Herbert?"

"I just want to check how the window is opened from inside the room."

"Okay."

Mark appeared at the window and waved.

"There's no one. Come on up."

We ran upstairs and entered the flat. We stepped into the room. Herbert went straight to the window and opened it wide. He checked inside and outside cautiously and looked down towards the street.

"Okay. I've got what I need."

As soon as Herbert said that, I looked at the grey suitcase lying on the bed. It was closed. I tried to open it, but it was locked.

"The painting is inside this suitcase if we're lucky," I told Herbert.

If I could just open the damn suitcase, we could have walked out of here with the painting through the living room. There was no one in the apartment now. But of course, anyone could walk in at any moment and see us with the large painting in our hands.

Herbert took the suitcase and shook it. There seemed to be something hard inside. I touched the bottom part on both sides of the suitcase and tried to feel it, pushing my fingers into the fabric of the suitcase. I couldn't tell if I detected anything.

"Let's get out of here before the bastard comes back," I said. Herbert placed the suitcase back where it had been, and we all rushed out of the flat. The whole operation took less than two minutes, and nobody saw us. Once we were downstairs, I sighed with relief.

"Oh, Herbert. I can move in this Sunday."

"Can you move in on Saturday? So I can take you with me after we retrieve the painting? I don't think it's a good idea to stay one more night here, next to the thief. If he finds out the painting is gone and you have something to do with it, he won't be too kind to you."

Herbert's words made sense.

"Okay. I think you're right. I will get ready by Saturday to go with you."

"I will think about a method of safely bringing down the painting through the window."

"Great. Thanks for coming by. See you."

"See you."

As Herbert left, Mark asked, "Kim. What does he mean, you can move in?"

"Oh, Mark, I'm sorry. I forgot to tell you I'm moving out. Herbert is letting me stay in a nice one-bedroom apartment next to his house, for less than half the price I'm paying for my room here."

"Oh, really? Where?"

"A few minutes walk from Stadtpark."

"Wow, lucky you. How did you know Herbert had an apartment to rent?"

"It was Axel. He asked Herbert."

"That's nice of him. So, you're leaving?"

"Yes. I'm getting the hell out of here. I'm really glad I will have my own place."

"Good for you. I have to go to prepare for the photo shoot now. See you later."

"See you later."

I went back to my room and spent the rest of the day packing. As well as the big suitcase, I had a small hand carrier with wheels. I decided to put the things I'd need until Saturday in it and the rest in the big suitcase. The noise of the door to the next room opening made me startle. Mark was out, so it could only be Anthony. I jumped to my feet. I got out of my room and stood in the living room, pricking my ears towards Anthony's room.

I entered my room again and found some paper and a pen, then I sat in the living room where I could keep an eye on Anthony's room. I waited patiently until his door opened. I was looking out for an opportunity to get into the room. I already had the key to Mark's safety suitcase to justify my entry to the room.

While waiting, I scribbled something on the piece of paper—something I had had on my mind for some time. I wondered what Hercule Poirot would have done in my shoes. My hero detective, extremely clever and meticulous. What would he have done? I recalled what he said to his friend Hastings.

'Order and method, my dear friend. And do not underestimate the power of observation. When you have a suspect in mind, never let him out of your sight. And do not hesitate to go outside of his room and peek through a keyhole. Yes. You think it's ungodly, but when it comes to hunting and catching a murderer, all possible methods are allowed. So, Hastings, never hesitate to watch through a keyhole. And, my friend, I do not approve of murder.'

Well, this was not an old-fashioned English house with a keyhole big enough to peek through, like in the days of Agatha Christie. But at least I could stake out his room and observe. And I do not approve of theft. It is the most wretched, barbarous, loathsome, eerie, selfish act I know. It's a violation. People with no morals and code of conduct steal from others.

The door was flung open. Anthony came out. He was wearing a T-shirt and shorts and had a towel over his shoulder. He was sweating like a filthy pig. He shot me a curious glance, but I ignored him and continued to write.

As soon as he had headed to the bathroom, I sprang up. I quickly stepped into his room and closed the door behind me. Once inside, I went straight to his clothes on the chair. There was a bum bag next to his jeans. I opened it and found his American passport inside. I found the page with the photo and his birth date. I rapidly wrote down his date of birth, July 28, 1969. I also wrote down his passport number. Any number that could open the damn suitcase. I put the passport back into the bum bag and replaced the bag carefully.

I dived under Mark's bed and reached out for his safety suitcase. It was pushed deep towards the wall, so I had to practically lie down flat to grab it. I struggled for a while until I managed to pull it out. I searched for the keyhole frantically and inserted the small key that Mark had given me. The key didn't fit well, so I wondered if Mark had given me the wrong key, but, after a moment of struggle, it finally opened. In between all sorts of equipment, I took two lenses. I left the safety case open and dashed to Anthony's suitcase that was lying on his bed. To my dismay, it was wide open.

I reached the bottom of the suitcase and searched for the painting. I wanted to see if I could touch anything hard, resembling the frame of a painting. My hands were shaking madly as I tried to feel between his clothes and various belongings.

I tried one side, but couldn't detect anything. I moved to the other side and frantically fumbled my hands around. My right hand felt something hard between the clothes. Although wrapped in some papers and clothing, it was the hard part of the edge of a frame. The painting was there alright. Bingo!

Approaching footsteps outside made me spring up. I

hurriedly smoothed the surface of the suitcase I had messed up. I sprinted towards Mark's safety suitcase, and as I was grabbing the two camera lenses, Anthony opened the door. He entered the room with a towel wrapped around his waist. As soon as he saw me, his eyes grew wide.

"What the fuck? What the hell are you doing in my room?"

I looked up from Mark's suitcase and held out the camera lenses.

"It's not your room alone, Anthony. It's also Mark's room, and he asked me a favour. He is out working, and he forgot these lenses and asked me if I could bring them to him."

I showed him the key to Mark's safety suitcase.

"See? He gave me the key."

He glared at me suspiciously, but I had all I needed to justify my presence in the room. He opened his mouth as if to say something, but nothing came out.

"Now, let me lock this safety suitcase, and I will be out of your hair."

I quickly locked the suitcase after I took the lenses, as the bastard was watching my every move. I pushed the suitcase further under the bed, then got up and walked past Anthony, who was still staring at me in doubt.

As soon as I got out of the room, I went back to my room and closed the door behind me. I collapsed on my bed, breathing hard. My hands were still shaking. I reached for the pocket in my jeans and took out the piece of paper with Anthony's passport number and birth date. Now I had some clues that might lead to my being able to open his suitcase.

I copied the numbers onto another piece of paper, folded it carefully, and slid it into my handbag. I looked down at the numbers. I had memorised the son of a bitch's birthday. It was quite an irony when I cursed the day the bastard was born!

~

After a long, fitful night, between weird dreams and sporadic interruptions, I woke up on Saturday morning. The window was ajar, and the noise of the cars and the busy street woke me up.

It was almost eight o'clock, and Dorothe was already gone. I got up slowly and looked around the room. My big suitcase was neatly packed, so full that I had to sit on it to close the zipper yesterday. I had finished packing most of my belongings yesterday, emptying all the drawers, the closet, and the wardrobe. There was only my hand carrier still open to be filled with the last of my belongings. A pair of fresh jeans, a clean T-shirt, socks, and underwear were neatly folded on a chair, waiting for me.

I needed coffee to fully wake up. When I stepped into the kitchen, Mark was preparing his breakfast—scrambled eggs, bacon and baked beans. And English breakfast tea, of course. The smell of eggs and bacon woke my senses. Poncho smelled it, too. He was at Mark's feet with his head held high in hopes of some treats.

"Good morning, Kim," Mark said cheerfully. And he added in a low voice: "It's a big day. I hope you are in good shape."

"Good morning, Mark. Yes, never been better. How are you feeling?"

"As good as I can be. Do you want some eggs?"

"Oh, no, thank you. I just need coffee."

I prepared the Italian Moka machine for a strong coffee, slid a slice of bread into the toaster, and took out butter and marmalade. I told Mark under my breath, "When you go out to walk Poncho, I will walk with you."

"Okay. I will go right after breakfast."

"Okay."

We had breakfast, talking cautiously to hide our words from the ears around us. After breakfast, I followed Mark out to walk Poncho. As soon as we were on the street and out of earshot, I said, "You know what? That sly son of a bitch, Anthony... I want to slap him hard. I just can't stand his smug face. I want to see him behind bars. I can't have him flee the country with a free flight ticket earned by stealing a painting. The bastard should go to prison."

"Oh, Kim. You want to make a permanent enemy?"

"Do you think it's okay for him to flee Vienna with no sort of punishment for what he did? The bastard is walking away from his crime and flying home free. I can't have that."

"Well, I don't know. Why don't you talk to Herbert? He is Austrian; he must know the law here."

"I say the son of a bitch should go to prison together with Matej, who gave him the idea. He is just as guilty as Anthony, if not worse."

"Okay, Kim. One thing at a time. Let's get the painting first. Then we will see, okay?"

"You're with me on this, right?"

"Yes, I'm a hundred per cent with you. I will do all I can to help you. Relax, Kim. You are so tense. We will get through this, alright?"

"Alright."

We took a long walk with Poncho and came back after an hour. I became unstable and jumpy during the day, pacing the apartment, with all my attention on Anthony's room. The bastard was in and out of the room all day and, not knowing how long he would be out, I didn't dare sneak into the room again and ruin everything before tonight.

I tried to calm myself by taking a long shower, letting the water pour over my body for quite a while, and trying not to think about the task. But when I stepped out, I ran into Anthony, face to face, outside the bathroom. He glared at me. I glared back.

Mark invited me to have lunch with him, Poncho, and his assistant named Dario, a young Austrian guy with a pleasant smile. We went to a deli near Naschmarkt. During lunch, chatting with them over Austrian specialities, I felt better. We strolled around the market afterwards, looking at all kinds of stalls loaded with fruits, vegetables, cheese, olives, fresh ravioli, and everything else Naschmarkt had to offer.

But in the end, my mind came back to my plans for tonight. As the hours passed by, I sensed a strange calmness, the kind that comes right before a huge storm. At around seven o'clock, I called Herbert.

"Hallo?"

"Hello, Herbert, it's Hyunah. Just calling to check if everything is alright for this evening."

"*Alles gut*. (Everything is okay.) We will be there at eight o'clock. I have everything we need."

"Alright. See you at eight."

"See you."

So, it's a go. We're doing it. I prayed to the saints, asking them to give me strength. I prayed there should not be any last-minute screw-ups. I went back to my room, finished packing my hand carrier, and checked for the tenth time if I had forgotten anything in the drawers, closets, or wardrobe.

Soon, a noise from the living room made me startle—the boys and girls leaving for the party, all dressed up and chatting merrily. The pub was near Schweden Platz, five minutes drive away, in an area popular for its sidewalk cafés and restaurants. I followed Mark to the door and waited until everybody left. It was not yet eight o'clock, but I waited for Herbert on the sidewalk. I scanned both sides of the street nervously, pacing, not knowing what else to do while waiting for them.

Just a few minutes after eight, Herbert arrived in his black Volkswagen and pulled the car up near the gym. Fortunately, there was a free space to park just a few metres away. Herbert got out of the car with Ulf and Karl-Heinz.

"*Grüß Gott*."

I greeted them as if they were my lifesavers. Herbert opened the trunk and took out a small toolbox and a long bundle of rope.

"I'm coming up with you," Herbert said, reassuringly.

Handling a rope was certainly better done by Herbert than me, with my shaking hands. Moreover, if the bastard showed up unexpectedly, it was better to face him with Herbert than alone.

"Sure, come on."

Showtime. Time to act. Time to take justice into my own hands. A wild surge of adrenaline started pumping into my blood. We ran up the stairs. The door to Anthony's room was locked. But I knew it already. Anthony wasn't going to leave his room wide open, and Mark had given me his key to the room before he left. I slid the key into the hole, but it didn't seem to fit.

"Let me try."

Herbert skilfully opened the door in a few seconds. Once inside the room, Herbert went straight to the window and opened it wide while I went to work on the suitcase lying on top of the bed. Looking at the piece of paper on which I'd copied the numbers from Anthony's passport, I dialled 2807. It didn't open. Okay. I tried 1969. Still didn't open. Alright, calm down. I tried the first four digits of his passport number. Nope. It still wasn't opening.

Herbert watched me calmly while I was doing it. I started sweating. He said, "If you can't open the lock, I have tools to open it manually."

"Wow, Herbert, you thought of everything, didn't you? Okay, let me try just one more thing."

I went to a drawer that held his papers; it was empty. Empty! The bastard didn't leave any paper trails. Shit. It came to my mind I should try the birthday in a different order. I tried 0728 instead of 2807.

It opened! I leapt with joy. Herbert spread out both sides of the suitcase. We both started removing clothes on both sides, fumbling everywhere. And soon enough, my hand met something hard. It was the edge of the painting. I removed everything that was on top and found the large frame carefully wrapped in a big woollen scarf. Frantically, I got rid of the scarf, and there was paper again, carefully wrapped around the painting.

Herbert ripped apart several layers of paper that were wrapped around the painting. The bastard knew what he was doing to keep it safe. When we finally got rid of all the paper, I found the painting coming out into the light, revealing itself completely in front of my eyes.

The painting was the most beautiful piece I had seen done by Axel. It was an alluring woman with long, blonde hair. She was sitting on horseback, attired in a light summer dress, revealing her shoulders and long, lovely legs, surrounded by green fields and big old trees on the right side. The background was blurry like in a dream, with pastel flowers over green grass. It was fantastic. At the same time, I felt a kind of nostalgia wash over me. Why I felt sad about this painting, I didn't know. I looked at the bottom right. It was signed *Axel*, with the initial of his middle name and his family name. This was his stolen painting alright.

Herbert said in an affirmative tone, "This is it."

"Okay, wonderful. Let's bring it down and get the hell out of here. Come on."

Unexpected voices from the living room made me jump. It sounded like two women. Was it Joanna? While Herbert was putting the rope around the painting, the telephone rang. It could be Mark telling me something had gone wrong. I came out of the room and ran to the telephone. It was Mark.

"Hello, Kim. Get out of there now! Right now! Anthony got himself into a fight with the people at the table next to ours, and the owner threw him out. He just left. He could be there any minute. Get out now!"

"Okay, thank you."

I hung up the phone. Joanna and Dorothe watched me curiously. They were late for the party, I guessed. I dashed into the room to tell Herbert.

"We have to get out of here now! The bastard is coming back. He's on his way. He could be here any minute!"

Herbert lowered the painting down with the rope while Ulf and Karl-Heinz stood on the street below, waiting to grab it. I put down the piece of paper with the note I had written to Anthony, leaving it on top of his suitcase. It said:

A note to the thief who stole the painting;

Your scurrilous act of robbery cannot go unchallenged. I know you stole the painting from the penthouse. I'm returning it to its rightful owner. And I will see to it that you will be punished for your horrendous crime. You are nothing more than human trash. The world would be a better place without you. Lawyer up, motherfucker; you will need a good one.

Your Eye in the Sky and secret observer.

As soon as the painting reached Ulf and Karl-Heinz below, we stormed out of the room. The suitcase was wide open, with clothes strewn all over the place, but we couldn't care less. Herbert locked the door with the key. As we ran towards the door of the apartment, the phone started ringing, but there was absolutely no time to answer it.

I took Herbert's toolbox and my hand carrier, while Herbert took my large suitcase. We went downstairs, heavily loaded. Ulf came to our aid and helped us carry the luggage. Karl-Heinz carried the painting safely to the car.

The door to the building downstairs burst open, and Anthony entered, with his face flushed scarlet. Well, he was about to get even angrier. We went past him, heading outside. Herbert loaded my luggage into the trunk of his car. I checked that the painting was safely placed in the backseat.

The next moment, all hell broke loose. I had wanted to pull this off quietly, but everything that came after was exactly the opposite. Sure enough, Anthony rushed out to the sidewalk, screaming at me, "You fucking bitch! You broke into my room! You opened my suitcase!"

It was like a slow-motion scene in a movie. Anthony raised his hand and threw a punch at me. Herbert pulled me back from behind, and I dodged the fist by an inch. At the same time, out of the corner of my eye, I spotted Ulf's brown hair brushing past me. Ulf gave Anthony a mighty punch to his belly and another one connected to his jaw. Anthony yelped with pain and fell to the ground. It was only then that I realised the son of a bitch had tried to hit me. Ulf had reacted fast and attacked him in response to his unforgivable act; the bloody bastard threw a punch at me, a woman. What kind of man hits a woman?

My blood boiled with rage. I couldn't believe he threw a punch at me. Without thinking, I kicked him hard in his belly, on the same spot Ulf had punched. I had sneakers on. The bastard screamed. I yelled loudly so that everyone around could hear what I said. "It was you who broke into the artist's room and stole his painting. We know you did it. We found it in your suitcase, you filthy thief!"

Soon people surrounded us, a crowd who had gathered to witness the commotion. Dorothe and Joanna came down and watched in dismay. Mark arrived as well. And Marcia and Klaus. They were all astonished. I lowered myself in front of Anthony, who was grimacing in pain with his hand on his belly.

"It was Matej who told you to steal the painting at the party, wasn't it? He offered you a free flight ticket home if you could steal it, right? Yeah, I heard your little conversation with your buddy in LA."

Anthony glared at me and tried to move, but Ulf and Karl-Heinz held him firmly from behind his back. He was cornered, and everybody watched him in disgust. That was when I did something I had longed to do for a long time. I slapped him hard. I slapped his hateful, smug face as hard as I could. My, that felt good, even though my hand hurt. I had never slapped anyone before, and I didn't know my hand could hurt so much. But it felt good. It felt so good that I wanted to do it again.

"Who is Matej?"

A low and familiar voice from behind my back reached my ears. I turned around brusquely to find Axel standing there, looking confused. I flinched with surprise. I jumped to my feet. Axel's beautiful face was frowning. He was wearing a blue-grey shirt and jeans. I found out later it was Axel who called just as we were getting the hell out of the flat. It was Dorothe who answered the phone and told him she had just seen me leave the flat with a man who had taken my big suitcase.

Axel was on his way back from Krems when he had made that phone call from a nearby gas station. He stopped to fuel his car and called me to say he was back and wanted to come by to see me. When Dorothe told him what happened, he came straight to me.

His eyes met mine. His brow was furrowed, and his forehead was tensed.

"Hyunah, I just came back. Tell me what's going on. Who is this guy?"

I answered him, pointing to Anthony, who collapsed on the floor. "He is the bastard who stole your painting. We just caught him with your painting in his suitcase."

Herbert told Axel something in German. Axel's face was calm, but a glint of rage flashed in his eyes. He sat in front of Anthony and asked, "Did you steal my painting?"

I detected fear in Anthony's eyes. Nothing came out of his mouth. "Answer the question, Anthony," I pressed him. Anthony's face was distorted with fear and pain, and he finally opened his mouth.

"Yeah, man, I did it."

Axel asked him, "Why? Why did you steal my painting?"

Anthony didn't dare meet Axel's gaze. He turned his face downwards. "It was Matej..."

"Who is Matej?"

"A booker. We were all drunk and high, man... it started as a joke..."

"A joke? Stealing my painting was a joke?"

"Yeah, I'm sorry, man. It was like a joke... a bet. Matej said if I could steal your painting right on the spot... he would... he would..."

"He would what?"

Anthony was definitely scared now. Axel's voice was calm, but it was the calm right before the storm. I knew it.

"He would pay for my flight ticket."

"You stole my painting for a flight ticket?"

"Yeah, man, but it was Matej's idea... it was Matej."

For a split second, I thought Axel was going to strike him. But he didn't. He was suppressing his anger with formidable self-control. He said calmly, cooling off his rage, "You're going to pay for what you did."

Axel stood up. He hadn't seen Anthony throw that punch at me. He must have arrived just in time to see me slap him. But for me, that wasn't enough. I had already lost my temper when the son of a bitch attacked me. If Herbert hadn't been there to pull me back, I would have received that bloody punch on my face. I could have had a huge black eye that might have taken days to heal. I was itching to see Axel give the bastard what he deserved. Yes, I was out for blood. My blood was boiling madly. I never knew I had such a dark side in me.

Axel turned to face me.

"Are you alright, Hyunah?"

"No. I'm not alright. This filthy bastard attacked me. He threw a punch at me. Give the bastard what he deserves!!"

Axel's eyes grew wide with rage. He faced Anthony, who was still sitting on the pavement.

"You attacked her?"

Anthony's face became white with fear. He didn't know what to say.

"You raised your hand to her? To hurt a woman?" Axel asked him. His calm voice was menacing.

"Get up. Hit me instead. Stand up and hit me."

"I'm not gonna hit you, man." That was all the terrified Anthony could manage. Now everybody was watching. The faint evening light was on Axel's enraged face. Herbert tried to say something to Axel to stop him, but it was too late.

Pulling Anthony by the scruff of his neck up to his feet, Axel threw a mighty punch at his chest, followed by an uppercut to his jaw, moving fast like a boxer. The next blow was aimed at Anthony's nose—it would have certainly broken his nose—but Herbert and Karl-Heinz both jumped on Axel at the same time. It was like a scene from a movie. Anthony collapsed on the sidewalk. Herbert and Karl-Heinz held Axel on both sides, and the people around watched with their jaws dropping. Some people cheered, saying, "The thief deserved it. Served him right."

Herbert was talking to Axel, trying to calm him down. Mark came to tell me, "I'm glad to see the bastard got what he deserved. I can't believe he attacked you."

A police car pulled up. Someone had called the police. Three police officers got out of the car and approached us. Herbert immediately started talking to them, explaining the situation in rapid German. I understood most of it. There was only one thing to do now. Axel had to press charges against Anthony for the burglary. He should report it to the police, and he had all of us as witnesses to the crime. I was willing to do whatever had to be done to put the bastard in jail before he went hiding in the American embassy. In Austria, theft, fraud, or any offence involving property can lead to up to six months behind bars, or a fine.

I turned to Axel, who had calmed down by now and was watching Herbert and the police officer having a serious conversation. I talked to him in a low voice: "You need to press charges against the bastard. He should not be allowed to walk free from his crime. Let's file a complaint against him now. I will accompany you to the police station. I will do whatever is necessary. Please, let's do this, Axel."

Axel looked me in the eye. After a moment, he nodded.

"Alright."

"We have retrieved your painting. Do you want to see it?"

"Yes. Where is it?"

"In Herbert's car."

I asked Herbert for the key to his car, as he was still talking to the police officer. He reached into his pocket and handed it to me. I walked Axel to the car and opened the back door. I lifted the painting carefully and removed the large cotton scarf Karl-Heinz had used to wrap around it.

Axel's eyes fell on his painting. I asked cautiously, "Who is this beautiful lady?"

I already knew the answer before he told me. His eyes welled with tears.

"My mother."

Tears trickled down his beautiful face.

"What happened to her?" I asked him, quietly and carefully.

Axel answered in a low voice, "She's gone. She died when I was ten."

Tears streamed down his face. His hands were shaking. I held him in my arms and pressed him against my chest. He buried his face in my shoulder and cried like a child.

It was the beautiful woman I had seen in my dreams. How could it be possible? In my dreams, I had seen Axel as a child and his mother when she was still alive. Was this a coincidence? I remembered how I saw my grandfather in my dream the day he died. Was it possible I could see things in an inexplicable way?

I held Axel tightly in my arms as he cried. He looked so small, like the child in my dream.

Demel and Schönbrunn

"*Haben schon gewählt?*" ("Has Madam/Sir already made her/his choice?")

The morning after the ordeal, Axel invited me for breakfast at the famous Demel, the oldest café and bakery in Vienna. He didn't go jogging in the morning. He was exhausted. It was not only the incredible trial on Saturday night but also the gruelling three days in Krems, trying to save the troubled horse called Poseidon.

What I understood, from what Axel told me and what I found out later, was that he had spent all of his time with Poseidon from the moment he arrived on Thursday morning. When he first encountered Poseidon, who was highly agitated and out of control, the horse lunged and reared, striking him with his hooves. Axel moved swiftly back, and the hooves missed him by a few centimetres.

Nevertheless, Axel never gave up. After two hours alone with Poseidon, the colt stopped bucking, neighing, and charging at Axel. I never knew what he did exactly to calm the furious horse inside the barn, but he didn't permit anyone inside, nor even to peek or make any noise outside the stall while he was with Poseidon.

It was only then that he paused briefly for a quick snack, gulping the iced cold beer his grandma brought him. He was sweating like hell. So was Poseidon. Axel spent the rest of the day with Poseidon, letting the colt out in the corral after the break. He let the colt trot around the corral and stood in the middle. He watched Poseidon spin around and around him for quite some time, lashing out his simmering anger and energy.

When the colt started to get tired and staggered, he finally stopped and stood to face Axel. He turned from the horse and walked away, and Poseidon followed him towards the gate. Axel slowly got out of the corral, and the colt trudged after him all the way to his barn, while his grandparents and two stable boys watched in amazement.

By early evening, the colt allowed Axel to touch him. That was when Axel gave him a holistic massage to relieve all the tension from his head, neck, shoulders, back and hind end, carefully avoiding the burn by the colt's hindquarters. To gain his trust, Axel spent the night in the stall with Poseidon. He only had a chair to rest on, until his grandma brought him a sun bed on which he could lie down at around midnight.

At dawn, Axel woke up with Poseidon licking the side of his face. Later in the morning, the owner of Poseidon, a middle-aged man named Moritz, came by to see the progress. He was impressed by the way Poseidon let Axel touch him, his head, his neck, and hind end, but the colt wouldn't let Moritz get anywhere near him, snorting and bucking again.

It seemed the poor horse was reborn by Axel and refused to have anything to do with the past and the accident. Axel never lost his patience with Poseidon and spent another day entirely devoted to him. By midday, Poseidon started eating. The colt accepted a carrot and an apple from Axel's hand but still did not allow anyone else near him.

When the vet came in the afternoon to treat his wound, Axel stayed with Poseidon the whole time, hiding the horse's eyes with his hands to calm him. While the vet was attending to the wound,

Axel whispered in the colt's ear comfortingly so that the vet didn't have to sedate him again.

Axel paused only a few times a day, and briefly until Poseidon regained his spirits and fed again. He spent another night with Poseidon in the stall, disregarding his grandma's request to return to the house for a decent night's sleep. By Saturday morning, the colt allowed Axel's grandma to approach him and accepted a carrot from her hand.

Later that night, after retrieving the painting, we all headed to a local beer joint. As we all drank away the tension from earlier, the conversation shifted as Mark mentioned Axel's fabulous Ducati and that everyone in the apartment called him Ducati Man.

Herbert asked, "Do you know how he got his Ducati?"

Ulf and Karl-Heinz smiled. Although they didn't speak English, they seemed to understand what we were saying.

"No, tell us."

"Two years ago, there was a photographer named Mario from Milan, who lived below the penthouse. He couldn't pay the rent for over six months because of a gambling problem. He had debt up to his neck, and Axel's grandmother threw him out but not before he paid up his rent and electricity and gas bills.

"He couldn't pay, so he proposed to Axel that he would give him anything he possessed. He showed Axel his professional camera and other expensive equipment. But Axel had something else in mind. When asked what Mario could offer him to cover the rent, Axel's hand pointed straight to Mario's Ducati parked in the garage. It was Mario's most precious possession. Mario paled with horror and uttered, "*Ma donna! Che cazzo*!"

We all laughed except Mark. He asked me, "What does it mean, '*Che cazzo*?" I replied, "It means 'what the fuck' in Italian."

Mark nodded. "Aha, that's how you became Ducati Man!"

And I asked, "So, what happened to poor Mario?"

"He had to give up his baby, of course," Axel answered. "Mario almost cried. He kept saying '*cazzo*'."

All of us roared again. Axel smiled for the first time that day.

"Mario made me promise to take care of his baby. And I gave him my word."

Mark burst out laughing, together with all of us.

When I scanned the details of the painting later, I found out Axel's mother was riding the horse without a saddle, only with a rein, and in her bare feet. She must have been one hell of a horse rider.

The famous and exquisite Hofzuckerbäckerei Demel café was founded in 1786 and ever since, it had been serving dishes and cakes carefully prepared by hand to traditional, centuries-old recipes.

A waitress wearing a black dress with a lace collar asked Axel if he had chosen a menu item. Axel ordered strawberry curd cake, sachertartlet (traditional Viennese chocolate cake) and Großer Brauner coffee (large coffee).

When the waitress was gone, I asked Axel, "What is this strange way of addressing the customers here?" My German was far from fluent, but good enough to notice the strange way in which the waitress spoke.

Axel nodded. "It is just like it was two hundred years ago. Guests are accordingly referred to in the third person when asked for their orders. The waitresses here are called *Demelinerinnen* by the Viennese. Demelinerinnen are often referred to as the last keepers of real Viennese traditions."

"So, they talk to their customers as they would have done two hundred years ago?"

"Yes. The cultivated impersonality is considered one of Demel's trademarks."

I considered this old-fashioned way of addressing their customers in Demel. A combination of discreet politeness with the slightest suggestion of distance. Quite different from Hawelka, frequently visited by intellectuals and artists with liberal-minded patrons, with its owner greeting you with a vigorous handshake at the entrance. Demel had always been a hot stop for the aristocracy and bourgeoisie.

"And also unique. Something that can only be found in Demel. I wonder if they laugh in the kitchen when they are not seen," I added, and Axel smiled.

"Maybe. All the cakes here are handmade—the famous Doboscake, cream slices, tea biscuits, ring cakes, and strudel. And some of them once used to satisfy the cravings of Emperor Franz Joseph."

"Oh, really? The Emperor?"

"Yes. He secretly had Demel cakes and pralines served during his tête-à-têtes with his lover."

"What about his wife? Sisi was his wife, right?"

"Oh, yes. Sisi was an unhappy wife. She was addicted to their legendary violet sorbet."

"At least she had something that satisfied her."

About twenty fresh mouth-watering cakes were presented in the pompous display case in Demel, and it was hard to make a choice. In the end, I opted for the strawberry curd cake, and Axel chose a Viennese chocolate cake. When the coffee and cakes arrived, we devoured them, tasting each other's cake like children. It was delicious.

Anna Demel was the first woman ever to receive the title of Councillor of Commerce in 1957 for strictly guarding and assuring those Viennese values, so Demel continued to be a portal to monarchic times until today. After Anna passed away, her son-in-law, Baron Federico of Berzevicsy-Pallavicini, shaped Demel's visual appearance with his fascinating window displays and playful designs. Some of his works were still preserved and visible on some of Demel's packaging.

It was a bit after 10:30 when we finally left Demel and emerged into the beautiful, sunny morning streets of Vienna. Axel said, "My grandma took me here for the first time when I moved to Vienna. She loved this kind of traditional and old-fashioned café, along with its delicacies."

"Well, I can only say she has excellent taste."

"I barely had time to talk to her when I was in Krems this time. I need to go back next weekend."

"So, how is Poseidon?"

"He is stable for now but not ready to go back to his owner. I'm not sure if he ever could. He went through a terrible shock and refused to face reality. He will be alright with my grandparents, but to be able to go back to Herr Moritz will take time."

Axel drove us back to his place on his Ducati. It was a lovely sunny day, and we strolled to the park across the street. The sky was blue and clear; a pleasant breeze brushed past us, and the trees had birds perched on their branches. We found a big, tall tree that scattered a blissful shadow. Axel gestured to me to sit down, and I sat next to him under the tree.

Axel seemed relaxed and calm, wearing a pink shirt and blue-grey cotton pants, his golden hair in a ponytail. I watched the tree carefully. This was the very tree under which I had been asleep when he came to find me. He lay on the grass next to me, with his arms folded under his head.

"You will get your nice shirt dirty," I said.

"It's alright. I've been mingling in the hay with a horse for three days. This is like a carpet to me."

"How is Frühling?"

"She's fine. I rode her on Saturday with Poseidon following us around the ranch. Poseidon is getting along well with Frühling. He has found a new friend."

"Tell me, what did you do with Poseidon while you were alone with him in the stall, to calm him down? He was dangerous, and yet you didn't allow anyone near you."

"The horse is a prey animal; they are not predators. When

confronted with a predator, all they can do is flee. They feel constantly unsafe and endangered. That's why they buck, bolt and swerve when they sense danger, to protect their most vulnerable part: the neck. Any predator would aim for their neck first, to kill them, and they know it. While what a dog wants from you is supper, what a horse wants from you is safety. I just told Poseidon he was safe with me, and I would not harm him. I'm his friend."

"But why did you have to be alone with him to let him know that?"

"Because, to let him know he was safe with me and bond a relationship, you cannot allow any other curious eyes to be around. The frightened animal is very sensitive and cannot have any distractions to make him feel unsafe. Poseidon already had doubts and mistrust towards me in the first place. He charged me when he first saw me, didn't I tell you?"

"Yes, you did. Weren't you scared when he struck out at you?"

"No, it was a normal reaction of a terrified horse. I left him in peace when he was agitated and uncontrollable. I just watched him across the stall, letting him know I was there."

"You just let him buck, snort, neigh, while you watched him across the stall?"

"Yes. When he was letting off his steam, I drew a picture of him."

"You drew a picture of the horse?"

"Yes. It's one of my methods to spend bonding time with a horse. If you don't approach the colt to harm him... if you allow him a safe distance, but let him know you are there... he will start to think you are no danger to him. That is the first step."

"And then?"

"When I finished drawing him, I slowly approached and showed him the picture."

"Oh, really? Do you think he knew it was him in the picture?"

"He knew I was no danger to him. At least I could see that."

He closed his eyes. I watched his beautiful long eyelashes, naturally curling as if a make-up artist had applied false ones. His face had seen some sun over the last days on the farm. His pale skin had turned slightly darker, giving him a healthy glow. It made a great contrast with his husky-blue eyes, making his eyes more sparkly and glittery. He was drop-dead gorgeous. His beauty didn't belong to the human species, but beyond that. Probably an elf. Secretly living among humans.

Last night, when he fell asleep, I lay next to him and watched him. I had never seen him so deeply asleep. My hands were itching to touch him—very carefully, without daring to wake him up, I stroked his hair and forehead. *Will he notice if I kiss him?* It was tempting, but I didn't dare.

And now, with his eyes closed, not moving, he seemed to be asleep. A gentle breeze passed through his golden hair. He looked serene, completely contrary to last night. I carefully caressed his hair, giving him a tender stroke over the side of his face. He smiled with his eyes still closed and gently took my hand with his right hand and drew it to his lips. And he kissed my hand.

This time, it seemed more intimate and alluring. His lips touched my hand with a quiet breath. He pressed his lovely lips to my hand, and kept hold of my hand, pushing it to his chest.

He whispered, "Lie next to me."

I was wearing a cotton summer dress, the only presentable attire I had in my hand carrier to wear to a fancy café like Demel. Axel pulled my hand gently towards him and, as I lay, he offered me his shoulder. I rested my head on his shoulder and lay next to him. He murmured, his voice like the sound of leaves up in the tree.

"Did I thank you for what you did for me—for the painting?"

"Um... I believe you thanked everyone involved last night."

"But did I thank you personally?"

"Um... not personally, I guess."

"Then I will."

He grinned with his eyes still closed. His profile showed his sharp nose, his high cheekbone, and beautifully carved lips. I stared at his lovely lips up close. *I would kiss him a thousand times if I were given a chance.* We lay next to each other under the shade of the tree for a while, listening to the birds chirping above, and smelling the scents of the flowers and plants the soft wind carried to us.

A dog barked nearby, and commotion erupted around us. A huge Labrador retriever was chasing after a frisbee that brushed past us. I got up. Axel opened his eyes, squinting at the noonday sun, and slowly got to his feet. He said, "Come and have lunch at my place. My grandma packed me enough food to feed ten soldiers."

I giggled. "She thinks you still have to grow."

Indeed, when we got home, Axel showed me various glass jars and stainless-steel containers with soups and Polish specialities cooked with love by his grandma. I wondered at how much she loved Axel... with undying and unconditional devotion... and how she must see her dead daughter's face in Axel.

We spent the rest of the day together, having *kwaśnica* (Polish sauerkraut soup with potatoes and root vegetables) and *baba kartoflana* (Polish potato pie) for lunch. They were delicious. His grandma was an excellent cook. *When would I have the pleasure of meeting her?*

My new flat was not dirty but dusty, having been left empty. It needed to be freshened up. We opened all the windows and cleaned the place, and Felix and Angela came over to watch. I was introduced to Herbert's two sisters; Klara, the elder sister who lived on the ground floor with her husband and her three-year-old daughter called Joë, and Ida, the younger sister who lived on the first floor, just below me. I watched Ida with bewilderment. She had absolutely no feminine side to her. She had very short hair, and even her voice sounded like a man's.

The next morning, I was soundly asleep when a soft knock on my door woke me up. The door opened. I had forgotten to lock it the night before. To my surprise, the door was opened by Pezzi, the Doberman. I found his black face with traces of beige right in front of me when I opened my eyes. I discovered later that Pezzi used to enter this apartment while Herbert lived here, by jumping on the doorknob with his front legs. I talked to Pezzi, still half asleep.

"*Mais, qu'est-ce qui se passe? Qu'est-ce tu fais là, Pezzi?*" (What's going on? What are you doing here, Pezzi?)

A familiar voice from the door fondled my ears. "*Elle veut te faire un bisou.*" (She wants to give you a kiss.)

"Axel?"

"I'm sorry I woke you up. I'll come back later."

"No, don't go. Come in. Come over here."

"May I come in?"

"Yes, come in."

He appeared in his jogging gear, sweating profusely. I had also forgotten to pull down the window shade, and the dazzling morning sunlight was lightening the room. I enjoyed the contrast between Pezzi's black face and Axel's Roman sculpture face as both looked down at me.

"Sorry, I intruded on your sleep."

"It's okay. What time is it?"

"Time for breakfast."

He had a bag in his hand. He had brought me breakfast.

"Did you come straight from running?"

"Yes. I wanted to bring you breakfast and join you."

"How nice, but you're all sweaty. You need a shower."

"I will give you time to wake up. I will go take a shower, change, and come back. Is that alright for you?"

"Sure. I will be up by the time you come back."

Axel disappeared with Pezzi in tow, just as fast as he appeared.

I got up slowly. Axel had left a bag on the table. I trudged to the table and opened the bag. There were semmel and Schwarzbrot as usual, and I saw something wrapped in a white paper. I opened it with curiosity. My eyes found *Oreilles d'abricot* (the French puff pastry with custard cream and apricots that I loved so much). It looked the same as the one I used to buy at Brioche Dorée in Paris. That woke me up to all my senses. I opened the window wide and let the fresh morning air into the apartment. Birds were singing high up in the trees as I looked across the garden below. Herbert was shepherding Felix and Angela to school.

When Axel came back, he had a shopping bag in his hand. He produced a bottle of mineral water, a jar of marmalade, butter, a few oranges, and a small box of loose tea leaves.

I said, "*Merci. Tu es adorable, mais il fallait pas...*" (Thanks. You are adorable, but it was not necessary...)

"*Je t'en prie. Ça me fait plaisir.*" (You're welcome. It is my pleasure.)

He said, "Oh, before I forget."

Axel took out a business card from his jeans pocket.

"I ran into the photographer downstairs this morning. He asked me to give this to you. He wanted you to call him. He has a job for you."

He handed me Mike's business card. There was no phone in my flat yet. As soon as we finished breakfast, we went down to Klara's place.

She greeted us with a big smile and let me use her phone. I called Mike.

"Hello."

"Hello, this is Kim. Is this Mike?"

"Yes, I wanted to talk to you about a job. Are you free on Wednesday? We're shooting the catalogue I told you about."

"Of course, yes, I'm free. What time do you want me to be there?"

"We will start at eight in the morning. Is it okay for you?"

"Sure. I will be there at eight. Do you need me as a make-up artist or as a stylist?"

"Just make-up."

"Okay, great. See you on Wednesday."

"See you, Kim."

"Thank you, Mike, 'bye."

The next morning, I started gathering all my equipment. I wanted to do a good job. It was the first job Mike had given me, so I had to be excellent. I had already set the alarm clock for six the next morning. I hated rushing and getting stressed in the morning when I had to work, so I needed to get up early and take my time.

While preparing my make-up equipment, I noticed one of my brushes was missing. It was a big brush for applying, evening out and wiping powder: one of my favourites I had paid a small fortune for in Paris. It was very soft and efficient, and I loved using it and always carried it around with me on every job. The brush was made from genuine *poiles d'écureuil* (squirrel hair), extremely soft to the touch and fine in texture. I even used it on myself. I always washed it carefully with soap and soaked it in alcohol, to remove all the dirt and possible fungus or bacteria after having used it on the models. And it always looked as good as new after being washed and dried. I rummaged through all my belongings, searching the apartment over and over again, but couldn't find my brush.

While I pondered on it, a man from the telephone company arrived to install the phone in my apartment. I let him do his job, and I arranged all my clothes in the wardrobe and the drawers, meticulously searching everywhere to find my brush. But nothing.

When Axel appeared at my door in the early evening, I told him about it. He suggested coming with him to his place and looking for it there. I might have left it there somewhere. Upon arrival at his place, I searched the guest bedroom while Axel looked around the rest of the penthouse. Neither of us found it.

"Please don't get so upset, Hyunah. We will find it. Focus on your job tomorrow."

"Yes, I know, I know. It's upsetting all the same. I like my brush. You have no idea."

"*Si*, I have an idea. Look, if we can't find your brush, I will buy you a new one."

"You don't know how expensive it is."

"I don't care. I will buy you one. I promise. Now, my lady. Can I interest you in riding with me?"

"Riding? On your Ducati, you mean?"

Axel nodded, with an irresistible smile. "It will do you good, come on."

He tilted his head toward the outside.

"Oh, alright then."

So, we went for a long ride around the Donau riverside and turned west. After about half an hour, we arrived at Schloss Schöbrunn, probably the most famous tourist attraction in Vienna, but I had never taken the time to go there. It was the main summer residence of the Habsburg rulers in Hietzing. The name Schönbrunn (meaning 'beautiful spring') had its roots in an artesian well from which water was consumed by the court. Schönbrunn Palace was closed for visiting; it was almost eight when we arrived there. Axel parked his Ducati, and we visited the beautiful garden with fountains, which was open to the public.

"We will come back during the day to look round the inside of the palace. This evening, we will go to Gloriette."

Axel led me along a zigzag path to the top of the hill on foot. I paused a moment to catch my breath. He offered me a hand. We hiked until we reached the Gloriette rooftop, which provided a fantastic view of Vienna.

I understood now why Axel had said, 'It will do you good' before we left. As was often the case, when he took me out for a ride, it was the perfect moment for a sunset. I forgot all the distress of the day when I'd whined about my missing brush.

Axel is all that matters to me. Not the damn brush I fussed about all day long.

I'm not sure if it was the wondrous, spellbinding light from the setting sun illuminating Axel's beautiful figure, revealing his sparkling blue eyes, his golden hair, his sharp nose, fascinating jaw and cheek from the flank of his face, or a sudden release of my tension from a stressful day. I was suddenly thrust into a trance-like state. An invisible power hypnotised me, and I lost control over my body. I felt dizzy, lost my balance and dropped to my knees. Axel swiftly took hold of me by the waist.

"Are you alright?"

He let me sit on the ground and sat next to me.

"Oh, it's just... I must have been too stressed out lately. I'm fine."

Axel stroked my head gently.

"Do you have pain in your head where you had the concussion?"

"No, just a little bit dizzy, that's all. I just need a moment."

He let my head rest on his shoulder and threw his arm around me. We sat there for a while, watching the setting sun from the Gloriette rooftop. I secretly pinched myself, feeling a sharp pain in my thigh. I was delighted. So this wasn't a dream, it was actually happening!

I wished with all my heart that time would stop there and then, suspending the flow of life.

The next morning, I was up before the alarm went off. I took a shower, brushed my teeth, got dressed, checked my make-up equipment, and left at seven, holding my precious square suitcase. I crossed the park as usual. Gentle winds complemented the overcast sky.

I had opted for a stylish black dress I had brought from Paris and a matching jacket, belt, and shoes—it was an ideal work outfit because I looked fashionable in it, and at the same time, it was comfortable to work in.

Axel was waiting for me for breakfast, already back from jogging, showered and dressed in a blue polo and jeans, looking gorgeous. We finished breakfast at a quarter to eight. Axel went to his atelier, and I went down to work.

As I rang the doorbell, a handsome male model exited the elevator. He was tall, with dark hair and green eyes, and looked Italian. He smiled at me.

"Good morning."

His accent was definitely Italian, so I answered, "*Buon giorno.*" (Good morning.)

His eyes grew wide in amazement. "*Parli Italiano?*" (Do you speak Italian?)

"*Sì, un poco.*" (Yes, a little.)

"*Brava! Mi chaimo Massimo, e tu?*" (Bravo! My name is Massimo, and you?)

"*Mi chiamo Kim. Piacere, Massimo.*" (My name is Kim. Nice to meet you, Massimo.)

"*Piacere, Kim.*"

Mike opened the door and greeted us cheerfully.

"Good morning. Come in."

I recognised a young assistant photographer in his twenties, and a woman and a man from Hanro who were in charge of the clothing.

"How are you, Mike?" I started.

"I'm good. Did I tell you what we are shooting today?"

"No. As a matter of fact, I was going to ask you."

"We're doing a catalogue for men's underwear and pyjamas for Hanro."

"Hanro? The Swiss underwear brand?"

"Yes. You know it?"

"Oh, yes, I know the brand. I have already worked for a fashion show for women's lingerie for Hanro."

"Good. We're doing men's underwear this time."

The doorbell rang. Ulrik, a tall Swedish boy with short blond hair entered. I assumed I would be working with these two guys today. They would pose mostly in underwear, so they would need only light make-up, to cover their skin evenly, and hide any blemishes. It was a relatively easy job. I started with Ulrik, since Mike wanted to shoot him first. He had fair skin with no particular blemishes, so I did light, natural make-up on his face, and powered most of his body slightly, just to remove the shiny spots for the camera.

Now it was Massimo's turn. Unlike Ulrik, who didn't speak much, Massimo was talkative, funny, and he gestured a lot. He was Italian, alright. He seemed to be glad to find someone who spoke some Italian.

"*Allora, dove hai imparato Italiano, Kim?*" (So, where did you learn Italian, Kim?)

"*Ho avuto un ragazzo Italiano.*" (I had an Italian boyfriend once.)

"*Davvero?*" (Really?)

"*Sì. Da dove vieni, Massimo?*" (Yes. Where are you from, Massimo?)

"*Da Roma. Ma vivo a Milano per lavoro. E tu, da dove vieni?*" (From Rome. But I live in Milan for work. And you, where are you from?)

"*Da Seoul, Corea del Sud. Ma ho vissuto a Parigi per alcuni anni prima di essere venuta a vivere qua.*" (From Seoul, South Korea. But I lived in Paris for a few years before I came here.)

"Ma tu ai viaggiato molto. Tu sei coraggiosa e bravissima." (But you have travelled a lot. You are brave and wonderful.)

"*E tu, hai viaggiato un po' in Europa?*" I asked Massimo. (And you, have you travelled a bit in Europe?)

"*Sì, Parigi, Londra, Amburgo.*" (Yes, Paris, London, Hamburg.)

"*E ti piace Vienna?*" (And do you like Vienna?)

"*No, non proprio. Preferisco Parigi,*" (No, not really. I prefer Paris), Massimo answered, with a grimace.

"*E perché?*" (Why?) I asked.

"*Si mangia meglio a Parigi che a Vienna.*" (You eat better in Paris than in Vienna.)

"*Sono totalmente d'accordo con te.*" (I totally agree with you.)

There wasn't much to do on his handsome face, so I was done with the make-up in no time.

"Now, show me your body."

Massimo grinned. There was a mischievous glint in his eyes. He removed his T-shirt and jeans, keeping only his underwear on. He was going to reveal his body just like this for the photo shoot, so I had to make sure his body appeared flawless. I immediately spotted a scar on his left shoulder and another huge one on his right thigh. I pointed at his thigh.

"*Mio Dio! Cosa ti è successo qui?*" (Oh, my God! What happened to you here?)

"*Un cane cattivo mi ha morso quando ero bambino.*" (A nasty dog bit me when I was a child.)

"Oh, no."

"*Sì, un cane cattivissimo. Bruto. Bruttissimo.*" (Yes, a very bad dog. Brute. Really nasty!)

Massimo's face distorted as he mimicked the mean dog. It was so funny I burst into laughter. I couldn't stop giggling as I started covering his scar with camouflage. He carried on with the dog story, and I went on laughing at him.

He said, "*Ti piace la cucina italiana?*" (Do you like Italian cuisine?)

"*Sì, certamente. Adoro gli spaghetti alle vongole.*" (Yes, of course. I love spaghetti with clams.)

"*Allora, conosco una buona pizzeria a Vienna. Sono sicuro che hanno gli spaghetti con vongole. Andiamo lì a mangiare stasera?*" (So, I know a good pizzeria in Vienna. I'm sure they have spaghetti with clams. Shall we go there this evening?)

Massimo stared down at me with a playful smile while I worked on his thigh. He was flirting with me. Flirting was common in my line of work. It was all part of the business. But in most cases, it ended when the job was done. And that was fine with me. Many handsome male models used to flirt with me, make jokes, make me laugh, hit on me, or sometimes even confide in me their troubles or secrets while I worked on them. But all this usually ended when we finished shooting. It was rare for them to ask me out afterwards. I had never been tempted to do anything like that, but I knew many did.

There was a commotion as the door opened, and a series of boxes and hangers with clothes were hauled into the studio, followed by two members of staff, a young woman, and a guy. They started to spread the contents of the boxes on the big table next to the ironing board.

I resumed working on his thigh without answering his question. The scar was deep, and it needed to be well hidden as if it never existed. Massimo cheerfully asked me again, "*Dimmi cosa pensi. Andiamo a mangiare una pizza staser?*" (Tell me what you think. Shall we go to eat pizza this evening?)

I didn't answer. I just giggled. Then a familiar, calm voice startled me from behind.

"Excuse me. Hyunah?"

I turned around to find Axel standing there, watching Massimo and me. His piercing eyes were on Massimo, and his forehead was screwed into a frown. He didn't like what he saw.

He had a brush in his hand—my missing brush.

"I found this in my atelier. Is it yours? Aga must have found it in the guest bedroom while cleaning the room, and she put it in my atelier."

I must have dropped the brush in the guest bedroom. Aga must have thought it was Axel's and brought it to his atelier without knowing the difference between my make-up brushes and Axel's paintbrushes. With all the fuss I had made about the brush, Axel had brought it to me the moment he found it.

The people arranging the items for the shoot, and the music, had distracted me from seeing Axel enter through the wide-open door. *How much did he hear of my conversation with Massimo? Maybe enough.* And the way I was bending towards Massimo's thigh to cover his scar, Axel could not have known what I was doing.

I jumped to my feet and took the brush from Axel.

"Oh, you found it! It must have slipped from my bag by accident. Thank you."

"No problem."

He was about to turn around and leave the studio when one of the female staff from Hanro pushed some underwear towards him, saying, "Do you mind trying this one first?"

Oh, dear Saints, this woman thinks Axel is a model.

I snatched the underwear from her hand and snapped, "Excuse me, he's not a model. Give it to me."

The woman, who was seemingly Austrian, looked embarrassed.

"*Entschuldigung*," she apologised.

Axel answered promptly, "*Kein problem.*"

As he walked away, I followed him out in a hurry.

"It's great you found my brush, thank you. See you later?"

"See you later."

He disappeared quickly. I came back to Massimo, finished disguising the scar on his thigh, and started working on the scar on his left shoulder. He opened his green eyes wide and began, "*Scusami, quello è il tuo ragazzo?*" (Excuse me, is that your boyfriend?)

"*No, è solo un amico.*" (No, he is just a friend.)

Theoretically, Axel and I were only friends. He was clear about it. And he had never kissed me. I could, theoretically, go out with Massimo if I fancied it, without feeling guilty. I saw no reason why I should say no. I was flattered by Massimo's honest advance. He made me feel like a woman. But somehow, I couldn't say yes to his invitation. He tried to convince me.

"*Dai, ti invito, non conosco nessuno a Vienna. Non voglio cenare da solo.*" (Come on, I will invite you. I don't know anyone in Vienna. I don't want to have dinner alone.)

"*Ah, non lo so.*" (Ah, I don't know.)

"*Okay, ecco l'indirizzo del ristorante. Sarò lì stasera alle otto. Vieni se puoi, sarà un piacere per me.*" (Okay, here's the address of the restaurant. I will be there at eight o'clock tonight. Come if you can. It will be a pleasure for me.)

He reached into a pocket of the jeans he had hung across the back of the chair. He produced a small card from the pizzeria and handed it to me. I hesitated but took it in the end. And then Mike called me. "Are you ready there, Kim?"

"Almost done. Give me five minutes for the finishing touches. We will be ready in five minutes."

While I was finishing, Massimo continued to talk, with a broad smile: "*C'è un vero pizzaiolo in quel ristorante che fa la vera pizza napoletana, è molto buono.*" (There's a genuine pizza maker in that restaurant, who makes very good Neapolitan pizza).

"*Sono sicuro che hai ragione. Fammi concentrare sulla fine di questo, per favour.*" (I'm sure you are right. Let me focus on finishing this, please.)

As soon as I was done, I sent Massimo to the Austrian staff for fitting. I moved to the shooting area. The photo session continued; Massimo went in front of the camera when Mike was done with Ulrik. I watched Massimo pose. He moved well. They had him come from Milano, especially for the job, and he was worth it.

Soon it was lunchtime. They had set up a makeshift table for a one-hour lunch break. The Austrian staff had ordered catered food and they spread the items across the table for everyone. There were mixed salads, fresh bread with cold cuts, and sandwiches with various ingredients. Everything looked good and fresh. They brought several bottles of mineral water and sodas.

I sat next to Mike, and Massimo came to sit next to me. I asked Mike, "Is everything okay? Did I do alright with the make-up?"

"Oh, Kim, you did great. The big scar on Massimo's leg is well hidden. You wouldn't even know it was there in the photos."

Mike showed me a few shots off the Polaroid. It looked as though the scar had never existed. I felt relieved. As soon as I finished my lunch, I excused myself and ran upstairs to see if Axel was there. No one came to the door, so I went downstairs to the garage. Hebert, Ulf, and Karl-Heinz weren't there, either. They must have gone out for lunch. Axel's Ducati was gone.

I went back to the studio; the makeshift table had been cleared, and people were finishing their coffee. Massimo came to me. "*Vuoi un caffè?*" (Do you want coffee?)

"*Si, grazie.*" (Yes, thank you.)

I sat on a chair next to the make-up table. Massimo brought me a cup of espresso, holding a cup for himself.

"*Grazie, Massimo.*" (Thank you, Massimo.)

"*Da quanto tempo sei a Vienna?*" (How long have you been in Vienna?)

"*Da dicembre dell'anno scorso.*" (Since December last year.)

"*Ti piace vivere qui?*" (Do you like living here?) Massimo asked.

I thought about his question a moment. If I liked living in Vienna, it was all thanks to Axel. Before I met him, Vienna was alright, if not a bit boring. It didn't have the alluring, glamorous and extravagant lifestyle of Paris, with its ostentatious people. Vienna was quieter, boring, safe, with rather reserved people. There was nothing exhilarating here like there was in Paris.

"*Va tutto bene, un po' noioso,*" (It's alright, a bit boring), I told Massimo.

"*Non so come fai a vivere qui, è così noioso qui. Sei stato a Milano?*" (I don't know how you live here, it's so boring. Have you been to Milan?)

"*Sì, solo per pochi giorni di lavoro. Tanto inquinamento e persone molto impegnate.*" (Yes, just for a few days for work. A lot of pollution and very busy people.)

Mike called me. Lunch break was over. We went on shooting. At around 5:30 pm, the work was over. I gathered my make-up equipment and got ready to go. Massimo came to say goodbye.

"*Spero che stasera tu possa venire a mangiare con me. Ci vediamo presto?*" (I hope you can have dinner with me this evening. See you soon?)

"*Oh, non ne sono sicuro. Non credo di poter venire. Ma grazie per l'invito.*" (Oh, I'm not sure. I don't think I can come. But thank you for the invitation.)

"*Ciao*, Kim."

"*Ciao*, Massimo."

Massimo left, and Mike said to me, "Thank you for the great work, Kim. I will call you as soon as I have the photos to show you. I think we will all get paid next week."

"Okay, great. Can't wait to see the photos. I'll see you soon, thank you."

I went upstairs and rang the bell. Axel came to the door, wearing the same blue polo and jeans from this morning.

"Just finished the job."

"How did it go?"

"Pretty well. Will you walk me home? I need fresh air and to get home to have a shower. It's been a long day."

"Sure, give me a second."

He went to his room and came back with a light denim jacket flung over his shoulder.

He took my make-up suitcase. "Give me that, let me carry it."

We walked through the park. The weather was getting cloudy, and the sky had become heavy with clouds. The wind was blowing lightly, moving the leaves. Axel seemed to be lost in his thoughts. I sensed something was bothering him. I told him about the Hanro underwear catalogue and explained how I had to hide the scars on Massimo, and how pleased I was with the Polaroid Mike showed me. He listened without commenting.

As we arrived at my place, he handed me back my make-up suitcase, and asked, "Are you going to have pizza with that Italian guy tonight?"

He didn't have the usual smile on his face. His eyes seemed to be sunken deeper, and his brows were pulled together in a frown. *So, this is what has been bothering him.* I met his eyes without answering right away. His lips tightened. He seemed restless. He went on: "You know he would just have his way with you, don't you? He would take advantage of you, and you would never see him again."

I held my breath for a while.

"You know, Axel. I'm a single woman. When a friendly guy asks me out for a pizza, I see no reason why I should refuse."

"Even if you know what he wants from you?"

"Axel, it was you who wanted us to be just friends. You made it clear, didn't you? And when a guy asks me out, why does it bother you?"

Axel fell silent. His eyes sank deeper, his cheeks flushed, and his jaw dropped. He looked astounded as if he had been struck by lightning. He was lost for words for a moment. Finally, he murmured, as if he was thinking out loud: "You are right... This is all my fault... I'm so wrong in all this... You are free to do as you want, Hyunah. I have no right to say anything... I'm sorry... please excuse me... I wish you a good evening."

His face was distorted with pain. He was not angry with me; he was angry with himself. He turned around and walked away. I called after him in despair.

"Axel! You can't walk away like that! Axel!"

He picked up his pace and disappeared quickly between the trees.

I stood there in dismay, not knowing what to do. The path between the trees had never looked so empty. With a painful knot in my stomach, I went up the stairs to my flat. I couldn't digest what had just happened. I collapsed on my bed and put my hands around my head. I wanted to scream, but my throat was so dry, that no sound came out. I got up and opened the fridge and gulped water directly from the bottle.

I got into the shower, hoping the sensation of the pouring water would make me feel better. It didn't.

I stayed under the water for quite a while, without noticing the passage of time. When I finally got out, with the towel wrapped around my body, I sat at the table. I looked down over the garden through the window. When I looked up again, it was around 7:30 in the evening. I dried my hair and went to the wardrobe. Going through all my dresses, one by one, I picked up a pale pink silk dress I had bought in Paris. I put it on and stared at myself in the dressing mirror. A pale and pathetic woman looked back at me.

'Why do you put all this make-up on your face? You look pretty without it. You have nothing to hide,' Axel told me once. I didn't put on any make-up. I already knew I wouldn't go to see Massimo for pizza.

I put on comfortable shoes that matched my dress. My

knotted stomach was hurting me. I peeked out of the window. The sky was becoming more and more cloudy and looked menacing. *Should I bring an umbrella?* But I had no idea where it was. And I wanted to get out as soon as possible.

I couldn't breathe in the confined space of my small flat.

When I went out through the gate, the blowing wind felt good on my face and bare arms. It reminded me of my childhood —the blissful wind that blew on my skin right before the rain, during the long rainy season in the summertime. I liked it so much that I would go out into the garden just to feel that wind on my face and my bare arms and legs, and I would stand there until it started raining, then run into the house, giggling with my brother. It was strange, the way this wind brought up my childhood memories. Now I was on the other side of the planet. I trudged along the road, between the trees. The street was deserted. Passing across the park, taking my time, I arrived on the other side towards Axel's penthouse.

It started raining. Strangely, it felt good. I ran into the building next to Herbert's garage and got into the elevator. I breathed deeply before I rang the bell on Axel's door. I pushed the button. No answer. I rang again, this time twice. No response. Axel wasn't home.

Where could he be at this hour? It was almost 8:30. I went down and stood outside. Rain was pelting down hard now. I was caught in a rainstorm, without an umbrella. I stood there, listening to the sound of the rain. I found the steady rainfall consoling and comforting. It sounded like a murmuring whisper, telling me a story—a fairytale or some ancient legend you heard when you were a child.

I leaned on the wall and listened and at some point, I looked up. There, about ten steps away, a tall figure of a man stood motionless, soaking wet. I blinked. It was Axel. He was drenched in the rain without an umbrella, staring at me.

Instinctively, I ran to him. I blurted out, "What are you doing in the rain, soaked like this? You know what? I wasn't done talking to you when you took off. Why did you run away? Don't you see? You are a fool! You are such a fool!"

He stared at me calmly. I couldn't read his face because of the rain.

Rain cascaded over us, and he pulled me hard towards him and pressed his lips on mine, without caring about the downfall in the slightest. It was as if the world stopped spinning and all the noise died out. It was just him and me in the world now.

I didn't realise, for one split second, that my long-awaited wish had come true. His wet lips tasted like a Granny Smith apple, sweet and fresh, like a fountain on a hot summer day or chilled morning dew on the leaves at dawn. I inhaled a hint of early May *muguet* (lily of the valley) from his lower lip, a scent I liked so much.

And something else happened deep inside me. The moment Axel's lips touched mine, I found myself instantly overwhelmed by love for him—a hit of thunder, a bolt of lightning awakening my senses. I wanted to kiss him again, kiss him all day, all night... And most of all, I felt at home. I had that strange sense of familiarity as if I had known him for a long time, as if I were used to his embrace. An inexplicable feeling indeed, since he had never kissed me before. Not this way.

Does it confirm we knew each other in our past lives? That we were related somehow? That we met again in this life to resume our ties?

He took my hand, and we ran into the building. We were both drenched to the bone. He pressed the elevator button and finally, we met each other's eyes. I asked him, "Where have you been in this rain without an umbrella?"

"I went to see you. You were gone. I thought you had already left to go to the pizzeria. It started raining on the way back."

"Why? You ran away without even listening to me. Why did you go back to see me?"

"Because I realised I was an idiot. I was wrong."

The elevator arrived, and we got in. Axel moved his wet hair off his forehead. His wet face, his mesmerising blue eyes, held a glint of desperation.

"When I saw you with that Italian bloke, I realised you could be taken away from me. It stung me sorely... so badly... It flipped me out of my mind... and instead of confronting it, I lost it and ran away... I'm sorry, Hyunah..."

With a *ting* sound, the elevator arrived at his floor. I pulled him out of the elevator and pushed him to the wall. And this time, I kissed him back. He responded passionately. My lips parted immediately. His lips divinely smelled of *muguet*, a pure white flower you see only once a year in early May in France, its shape like a bell.

He kissed me hungrily, as if he had been starving for days, and tasted my lips as if he wanted to quench his thirst. An endless thirst he seemed to satisfy only out of my lips. As soon as he opened the door, and once we were inside, Axel held my face and looked me in the eye.

"I'm sorry I embarrassed you when you offered yourself to me. I denied you... but please... give me a chance to explain... will you? I care about you, Hyunah... I really do... please, let me make it up to you."

"Oh, yes, you denied me alright. It's going to cost you, Axel... you are going to pay for what you've done...."

Soaked as we were, we undressed each other by the door before we drenched the whole floor. It was not easy to undress when all our clothes were wet—they stuck to our bodies. We brought our wet clothes to the bathroom and left them in the bathtub. Both naked, we got ourselves into the shower together.

Axel turned on the shower and let the water run over our bodies, washing the rain off. His arms were around my body. His left hand held me by the waist and, with his right hand stroking the back of my neck, he kissed me again, and this time his body pressed tightly against mine. The wall of the shower booth was hard against my back as he kissed me.

His divine scent of *muguet* made me dizzy, my heart

pounding so loudly, that it seemed about to burst out of my chest. His lovely lips tasted like green apple, its freshness like the morning dew at dawn. The blissful warm water streamed down over us. His lips moved to my earlobe, my neck, and my shoulders, exploring every surface of my skin.

We couldn't quite get to wash ourselves properly, but Axel poured a bit of men's shower gel and rubbed it against my body. I caressed his athletic, dreamlike body, making foam, feeling his muscles with my hands. My eyes discovered his naked body for the first time. He had a physique I had rarely seen on a man. His naturally toned body, trained from horse-riding, fencing, and running, was carved like a Renaissance sculpture in Florence. He had long arms and legs, perfectly proportioned. His long legs were slender and beautiful, and he had perfect shoulder blades with athletic biceps and triceps developed from years of training. His amazing chest and flat stomach were all muscles without a trace of fat. His buttocks were tight and firm. Over to the front, he had a delight and feast for my eyes, ornamented with golden curly hair.

He would have made a perfect model for Hanro underwear today—much better than Ulrik or Massimo. I wanted to touch his fair golden hair, so I let him sit on the floor of the shower booth and shampooed his hair. He let me do what I wanted, so I gave him a gentle scalp massage while watching his closed eyes showing off his long eyelashes. He was a dream... A dream come true.

I removed the shampoo from his hair, splashing water over his head using the showerhead. While I was doing it, he drew me closer by holding my legs, stroking them slowly. I felt his hands over my thigh, gliding up and down, his artist's fingers on my legs. When he reached my knees, I spasmed out of intense stimulation. He must have noticed my knees were my erogenous zone. He kept his hands on them with a pixyish smile on his face.

As the mousse from the remaining shampoo washed off, he circled my left knee with the palm of his hand, with slight pressure but good enough to stimulate me. He took the showerhead from my hand and hung it up, and pulled me down at his side, still keeping his palm over my knee. He let me sit across from him, drawing my knee to his chest, and he kissed it. As his lovely lips pressed on my knee, I felt a wave of exhilaration spread across my body.

I grabbed his shoulder, as he whispered in my ear, "Is there anything I can do for you, my lady?"

"Yes..."

"Tell me."

He continued stroking my knee.

"Don't stop... please."

"And? Anything else?"

He kissed my earlobe while whispering. I could barely breathe. I was panting and craving his touch. At the end of my breath, I managed a few words.

"My heart asks for pleasure."

"I will please you, my lady. I will. You shall have me as if there is no tomorrow."

He kissed my lips. Slow, enamouring, and spellbinding. The moment was so sweet and arousing, spreading a wild, uncontrollable thirst across my body. After the rain was washed off him, his lips still tasted sweet but with a hint of mimosa. I inhaled his divine scent, fresh *muguet* with underlying rosemary and sandalwood. His hair smelled of shampoo—masculine, clean, with a hint of early morning fresh air.

Water stopped running. Axel opened the shower booth door, took a fresh towel, and wrapped me in it. Then he put on his bathrobe. He found another small towel and dried my hair, rubbing it quickly against my head. We made eye contact. His blue eyes were as beautiful as ever, with a fabulous glint that made my heart thump uncontrollably.

"Are you sure, my lady? Will you have me?"

"Yes. More than anything... please."

Axel lowered his lips to my ear and whispered, "Say you will have me."

"I will have you, my lord. Please allow me the pleasure of your company. I shall have you as if there is no tomorrow."

With one graceful movement, he lifted me in his arms with the towel still around my body. He took a few steps and laid me on his bed. His hair was still wet, so I took my small towel and rubbed it against his head. He shook his head at the same time, and it made me giggle. He grinned.

He shrugged off his bathrobe, revealing his fantastic torso. And he kissed me. He climbed on top of me, supporting himself with his arms, trying not to crush me with his body weight. He kissed me slowly, awakening all my senses. He moved towards my neck, my shoulder, and my breast. He removed the towel wrapped around me with one swift movement, and his lips perched on my left nipple.

First, he pressed his lips on my nipple ever so gently, and his tongue slowly circled it. It stimulated me right away, and I couldn't help but groan. He took my right hand, squeezing it as he kept on arousing me. He sensed I liked it, and he stayed on it for a good moment and moved to my right nipple.

As he started kissing my right nipple, I squeezed his hand hard, not even knowing I was holding it. I was already hypnotised and inflamed. I completely lost track of time. After a moment, he moved lower. His lips explored my belly, thigh, loin, and down to my pelvis. He started shyly, as if going down there was a taboo. And he moved around but kept coming back, stimulating me even more that way. I moaned and groaned. He stayed there, moving slowly and delicately, slightly increasing the pressure. I was overwhelmed by his gesture of giving himself to me.

Yes, he was giving. He was devoted to giving himself to please me. He seemed as though he didn't care about his own desires. Julian hadn't taken his time like this before he took me.

But Axel was different. He put his lust to one side and seemed to focus on giving me pleasure first. He took his time, observing me closely to see and learn what would please me the most. When he noticed I liked certain things, he didn't hesitate to concentrate on them as long as I wanted. He was absolutely selfless, kind, and loving, thus even more charming and irresistible.

As he slowly, but persistently, increased his pressure and pace, I felt something I had never experienced before. My whole body shuddered in wavelike spasms. Only later, I learned it was my first orgasm. It didn't last too long, but it was like having fireworks within my body. I was sweating, my entire body on fire. I knew I would always come back for more, now that I knew what it felt like. It was like tasting ambrosia, drinking the nectar of manna from an immortal fountain.

Axel finally looked up and stared down at me with a pixyish smile, his beautiful eyes glistening with joy, his hair still half-wet, flowing freely on his shoulders. And I begged him to take me.

"Please... I want you inside me... now."

He peered at me as he whispered, "You are beautiful..."

He obliged my wish as he fell towards my shoulders. He moved slowly at first, letting me adjust to him before he picked up his pace and advanced towards me rhythmically. The feeling of his body against me was dazzling. His blissful scent and divine motion wrapped around me like a silk gown.

Sweat formed on his beautiful forehead. I could not describe the feeling of having him inside of me—our two hearts beating as one, enthralled, enamoured, captivated like slaves to each other. As we entwined in each other's arms, becoming one, a strange, familiar sensation of déjà vu formed in my mind. *I had already done this many times before, probably in my previous life. Did I meet him in my previous life? Was he someone close to me in infinity?*

At one point, I screamed, and he paused a moment, looking down at me.

"*Regarde moi.*" (Look at me.)

I heard his whisper. I looked into his eyes.

"Are you alright, my lady?"

"Yes."

"Really?"

"*Oui*." (Yes.)

He lowered himself towards my ear. He kissed my earlobe gently.

"Shall I go on, my lady?"

"Yes."

"*Dis moi oui*." (Tell me yes.)

I said again, holding my breath and panting: "*Oui*, Axel."

"Really?"

"*Oui, oui*."

"Say it again."

"*Oui, oui, oui*. Don't stop. Go on. I want you to go on."

And he let go of himself. His half-wet, ruffled hair was whipping back and forth, his athletic body moving like a dancer. His sweat became a stream. He was soaked again, this time with his own sweat.

Rain was still pattering outside. Axel was panting, *à bout de souffle*. (Breathless.)

After having blessed me with multiple ecstatic and rapturous moments, he collapsed next to me on his back. He was breathing hard. I lay next to him, panting.

For a while, we lay motionless, listening to the rain outside. I took a small towel and wiped the sweat from his face and chest. He took my hand and drew it to his lips. He kissed my hand with his eyes on me. He grinned. I found a bottle of mineral water on the bedside table and handed it to him. He gestured for me to drink first. I gulped half the bottle and brought the bottle to his lips. He drained it in a few gulps.

"Come here." He offered me his shoulder. I leaned my head on his shoulder. He stroked my hair ever so gently.

"Will you forgive me?"

"For what?"

"For having misled you. I have confused you since the day we met. I told you we should be friends, then acted differently sometimes. I have been ambiguous. But I didn't do it on purpose... it seems I am incapable of thinking clearly... reasoning... acting with my brain, not with my feelings. For that, I owe you an apology."

I met his eyes. They glistened. A few strands of wet hair fell over his beautiful face.

"It's alright, *mon petit chou*. Apology accepted. But it's going to cost you, I told you already."

Axel smiled. "What shall I do to oblige you, my lady?

"You promised to be my humble servant. You will show me with actions, not with words."

"I'm listening."

"You will wake me up every morning with a kiss."

He grinned.

"And?"

"And you will..."

I played with his damp hair.

"You will..."

"You will what?"

"You will serve me."

I smiled wickedly.

"How will I serve you, my lady?"

"Every morning, you will..."

He smiled with a question mark on his face.

"Every morning, you will serve me breakfast with hot tea and fresh bread."

Axel's eyes twinkled.

"That can be arranged, my lady. Anything else?"

"I forbid you to walk away from me when I haven't finished talking to you."

"It won't happen again. I promise."

"You promise? You will give me your word?"

"I give you my word."

And Axel kissed me—a sweet, gentle kiss on my lips and my earlobe.

"You have my word, my lady."

The pouring rain halted, softening to a murmuring sound.

Axel got up from the bed and put his bathrobe on, and asked, "Did you have dinner?"

"No."

"Are you hungry?"

"A little."

"Then I will make you something."

He took a fresh T-shirt out of a drawer and handed it to me. I pulled it over my head. And I thought of my wet dress—while he headed to the kitchen, I went to the bathtub and put the dress on a hanger to let it dry in the small laundry room.

Something mouth-watering was cooking in the kitchen. Axel was making an omelette—with tomatoes, onions, and mushrooms. It smelled delicious.

"Wow, it smells good in here. Now I'm hungry," I said, as I joined him in the kitchen.

I went behind him and drew my arms around his waist.

"I hope you're not regretting the pizza."

"Are you jealous, *mon petit chou*? How could you possibly be jealous when you look like you do? Look at yourself in the mirror. You look like a Greek statue of Narcissus."

"Narcissus? A Greek hunter who fell in love with himself after refusing all romantic advances? It's pathetic. He died watching his own image reflected on the pond. Don't call me that. He's pathetic."

He took out a bottle of Weizenbier (wheat beer) from the fridge. He opened it skilfully with a fork. "Do you want a sip?"

The sight of beer made me thirsty. I took a few sips directly from the bottle. Axel gulped it afterwards. He sprinkled freshly chopped parsley on the omelette and served it. It was delicious, probably the most delicious omelette I ever had. I never knew a simple omelette could be so tasty.

"This is so good. Where did you learn to make an omelette like this?"

"My grandma. I always hung around in the kitchen when she cooked."

"She's such a good cook, your grandma."

"Yes. I'm going back to Krems this weekend. Do you want to come with me?"

"Oh, really? Are you inviting me?"

"Yes, it will do you good to get some fresh air in the countryside. I need to spend some time with Poseidon and the other horses. If you don't mind hanging with me in the stalls and the corrals with the horses, you're welcome."

"Oh, I would love to. But what about your grandma? She wouldn't mind me coming?"

"She is looking forward to seeing you. She cannot wait to meet you."

"Alright then. I will come with you."

Axel grinned. "It will be a great pleasure for us, Hyunah. My grandma will be thrilled."

"If she always cooks as well as this, I will put on two kilos over the weekend."

"Come on, Hyunah. You're just skin and bones. In any case, we will go riding every day. You won't have time to put on weight."

"Go riding? I've never been on a horse in my life."

"Oh, you will, on our ranch. I will teach you. I will make sure you get your daily exercise in the fresh country air. You will discover the beautiful landscape of Austria."

"That sounds wonderful. I'm already excited. To get out of Vienna... breathe the fresh air in nature with the horses. A weekend getaway..."

"I'm planning to leave on Friday. I hope you are not working on Friday?"

"For the moment, I have nothing booked."

"Good."

We finished the omelette and cleared the table. Axel opened the fridge, took a bowl of strawberries, and laid it on the table. He gestured to me to come and sit on his lap. As I settled down on his lap, with my arm around his shoulders, he brought a strawberry towards my mouth. I accepted it, eating it out of his hand like a pet. He took one for himself and smiled. He kissed my earlobe, whispering.

"*È vero che ami gli spaghetti alle vongole*?" (Is it true you love spaghetti alle vongole?)

I was taken by surprise by his fluent Italian. I realised he had listened to a good part of my conversation with Massimo. I wondered how much. I answered.

"*Sì, lo adoro. Lo ordino solo quando sono nel ristorante Italiano.*" (Yes, I love it. It's the only thing I order at Italian restaurants.)

"*Poi conosco un buon ristorante Italiano a Vienna. Ci sono andato una volta con Mario di Milano, il fotografo. Vorrei invitarti lì. Ma senza Massimo.*" (Then I know a good Italian restaurant in Vienna. I went there once with Mario from Milan, the photographer. I would like to invite you there. But without Massimo.)

"*Ma perché senza Massimo?*" (But why without Massimo?)

I smiled at his ridiculous jealousy. I admired his boyish charm.

"*Perché ha cercato di rubare la mia principessa. La prossima volta che ci riprova, morirà con la mia spada.*" (Because he tried to steal my princess. The next time he tries again, he will die by my sword.)

"*Ma senza Massimo, non mi avresti mai baciato.*" (But without Massimo, you would never have kissed me.)

"*Poi lo ringrazio perché è stato bravissimo, ma ancora non è invitato.*" (Then I thank him because he was wonderful, but he is still not invited.)

I burst into laughter, and he grinned boyishly. He picked one big, pretty strawberry and moved it to my lips. I ate it directly from his hand. And I added, "*Questo è così buono, perché è dalla tua mano.*" (This tastes so good because it's from your hand.)

He took another big strawberry, slightly larger than the last, and drew it to my mouth. The moment I took a bite, he bit the strawberry from the other side. Our lips met, and he kissed my lips while we both had strawberry in our mouths. And he whispered, "*E questa fragola è ancora più dolce perché l'hai baciata.*" (And this strawberry is even sweeter because you kissed it)."

And he fed me another, and another. We kept kissing, tasting the strawberries until the bowl was empty. And those were the most delicious strawberries I ever had in my life.

~

The morning after, the rain had a magnificent effect on the weather. The sky was clear and blue, the air was crisp and invigorating. Axel woke me up with a kiss on my forehead in the early morning.

"*Buongiorno mia principessa.*" (Good morning, my princess.)

I opened my eyes. Those beautiful, sparkling blue eyes peered down at me. A fresh breeze rustled from the open window. I looked around the room and stretched my arms.

"*Buongiorno mio principe.*" (Good morning, my prince.)

Axel asked shyly, "My lady, I have a question, and I hope you will oblige me with an honest answer."

"Yes. Tell me."

"Did I please her ladyship last night?"

His eyes were wide with curiosity.

"Oh, my lord. Yes, you did. Very much indeed."

"Really?"

"Yes, my lord. Her ladyship was greatly pleased."

This time, I smiled bashfully. He kissed me—a sweet, slow kiss with quiet breathing as if the fresh morning breeze from the window perched on my lips. He locked his gaze on me, and I found myself blissfully lost in his blue, endless, immortal fountain. I remembered his beautiful mother on horseback. She had those magical blue eyes and an immortal gaze, just like Axel's.

He shifted his body and lay next to me. He was staring at the ceiling, and his smile was gone. I turned to face him—his sharp nose, high cheekbones, lovely lips, long eyelashes, and amazingly sculpted jaw—and wondered what was going on in his mind.

"What are you thinking?" I asked.

With his eyes still in the void, he spoke softly: "There's something I need to tell you."

His voice was calm as usual, but something in his tone gave me a chill.

"I know it's not going to be easy for me. I have been dreading this moment. But after all the wrong I've done to you, I think I owe you an explanation. At least you deserve that much, after all you've done for me."

"I haven't done much for you."

"Yes, you have, Hyunah. You have risked a great deal to retrieve my painting. I cannot thank you enough. Herbert told me you were the driving force behind all this and the mastermind who orchestrated everything. You have no idea what that painting means to me. It may be the only thing I have left of my mother."

"I'm listening."

"I don't know what you think of me now, but you might change your mind about me after you hear what I'm going to tell you. That's fine with me, as long as you're honest with me and with yourself. All I expect from you is your honesty. Once you hear me out, you will tell me what you think. You can judge me if you wish, but what you will tell me afterwards... let it be the truth and nothing else. Am I clear enough for you?"

"I shall never judge you, Axel."

"Even if you do, I don't mind. As long as you will say what you truly have in your mind."

"I can tell you already that nothing you say now will change my mind about you. I really like you, Axel, and I care about you. Nothing can change that. You can tell me anything, please."

He blinked a few times and started talking. "When I was five years old, my mother eloped with another man. She ran off one day—just disappeared into thin air, leaving my father and me behind. Quite a difficult thing to understand for a five-year-old boy, so I grew up confused about my mother. Of course, I hated her for leaving me, whatever the cause was. Every night I went to bed crying and hating her, asking myself why she did that to me.

"When I turned six, my father got himself a woman from Prague. He was from Prague himself—he was Czechoslovakian. I didn't get along with the woman, so I spent more and more time with my grandma at the ranch. Eventually, I spent all my weekends and school holidays there with my grandparents.

"One day, when I turned eight, my mother came back out of the blue. She had been watching me at a distance from the schoolyard for quite some time. And she appeared in front of me when I had finished school. She told me she had never spent a day without thinking of me, and she begged me to forgive her... she would do anything for me if she could have me in her life again. I was confused and troubled. I didn't know what to say to her.

"But before I could answer her, my father arrived. He reacted with fury. He told my mother she had no right to talk to me after what she had done. He took me away in a rage, leaving her behind in tears. I still cannot forget her face, contorted with despair, tears streaming down her face. She just stood there hopelessly, watching me get taken away from her. But she kept coming to the school, and I remember one afternoon she managed to exchange a few words with me. She said she would like to ride horses with me again and told me to think about it. I said I would like that. But again, my father arrived and chased her away.

"I hated the way he treated my mother. He always ruined everything. At that time, I was too young to understand. I never knew what was going on behind the whole struggle. Everyone around me considered I was too young to digest the situation and kept on feeding me lies. My father didn't help me in any way. He went on and on, denigrating my mother. What a horrible mother she was, to have abandoned me the way she did, that she was unforgivable, and I should never talk to her again.

"I knew he was deeply hurt by my mother. He couldn't handle his fury and kept on lashing out his wrath at me. He always managed to come earlier than the end of the school day and blocked all my mother's attempts to approach me. But I knew she was there, peering at me from a distance—hiding behind a tree, with a hat and sunglasses so that my father couldn't recognise her. She kept coming, and sometimes when I saw her, she waved at me.

"In the meantime, my grandma had no idea what was going on. My mother never told her anything. She was ashamed of what she had done, and she didn't dare contact my grandma. Then one day, probably a year later, I confronted my father. It was taboo to talk about my mother in the house, but I did. I told him I wanted to see my mother and he shouldn't get in the way. He was furious, and instead of talking to me, he hit me. He slapped me hard. The next day, when I packed my rucksack for school, I added something. I took my pencils and my favourite paintbrushes and an extra pullover. Instead of going to school, I took off. I wanted to go to my grandma's with the horses, and I never wanted to see my father again.

"My grandma lived fifteen kilometres away on the other side of the river, so I got lost on the way. I don't remember how I did it, but I managed to arrive at the ranch by nightfall. The teacher at school called my father, telling him I never showed up at school that day, and the whole village went looking for me. The police got involved as well, and they sent out a search party with dogs, looking around the area.

"Nobody knew I was at my grandma's barn by nightfall. I fell asleep in one of the stalls. The next day, my grandma found me early in the morning, sleeping between the huge hooves of a mare called Frühling. It was as if the mare was protecting me."

Axel paused, and I barged in.

"That mare is Frühling?"

He smiled faintly.

"Yes. That mare has become my best friend and companion."

"Wow, how old is she now?"

"She is two years older than me. She is twenty-four. She was my mother's horse and mount. That's her you see in the painting you retrieved for me. When my mother eloped, she left Frühling at the ranch. Frühling became my horse. I grew up with her all my life. She's still in good health, although she cannot run as fast as she used to... she's perfectly fine for a stroll. You will get to meet her this weekend."

"So, what happened when your grandma found you in the stall?"

"She woke me up and brought me to the house, and I asked her if I could stay with her. She took me in her arms and said I was always welcome in her house. And I never left. I have never gone back to my father."

"Did your father try to bring you back to him?"

"Yes, but I refused. I wouldn't even talk to him. I could never forgive him for meddling between my mother and me. I mean, she was my mother after all, whatever she had done... and I had a right to see her if I wanted to. It was up to me to decide to forgive her or give her another chance to have me back. My father took that chance away from me. He had no right to decide that for me."

Here comes the origin of Axel's Oedipus Complex: remorse for his mother and murderous rage for his father.

"I agree with you. He had no right. And he took another woman. He seemed to have moved on. Why did he act so badly?"

"We all have our way of dealing with hurt and anger. Everyone reacts differently. My father didn't react well. But that's all in the past now."

"Did you see him again?"

"Only at my mother's funeral."

"Did you make peace with him, then?"

Axel took a deep breath. His eyes glinted, filled with agony.

"No."

"No?"

"No. I'm not on speaking terms with him. He moved to Prague a few months after the funeral, and I haven't seen him since."

"Oh, I'm sorry to hear that. Um... how did your mother die?"

Axel shifted his gaze around the ceiling, blinked, and inhaled deeply.

"After a year or so, my mother stopped coming to my school. She never managed to talk to me, because of my father. I guess he must have used all his means to stop her attempts to see me. I can never forgive him for that. Never. And my grandma put me in another school near her ranch after the summer holiday. I told my grandma all about my mother and what happened at school.

"My grandma had searched for her everywhere. She even hired a private detective to find her, but all in vain. Nobody had seen her or heard of her. About a year later, when I turned ten, the body of a woman was found in a cemetery in Wieliczka: a small town, sixteen kilometres south of Kraków. A Polish constable from the police office there contacted my grandma. Among the effects of the dead woman, they found a letter addressed to my grandma along with the photos of me on horseback. My grandma was asked to come to identify the body.

"My grandparents took me with them to Wieliczka to see the body. She was under a false Polish identity when she was found. The only connection that led her to my grandma was the letter addressed to her on our ranch in Krems and the photos of me she had kept in her purse. And the dead woman was identified as my mother. The police determined her death was suicide. It turned out she had been a patient in a psychiatric hospital in Kraków for a few months, due to severe depression and suicidal attempts. How she escaped from the hospital and found herself in the cemetery in Wieliczka was unknown at that moment.

"It was clear her mental state was deteriorating long before she was diagnosed by a Polish doctor as showing symptoms of schizophrenia: thus not able to live a normal life in society. How she found herself in Kraków disguised as a Polish woman was not yet known. My grandma found out later that my mother's paramour, the man she had eloped with, had died earlier under tragic circumstances, and was buried in that cemetery where my mother's body was found.

"Before my mother had started suffering from depression, she had made sure no one could find her, by using fake identification. She didn't want anyone to know she had abandoned her son and eloped with another man. She felt deeply guilty about it. Her body was repatriated to Krems for the funeral. She now rests next to my great-aunt, the elder sister of my grandma."

Axel paused. Tears welled up in his eyes. He blinked once, and the tears trickled down his cheek. I wiped his tears in silence, stroking his hair. For the first time since he began talking, he looked me in the eye. He took my hand that had wiped his tears and drew it to his lips, kissing it.

"And you should know, Hyunah... I might have inherited my mother's insanity... I heard it's hereditary. I have already suffered a series of episodes of depression and that's why I decided we should stay as friends, not more. It was not fair for you to have to share this burden with me. I'm... um... mentally unstable... according to the psychiatrist who was in charge of me. There were times I needed help... And I thought that if we stayed as friends, you wouldn't have to know all this about me... this dark side of me... and my past."

As I watched him talk, I felt him with my whole heart. His beautiful face was pale and distorted with years of agony. I stared at his sad but indescribably beautiful eyes and said, "Nonsense, look at me, Axel. Who could stay sane and perfectly well after what you have gone through? You're perfectly normal and perfectly human. And I'm crazy about you. See? I'm crazy. We're all crazy."

Axel's tearful face lightened up slightly. "You are crazy about me?"

"Yes, more than ever. I'm hopelessly, incurably, crazy about you."

"And I don't want to lose you."

"You won't. I'm here, Axel. I'm not going anywhere."

I moved towards him, and he held me in his arms, squeezing me tightly, and I drowned in a surge of empathy for him. He lifted me and laid me on top of him. His face found his usual calm, although his beautiful blue eyes were still wet.

He whispered, "My lady, I think I have done enough confiding for one day."

"Yes, my lord. Now, please bless me with your heart and kindness."

"How can I do that, my lady? Enlighten me."

I answered without thinking.

"*Dammi Mille Baci.*" (Give me a thousand kisses.)

Axel smiled. His face brightened up.

"*Certo, bella mia,*" (Of course, my beautiful), he answered, his low voice melting my heart again. He started counting. He began with a kiss on my forehead.

"*Uno.*" (One)

Axel shifted his body and rolled me to his side.

"*Due, Tre...*" (Two, three...)

His kisses fell on my cheeks.

"*Quattro, cinque, sei...*" (Four, five, six...)

He continued on my neck and earlobe, counting softly.

"*Sette, Otto, Nove...*" (Seven, eight, nine...)

He went down on my lower neck.

"*Dieci, undici...*" (Ten, eleven...)

And he came back to kiss my lips again. As our lips touched, his hand slid under my T-shirt, touching my waist. He pulled my T-shirt off over my head. As I became naked again, I met his eyes, looking down at me as he moved on top of me, grinning. I removed his white cotton T-shirt and marvelled at his fantastic torso. His lips pressed against my shoulders.

"*Dodici, Tredici, Quattordici...*" (Twelve, thirteen, fourteen...)

This time I counted.

"*Quindici, Sedici, Diciassette...*" (Fifteen, sixteen, seventeen...)

His lips pressed on my breast, slowly going down towards my left nipple.

"*Diciotto, Diciannove, Venti...*" (Eighteen, nineteen, twenty...)

His blissful kisses continued as his body flowed smoothly over my belly and legs, sliding gracefully, his hands stroking my legs up and down. I felt dizzy while being swept with pleasure, opening the door to heaven and the taste of manna. He kept on counting, and his lips moved down to my waist.

"*Trenta... trentasette... quarantanove...*" (Thirty... thirty-seven... forty-nine...) he whispered in my ear as he slowly caressed my knee. As soon as he touched my knee, thrills spread through my body. I shuddered. Every gesture he made was evocative and sensual.

"*Cinquantotto... Sessantasette... Settanta...*" (Fifty-eight... Sixty-seven... Seventy...)

I lost myself in his embrace.

And this was it... my happiest morning since meeting Axel.

Afterword

Vienna Calling is based on a true story that happened to me when I lived in Vienna a long time ago. It is a story that I had buried deep inside of me. Had it not been for the pandemic and the death of my father thrown at me in the middle of it, I would not have written the story. When my father passed away, and I couldn't even attend his funeral, I suffered a period of depression, and it opened a scar, an old wound that I could never get over, even after all these years. And that was it.

I started writing about my encounter with a mysterious young artist I had met in Vienna and how it had positively changed and influenced my life.

What is art? How does one become an artist? Those are among the questions I asked in my story. I found it strangely therapeutic to write this story, and I want to share it with you. It will be my greatest pleasure to see people read my book and share my ideologies. Although it is based on true events, I got liberal with a few details and let my imagination carry me away. I made it my mission to make the story compelling. After all, I can't have my readers bored for the sake of realism, can I?

Since this happened in the culturally rich and diverse Austrian capital, you will discover Vienna in a unique way through my eyes and memories. The story also reflects the multi-cultural aspects of Europe, with its different languages. I hope the translations of the languages I used aren't too limited, but I'm sure you'll find it quite easy to understand. You may even end up practising a new foreign language!

There will be *Vienna Calling 2*, with a subtitle, *Ultra Mortem in Aeternum*, (Beyond Death in Eternity), following soon...

Thank you all so much.

About the Author

After graduation in the university in Seoul, having studied English literature, I adventured myself to Europe, where I have been living a good majority of my life until now. I went to a fashion school in Paris, and started working as a makeup artist and a stylist in Paris. Then I moved to Munich, and to Vienna, where I met Axel, where the inspiration for my book was born.

My journey constantly kept me going from Europe, back to Korea, then to Australia, and New Zealand, and to Hong Kong. Then I moved back to France, here in Antibes, in beautiful Côte d'Azur since 2019.

~

To learn more about Hyunah Kim and discover more Next Chapter authors, visit our website at www.nextchapter.pub.

There Are No Innocents
ISBN: 978-4-82415-086-8

Published by
Next Chapter
2-5-6 SANNO
SANNO BRIDGE
143-0023 Ota-Ku, Tokyo
+818035793528

14th September 2022

CPSIA information can be obtained
at www.ICGtesting.com
Printed in the USA
LVHW111051101122
732809LV00003B/32